Assassin

Also by Tom Cain

The Accident Man
The Survivor

Assassin

TOM CAIN

BANTAM PRESS

LONDON • TORONTO • SYDNEY • AUCKLAND • JOHANNESBURG

TRANSWORLD PUBLISHERS
61–63 Uxbridge Road, London W5 5SA
A Random House Group Company
www.rbooks.co.uk

First published in Great Britain
in 2009 by Bantam Press
an imprint of Transworld Publishers

A CIP catalogue record for this book
is available from the British Library.

ISBNs 9780593062319 (cased)
9780593062326 (tpb)

Addresses for Random House Group Ltd companies outside the UK
can be found at: www.randomhouse.co.uk
The Random House Group Ltd Reg. No. 954009

The Random House Group Limited supports The Forest Stewardship
Council (FSC), the leading international forest-certification organization. All our
titles that are printed on Greenpeace-approved FSC-certified paper carry the FSC logo.
Our paper procurement policy can be found at
www.rbooks.co.uk/environment

Typeset in 11/14pt Caslon 540 by
Falcon Oast Graphic Art Ltd.
Printed and bound in Great Britain by
CPI Mackays, Chatham, ME5 8TD

2 4 6 8 10 9 7 5 3 1

Mixed Sources
Product group from well-managed
forests and other controlled sources
www.fsc.org Cert no. TT-COC-2139
© 1996 Forest Stewardship Council
FSC

For my children

1

Lara Dashian was as pretty as a pixie, as fresh and full of life as a wildflower meadow on a sunny spring day. At the age of eighteen, she was loving, dutiful and unsullied, her parents' pride and joy. Then she left her hometown of Armavir in western Armenia and caught a bus to the capital Yerevan to meet a man her aunt had said could get her a good job in the West. When her supposed benefactor took her papers and her meagre savings and then shut her in a cellar beneath a suburban bar, Lara learned the hard way that some people will sell their own family to buy a new TV.

The naive, innocent girl that she had been until then did not exist any more. She had been ripped apart by the process of repeated sexual assault, punishment and intimidation that people-traffickers call 'breaking in'. Its purpose is very straightforward: to accustom young women to the inevitability of rape and the absolute necessity, for their own self-preservation, of acting as though they enjoy it. Lara had cowered in terror as another girl, brave enough to resist, was beaten to death before her eyes as a warning to the other unwitting slaves with whom she had been imprisoned. Her old self had been left behind for ever as a new Lara obeyed her tormentors and stepped aboard the plane that would take her, via Munich, to Dubai.

She had no idea where Dubai was, no more understanding of her final destination than a sheep has of the slaughterhouse. And just like an animal, she was traded along the way. The deal was done in a coffee shop at Munich airport between the trafficker who had flown her from Yerevan and another man, heavily built, with a puffy, unshaven face, heavy gold chains around his neck and wrists, wearing a black leather jacket.

'This is Khat,' the trafficker had said.

Lara sat in silence while the two men haggled over her selling price. While they batted numbers back and forth – laughing, switching from coffee to beer, enjoying themselves – Lara tried to come to terms with the unreality of her situation. One man had brought her to the café, and another would take her away: her new owner. She rolled the words around in her head – 'my owner' – but could make no sense of them. It seemed impossible that such a thing could happen as all around her the life of the airport carried on regardless, still less that she would simply sit there and allow herself to be bought and sold. And yet it had been so.

Now she was bought and sold every day.

In the past week alone Lara had been with at least thirty men, maybe more. She did not count them any more, just the money they gave her. She had to make fifteen hundred dirhams a night, roughly four hundred US dollars, or two-seventy in euros: Lara was rapidly acquiring a head for currency calculations. If she succeeded, Khat would let her microwave a cheap frozen meal before he locked her away in the bare room where she and his three other prostitutes passed their days. If she failed, he would hit her with vicious jabs to the stomach that left her lying on the cheap nylon carpet, winded, weeping and retching.

Now another sale was in prospect. That evening, when Khat came into the room, he seemed upbeat, but also edgy. He looked the girls over, considered for a moment and then pointed at Lara.

'You,' he said. 'Get dressed, your best clothes. Take extra care when you paint your face. You're coming with me.'

On the way out, Khat told her that a wealthy Englishman had arrived in Dubai. He was very well connected to the city's most powerful men. He was looking to buy a girl for his own, exclusive use. And he was willing to pay up to thirty thousand euros to get exactly what he wanted.

Lara had gasped at the figure. Despite the income that prostitutes could generate, the sheer number of women on the market meant that they could usually be bought for less than the price of a rusty old second-hand car. In Munich she had fetched just 2,800 euros, inclusive of airfare. No wonder Khat was tense. If Lara caught the buyer's eye, he stood to make back more than ten times what he had paid for her.

'But if I have to bring you back here . . .' He gave her a cold, leering smile like a wolf eyeing its prey. '. . . I will hit you so hard, it will make all the times before seem like I was only tickling.'

2

Fifty years ago Dubai had been a dusty, insignificant speck on the map of the Persian Gulf. Yet by the time the twenty-first century dawned it was said to be the fastest-growing city in the world. Barely a week had gone by without the opening of another new five-, six- or even seven-star hotel, each claiming to be more luxurious, more outrageously indulgent than the last. Amidst this brash, relentless extravagance the Karama Pearl, an unimpressive structure barely a dozen storeys tall, was not the most obvious place for a wealthy visitor to conduct his business. It had one feature, however, that marked it out from anywhere else in Dubai: a night-club that was one of the city's prime locations for picking up prostitutes.

Tonight, as always, there were tarts wandering from table to table looking for business, but they were just the supporting cast. The stars were up by the bar that snaked down one side of the club. There stood six pimps, each with their most desirable property: six stallholders touting for a foreigner's custom in a human souk.

The girls who were coming up for sale cast quick, competitive glances at one another, each as fearful of failure as Lara, knowing only one of them could succeed. They toyed with their hair and tossed their heads. As they shifted nervously from foot to foot, their heels tapped against the floor like the shoes of skittish race-horses coming under starter's orders.

Across the room, on the far side of the club's dancefloor, sat the man for whom the whole display was being staged. Lara guessed he was probably in his late thirties. He was simply dressed in a white shirt, the sleeves rolled up below his elbows, faded jeans and loafers. He wore no jewellery besides his watch. He had short dark hair and a face whose sharply defined features suggested that the body beneath his clothes was lean and fit. Only his mouth, with its full lips and sullen expression, jarred with his clean-cut features. Lara had become an expert in reading men's faces. This one, she thought, might have a cruel streak. Yet he was handsome, there was no denying that, and rich, too.

She wondered why he had to buy a girl when plenty of women would happily give themselves to him for free. Perhaps he already had a wife, or simply preferred to pay for what he needed. Some of her regular clients thought sex was simpler that way. All women cost money, they said, but at least with a whore you knew the bill in advance.

It still seemed strange to Lara, even now, that when they talked about a whore, they meant her.

Next to the buyer lolled an Indian, whose chubby physique and plump, smiling cheeks could not disguise the sharp, predatory glint in his eyes. Khat had pointed him out when they first walked into the club.

'That is Tiger Dey. He controls much of the market for foreign labour in Dubai: the labourers on building sites, the cleaners in hotel rooms . . .' Khat had given her a wry, almost resigned look she had never seen on his face before. 'He controls you and me, too. Every night, you give me the money, but in the end, Tiger Dey is the one you are working for.'

Now, Lara saw, Dey and the Englishman were looking towards the bar, running their eyes along the line of candidates, pausing from time to time to confer with one another. She could see Dey trying to be persuasive, emphasizing his points by gesturing with his right fist. There was a bright-red cocktail cherry, taken from the drink in front of him, dangling between his thumb and forefinger. It looked absurd hanging there. Maybe that was why the other man was laughing as he held up his hands in mock surrender, letting Dey win the argument.

The Indian leaned back on the velvet banquette, popped the cherry into his mouth and threw away the stalk. Then he raised a finger to summon one of the bodyguards who were deployed around his table, pointed at the bar and dispatched him.

Lara soon discovered why Dey had been so insistent. One of the other prostitutes was Indian. She was a beautiful creature, with lush curves, heavy, sensuous features and turquoise eyes that dazzled against her flawless brown skin. The bodyguard stopped by her and jerked his thumb back towards the table where his boss was sitting. As she trotted away, her owner pumped his fist in triumph.

Khat snorted contemptuously. 'It will not be her.' He looked across the room to where the girl was arriving at the buyer's table. 'That one prefers white meat. I can tell.'

A few minutes later, he was proved right. The Indian girl came back to the bar, her haughtiness replaced by a look of desperate ingratiation. Her pimp screamed abuse at her and then slapped her hard in the face. As she began to cry, he grabbed her upper arm and pulled her towards the exit; she pleaded with him frantically, her words punctuated by sobs. No one moved a muscle to stop him or help her. Whatever a man wanted to do with his property, that was his business.

Lara had no time to speculate about the fate that awaited the Indian girl. At the far table, the Englishman was pointing at Dey, as if to say, 'I told you so,' and it was his host who had to shrug and admit defeat. Again the bodyguard was sent over to the bar.

This time he pointed at Lara.

For a second she could not move. Then Khat gave her a stinging spank on the backside that sent her skidding across the polished wood of the dancefloor until she managed to stop, compose herself, tug her tiny skirt tight against her upper thighs and walk towards the men who now held her life in their hands. They were grinning broadly, amused by her attempts to restore a little dignity.

Lara hoped that was a good sign. She did her best to smile back.

The Englishman patted the dark velvet upholstery to the right of him, indicating she should sit there. Lara did as she was told, turning her body towards him. She placed her right hand on his inner thigh and leaned towards him, feigning a little gasp of pleasure as her left breast brushed against his arm.

Lara waited for a second, expecting the reaction that such a blatant display of availability usually provoked. But when the man put his hand around her wrist, it was not to guide her fingers higher towards his crotch, but to gently push her back until she was sitting upright on the banquette. Lara could not stop the fear of rejection flickering across her face, but he smiled, much more softly this time, and said, 'It's OK, don't worry.' Then he looked at her quizzically. 'You do speak English, right?'

'Little bit,' said Lara, who was rapidly adding a whole new vocabulary to the smattering she had learned at school.

'OK then, what's your name?'

'Lara.'

'Hi,' he said. 'My name's Carver.'

3

The Englishman called Carver looked Lara up and down. His face betrayed no indication of what he thought of her.

'I very good at sex,' she blurted, not knowing what else to say. 'You take me please, we have good time.'

Now Carver laughed. He looked past her, towards Tiger Dey, and said, 'I'll give the girl one thing, she's enthusiastic.'

As the Indian smiled in agreement, Carver looked at Lara again, leaned towards her and, almost to himself, murmured, 'But you're not enthusiastic really, are you, Lara? I can tell.'

Lara felt confused, unable to decide if she was doing well or badly. She could not read this man's eyes. At first she had thought they were blue, but close up she wondered if they might be green. In the dim light of the club it was hard to tell. Either way, there was something not quite right, almost unnatural about them.

Before she could pin it down she was distracted by a movement at the very edge of her peripheral vision. Even while he gazed at her face, Carver seemed to be doing something with the drink on the table beside him, though she could not tell what it was.

Then suddenly the spell was broken.

'I like her,' said Carver, relaxing back into the seat and talking to Tiger Dey again. 'She'll do . . . my little Lara,' he continued, giving her bare thigh a friendly squeeze.

She gave him a nervous smile, hardly daring to believe that he had chosen her, still uncertain that the deal was done.

'What do you think that ape is going to want for her?' Carver asked.

Tiger Dey smiled. 'He will want whatever I tell him to want. You will give me thirty thousand, and I will give him half of that. He will not dare to complain.'

'Excellent,' said Carver and Lara, watching him, was struck again by the sense that something about him wasn't quite right. She realized that Carver was acting, just as she so often did. He was giving a performance. But why, and what would it mean for her?

She knew at once that such questions were futile. Her only hope was to make him like her. So Lara put a happy look on her face and giggled sweetly when Carver asked her if she wanted a drink to celebrate. She laughed again when Carver told the waiter to put a cherry in it.

'Don't worry, darling, it's not for you,' he said. 'It's for Tiger. He can't resist those cherries, can you, mate?'

'Indeed, they are my fatal weakness,' the Indian agreed.

'Hang on, what have we here?' said Carver, reaching into his own, empty glass and pulling a waxy red fruit out by its stalk. 'There you go, have a cherry on me!'

He lobbed it over the table. Tiger Dey caught it one-handed and popped it in his mouth, to a cheer from Carver and an excited squeal and burst of applause from Lara.

As the merriment subsided, Carver reached into the inside pocket of his jacket, took out a tightly stuffed envelope and slipped it across the table. 'Thirty grand in five-hundred-euro notes,' he said as Tiger Dey picked it up. 'I won't even try to beat you down.'

'You would only end up paying even more. In any case, this one is worth the money.'

Within minutes, Khat had been led across to them and given his share. Lara could see him biting back the urge to complain.

So he is scared too, she thought, relishing his fear. Then she heard Tiger Dey telling Carver, 'She is yours, my friend. Do with her as you will.'

'In that case, I'm going to find out exactly what I've just bought.' Carver looked at Lara and, mimicking the patronizing tone of a husband to his wife, said, 'Finish up your drink, darling, I think it's time we left.'

He took her by the hand as he helped her up from the table and then slipped his arm around her waist as they left the club, crossed the lobby and took the lift up to his top-floor suite.

It struck Lara as Carver held the door open and ushered her in that she would never be going back to Khat's apartment, the locked room and the beatings. She did not have to make fifteen hundred dirhams tonight. She just had to persuade this strange, disturbing, handsome man that he had been right to buy her, and that he wanted to keep her. Perhaps, if she were very good, he might want to make her his proper girlfriend, or even his wife. Her eyes welled up, though she did not know if it was from relief, from hope or just because she was a young girl, far from home and weary to her bones.

Carver ran a finger under her eyes, wiping away the tears. 'Don't cry,' he said. Then he took her in her arms.

It began as a hug of consolation, but soon he pushed a little harder against her, and Lara found herself pushing back, although she could not say why. In all the times she had been with men, she had only ever given them what they wanted – no matter how much it disgusted her, no matter how badly it hurt – because the consequences of not doing so were even worse.

So was it fear that made her long to please the man who was taking her now? When he picked her up and carried her across the room, she wrapped her arms around his neck and pulled her mouth to his, so that he had to jerk away, laughing, just to see where he was going. And then, very gently, he lowered her down to the bed.

4

Lara lay with her eyes shut, expecting at any moment to feel Carver's weight upon her, wondering if this would feel different to all the other times. It took her a few seconds to realize that he was not joining her on the bed. She opened her eyes to find him still standing, fully clothed, taking more money from a leather wallet.

'This is for you,' he said, placing the money on the bedside table. 'Twenty thousand dirhams. Now I must go.'

It took a second or two for Lara to understand what he meant. He was leaving her. She had failed somehow. He was going to return her to Khat and demand his money back. She sat upright, terrified, pulling a sheet across her chest.

'I no good?' she asked. 'No please you?'

'You were very good,' he said. 'That's why I'm setting you free.'

'But Khat, Mr Dey, if they find out—'

Carver held two fingers to her lips. 'Shush, don't worry, they won't cause you any trouble. Do you understand?'

Lara did not. All she understood was the price she would pay for failure. Her tears had returned as he took a hotel Biro from the table and wrote on a scrap of headed paper.

'Listen,' he said. 'This is important. Are you listening?'

She nodded miserably.

'Good. This is the address of a place called the House of Freedom. It's a shelter for women who have been trafficked. That means forced to come here, forced to go with men. It's in Jumeirah, not far from here. I want you to go there. In a few days, the police will come to speak to you. It's nothing serious, they just want to check you really were trafficked. But don't tell them about me, OK? That's important. Say that you escaped from your owner. Say that you want to go home. They will help you.'

Lara looked at him in bleak desperation. 'Can't go home. My family will say I am bad girl, I am whore.'

'Here,' said Carver, pulling more notes from his wallet. 'That should help change their mind.'

Lara wiped the tears from her eyes and the snot from her nose. Then she asked the question that had been troubling her since they first met in the nightclub. 'Who are you? Why you do . . . all this?'

Carver smiled. 'I can't tell you what I do, or why,' he said. 'But my close friends call me Pablo. Why don't you do that?'

'Don't go, Pablo,' she said. 'Please . . .'

'I'm sorry, I've got work to do. But you can stay here for a while if you like. Have a shower. Get something to eat. Don't worry about the bill. But don't stay more than one hour. In sixty minutes, you go, OK?'

Lara nodded. 'One hour, maximum.'

'Good girl.'

He walked over to the door, half opened it, then paused. 'Goodbye, Lara,' he said. 'And good luck.'

Before she could say, 'Goodbye, Pablo,' he was gone.

Over the next few hours, Tiger Dey was gripped by violent stomach pains. These were the first effects of ricin poisoning. The

1-milligram dose – several times the estimated minimum required to be fatal – had been concealed within a sugar-coated pellet less than two millimetres across, designed to melt at human body temperature. This, in turn, was secreted inside the maraschino cherry given to him by an assassin he knew as Carver.

Ricin acts by breaking down proteins within cells, causing them to cease to function. There is no antidote to the poison, which is swiftly metabolized in the body, leaving no trace. It is, however, identifiable by its effects, which are incurable. In Tiger Dey's case, these progressed to repeated vomiting and bloody diarrhoea. Within two days his kidneys, liver and spleen would all collapse.

Dey's semi-legendary status, the controversy that surrounded him and the gruesome predictability of his demise attracted the kind of blanket media coverage that Dubai's rulers do not particularly enjoy. Outside the hospital, cameramen and reporters jostled for position. Inside, Dey's doctors tried their best to ease his pain. That aside, there was nothing they could do. There are few good ways to die, but this is arguably one of the worst.

Khat, whose given name was Kajoshaj Bajrami, met a swifter, more merciful end. He was shot in the back of the head, at point-blank range, when he went to collect his car in the lot behind the Karama Pearl hotel. No one heard the silenced shots or saw his assailant. His wallet was missing, however, and several witnesses testified to the fact that Khat had spent the evening at the bar in the basement club, boasting to anyone who would listen that he had just taken fifteen thousand euros in cash off Tiger Dey for a whore he'd bought for less than three thousand and was past her best earning days. The motive for his murder was therefore obvious, even if the culprit was, as yet, unknown.

At around 1.55 a.m., the man who had called himself both Samuel Carver and Pablo stopped by a dumpster behind a fast-food restaurant in the Deira district just north of the airport. He deposited a brown wig within the dumpster, making sure that it was well covered by a thick pile of stinking waste. He had already flushed his green contact lenses down a lavatory and swapped his white shirt for a black one. Back with his natural colouring of deep red hair and icy blue eyes, he made his way to Dubai International. Having checked in online and carrying only hand baggage he was in plenty of time to walk straight through security and on to the 2.45 a.m. Emirates flight to London. His ticket had been issued in the name of Damon Tyzack.

Tired by his hard work, but delighted by its outcome, Tyzack settled himself into a first-class private suite, lay back and soon fell into a deep and dreamless sleep.

5

Several thousand miles away to the west, Samuel Carver was hurtling across the night sky like a human dart. With every second that passed he travelled 175 feet forwards through the air, and fell 50 feet closer to the surface of the earth.

For six weeks, Carver had been planning and training, gradually dropping out of sight, going off-grid. Nobody who knew him knew where he was. The people who had encountered him lacked any clue to his true identity. The chartered De Havilland Twin Otter aircraft from which he had just jumped, almost five miles up, was routed from Richmond, Virginia to the island of Bermuda, several hundred miles out to sea. The crew were men who worked on the same principles as Carver. They did the job, took the money and kept their mouths shut. They did not know or want to know what he intended to do once he left their aircraft. They got him to a specified point at the time required, and then they flew away.

Now he was lying face down with his back straight and his head tilted slightly downwards to streamline his shape and encourage maximum velocity. His arms were extended behind him at forty-five degrees from his body and his legs were wide apart. Thin membranes of rip-stop fabric formed wings that stretched between his arms and his torso, and from his crotch down to his ankles. There were four minutes to go before he hit his drop zone. But there were a myriad ways he could die before he got there.

The higher you go, the colder it gets: a little less than two degrees centigrade for every thousand feet of altitude. Speed merely adds to that problem by generating intense wind-chill. Carver faced roughly the same risk of death from hypothermia as if he'd walked out of the Amundsen–Scott research station, down at the South Pole, straight into an Antarctic blizzard, but his only protection from the intense cold came from two layers of full-length thermal undergarments beneath his nylon flying suit.

Altitude also thins the atmosphere. This can lead to hypoxia, or oxygen starvation, which in turn causes blackouts. An unconscious man in a wing-suit will lose control and tumble helplessly down to earth like a stricken aircraft. Carver's chute was set to deploy automatically at around two thousand feet, but if his body position was unstable his lines and canopy could wrap themselves around him like a spider's web round a fly. And then they'd just be shrink-wrap for his shattered corpse.

To combat hypoxia, Carver was using a personal oxygen supply. But the extreme cold can play havoc by icing up an oxygen mask, leaving the user blind and disoriented. That, too, can lead to a fatal loss of control.

Buffeted and deafened by the air being forced around his body as he plummeted, and as numb with cold as a deep-frozen T-bone, Carver wondered how much difference blindness would make. If he looked straight down, there was nothing below him but the infinite blackness of the Atlantic Ocean. But then out of the corner of his right eye, he saw a sparkle of light, far beneath him, that expanded and brightened with every second that passed, and now he was able to get his bearings.

He was travelling from east to west, towards the eastern seaboard of America, still so high that he could detect the curvature of the earth. To his left, a dusting of lights from roads and buildings and a faint line of pale grey marked the sandy shoreline of the Outer Banks, the ribbon of barrier islands that curved around the North Carolina coast, enclosing a great stretch of water between them and the mainland. To his right, looking north across the Virginia state line, the lights he had seen glittering against the black earth were the cities of Virginia Beach, Norfolk, Hampton and Newport News.

Few places on the planet held more concentrated military fire-power than that coastal conurbation, packed against the shoreline where Chesapeake Bay opened out on to the Atlantic Ocean. The US Coast Guard, Navy and Air Force owned thousands of acres, given over to bases that housed hundreds of combat aircraft and massive fleets of warships: aircraft carriers, cruisers, destroyers and nuclear submarines. But Carver was all alone in the sky, aiming for the man who was his target, the man all those armed forces were paid to protect.

6

'See that picture over there?' President Lincoln Roberts pointed at an antique photograph mounted in a stained-wood frame, one of a collection of personal mementos on the wall of the private study at Lusterleaf, his family home near Knotts Island, North Carolina. The monochrome print showed about twenty African-Americans gathered in front of a building made of crudely nailed wooden planks. A couple of them were grown men, the rest women and children, ranging in age from grandmothers to babes in arms.

'Sure,' said Harrison James. 'You've had it there as long as I've known you.'

'That's right, but I never told you about it, I don't think.' The President grinned unexpectedly, his face lighting up with almost boyish mischief: fifty-six going on fifteen. 'See, all those people there are slaves. The photograph was taken on the Gloucester Hall Plantation in Bertie County, across the sound from here, in 1860, maybe '61 – round about the time of the secession, anyway. Look at the woman in the middle, sitting on that bench, holding her baby. Her name was Hattie MacInstry. Some Scots folks owned the place, she took her name from them. The little kid on her lap is Adelaide MacInstry. Her married name was Roberts. I'm her great-great-grandson. Her dad was the plantation overseer, man by the name of Obadiah Jakes. White man.'

His Chief of Staff whistled softly to himself, shaking his head. 'My God, Linc, that's a helluva story! From the plantation to the White House. I mean, that's . . . that's America, Linc, right there. What an image! Wish we'd had that in the campaign.'

'That's why I didn't tell you about it sooner. I knew you'd want it. But we couldn't have run a campaign that was all about moving beyond racial divisions and then shown people pictures of my great-great-grammy on a slave plantation.'

'So why are we talking about it now?'

The President looked him right in the eye. 'Because I aim to make the fight against slavery one of the central pillars of my foreign policy. I want to start a worldwide crusade for freedom, use the power of our great nation for good.'

Whatever Harrison James had been expecting, it certainly wasn't that. 'You know, you coulda told me this earlier. I mean, you just said we didn't want to campaign on race. Well, we sure as hell don't want to base our first administration on race.'

'We're not going to, because this isn't about race,' said Roberts, totally serious now. 'It's about humanity. Africans, Europeans, Indians, Chinese – all the children of the earth – are being bought and sold in every nation on the planet, including our own, in a slave trade worth a minimum thirty billion dollars a year. You know how many slaves were transported from West Africa to this country in the four centuries before the trade was abolished? About six hundred and fifty thousand. You know how many people are being trafficked across national borders every year, right now, in the twenty-first century? Eight hundred thousand. The current United Nations estimate for the number of men, women and children living in conditions of slavery today, worldwide, is almost thirteen million. Some people think the true figure's twice as high. It's an abomination, Hal, a stain upon all our consciences, and I aim to stamp it out.'

The President's voice had been gaining in intensity as he spoke. He was tall and strongly built, blessed with the presence of a born commander-in-chief and the captivating oratory of a gospel preacher. Once he built up a head of steam Roberts became an unstoppable force. Harrison James tried to pull on the brake while there was still time.

'But, Linc, it's not like this is new. The State Department's been issuing reports on trafficking for years. We've been putting pressure on other nations, spending hundreds of millions of dollars on enforcing action against criminals—'

'Well, exactly, we spent hundreds of millions, in total, over several years,' Roberts interrupted. 'But we spend hundreds of billions on defence and the war against terror every single year, thousands of times as much. It's time we looked at the world a different way. We've got to do something good, something that makes us feel proud of who we are and what we stand for. There are countless thousands dying and suffering every day because of slavery. What's more American, what's more patriotic, than standing up and saying, "That's not going to happen on my watch"?'

Now, for the first time in a while, there was a rueful half-smile on Harrison James's face. 'You sound like you've been working on that speech a while. I guess we better work out a way to sell it to the Hill, the American people and the whole damn world.'

'I already did,' said Roberts. 'There's a conference on people-trafficking in Bristol, England, next month.'

'Sure, we're sending a delegation.'

'I want to address that conference.'

'Next month? But, Linc – Mr President, your schedule's already fixed. I mean—'

'Screw my schedule. Make it happen.'

The Chief of Staff's face drained of emotion as friendship was forgotten and he became a subordinate taking an unwanted order from his boss. 'Yes, Mr President.'

The room fell silent, the tension between the two men charging the atmosphere. Then the mood was broken by a knock on the door. It was already opening as Roberts said, 'Come in,' and a man with bland, clean-cut features, his mousy hair cut in a short, conservative, corporate style came in. He wore a black suit, white shirt and sober blue tie. A wire by his neck revealed the presence of an earpiece.

'Any news?' asked the President.

Special Agent Tord Bahr of the US Secret Service nodded. 'Yes, sir. And I have to advise you, Mr President, that I strongly recommend evacuating you immediately. Our latest intelligence indicates a high probability of an attack on you tonight. There's still time to get you away.'

'You're certain of the threat?'

'Yes, sir.'

'And you're totally prepared?'

'Absolutely. As much as anyone can be.'

'And my family are quite safe at the White House?'

'Yes, sir.'

'Then I'm not going to cut and run. It doesn't look good, the leader of the free world hiding at a moment of crisis. Are we clear?'

Bahr's jaw clenched for a second before he replied, 'As crystal, Mr President.'

'Thanks, Tord, I have total confidence in you and your team.'

Roberts looked out through the bullet-proof glass that had been fitted to all the windows of his house. 'Guess it's going to be a long night,' he said. But his Chief of Staff had already followed the Secret Service agent out of the door and was setting about his business.

7

Carver crossed the coast of North Carolina at an altitude of 15,000 feet, seeing down below him a narrow stretch of uninhabited scrub, less than a mile wide. He passed over it in twenty-five seconds, during which time he fell another 1,200 feet. Now he was over the inland waters of Back Bay. This was the longest section of his journey: four miles of open water, dropping all the time till he could feel the air getting warmer and richer, so that he no longer needed any oxygen. He knew exactly where he was and for now his flight was smooth and untroubled. He had a couple of minutes to make the best of it. After that, things would turn very nasty again.

To his left was Knotts Island. It was about five miles long by four miles across at its widest, southernmost end. A thin ribbon of land connected it to the Virginia mainland, splitting two stretches of inland water: Back Bay and Currituck Sound. The Roberts estate lay on the ribbon, with the main house right up against the Currituck shoreline.

Carver flew a few hundred yards to the north of the estate. He was getting nervous now. The strong following wind which he'd counted on to carry him on his way had slackened and he was losing airspeed, not covering enough distance relative to the height he was losing. His altimeter started beeping in his ear, telling him that he was down to 3,000 feet. In no more than twenty seconds, he would have to open his chute. It was an illusion, he knew, but the ever-nearing roofs and trees below him seemed almost close enough to touch. Surely he would be seen. He felt the gaze of unseen eyes and his body tensed, waiting for the sound of gunfire. Yet none came.

And then he was back over water, not much further to go.

He banked hard left, turning through 90 degrees on to a southerly course that would take him over Currituck Sound, back down towards the estate. Then he passed 2,000 feet; the parachute opened; he felt the massive G-forces imposed by instant, radical deceleration, and after all the dangers he had overcome to get this far, Carver prepared for the deadliest part of his journey.

For the next ninety seconds, he would be drifting over enemy airspace. Both he and his chute were covered in black, non-reflective material, making him very hard to spot. But even so, he knew from personal experience just how vulnerable a man felt hanging from a chute with hostiles armed with guns beneath him. It was a noxious cocktail of bowel-juddering fear, mixed with the exposure of a nudity dream, going out in public naked from the waist down. As he steered towards the sound, Carver didn't feel any better about it than he had on any previous occasion. He had his pants on all right, but somehow his balls were still dangling in the wind.

Up ahead there was a tiny island, just a few yards wide, poking up out of the sound, about a thousand yards from the shore. Carver, however, had no intention of landing on it. He would be far too visible, even if he could hit it and stop himself before his momentum carried him right over the far edge. His aim had always been to touch down in its lee, out of sight of the Secret Service personnel guarding the Roberts estate. And that meant landing in the water.

Even for a regular parachutist, that is a tricky enough procedure. The key issue is to know exactly when to detach the parachute canopy. Do it too soon, while still too far above the water, and you'll hit the surface too fast and just keep going down unstoppably into the depths. Plenty of special forces men have perished that way, dragged to their deaths by the speed of impact and the excess weight of their gear.

Anyone who waits too long, however, risks becoming tangled in lines and canopy fabric. Unable to swim, they will then drown like a dolphin trapped in a tuna-net. The Goldilocks knack is to release the canopy not too high and not too low, but just right: 'When you feel the water on the tips of your toes,' as one of Carver's instructors had told him.

He might also have added, had he known what his pupil would one day attempt: 'And for Christ's sake don't wear a wing-suit.'

It's hard enough to swim when your arms are prevented from moving more than 45 degrees from your body because you're dressed like a man-sized bat. When your legs are hobbled by a triangle of tough, unyielding material it's absolutely impossible. So long before Carver got rid of his parachute, he had to deal with his wings.

A thousand feet above the water, he pulled on the cutaway handles that released his arm wings. He felt the ripping sensation of opening Velcro, raised his arms, yanked them outwards and exhaled with relief as the two black triangles fluttered like flags on the wind before disappearing into the night.

His leg wing had no instant cutaway system. It had to be released by its zip. Carver raised his knees towards his chest, felt for the zip handle and tugged. Nothing happened. He tugged again. Still no response. The zip was jammed.

Carver was twenty seconds, maximum, away from impact. He forced himself not to panic, but to think clearly and act calmly. All was not lost. Attached to his suit he had a lightweight combat-utility knife with a titanium handle and a steel blade, hardened with tungsten and carbon-diamond. It could cut through the toughest fabric as easily as it could cut through a man. Carver had counted on being able to do both.

He grabbed the blade, reached down and started slashing desperately at the tough black material between his legs. The bottom end of the wing was reinforced with a panel of extra-stiff fabric, designed to increase stability and rigidity during flight.

The water was rushing towards him. The knife was sawing back and forth across the panel. Carver cut through the final strands just in time. His legs were free, even if there were now two strips of fabric flapping round them like a pair of seventies disco flares. But then he realized something else. He had to release the parachute, which he could not do with a knife in his right hand. Nor could he risk hitting the water holding a deadly blade.

With a muttered, 'Shit!' Carver threw the knife as far away from himself as he could. He had lost one of his most valuable weapons. But there was no time to waste worrying about that. He pulled at the release-cord and freed himself from his canopy.

An instant later, he hit the water. And he kept going down.

For a second or two his momentum seemed undiminished, but then his descent slowed, he kicked out with his legs, pulled at the water above him with his hands and slowly, oh so slowly, he felt himself rise up towards the surface.

At last he broke through and felt the glorious rebirth of that first desperate breath of fresh air. He was down. He was alive. Now he swam to the island and scrambled on to one of the rocks that surrounded it, taking care to stay well out of sight of the far shore, and the men guarding Lincoln Roberts.

Carver had an equipment pouch strapped to his stomach. Inside it, he'd packed a shortened Heckler and Koch MP7 sub-machine gun. It was the updated version of the MP5 he had used in the past, designed to penetrate body armour, but he was still keeping out water the old-fashioned SBS way: with a condom stuck over the barrel. Next to it in the pouch were a selection of small explosive charges, a snorkel, a diver's mask and a pair of fins. He removed the oxygen mask he had worn for the jump and threw it into the water, along with his parachute harness. He put on the sub-aqua gear. Then he slipped back into Currituck Sound, made his way around the island and started swimming towards the shore.

8

Carver had spent his professional lifetime training himself not to think about the rights and wrongs of the work he did. It was not that he lacked a moral compass. It was just that there was no point in wasting time on matters over which he had no control. He'd learned that in the Royal Marines. Politicians started wars. Senior officers then had to prosecute them. They gave orders and men like Carver obeyed them. All along the line, people had reasons for what they did. They all thought they were doing the right thing. For the people at the sharp end, however, the issue wasn't right or wrong. It was doing everything you could to kill the other guy before he got you.

The same principle applied outside the armed forces. Carver had never been on a job, even the ones that seemed beyond all justification, that someone, somewhere didn't believe was the right thing to do. He'd fought a man who was willing to bring down the wrath of God upon the world and provoke the end of days in the sincere and absolute belief that this was the road to salvation. Granted, he was crazy. But his conviction was no less total than that of men who'd claimed to be sane.

So now he didn't think about anything as he swam just beneath the surface of Currituck Sound, aside from the immediate, practical realities of his situation. He had several hundred yards to cover, through water that was virtually tideless, so currents were not a problem. The wind, now freshening once more, was against him, making the surface choppy. Although that slowed him down a little, he was virtually submerged, and the broken water surface only helped hide him from anyone watching from the shore. But having just overcome the threat of hypothermia, his biggest problem now was heat. His flying suit was acting as a dry shellsuit, but the multiple layers of undergarments essential to keep him alive at high altitude were putting him in danger of overheating. The process would begin with the swelling of his hands and feet, moving on to cramps and heatstroke, which could leave him disoriented, hallucinating and even comatose.

For SBS operatives, who regularly have to shift from the extreme cold of, say, an underwater drop-off from a submarine to the intense exertion of a long swim, followed by a climb up a ship's hull or oil platform, heat is a familiar adversary. So Carver took the swim slowly, regularly pausing to get his bearings and keep an eye out for hostile vessels. He presumed that the Coast Guard would be patrolling the sound, in the knowledge that al-Qaeda had made deadly attacks on US forces by speedboat before and might easily do so again.

Sure enough, he twice heard the rumble of screws in the water. There was nothing to do but stop swimming and remain as still as possible, treading water just enough to prevent himself sinking, with his snorkel-tube just an inch or two above the surface of the water. The first time, the cutter passed by a good hundred yards away. The second time the deep rumbling in the water intensified until Carver knew it was headed directly for him.

His eyes desperately widened to catch any scrap of light, he peered out into the black, murky water and then, suddenly, there it was, a foaming mass of bubbles streaming from the onrushing grey blade of a ship's bow. Carver took one last breath and dived, frantically kicking out with his fins as he fought to escape the inexorable avalanche of steel now bearing down upon him.

It was no good. He wasn't getting away. The bow was going to hit him. And then, just as he braced himself for the impact, an unseen force picked him up and flung him sideways, displacing him along with the water being forced away from the ship and he was caught up in the wake as it flowed away from the hull, and then, like iron filings attracted to a magnet, was drawn back towards the vessel.

Carver was hurled towards the flank of the cutter. He saw the diagonal red, white and blue stripes painted on its side and aft of them the words 'US COAST GUARD' printed in white capital letters. He hit the hull just under the final 'D', taking the blow on his left shoulder, arm and hip with a force that knocked the breath from his body, before the current swirled away again and left him bobbing in the open water as the stern of the cutter disappeared into the night.

Carver ran his hand over his body, pressing with his fingers to detect any broken bones. He felt shaken up and bruised, but his arm was still mobile and his chest only ached when he breathed, without the sharp, stabbing pain of a broken rib. He was fit to go on.

Fifteen minutes later, he was treading water beneath one of the two L-shaped walls that stretched out from the shore to form the dock. The entire structure was about sixty feet wide and twice as deep. Right next to Carver, facing out to sea, was a gap in the wall, about thirty feet wide, to let boats in and out. A man dressed in black fatigues, with a black flak jacket, boots and cap, was patrolling the wall on the far side of the gap, walking to and fro, pausing every so often to raise his night-vision binoculars and look out over the water.

Through the opening into the dock, Carver could see a yacht, moored to a floating pontoon at the foot of the far wall, its bow pointing towards him. This must be the *Lady Rosalie*, a 42-foot sloop loved by the President almost as much as the wife after whom she was named. He took a deep breath, dropped beneath the surface of the water and started swimming towards her.

Carver surfaced on the far side of the bow, in the narrow gap between the hull of the *Lady Rosalie* and the wooden planking of the pontoon floating beside her. At the far end of the pontoon a set of stone steps marched diagonally up the side of the dock wall. Still staying below the level of planking, Carver made his way along the hull. He ducked behind the yacht's stern, breathed deeply once again and dropped below the surface of the water. A good sixty seconds passed before he reappeared and looked back along the hull towards the guard. He had walked out along the wall, his back was turned and his attention was now focused out to sea. Still in the water, Carver pulled off his mask, snorkel and flippers. He pulled himself out of the water on to the dock and scurried across to the steps.

Crouching in the shadows, he reached into the pack on his chest and removed the Heckler and Koch. It was compact and snub-nosed, little more than a foot long, but plenty big enough for the job he would ask it to do.

Carver closed his eyes, regulated his breathing until it was slow and easy. His mind was running over the plans he'd memorized of the grounds of Lusterleaf, and the main house itself, no more than a hundred feet away across the grass that ran up to the dock. About twenty feet shy of the house ran a low stone wall, with a flower-bed in front of it, and a stone terrace behind, furnished with tables and chairs, that ran up to the back of the house.

Carver assumed that there were lookouts on the roof of the house. He also took it for granted that there would be agents inside the building, and that the lawn would be covered by motion-detectors, pressure-sensors and cameras with thermal-imaging capacity. There was no way he was going to get across that open space undetected. He just had to get across it fast.

The way Carver looked at it, the odds weren't really too bad. It would take less than four seconds to cross the open grass, hurdle the wall and get to the building. The man on the dock wasn't likely to pick him up straight away, and even if he did, he would have to be damn good to hit a running man from where he was standing. The agents up on the roof would be hampered by basic geometry. They would have to shoot downwards, and the closer he got to the house, the tougher that shot would become. And again, they would have to react with remarkable speed.

There were two possible ways into the house from where he was positioned: French windows leading into the main living-room and a back door by the kitchen. If Carver could get to either of those entrances, blast them open and then start shooting, he backed himself to take down anyone he met inside, including Lincoln Roberts.

So he crouched by the foot of the steps, as tense as a sprinter on the blocks, took three deep breaths, then sprang upwards over the stone and on to the grass. And then he just ran like hell.

Carver didn't need Einstein to tell him that time was relative. Four seconds feels like a lifetime when it only takes a fraction of one of them to trigger the alarm system that sets bells ringing and lights blazing ... and suddenly you feel as if you're running through treacle. Warnings are being shouted from all directions. Guns are being raised. You're trying to jink and swerve to unsettle the shooters, but every sidestep only slows you down. Then the firecracker explosions of small-arms fire rip through the screaming of the alarm bells, and you wait for the first bullet to tear your flesh, but none comes, and then you just throw yourself the last twenty feet, and ...

Carver hit the ground, ducked into a forward roll and made it alive to the wall of the house. The French windows were just ahead of him. A shaped charge was in his hand, ready to blow them open, and then the gunfire and bells both stopped, instantaneously, and his ringing ears heard a voice shout, 'Drop your weapons, now!'

Carver did as he was told. Slowly, without giving anyone any cause for alarm or reason to shoot, he placed the gun and the explosive charge on the stone flagstones at his feet.

'Now place your hands behind your head.'

Again, Carver obeyed the instruction.

'Turn around. Nice and easy.'

Carver turned and came face to face with Special Agent Tord Bahr. There was a hint of a smirk playing round the corners of his mouth. And there was a look of real pleasure in Bahr's eyes as he raised the pistol in his right hand, aimed it directly at Samuel Carver's unprotected chest. And fired.

9

Carver spent the small hours on a bunk in the estate's staff quarters, his chest unharmed by the blanks that had been fired at it. At six thirty in the morning, after three hours' sleep, he was in the dining-room, with one hand round a mug of strong coffee and the other holding a steak sandwich, the bread richly infused with blood and melted fat.

The Secret Service had fixed Carver up with a dark blue T-shirt and a pair of athletic grey sweatpants. They'd given him a toothbrush but no razor, nor a hairbrush. He was looking pretty much the same as any other man on a Saturday morning after a hard Friday night. That was the way he liked it, appearing so normal as to be almost nondescript.

Carver wasn't especially tall, just a fraction under six feet. He didn't ripple with muscle, or exude the air of physical menace that characterized so many men who dealt in violence for a living. He was happy to blend into the crowd and go about his business unnoticed. Only the most sharp-eyed observer would spot the controlled athleticism of his walk, the set furrow of his brow or the way his eyes, so clear and so green, snapped into focus when his concentration was engaged. Right now, though, the only thing they were focused on was his sandwich.

On the other side of the table Tord Bahr was eating a bowl of granola with skimmed milk and sliced banana. He was already dressed in a suit and tie, his earpiece and wrist-mike in place, showing no sign whatever of the night's exertions. The only scintilla of human weakness Bahr allowed himself was the expression, dangerously close to an actual smile, that conveyed his deep satisfaction at the way the dummy attack, designed to test his men's readiness, had panned out. From Bahr's perspective, the night had been a total success. Carver had provided a tough test, but then lost.

'The wing-suit,' he said, having first made sure that his mouth was completely free of granola pieces, 'what gave you that idea?'

'Process of elimination,' said Carver. He was now leaning back in his chair, side-on to the table, looking out of the dining-room's open French windows. 'I thought about conventional HAHO and HALO insertions, but then . . . hang on . . .'

Carver got up and walked over to the windows. The *Lady Rosalie* was out on the water, heeling over in the fresh breeze, her sails dazzling white in the low morning sun. There were two speedboats flanking her, a helicopter hovering above.

'Who's taken the yacht out?' he asked.

'The President,' Bahr replied. 'He's been here all night.'

'The President?' Carver tried hard not to splutter meat and coffee all over the floor. 'What do you mean, he's here? I thought this was just a training exercise. Is that regular procedure, having him on-site?'

'No, it is absolutely not regular. It's beyond irregular. We have a training division with its own facility. Anything we need to train for, we can pretty much do it right there. But the President had his own views and of course we, ah . . . we respected those.'

Carver said nothing. He turned back to the window and watched for a few seconds, before looking back at Bahr. He seemed to be on the verge of saying something.

'You got something on your mind?' asked Bahr.

'Come here,' said Carver.

'Lemme just finish my granola.'

'No, I think you should come here.'

Bahr sighed, shook his head, then got up from the table and began walking towards where Carver was standing. He had only taken a couple of steps before an explosive crack split the air.

A tiny figure in the cockpit of the *Lady Rosalie* rushed to the stern as the boat turned into the wind, its sails flapping uselessly as it slowed almost to a halt. The speedboats were already racing towards the yacht.

'What the fuck—?' shouted Bahr.

He raced the last few feet towards the window, and then kept going till he was standing on the grass outside. Carver saw him put a finger to his ear and bark into his wrist-mike.

'I don't get it,' he was saying. 'What are you saying? What do you mean the sea has turned red?'

Up in the helicopter the pilot was looking down on a crimson stain spreading out around the *Lady Rosalie*.

'It's like blood, man, like the whole frickin' ocean is turning into blood.'

Bahr turned back to the staff quarters and glared wide-eyed at Carver. 'Don't you go anywhere!' he yelled, his composure shattered. 'Consider yourself under arrest!'

Then he started running towards the dock.

10

Carver stood in thoughtful silence watching the chaos as the President was helped off his yacht on to one of the speedboats. His place at the *Lady Rosalie*'s helm was taken by a black-uniformed figure and then the speedboats turned and raced for the shore, shadowed by the helicopter.

'Step away from the window.'

Carver turned and saw a young Secret Service agent standing by the internal door to the dining-room pointing his gun right at him. The agent looked as though he was having a hard time holding on to his composure. His nerves were fraying. If they snapped, he might do something foolish. With the minimum possible fuss, Carver did as he was told.

'Now sit down at the table, hands on the table-top, palms down.'

'Sure,' said Carver and once again obeyed.

For a while, nothing happened. From where he was sitting, Carver could look past the agent, through the door and into the corridor. So, when footsteps sounded outside the room, he was the first to see the tall, commanding figure dressed in jeans and a windcheater with the presidential insignia on the left breast standing framed in the doorway.

Automatically Carver got to his feet.

'Sit down!' screamed the agent, his head suddenly jerking to one side as he realized that his President was in the room.

'Take it easy, son,' Roberts said.

Tord Bahr was following right behind the President. He went up to the agent and said a few words in his ear, sending him from the room.

Lincoln Roberts turned his attention to Carver. He stood still, saying nothing, just weighing him up. Finally he said, 'Sit down.'

Roberts strolled over to the coffee jug and poured himself a cup, nice and easy, just as though this were a casual social visit between friends. After all that had just happened there was something almost unnatural about his aura of calm self-control. His drink fixed, he sat down opposite Carver in the chair that Bahr had been occupying no more than ten minutes earlier. He moved the bowl of cereal out of his way, leaving the table clear between him and Carver. Bahr very deliberately remained on his feet, evidently determined to reassert his unbending sense of duty.

Roberts took a sip of coffee. 'Mmm, that's good,' he said appreciatively. 'Your sandwich OK?'

'Yes, sir.'

Carver wasn't a man who often felt awed by anyone else's presence. But then he'd never sat down for coffee with a US president before, let alone one he was willing to risk his life for. Most politicians he'd met, he wouldn't have jumped from a plane at 25,000 feet just to test their security systems. He'd have chucked them out of it, instead, see how that worked.

Roberts, though, had something different about him. When he talked about trying to change things for the better he sounded as though he truly meant it. Maybe he was just a better actor than the rest of them. What was that saying? If you can fake sincerity, you've got it made. That could be his secret, though Carver hoped it wasn't. Time would tell. Meanwhile, Carver resumed chewing on his steak, waiting to see what the President wanted to say.

'You like my yacht?' he asked.

'Yes, sir,' Carver replied. 'She's a beautiful boat.'

Roberts nodded over his coffee mug. 'I agree. She's thirty years old, you know, got a Brazilian hardwood hull. I had her restored a while back. When I get her out on the water, feel the wind in her sails, breathe in that salt sea air . . . well, I guess that's when I'm most at peace with the world.'

The President leaned forward and looked Carver in the eye, and now he wasn't anyone's friend. He was a man who had the ambition, the drive and the ruthless focus required to work his way from obscurity to the most powerful job in the world.

'You want to tell me what you thought you were doing wrecking that peace?'

'Keeping you alive, sir – making sure you never became another Mountbatten,' Carver replied. 'In 1979, the IRA killed Lord Louis Mountbatten, Prince Charles's "Uncle Dickie", by blowing up his yacht. Last night, I attached a dummy device to the hull of the *Lady Rosalie*, right beneath the cockpit, about sixty seconds before I ran like a lunatic across that lawn out there. There was a sensor attached to it that measured boat-speed through the water, wired to explode once the boat reached eight knots. Nothing serious, just a great big bang and a lot of red dye, but I think it made my point.

'Of course, if I'd been a real assassin, I wouldn't be sitting here opposite you now. I'd have sneaked back out of your dock, the same way I came in, swum down past the boundary of your property and come ashore. Then I'd have got into the sand-coloured Saturn Astra that's parked in the lot at the Knotts Island Market, just a mile or two down the road from here, driven to the nearest airport and got a ticket out, bound for any destination on earth. I'd be gone before you even knew what I'd done.'

'So why attack the house?' asked the President.

'I wanted to make a point, sir. Special Agent Bahr asked me to stage an assassination attempt as an exercise to test his agents' readiness. So I gave them a very obvious assassin, right there in everyone's face. Once he'd been taken out, they all thought the exercise was over. I don't blame them: it's only natural. This morning, they were relaxed, feeling good. The last thing anyone expected at that point was the actual hit. But that was the point: if anyone does this for real, it's going to be unexpected. Maybe in movies you see nut-jobs posting threatening letters, making the hero run round the streets chasing messages on payphones, letting everyone know there's a killing on the way. But the guys at the top of this business just come in quietly, do the job, and half the time no one ever knows that there even was an assassination. They think it was an accident.'

'You sound awfully like a man who's talking from experience.'

'Let's just say I was very well trained, Mr President, and I served in various units with a wide range of duties.'

Roberts did not reply, just drank his coffee. He swallowed, grimaced and murmured, 'Hmm . . .' Then he got up from the table and held out a hand. As Carver shook it, the President said, 'It's been very interesting meeting you, Mr Carver. You gave me a lot to think about. You mind if I give you some advice in return?'

'Of course not, Mr President.'

'Those things you said about assassinations . . .'

'Yes, sir?'

'I'd advise you very strongly not to put any of your ideas into practice.'

'No, sir, my work these days is based entirely on keeping people safe from harm. I sleep better that way. One thing I learned from active service was that every time you cause someone else to be killed you kill a bit more of yourself. Gets to the point where there's barely anything left. It's not a good place to be.'

Roberts frowned. 'Goodbye, Mr Carver,' he said. 'Have a safe journey home.'

The President left the room, but Bahr stayed behind. When the two of them were alone, he told Carver, 'No one ever finds out about this, do you understand? No one. Ever. As far as we're concerned – far as the whole world's concerned – the President came down here, had a peaceful weekend, just like any other. You are way off the record. You want my advice, you'll keep it that way.'

'Fair enough,' said Carver. 'Can you get me a lift to my car?'

11

Carver drove back up to Richmond, getting there just in time for a ten o'clock flight to Chicago. He was feeling good about the way the Lusterleaf job had gone. He'd decided to ride his luck, see if it worked for women as well as presidents.

As he sat at the departure gate, he was looking at a text message on his phone. It read: 'Hey you! 2 long. How come no call?! Maddy xox'.

It had come in three weeks ago, automatically and untraceably rerouted from his standard contact number. Carver thought about the first time she'd left him a message, a scrap of paper left on a bedside table at a hotel in the South of France that read, 'If you're ever in Chicago . . .' with a number and the same sign-off, 'Maddy xox'. He'd found it when he woke up and discovered he was alone in his bed. The night before, Madeleine Cross had just about saved his life.

They'd met in the bar of the Hôtel du Cap. Her husband, who'd made millions selling medical supplies to hospitals, had gone off to a casino in Cannes. It said everything about the state of their marriage that he hadn't invited her to go with him, and she hadn't invited herself.

Carver, meanwhile, had just watched his whole life falling apart around him. Alix Petrova, the woman he loved, had told him she'd married another man. She swore that someone had told her Carver was dead. It was a complicated story. But then, he thought, everything about his relationship with Alix had been a complicated, painful, impossible bloody story.

Madeleine had been sitting by the bar, watching the whole charade of his conversation with Alix and her subsequent departure. Left alone and defeated at his table, Carver had been too lost in his own self-pitying misery even to notice another woman. He'd walked up to the bar to get a double whisky and it was only then he heard someone say, 'So it didn't work out, huh?'

He turned and saw an immaculately glossed and painted brunette, whose scarlet dress was perfectly cut to reveal the swell of her breasts, the slenderness of her waist and the flawless line of her caramel-tanned thighs. That much Carver caught at a glance. It took him a while to notice the knowing, feline tilt of her eyes or the sharp, dry mind that lay behind them.

Since both their partners had let them down, they decided to find out how well they could make it work together instead. Pretty well was the answer, but it had only ever been the one night. A fair amount of time had passed, long enough for Carver and Alix to get back together, try to make it work and fail. Since then he'd exchanged occasional texts and emails with Maddy. It had all been friendly, but nothing more than, and they'd never got round to meeting up again. Maybe it was time to change that. He made the call.

'Hello?' Her voice was sleepy. Damn! Had he woken her up?

'Hi, it's Sam . . . Samuel Carver . . . You texted me a while back. I couldn't get back to you till now.'

'Sam . . . ? Oh, Sam! Hey, great to hear from you. Where are you?'

'I'm at Richmond airport, Virginia, thought I'd take a plane to Chicago. Fancy some brunch when I get there?'

'No, I don't think that would be possible . . .'

Carver was shocked to discover how sharp the pain of disappointment felt. 'Oh . . . Right . . . Look, I'm sorry if I disturbed you, I—'

'No, it's fine, you didn't disturb me at all . . .' He could hear the smile in her voice as she admitted, 'OK, you did, but I don't mind. It's just I'm not in Chicago.'

He gave an exhausted, ironic laugh. 'Oh God, I don't believe it . . . Where are you then?'

'On my ranch. It's a few miles out of Cascade, Idaho. It's where I come from. I told you, remember?'

'Yeah, maybe, I think so. But excuse my ignorance, where exactly is Idaho?'

'Where's Idaho?' She sounded outraged by his ignorance. 'I should put this phone down, right now, just for that.'

'Seriously, how do I get to you?'

'You'd do that? Really?'

Now he detected something else: she wanted him to make the effort.

'Sure. In the past twelve hours I've parachuted 25,000 feet, swum about a thousand yards and driven 120 miles. What's one extra flight?'

She laughed. 'OK, action hero, when do you get to O'Hare?'

'About eleven.'

'Perfect. There's a United flight to Boise, that's the closest airport to me. It leaves around midday, gets in early afternoon. Why don't you take that?'

'Sounds like a plan.'

'And if you're very good, I'll meet you at the airport.'

Now Carver knew his luck was in. As the first call for passengers was being made he dialled a number in Oslo, Norway. It belonged to Thor Larsson, the eccentric Norwegian who was both his closest friend and the supplier of much of the surveillance equipment, computer hard- and software and assorted gadgets Carver needed to carry out his assignments.

'Hi, it's me,' Carver said when the call was answered. 'Look, I'm sorry it's taken me a while to get back to you. I've been under the radar. Just wanted you to know that little gizmo you just made me – the one with all the red ink . . . Yeah, that one. Well, it worked a treat . . . No, I can't tell you where I used it, not unless you want us both to get shot! . . . Of course I haven't forgotten your wedding. Unless you're telling me the bride changed her mind. Can't say I'd blame her . . .'

Carver smiled as he heard what the voice on the other end of the line had to say. 'Well, that's good news. I'd better start working on my speech . . . Yeah, I'm great, just off to Boise, Idaho, if you can believe that . . .

'What do you mean, you don't know where that is?' He laughed. 'Miles from anywhere, that's where! And yes, of course there's a woman involved. Why else would I go to Boise bloody Idaho?'

12

Damon Tyzack was back in London, sitting at a table outside a café on Brompton Cross. He watched the glossy Eurotrash girls passing by, babbling into their mobile phones, while bankers' wives and trust-fund totties wandered in and out of Joseph and the Conran Shop as if they'd never even heard the word 'recession'. These were the women he had been born and raised to possess.

He should have been properly settled by now, with a family in the home counties, a flat and a mistress in town, and an agreeable life all round. Instead, he'd suffered disgrace, been disowned by his family and forced to spend years doing squalid work for ignorant, lowlife scum. And that had all been Samuel Carver's fault. His small-minded attitude – a determination to play by the rules and regulations that was, quite frankly, proof that he was common as muck, for all his attempts to pretend otherwise – had cost Tyzack everything he held dear. Now that, entirely through his own efforts, he was in a position to exact some measure of revenge, Tyzack intended to make the most of it. Years ago, he might have acted out of anger or bitterness. But now, having had plenty of time to reflect, he was going to treat the whole thing as a game, a treat to be savoured and enjoyed.

A waitress came to take his order. She was a pretty enough thing, with blue eyes and an engaging smile. Carrying about five to seven pounds of extra weight, Tyzack estimated, but tighten up that stomach a little and firm up the jawline, stick her in a studio flat off the Gloucester Road and you'd be looking at two to three hundred quid an hour, twelve hundred for an overnight.

When the girl asked if he was ready to order, Tyzack's face broke into a friendly, open smile and he looked at her as if there were no one in the world he was happier to see standing in front of him than her.

'Absolutely,' he said. 'I'll have scrambled eggs and smoked salmon, brown toast, a nice big glass of fresh orange juice and a double espresso, please.'

As she was writing it down he asked, 'What's your name?'

The girl smiled shyly. 'Agnieszka.'

'What a lovely name. Where do you come from, Agnieszka?'

'From Łódź, in Poland.'

'Well, I feel very sorry for all the boys from Łódź, then.'

She frowned, not quite sure where he was going, but unable to resist the obvious question: 'Why?'

'Because they don't have a beautiful girl like you to look at any more! Still, very good news for us boys in London, isn't it?'

The lines were ridiculously corny, but it didn't matter. Tyzack had charm, a gift that stupid people always saw as a sign of warmth, when so far as he could see it simply involved a cold-blooded knack for sensing what other people wanted and then giving it to them.

Agnieszka giggled, right on cue, flashed him a coy, heavy-lidded glance and walked away with an extra little swing in her step.

Not bad, thought Tyzack, watching her rump in her tight black skirt. A good little earner if she did what she was told. She would, of course, once he'd persuaded her. That was always the enjoyable part of the process, establishing who was in charge. Tyzack contemplated precisely how long it would take to beat the light out of those bright-blue eyes: experience had given him an almost mathematical appreciation of the effects of time and abuse. His mind drifted back to Lara Dashian. When she made her pathetic, stumbling way to his table, he'd immediately felt that essential deadness, overlaid with a dusting of fear and desperation, like the icing sugar on a sponge cake. Obviously seeing him as the lesser of two evils, she'd tried so hard to please; he'd been tempted to chuck her back to her pimp, just for a laugh. On balance, he decided he'd have more fun keeping her. As they went upstairs, he watched her fear melt away and for a moment he regretted his decision and wondered if he'd better give her something to be scared of himself.

But then he remembered he was playing the part of Samuel Carver. And that pathetic little man would never have taken advantage of a screwed-up teenage whore. He'd have behaved like his dismal, suburban idea of a gentleman. And there was something else, too. As he chucked her on the bed it suddenly occurred to Tyzack that the silly bitch might actually want him to screw her. All the more reason, then, not to.

Tyzack's phone rang. He saw the number come up on his screen and gave an exasperated sigh. 'Yes, Foster, what is it?'

'It's that container, guv. It's fallen off the ship.'

Tyzack closed his eyes and inhaled slowly through his nose, trying to ease the tension that had suddenly clamped around his temples. He let out his breath and asked, 'What do you mean, "fallen off the ship"? Tell me, Foster, how exactly does a container just fall off a ship?'

'Storms, innit? They had, like, force ten winds in the North Sea. Blew a dozen of the bastard containers right into the water. One of 'em was ours.'

'This is the cargo from Hamburg?'

'The Chinkies, yeah.'

Tyzack leaned forward, putting a hand over the receiver to hide his mouth, and hissed, 'Are you telling me that seventy of our little yellow friends are currently sitting on the bottom of the North Sea?'

'That's about the size of it, yeah.'

'They're not going to pick much fruit down there, are they?'

'Nah . . .'

'So what do you plan to do about that? When I get a couple of extremely irate gangmasters on my hands, wondering where all their farm labour's gone, what am I going to tell them?'

'We can cover it, guv. We got them Somalis down Plaistow, yeah? That's twenty-odd right there. Couple of trucks coming in from Bulgaria this week, pikey scum, obviously, but we can knock them out to the farms 'cause there's piss-all for them to do on the building sites. Bring in a few others we got lyin' around. No worries.'

The waitress, Agnieszka, had discreetly sidled up to the table and placed Tyzack's food in front of him, along with the juice and coffee. He gave her a flickering smile of acknowledgement, took a forkful of egg and salmon and went on with his conversation.

'Well, I certainly hope not, Foster. I'm supposed to be getting on a plane for America in less than four hours' time. I have important work to take care of and I don't want any distractions. Which reminds me, those Pakis up in Bradford, were you able to explain that they really could not be allowed to operate in our market?'

'Oh yeah, me and a few of the lads went up north, gave 'em a proper kicking. Happy days.'

'And the merchandise?'

'Yeah, we took the slappers, obviously. Stuck 'em in our places. Got 'em workin' the same night.'

'Excellent. Glad we got that sorted, at least. Now, piss off and replace the seventy Chinese. Chop-chop!'

Tyzack hung up. Foster Lafferty was a shaven-headed thug from the East London end of Essex, but dealing with him was really no different to maintaining control over a stroppy, rather insolent sergeant-major. In fact, running a criminal gang, Tyzack had discovered, was very much like being in the forces: the fact that he'd been killing people for drug-runners and traffickers rather than Her Majesty was really just a technicality. His success had, over time, enabled him to start up his own small firm, much like a platoon.

This had grown in size and power so that he could now regard himself as the colonel of his own private regiment.

There were, of course, still more senior men from whom he took orders and for whom he carried out assignments. They were hardly the kind of individuals for whom he would have chosen to work, all things being equal, but at least there was always the professional satisfaction of a job well done. By poisoning Dey, for example, he had both removed a competitor and framed an enemy. And the cocktail cherry, that had been a sweet touch. After that, putting a bullet through the back of the pimp's head had been the perfect way to round off the evening.

As he sipped at his espresso, Tyzack wondered whether Carver felt the same way. Was it a pleasure to him, too? Deep down, perhaps, but a man that obsessed with his own righteousness would never admit it. Tyzack had gone to considerable trouble and expense to compile a detailed dossier on his old enemy's activities. He'd pulled a few strings, called in some favours and found his way to Percy Wake, the pompous old poof who'd run the Consortium, the secret group of wealthy, powerful individuals who'd given Carver most of his jobs and by doing so made him rich. Wake was living down in the country now, in disgrace, missing the old days, bored out of his mind and longing for some malice and intrigue to brighten up his life. When Tyzack had asked for his help to get at Samuel Carver, Wake had been only too happy to help. He'd spilled the beans about Carver's old operations and working methods. He'd even done a spot of recruiting on Tyzack's behalf. It had all worked out very nicely.

'Can I get you anything else?' The waitress had returned to the table.

'How kind of you to ask, Agnieszka. Just the bill, thanks.'

He bestowed another one of his smiles upon her, wondering if it was worth slipping the manager half a dozen fifties and taking her away right now. He looked at his watch as she put his card through the machine. No, he really ought to be on the way to Heathrow. He had one man to kill, another one to screw up. So he tapped out his pin-number on the keypad, left the girl a generous tip and walked off down the Fulham Road.

Work, work, work, thought Damon Tyzack. I deserve a nice break.

13

The first morning at the ranch, Carver woke up with something tangled round his right foot. He reached down and felt a length of satin ribbon attached to a sliver of silk and lace. He remembered pulling that ribbon and its twin, and a sleepy grin crossed his face.

He was alone in the bed. Carver reached for his watch and was startled to see it was gone ten in the morning. He brushed his teeth, put on his jeans and wandered downstairs, expecting to find Maddy, but the kitchen and living-room were empty. The previous day she'd given him the guided tour of the house and its out-buildings. It struck him she might be out at the stable, tending to her horses, so he fixed himself a coffee, grabbed a pair of dark glasses and went outside.

The air was already warm, well on the way from the relative cool of early morning to the pure, dry heat of midday, and the sun was bright enough to make him glad of the shades. He stopped for a second to look at the forest-covered mountains ringing the horizon, their jagged peaks stabbing into the cloudless blue sky. Carver lived in Geneva, he was used to a spectacular backdrop, but that didn't make this one any less impressive.

The stables were empty, but as Carver came back outside he heard country music coming from the open-fronted, three-bay garage nearby, so he ambled across the compound till he came to a radio, left on a concrete floor next to a plastic bottle of mineral water and an open toolkit. Maddy's German Shepherd, Buster, was lying asleep beside them. Her open-top, metallic champagne Ford Bronco truck was lifted up on jacks just beyond him.

A pair of feet in battered old workboots poked out from underneath the truck, attached to legs encased in oily blue dungarees. Carver took a sip of coffee, put down his cup and peered under the Bronco with an inquisitive frown on his face.

'Hello?'

There was a muffled, high-pitched 'Shit!' then the boot-heels pushed down on the concrete and pulled their owner out from under the truck on a low mechanic's trolley.

Maddy got to her feet. One hand held a wrench, the other was making a futile effort to neaten the hair pinned up on the back of her head. Rebellious dark brown strands had escaped and fallen either side of her face, which was bare of make-up, other than a few smears of motor-oil. The top of her dungarees was tied around her waist. All she was wearing above that was a cap-sleeved white T-shirt with the words '[semi]sweet' written across the chest. The shirt was lightly speckled in dust and grime, as was the strip of flat, caramel-tanned tummy peeking out beneath it.

'Shit!' she repeated. 'I was hoping to get this done before you got up. Figured you'd be out for hours, the way you were lying there, snoring like a big ol' hog.'

She stopped for a moment and looked at Carver. He suddenly realized he was grinning like a village idiot.

'Yeah, go ahead, laugh,' she said. 'I know I look like crap.'

'No, you don't, you don't at all,' he said, slowly shaking his head, but still unable to take the smile off his face. 'You look great.'

'I do?'

Now she was smiling too and the way she was looking at him had changed. Carver was suddenly uncomfortably aware that not only had he not bothered to shave before he came looking for her, he had not brushed his hair or even put on a shirt.

Maddy pulled off her gloves and ran a single finger down Carver's chest. 'Well, you don't look so bad yourself, Mr Six-Pack. Couldn't resist showing it off, huh?'

Her finger was still moving down.

He reached out for her backside and pulled her towards him.

'We can't!' she said, giggling. 'Not in front of Buster!'

'He's asleep,' he said, and kissed her bare neck. 'How about the back of the truck – reckon the jacks'll hold us?'

Carver started nibbling Maddy's ear. She squirmed with pleasure and whispered, 'You'd have to take it real slow and gentle. Think you can manage that?'

'I can try,' he said.

He let go of her for a moment, clambered up into the back of the Bronco, then turned to give her a hand as she climbed up to join him.

The last words she said before his mouth covered hers were, 'Remember, slow and gentle . . .'

A while later they walked back up to the house, arm in arm, with Buster bounding along beside them, wagging his tail so hard it was making circles in the air. He didn't seem too traumatized. They took a shower that seemed to take a little longer than the business of getting clean necessarily required. Then Carver sat on the edge of the bed and watched Maddy dry and brush the tumbling mane that fell halfway down her back.

She looked at him over her shoulder and said, 'So, you freaked out by a girl who does her own auto-mechanics?'

'Not at all. I respect all forms of competence. I like people who are good at things.'

There was just the hint of a dirty undertone in his voice as he said that.

'I agree, skill is very important,' she said with impeccably lady-like cool.

Carver wasn't sure he had the strength to take that thought any further, so he took the conversation on to safer ground: 'Seriously, how did you learn all that stuff?'

'I was an only child. I guess Dad didn't have anyone else to pass on his knowledge to, so he took me hunting every season for deer, pheasants and grouse. I learned how to shoot, how to keep a weapon properly maintained, how to service his truck. Maybe he thought I could be the boy he never had . . .'

'Not too much like a boy, thank God.'

Maddy was silent for a few moments, brushing her hair, her mind elsewhere.

'Suits you, being single,' he said. 'You look more relaxed, like you're a real woman, not someone's prize possession.'

Maddy gave her hair one last brushstroke, ran her hands through it to get precisely the right degree of artless tumble, then got up from her dressing table.

'Feel like some brunch?' she said.

'Thank God,' said Carver, 'I thought you'd never ask.'

14

Bill Selsey was sitting at his desk at the headquarters of the Secret Intelligence Service, otherwise known as MI6, at Vauxhall Cross, London. If he got up and walked to the windows looking out on to the river Thames he could see the Gothic towers and spires of the Houses of Parliament across the water, a few hundred yards downstream. He had given his entire working life to this agency, protecting the values that parliament embodied. Now he was about to betray it all. True, it wasn't as terrible a deception as those of some of the traitors who had gone before him. He wasn't working for enemies bent on his country's destruction: he was just doing favours for a gangster. But in a way, that pettiness only made it worse. He couldn't claim he was working for any great cause. He was simply selling out.

It had all begun with Sir Perceval Wake. Selsey had helped destroy Wake's Consortium and consign him to an enforced, ignominious retirement, deep in the Shropshire countryside. But the old man had always been a compulsive networker and the love of intrigue had never left him. He had enticed Selsey down to his modest farmhouse with the promise of new revelations about the Consortium's activities. Wake had thrown Selsey a few titbits of useful information, just so that he did not return to his superiors empty-handed. That task accomplished, it had proved simple – surprisingly so, to both men – to persuade Selsey to carry out a few straightforward orders for which he would be rewarded on a scale that far outstripped his modest government salary.

Money, of course, has always been a motive for treachery. As Selsey well knew, it provided the 'M' in 'MICE', the intelligence-business acronym that described the four motivations through which undercover spies could be recruited: the other three being 'ideology', 'coercion' and 'ego'. Neither ideology nor coercion applied to Selsey. But ego, he admitted to himself, yes, that might have had something to do with it.

For years, Selsey had been a loyal second-in-command to Jack Grantham, a younger but more brilliant, more driven man. Selsey had always told himself, and anyone else who asked, that he was happy to leave the heavy lifting to someone else. Let Grantham suffer the stresses of leadership and the poison of inter-departmental politics: Selsey was happy to do a good day's work, then head home to a quiet life in the south London suburbs. But much like a loyal spouse, too long taken for granted, Selsey had begun to harbour feelings of bitterness and an urge to upset the status quo. When he was offered the chance to go behind Grantham's back, to withhold secrets and to mislead him with false information, it was as enticing as a pretty young woman offering the promise of an affair.

And it was, after all, such a little thing that had been asked of him. At some point, as yet to be determined, a mechanism would be set in motion that would end in Samuel Carver's death. Selsey had no particular reason to feel any loyalty to Carver. Nor would he be responsible for any harm that Carver suffered. He would just be one cog in a much bigger machine, one step on a long road, and for this small favour he would receive a total of two hundred thousand pounds, tax-free, in a Cayman Islands account.

The first fifty thousand was already sitting there, enough to enable Selsey to think, I've earned more than you this year, old boy, whenever Grantham's casual arrogance became more than usually irritating. The second instalment would soon follow. For Selsey had just received his first instructions.

He was ordered to investigate the poisoning of an Indian people-trafficker called Tiger Dey. To help him in this task, he was advised to examine the passenger manifests of an Emirates Airlines flight from London to Dubai, and to check relevant CCTV footage at both Dubai and Heathrow airports. He was also given a contact in the Dubai police, who would provide him with access to the official investigation of Dey's murder – an investigation that had, un-usually, begun while its subject was still, just, alive. Finally, he was supplied with the number of a recently opened account at a Zurich bank, and the name of a former prostitute who would be able to assist in his inquiries.

Taken together, he was assured, these leads would provide a great deal of information. All he had to do, for now at any rate, was to use this information to arouse Jack Grantham's interest, and persuade him that Samuel Carver had started killing again. From then on, events would take care of themselves.

Selsey had assigned a junior agent to do the donkey work. Provided with the passenger list he had quickly spotted the name 'James Conway Murray' and recognized it at once as one of Carver's known aliases. He had the relevant footage pulled from Heathrow Terminal Three's cameras. As always, the footage was infuriatingly indistinct, but there certainly was a man who answered to Carver's general description, carefully keeping his face away from any direct exposure to the cameras with a skill that only an experienced professional would possess.

Selsey asked for any records of further flights by Murray and was rewarded with a BA ticket to San Francisco, leaving three days after the Dubai job. There was no flight yet between Dubai and London – he would have to keep looking for that. Meanwhile

Murray had gone to the States. That would be a lead worth following in due course.

He put in a call to Dubai, beginning the negotiations that would get him the police reports. The local detectives had already concluded that Dey's killer must have been the Englishman who had sat with him at the Karama Pearl Hotel. They had interviewed Dey's bodyguards without success: they would not squeal to the police, not even on their boss's killer. But Selsey's call made the Dubaians suspect that someone in London knew who the man was. So the deal was obvious: the reports in exchange for the name. Selsey told them he would think about it.

He also had to start the process of extracting information from the Swiss bank. With any luck the people there would be co-operative: the Swiss were far more open than they used to be. Otherwise he'd have to use more underhand methods. He also needed a way into that refuge where the prostitute was hiding. All that would require resources, and for that he needed Grantham's approval. It was time to approach his boss . . . and start lying in his face.

Jack Grantham sat back in his chair and rubbed his forehead, trying to ease his tension and fatigue. He let out a long slow exhalation, then leaned forward and looked at Selsey standing on the far side of his desk.

'I'm sorry, Bill, but I just don't buy it. The last I heard, Carver was doing high-end security work. He tells nervous billionaires and politicians how to keep themselves safe. He even does dummy attacks, just to test their protection. The pay's good. There's no danger. He doesn't feel like shit thinking about what he's done. Why would he want to go back to wet jobs?'

'Maybe he's strapped for cash. Plenty of people are these days. I don't really know why he's done it. I'm just looking at a pile of evidence that says he has.'

'Well, how did we get dragged into this anyway?'

'A private call from Dubai,' said Selsey, pleased that he could now stick to something that had a grain of truth. 'The authorities there already know that Dey's killer is British. They think it would be good for the continued friendship between our two peoples if we helped identify him.'

'Forget it. We're not going to do their bloody plod-work for them. If they arrest a suspect and he happens to be British, it's a straightforward Foreign Office matter, nothing to do with us.'

'Unless he actually is Carver,' mused Selsey, delighted that Grantham had given him an opening. 'We wouldn't necessarily want him falling into anyone else's hands, would we? Not with what he knows.'

'No, we bloody wouldn't . . .' Grantham muttered. He had made deals with Carver, deals that would be very embarrassing indeed were they ever to be made public. It wouldn't be good for a senior MI6 officer to be exposed as a close associate of a paid killer. He shook his head. 'I still can't work out what's really happening here. I mean, what if someone's framing Carver, using him as camouflage to hide what they're up to?'

'Seems a bit elaborate,' said Selsey, trying to sound a lot more relaxed about the speed of Grantham's thought processes than he actually felt.

'Maybe, but even so, I'm not entirely sure about this.'

'Still, there's no harm in looking a bit deeper, eh? We might as well find out what's going on, just to keep our own back well covered.'

'That's always worth doing,' Grantham agreed. 'All right, Bill, dig around. Tell me what you find. And don't tell anyone else.'

'Of course not,' said Selsey. 'You can count on me.'

15

Harrison James put the phone down on a furious senior senator from Florida, having just informed him of the cancellation of a planned presidential trip to Miami. Officially the President had been going to visit the National Hurricane Center and lunch with local business leaders; unofficially he was repaying the senator for his endorsement early in the primary season. James had given the senator a vague explanation of the President's change of plans, saying that he'd be making an overseas trip with significant national security implications that made his destination confidential for the time being.

When the pork-barrelling old bastard asked, 'Are we talking Afghanistan, here, Hal?' he'd replied, 'Well, I can't comment on that, Javier. But I'll tell you this, the President has dynamic, far-reaching plans for the projection of US power around the world. If you can help make those plans a reality, he will not forget your sacrifice.'

Christ, the shit you had to talk just to smooth old men's egos, James thought, putting down the phone. Seconds later, the red light was flashing again.

'It's the British ambassador,' James's personal assistant informed him. 'He wants to talk about the Prime Minister's role in the President's visit.'

'I'll bet he does,' muttered James, then forced a smile into his voice as he said, 'Sir Michael, good to hear from you. What can I do?'

'Morning, Hal, it's just this whole Bristol business. The PM's delighted the President is coming to see us, naturally. Can't wait. And, of course, bearing in mind Britain's historic role in the abolition of slavery, he's absolutely supportive of any effort to stamp out this vile business today. He's just concerned that our presence is acknowledged, as it were.'

'You mean he doesn't want to be totally upstaged in his own back yard.'

'Absolutely, Hal, I knew you'd understand. And if you need a royal or two to greet the President off the plane, or host a spot of lunch, you only have to ask.'

'That's great, Sir Michael,' said James, wondering how the Brits managed to sound so damn condescending, even when they were kissing your ass.

No sooner had he got rid of the ambassador than the light went on again.

'It's Bobby DiLivio in the speechwriters' office,' came his assistant's voice. 'He wants to know if you can spare him five minutes to look over the opening paragraph of the President's speech.'

The men who make tens or even hundreds of billions of dollars a year from organized crime do not possess the intelligence agencies – with electronic infrastructure capable of spying on virtually any communication, anywhere – available to the world's richest nations. They can, however, pay for the very best private-sector specialists in every form of surveillance and investigation. They also have the advantage that they do not even have to pretend to be bound by the law. They are thus free to bribe, blackmail, coerce and otherwise extort information. They routinely use assassination to further their aims. And they can, like any other spy network, insert their people as sleeper agents into legitimate occupations.

Bobby Kula, for example, was a highly regarded computer wizard who played an invaluable role developing and maintaining the operational software that enabled the Department of State to do its job. He was an Albanian-American, a fact of which he was proud, having arrived in the US with his parents when he was just four years old. He was equally proud of his doctorate from 'Course 6', otherwise known as the Electronic and Computer Science department of the Massachusetts Institute of Technology. His security-clearance procedure had shown no record of any criminal activity; no predisposition to aberrant behaviour of any kind; no reason at all to suspect that he posed any risk to the security of his adopted country. It would have taken a detailed understanding of Albania's clan-based culture to understand that Bobby Kula was distantly related on his mother's side to a senior member of a gang run by the Visar clan, which had become one of the biggest international players in the trafficking of drugs, weapons and, above all, people. The importance of this family tie had been drummed into him from his earliest boyhood: both the advantages that it offered and the duties it involved.

It was pure chance that Kula overheard two State officials talking about the President's proposed war on slavery while sitting in a men's room cubicle, invisible to the officials standing at the urinals. His response was anything but random. He understood at once how the new policy could impact on the family business and conducted a private trawl through the department's computers, easily bypassing the security systems that he himself had helped develop and install, to find out more about it.

Having come up with a date and a place for the President's announcement, Kula called a friend at the Albanian embassy in DC and asked him and his family over for a barbecue he and his wife Cindy were having that Sunday afternoon. The invitation would have aroused no suspicion, even if Kula were being watched, which he was not: Albania is an ally of the US and it is perfectly normal for diplomats of all nations to make social contacts in the cities where they are posted. It is, in fact, their job. That this particular diplomat was also connected to the Visar clan was a detail of which the American security agencies were unaware. But even if they had been, there are few agents able to speak *Gjuha shqipe*, the language of Albania, particularly not in the colloquial north-western Geg dialect in which Bobby Kula and his contact were chatting over the franks, slaw and Coors Lights. The contact used the same dialect when passing the news on to the palatial villa in the hills of Nueva Andalucía, looking over the Spanish resort of Puerto Banús, where Arjan Visar was spending the weekend.

Visar was an intellectual among gangsters. He had a chess-player's mind, was able to think several moves ahead, devising strategies of his own and anticipating those of his opponents. He came to a swift conclusion about the implications of the inform-ation he had received and what needed to be done, but not wishing to act rashly, he gave himself a further hour to let his mind settle. Then he reconsidered the problem and concluded that his initial response was the correct one. Only at that point did he start giving orders.

16

Damon Tyzack was invisible to anyone driving by less than fifty yards from where he lay on the grassy slope. But he could see the cars and trucks on the narrow local road, just off Highway 88 in Amador County, northern California. And he could hear the tyres whispering on the blacktop, like waves on a shingle beach.

The landscape, too, possessed a gentle, rolling swell, and the foothills of the Sierra Nevada were softened to a smoky grey by the dying light of a summer dusk. The tourism people hereabouts called their patch the Heart of the Mother Lode, in memory of the forty-niners who'd thronged there during the Gold Rush. These days the mines were gone, or converted into visitor attractions, and the land was given over to vineyards and ranches, like the one that sprawled for a couple of thousand acres on the far side of the road.

The owner was a financier by the name of Norton Krebs, whose business was based in San Francisco, 125 miles away. For the past five years, Krebs had handled investments for corporations controlled by Tyzack and his associates. These investments had lost a great deal of their value and the kind of clients Krebs had cultivated took a less forgiving view than the average investor of a financial adviser continuing to pay himself large fees while delivering poor performance. They saw the destruction of their wealth as, in every sense, a capital offence. So Krebs was marked for death.

The hit would go down within the next few minutes, but the hard work had been done over the past several days. The morning after he'd arrived in San Francisco, Tyzack had ridden Amtrak's California Zephyr train to Salt Lake City, then caught a bus to Boise. There he'd bought a second-hand Toyota Tacoma truck, for cash, using fake ID in Carver's name. He drove it back down to Amador County and spent three full days familiarizing himself with the details of Norton Krebs's life, movements and environment. He took care to speak to people in the towns of Jackson, Iona, Sutter Creek and Amador City, nearest to the Krebs ranch, both to gain information and leave a memory in their minds – a memory of a dark-haired, green-eyed Englishman.

Late on Saturday night, he'd driven across northern California and into Nevada, to the parking garage of the Lake Tahoe casino where Krebs was spending the weekend. That was where Tyzack had replaced the tyre-valves of Krebs's Escalade with valves that looked identical to any casual inspection, but which contained a radio-activated explosive filament. When triggered, they were enough to cause a blow-out that would, if carefully timed and located, cause any but the finest driver to lose control of their vehicle.

The booby-trapped valves were an old Russian trick, but Tyzack had been taught about them when he had served in the British Special Forces. Tyzack hadn't spent long serving Her Majesty. But he'd learned a very great deal.

Beneath him the road curved sharply to the left, following the line of the valley. Just before the turn, the land fell away from the road into a minor ravine around thirty feet deep. A live oak tree grew by the side of the ravine, centuries old to judge by the mighty girth of its trunk and the spread of its evergreen branches.

Between the road and the ravine stretched a barbed-wire fence. Norton Krebs was a perfectionist. He prided himself on demanding nothing but the best. He'd spent a fortune upgrading the boundary of his land with wire that was strong enough to stop a charging bull, stretched tight between posts bedded firmly in the ground. Tyzack was counting on that perfectionism to kill his target.

Krebs, he calculated, was going to approach the left-hander with the confidence and speed of a man who knew the route so well his driving was virtually automatic. His concentration would be impaired by fatigue and the after-effects of the alcohol, cocaine and ecstasy he'd been consuming through most of his waking hours since Friday evening.

Now a car was coming down the road towards Tyzack. Its Xenon headlights were on, but there was still enough ambient light for him to be able to see beyond them and make out the domineering bulk of the Escalade, the Diamond White paint-job and 22-inch chrome wheels identifying it as Krebs's.

Tyzack took his time. He waited until Krebs was just fractionally short of the point where he would have to brake, the car's speed up around 70 mph, before he depressed the control that sent a radio signal to the explosive valves. Then he just let events play out of their own accord.

Just two of the charges detonated. The driver's side tyres remained intact. But that only added to the catastrophic effect of the other explosions, as the functioning wheels kept driving, pushing the car away from the centre of the road, towards the hazards beyond.

Krebs's reactions were as sluggish as predicted. He'd been driving along a dry road on a warm, clear evening with very little traffic about, so there'd been no reason to anticipate any problems. The simultaneous disintegration of two tyres and the immediate, total loss of steering and brakes took him entirely by surprise.

His eyes widened, his mouth dropped open and the Escalade swerved across the tarmac, its high body lurching from side to side.

It rocketed off the road and hit the cattle wire at full tilt. The fiery rasping of wheel rims on the road was replaced by the screech of the wire on the car's bodywork as it rode up the radiator grille then over the high, bulbous bonnet, stretching like a bowstring as the nearest fence-posts were torn from their footings.

Then, as the massive white machine approached the edge of the ravine, an invisible hand seemed to let the bowstring loose and it cut through the first six feet of the Escalade's cabin as easily as a wire through cheese, slicing Norton Krebs clean in two below the shoulder. Only then did the barbed wire snap. The release of tension catapulted the Escalade towards the oak tree and then sent it pinballing off its trunk into the ravine, where it finally came to rest, as ripped and lifeless as its owner.

Tyzack let out his breath and gave a slight shake of the head. Then he turned away from the scene of the crime. The un-exploded tyre-valves were still down there in the wreckage, but Damon Tyzack did not make any move to retrieve them. He walked away down the road, towards the truck he'd parked half a mile away, without a backward glance.

17

Carver was not a horseman. He'd always left that kind of thing to the fancy-dressed toy soldiers in the Household Cavalry, keeping the tourists happy at Buckingham Palace with their shiny breast-plates and plumed helmets. But since arriving at the ranch he'd grasped that if he wanted to know Madeleine Cross and under-stand who she really was, he'd have to change his ways.

One morning, lying in bed with her head nestled on his shoulder and her legs wrapped around his, the heat of her on his thigh, she started telling him about her childhood.

'We were absolutely blue-collar,' she murmured. He could feel her breath on his skin, and her own skin was smooth and warm against the arm he'd draped around her. 'My father took jobs wher-ever he could find them, working the fields as a farmhand, or on construction sites. I wore hand-me-downs from the families Mom cleaned for.'

'If you were so poor, how come you learned to ride?' Carver asked.

'I had a horse called Blaze. Well, he belonged to our neighbour, but to me he was mine. I used to ride him bareback in the summer. When I'd dismount you could see the sweat-prints from my legs on his back. You know, it's crazy, but even now, when I talk about Blaze, or just think about him, I can smell him, that horse-smell, the leather and sweat.'

'There you go,' said Carver, 'horses smell. No wonder I can't stand them.'

She propped herself on her elbows and he shifted under her, so that they were face to face.

'But you can stand me, right?' she asked.

'Oh yes,' he said, a greedy smile on his face, his hands moving down to her buttocks, pushing her closer to him.

'And you desire me very much . . .'

'I think that's pretty obvious.'

She gave a little wriggle. 'Mmm . . . seems to be.'

'So are we going to do something about that?'

He moved his mouth towards hers, closing his eyes, expecting her to meet him. Instead, she pushed away with her hands, slipped out of his grasp and off the bed. By the time he looked up, she was standing several feet away, her naked body glowing in the light that filtered through the bedroom curtains.

'No!' she said. 'We don't do anything until you at least try to ride one of my horses.'

'You're kidding . . .'

'Not at all,' she insisted, opening her underwear drawer and pulling on her knickers.

Carver got out of bed, never taking his eyes off her and stood in front of her, half a head taller and sixty pounds heavier. She remained motionless as he ran his strong hands down the sides of her body, pausing for a moment on her waist before continuing downwards, his fingers spreading over her hips and sliding under the flimsy strips of fabric they found there.

'I could rip these off right now,' he said.

'Don't,' she said, quietly, but with absolute seriousness.

Carver's pulse was racing, his breathing heavy. His hunger for her was overwhelming and he was certain that she wanted him just as much. If he took her now there would be absolutely nothing she could do to stop him, but her trust and faith in him would be lost. Without that, they would have nothing.

So he stepped away from her, slowed his breathing and even let a wry smile play across his mouth as he said, 'All right then, where are the gee-gees?'

Carver fell off more than his jarred bones, aching backside and injured dignity would have liked, but Maddy taught him to ride Western-style, leaning back in the saddle, the reins in one hand, his stirrups so long that his legs fell straight down the flanks of his horse. With Buster bounding along beside them, they rode out across the open land that took up most of the ranch's 120 acres and picked their way uphill between the pine trees, where the air was cool. In the early morning, with the dew still glistening under the horses' hooves, the pines gave off a scent that was as sweet as a pina colada. Carver could smell vanilla, too.

'Some folks call them Sugar Pines,' Maddy said.

While they'd been riding through the woods, Buster had suddenly started barking. He'd dashed away into the undergrowth, stopped dead, and then begun digging at the earth with his front paws, growling excitedly. Carver had felt a tremor of danger from a source he could not place, an indeterminate, undefined threat. But then Maddy smiled at him, and the feeling vanished like the shadow of a cloud when the sun comes out, burned away by her presence.

'He's just chasing rabbits,' she said, kicking her horse into a walk. She called the dog. Reluctantly, Buster stopped his digging and trotted after them. A minute later, the whole episode had been forgotten and the main thing on his mind was trying to work out exactly what he had going with Maddy. Whatever it was, pretty soon he'd have to leave. It was going to take three flights and the best part of twenty-four hours to get him to Norway and Thor Larsson's wedding.

Standing in the kitchen a few hours later, watching Maddy cook supper, a thought struck him.

'I've been invited to a wedding,' he told her. 'Would you like to come?'

'OK, weddings are good, so long as they're not mine . . .'

'No, it's a mate of mine called Thor Larsson. He's this ridiculously tall Norwegian with a big mop of ginger hair. He looks like a Viking Rastaman. We've done a lot of work together.'

'Really? What kind of work?'

Carver shrugged. 'Hard to describe – security consultancy, that sort of thing. Anyway, Thor's lived in Geneva for years, like me, but he's Norwegian and so's Karin, the girl he's marrying. The wedding's going to be in Oslo. Do you want to come?'

'Of course I'll come, that would be great. I guess I'll have to get someone in to look after the horses, but, oh my God . . . what am I going to wear?'

She was laughing as she said it, but Carver kept his face deadpan.

'We have to change planes in Paris,' he said thoughtfully. 'If we left early we could stop off for a night, do a little shopping in the morning. I need a suit. Maybe you could find something too. My treat.'

She sighed happily, then wrapped her arms around him. 'You just earned yourself a really fun night,' she said.

18

Damon Tyzack was in the field next to the house, spying on the lovers through high-powered binoculars. They'd been standing right in front of the kitchen windows, without any inkling that they were being observed, when the Cross woman took Carver in her arms.

The neckline of her thin cotton top was elasticated and she had pulled it over her shoulders, leaving them bare, so that her sleeves were puffed around her upper arm. He imagined what it would be like to stick his fist in her face, put a knife to her throat, hear her begging him to stop.

Tyzack had never caught quite such an intimate glimpse of Carver and his piece before, but he knew all about their little love nest. One afternoon, when the pair of them were off on yet another ride, he'd left his hide among the trees and come down for a tour of the place.

'My God, it's the little house on the prairie,' Tyzack had muttered to himself, examining what struck him as a distinctly modest, unimpressive property. It was wood-built, with an awning surrounding it on all four sides, supported by rough-cut timbers and hung with baskets of mountain flowers. Inside, the ground floor was all stone-flagged. The walls were treated with some sort of wash to make the wood seem paler. Vases, knick-knacks and piles of embroidered cushions proclaimed that the place belonged to a woman. But it wasn't hard to see that there was a man about the house.

A big, brass-framed double bed stood in the bitch's room upstairs. A pair of men's trousers was draped over one end of the frame. A five-blade razor rested in a mug by the bathroom sink. Carver had made himself right at home.

Later, Tyzack had gone down to the garage where Cross kept her gaudily painted old truck and slipped a small, magnetized tracking device inside one of the rear wheel arches. He wanted to be able to follow the lovers if they ever left their little nest. He, meanwhile, would remain completely undetected, just as he had been when the two of them had been up in the woods, sitting on their horses just yards from his hide, babbling inanely about the trees smelling of vanilla.

The worst of it was, Tyzack could see that Carver was having a high old time. He'd tucked away a nice little pile of cash. He had a pretty girl making goo-goo eyes at him. He was getting his meals cooked. Oh yes, our Samuel was as happy as a sandboy. That happiness angered Tyzack more than anything. It wasn't right that the man who had wrecked his life should be so at peace with the world. He couldn't just lie there doing nothing about it. The situation demanded a fly or two in the ointment.

Tyzack put away his binoculars and went back up to the woods. Then he cleaned up his hide, covered his traces and went on his way.

19

Jake Tolland drove past the endless blocks of Dubai's building sites, each tower higher than the last, its design more flamboyant, its promises to prospective tenants more outrageous. Yet many of those glittering towers lay empty; many of the building sites were idle. The boom was over, the miracle exposed as a financial sleight of hand. The giant steel skeletons looked like a dinosaur graveyard, Ground Zero for the global economy.

Tolland turned into a quiet residential street in the Jumeirah district, parked his car and approached a metal door set into a high concrete wall. He pressed the button on the intercom and then said, 'Hello? This is Jake Tolland, from the London *Times*. I have an appointment to see Mrs Khan.'

There was no response, just a buzzing sound as the door unlocked. Tolland, a tall, bespectacled stringbean in his mid-twenties, with the first signs of hair loss already eating away at his temples, made his way across a dusty yard, dotted with spindly trees. Three small children were playing a game in the dirt, scattering the ground with cheap, brightly coloured plastic toys.

A flight of concrete steps led up to a small, boxy, modern villa.

Tolland rang the bell beside the glass front door and watched as a woman, dressed in a plain black trouser suit, her head covered by a grey scarf that wrapped around her neck, crossed the tiled floor of the hallway and opened the door.

He gave a friendly, ingratiating smile. 'Good morning,' he said. 'I'm—'

'I know who you are, sweetie,' said the woman in the hallway, in an accent that came direct from the back streets of Brooklyn. 'I read you all the time online. Why don't you come right on in?'

Jake Tolland had always wanted to be a foreign correspondent. Reckoning that a significant proportion of all the bad news – and thus good stories – in the world came from a bloodstained smear of revolution, war, disorder and crime that stretched from Russia, through the Balkans and into the Middle East, he had studied Russian at Cambridge University and then learned Arabic at the Language Centre of London University's School of Oriental and African Studies. Armed with these two qualifications and an inquisitive nature, Tolland soon amassed an impressive portfolio of freelance articles and a couple of well-received books that earned him a contract at *The Times*.

His work also brought him to the attention of talent scouts at MI6, who have long used Fleet Street journalists as auxiliary spies. For the past three years, Tolland had been carrying out low-risk intelligence jobs, gathering information and acting as a conduit between field agents and London. So he had not been in the least surprised to get a call from Bill Selsey, tipping him off to a juicy little yarn about a mysterious Englishman who had been buying and then freeing trafficked prostitutes in Dubai.

'Go to a place called the House of Freedom,' Selsey had told him. 'It's a refuge run by an American woman called Sadira Khan. She's married to a Pakistani, hence the name. We think there's a girl at the refuge called Lara. She was sent there by an Englishman, who appears to have bought her at some sort of slave auction and then freed her – proper Scarlet Pimpernel stuff. We're interested in him, so be a good chap, see what you can find out, pass it all on to us, and get yourself an exclusive. All I ask is have a word with me before you file. Let me run an eye over what you've written, make sure there's nothing in there we'd rather keep private.'

Like any refuge, the House of Freedom was filled with vulnerable, traumatized women. It had taken Tolland an hour of patient persuasion on the telephone to arrange an appointment, and still more negotiation, sitting around a dining table in a bare, magnolia-painted room, before Sadira agreed to speak to Lara Dashian on his behalf.

'But I'm not promising anything,' she said. 'If Lara doesn't want to talk, that's it, you leave. And even if she does talk, there are no names, no photographs, nothing that could identify her. I don't know how much you know about the men who traffick young women like Lara, but there is nothing, absolutely nothing they won't do. Her life is at stake.'

'I understand,' said Tolland, cheerfully imagining how well Sadira Khan's warning would read, suitably framed by his own dramatic prose, right up at the top of the piece. For the next twenty minutes, he waited in the room before Sadira Khan reappeared with a tiny slip of a girl whose dark, almost black hair framed a pretty, fine-boned face. Two huge brown eyes peered out from beneath her fringe. They were lovely eyes. They should have shone with life. But all Tolland could see was a veneer of blank numbness, stretched tight over a limitless depth of pain. In that moment all his professional, cold-hearted objectivity disappeared through the window. He could understand precisely why the man Bill Selsey had described as a Pimpernel had paid so much to free her. Tolland would happily have done the same himself. He wanted to take her under his wing, to be her knight in shining armour. And because he was above all else a reporter, he wanted to tell her story.

Gradually, gently, with infinite care, Tolland led Lara down the road from innocent schoolgirl to brutalized prostitute. He made no attempt to hide his shock at what he was hearing, his anger at the

vile obscenities of which his fellow-men were capable, or his com-
passion for the suffering Lara Dashian had endured. Yet all the
while, another part of him was exulting. He knew that she was
telling a tale that would make his name. And now they came to the
final act.

Lara told him about the nightclub. She described her encounter
with an Indian, Tiger Dey, and an Englishman who called himself
Pablo. She talked about the moment she knew she had been
bought and the walk up to the Englishman's suite.

'Did Pablo ever tell you his full name?' Tolland asked. 'What was
he called?'

Lara chewed at her lips. It was obvious that she had been given
a name.

'You can tell us, it's all right,' said Tolland, his voice reassuring
yet quietly insistent.

'He was kind to me. I do not want to get him into trouble with
the police.'

'But I am not a policeman. I will not tell them anything.'

Tolland saw Lara looking at Sadira Khan, silently begging for her
guidance. He willed himself to stay silent, not even turning to see
the older woman's response.

'It's all right, honey, you can tell him,' she said.

Lara looked once more at her protector, seeking a last iota of
reassurance, then her eyes returned to Tolland. He could tell she
was still nervous, not yet quite convinced that it was wise as
she murmured, 'He said his name was Carver.'

20

As soon as he had returned to his car, Jake Tolland got out his BlackBerry and sent a brief summary of the conversation to MI6. Selsey mailed him back with congratulations and one simple instruction: 'Essential NO mention name Carver in story.' Minutes later, Selsey was in Jack Grantham's office.

'It was Carver,' he said. 'I just heard from Tolland. She also said he told her to call him Pablo.'

'You hadn't primed him in advance?' Grantham was groping for straws.

'No,' Selsey insisted. 'I gave him the names of the woman who ran the refuge and the girl. But I didn't say a dickie-bird about Carver, or Pablo. The only way he could know that name is from the girl.'

'And the only way she could know . . .' Grantham conceded.

'I've managed to get the bank information out of the Swiss,' Selsey went on, ramming home his advantage. 'A man answering Carver's description recently opened a new account. He gave his name as Dirk Vandervart, which is—'

'Another one of Carver's known aliases,' Grantham cut in.

'Exactly. And four hundred thousand US dollars have been deposited in that account, in two payments. The first, two weeks before the Dey poisoning, the second on the day he died.'

Grantham nodded. 'OK, you win, Carver's gone back on the game. I can't say I'm too bothered about him hitting a piece of work like Tiger Dey. And I don't foresee a problem with the Dubaians, not in the short-term, anyway. We'll just tell them we have no criminal records for a James Conway Murray. But I don't want Carver running around bumping people off whenever the mood takes him. So I'm going to tell you what my mum used to tell my dad when she thought I was up to no good.'

'What was that, then?'

'Find out what that boy's doing. And tell him to stop it.'

21

Sooner or later they had to leave the ranch, and Maddy insisted on making a day of it. She told Carver she'd figured out an itinerary. He couldn't think of any good reason to say no, other than bone idleness, so he went along for the ride. Maddy drove them up to Lake Cascade, where they swam in cold, fresh water and lay on the shore, side by side, letting the sun dry their bodies. Carver had to admit the itinerary was working well so far. He couldn't work out why he'd not spent more mornings like that. What had he been doing all his life that was so much better?

Afterwards they headed into Cascade itself, a low-rise cluster of homes, stores and business units either side of the broad, dusty highway. Maddy parked next to a hot-dog stand: a caravan with fabric awning stretched over it, sheltering a bunch of green plastic garden chairs and camping tables. 'Make mine a chilli dog,' she said.

'Yes, ma'am.'

Carver got out of the Bronco and walked over towards the caravan. There was a counter with a middle-aged woman in a floral top standing behind it. From the corner of his eye, Carver saw another car pull into the lot, a silver-grey sedan. He had a feeling he'd seen it on the road earlier that day, but maybe not. It was just another boring car, there must have been millions just like it.

'What can I get you?' the woman asked.

'One chilli dog, please, and I'll have . . .'

There was a man getting out of the car. He was heading towards the Bronco. Carver couldn't see the man's face: he was bearded and wearing shades and a New York Yankees baseball cap. But there was something about him that seemed to nag at his memory. The way he walked, maybe: Carver couldn't place it.

'You made up your mind, hon?' said the woman, putting the chilli dog on the counter in front of him.

Carver frowned, sighing, trying not to lose the path back to his memory of this man. It was there somewhere, he was sure. But no, too late, it had gone.

'Ah . . . give me another just like that,' he said, pointing at the chilli dog.

The man was talking to Maddy. What the hell was going on?

Tyzack had used the tracker to follow the lovebirds out to the lake and then into town. The moment he saw Carver get out of Cross's truck, he decided to make his move. He walked across to the Bronco.

'G'day,' he said. His Australian accent wasn't the best in the world, but he was sure it was good enough to fool a Yank. He walked alongside the car and sidled up close to the woman still sitting in the driver's seat, leaning forward a little to invade her personal space and make her nervous.

'Can I help you?'

Her voice was steady, just an edge of irritation. She wasn't the kind to panic. Tyzack liked that: made her more of a challenge, more enjoyable to break.

'Yeah, I just wondered . . . I'm trying to get up to Meadows, is this the right road?'

'Sure. Just keep right on up through Donnelly and McCall, it'll take you straight there.'

'Thanks, love.'

He didn't move, just stood there, looking at her.

'Anything else?' she asked. ''Cause my boyfriend's just about to come back with our order, and you wouldn't want to upset him.'

'Strewth, is he a fighter? Glad you warned me, love. And listen, if he ever gets bored with you, the sloppy seconds'll see me right.'

'Get lost, jerkoff.'

'Don't spit the dummy, I'm going. Don't want any aggro with that bastard boyfriend. Cheers!'

Then Damon Tyzack turned and strolled back to his car, barely able to keep the grin off his face.

'What was that about?' Carver asked, handing Maddy her dog.

'Just some creep. Forget about it.'

Maddy took a bite out of her hot dog, floored the accelerator and swerved out of the parking lot with one hand on the wheel, racing away like a getaway driver leaving a bank-job, taking her anger out on the road. Carver couldn't help but notice that as furious as she was, she remained in total control of the car. Maybe her dad had taught her that, along with the mechanics. Or maybe she'd learned from someone with a professional interest in developing her skills.

They were heading south out of town, back towards the ranch, when Maddy shouted at him over the roar of engine, tarmac and wind, 'I thought we'd start the day nice and easy. You ready for some action now?'

They rafted the North Fork Payette River down from Cabarton Bridge to Smith's Ferry, riding rapids that provided the perfect amount of heart-pumping, drenching excitement to put smiles back on both their faces. The wooded banks of the canyon ran with wild deer. Bald eagles and osprey wheeled in the sky above the near wilderness. By the time they got back to the car, they were mellow with the contented exhaustion induced by hard but pleasurable physical activity. Carver had a powerful urge for a cold beer and a big, fat cheeseburger. They pulled into the first roadside place they could find. It didn't look fancy, just a windowless one-storey unit surrounded by a parking lot, but he wasn't feeling choosy.

Maddy went to the ladies' room while Carver went to the bar, ordered two beers, a burger and a chef's salad, then took the drinks over to a quiet table in the corner. Maddy returned, they chinked their glasses together and sat for a while in what seemed to him like companionable silence till she asked him, 'OK, what's the matter?'

'Nothing, I'm really happy.'

'You don't sound it.'

Carver gave a rueful chuckle. 'Sorry. I'm just not used to it, you know, happiness. Don't know what to do with it.'

'How do you mean?'

He screwed up his face, had some more beer and said, 'I was given away when I was a baby, by my mother. I was adopted. My new parents tried their best, but their hearts weren't in it.'

She reached across and touched him: 'I had no idea . . .'

'How could you?'

He paused for a moment while the waitress brought their orders. As she left the table, Carver watched her for a second and then caught the eye of a massive lump of muscle sitting up by the bar dressed in jeans and a black leather biker's waistcoat. He had razor-cut blond hair, a beefy, sunburned face and a neck so thick it seemed to flare out in a single diagonal line from his jawline to his shoulders. It was very possible, Carver thought, that the man's collar-size was higher than his IQ, and the guy next to him didn't look any smaller or more intelligent. The only thing different about the second man was that he didn't wear a waistcoat, but he did have a close-cropped beard. Now he saw Carver too. Both men raised their shot-glasses mockingly, downed their drinks in one and then stared leeringly at Maddy.

'Ignore them,' she said. 'Go on with what you were saying.'

'Well, I left school and went into the Marines. Just as I was coming to the end of my time, I met this girl called Kate. We were going to get married. Only that never happened . . .'

Maddy said nothing, knowing the effort it was taking Carver to reveal himself, knowing also what it said about his feelings for her that he thought she was worth it.

He turned his head away. The guys at the bar had finished their second drinks and were ordering another round with the grim relentlessness of men aiming to get very drunk, very fast.

Carver turned back to Maddy. 'She died,' he said. 'Well, she was killed, a hit-and-run driver. They never caught the bastard.'

'So you were abandoned again,' Maddy said. 'And the night we met, same thing. Do you remember, I said I'd got you on the rebound? You went, "You got me sooner than that. I hadn't finished hitting the wall."'

Carver was grateful for the chance to laugh. 'That sounds right. We got back together, you know, me and Alix.'

Maddy tried to make her voice sound casual as she asked, 'What happened?'

'It didn't work out. We loved each other, but we'd never had a normal life together. It had always been crazy. And that was painful, a lot of it, but at the same time, it was exciting. It turned out we were fine with crazy. It was the everyday stuff we couldn't handle.'

'So do you still see her?'

'No, the last I heard she'd gone back to Moscow – she's Russian. Anyway, she's very successful now. Very rich.'

'Uh-oh, I can't compete with that!'

'You don't have to. It's the everyday stuff that I really like about you. That's what's making me happy.'

'And making you happy is what's getting you all messed up?'

'Among other things.' Carver frowned. 'I think we've got company.'

22

The two gorillas lumbered across the room, their eyes fixed on Maddy, looking dumb, drunk, mean and horny. Maybe if they'd had any wits about them they'd have noticed that the guy sitting next to the sexy little lady didn't seem too scared by the sight of them heading towards his table with nothing but trouble on their minds.

Carver got up and took a couple of paces towards the men, holding his hands up in front of him in the universal gesture of conciliation.

These boys didn't do conciliation.

The one in the waistcoat jabbed out a meaty paw and shoved Carver aside with a grunt, barely sparing a glance as Carver staggered backwards into an unoccupied table.

There were menus on all the tables, just sheets of paper laminated in plastic. Carver picked up a menu and rolled it up nice and tight. Then he calmly stepped up behind the two men, who were too busy introducing themselves to Maddy to pay him any mind, and tapped his left hand on the back of the leather waistcoat.

Its owner turned round and managed to say, 'What the f—' before his speech was turned to a wordless, retching struggle for air as Carver's right arm flashed forward holding the rolled-up menu and caught him right on the Adam's apple. The man bent double, clutching his throat and that was when Carver kneed him in the face and laid him out on the floor.

That seemed to annoy his bearded pal. He pulled a knife, strode towards Carver and stabbed upwards, right at his guts.

Carver just bent his shoulders forward, sucking in his stomach muscles to avoid the blade, and stuck his arms out in front of him, one hand crossed over the other to block the stab. Then Carver grabbed the onrushing knife hand and twisted it round behind the other man's back, following it round so that he was now behind his assailant. He lashed out with a foot into the back of the bearded man's knee, causing his stance to crumple, then, still holding off the knife with one hand, he grabbed the back of the stubbly blond head with the other. Carver smashed it down, face-first into the table-top, knocking the man out cold.

The entire fight had taken less than ten seconds. Carver hadn't even broken sweat.

He looked down at the table, where Maddy was just staring at him, speechless, stunned by Carver's capacity for efficient, cold-blooded violence.

'Damn! I only ate half my burger,' he said. And then, 'We'd better go.'

He led Maddy past all the staring, dumbstruck drinkers, then peeled off half a dozen fifty-dollar notes and handed them to the barman.

'That's for our bill.' He nodded at the people behind him. 'Buy 'em all a round on me. Keep the change. And please, don't bother calling the police. I don't want to press charges.'

The barman gasped, 'But . . .'

'They attacked me. You saw that.'

'Sure, sure,' babbled the barman, taking the money.

'See what I mean?' said Carver to Maddy as they walked out into the lot. 'How are you supposed to stay happy when so many people just want to screw it all up?'

She got into the Bronco, still not saying anything. As they headed for the road Carver noticed a nondescript grey sedan parked at the far end of the lot. It looked like a million others. But he was absolutely certain it was the same one that the guy at the hot-dog stand had been driving. It could have been a coincidence. But Carver didn't believe in coincidence, any more than he did in accidents.

When Carver and the woman had gone, Tyzack got out of the car and went to see what had happened. He had spotted the two red-necks as they arrived and decided on the spur of the moment to use them in a little experiment. He told them his wife was inside, having a date with another man. He said he wanted the two of them taught a lesson and offered five hundred bucks, up-front, for the job. The idiot duo had been only too happy to oblige, unaware that they were being used as lab-rats. Tyzack was curious to see what kind of shape Carver was in. Fifteen minutes later, Carver walked out without a scratch. The lab-rats, Tyzack soon discovered, had taken part in a very swift, very brutal experiment. Carver, it seemed, was on excellent form.

Tyzack was delighted. It wouldn't be half so pleasurable taking down a man who couldn't put up a good fight.

23

Tord Bahr was sitting in front of a screen in Washington, DC, looking at water features in Bristol, England. They ran down the
middle of Broad Quay, the waterside area at the city's heart that was
once one corner of the Golden Triangle of the British slave trade.
Three centuries ago, ships left Broad Quay for Africa, laden down
with trade goods that would be exchanged for human beings. This
living cargo was shackled with iron chains and kept in conditions so
vile that more than twice as many Africans died on the journey as
survived to be sold in the markets of Maryland, Virginia and the
Carolinas. The money raised by their enslavement was used to buy
sugar, molasses, cotton and tobacco to take back home to Bristol.

Given all that, Bahr understood why the President wanted to
make his public address from a stage at the end of the quay. He
could see the symbolic significance of starting a war against modern
slavery from that point. But that didn't mean he liked the
President's sudden decision to go there, not when it was his job to
keep Lincoln Roberts alive. An overseas presidential visit required
a massive amount of planning, involving as many as two thousand

bureaucrats, servicemen and women, presidential staffers and politicians, not to mention the bomb dogs that would sniff every square inch of the ground the President would cover. Under normal circumstances, a Presidential Advance Team would be sent out months in advance to consider every possible eventuality that might occur during a visit. Now Bahr was being given days, not weeks, to do the same job.

There was at least the minuscule consolation that any potential threats to his boss's life would be working at equally short notice. An assassination typically requires at least as much planning as its prevention, but even so, killers are as capable of being spontaneous as anyone else. So now Bahr was looking at dozens of water-spouts, no more than six inches tall, arranged in rows along a series of shallow, flagstoned basins down the centre of the quay. Assuming that the whole area would be packed with people – and when you had a president who made rock gods and supermodels look like minor local celebrities, every area was always packed – those basins would be as filled with people as the cobblestoned areas around them. And Bahr couldn't have people falling over and suing the President, any more than he could have them shooting him.

He gave a deep, frustrated sigh, ran a hand through his hair, momentarily ruffling its immaculate neatness as he scratched his scalp, and spoke to one of his subordinates. 'OK, Craig, you're gonna have to talk to the local people here, because all these fountains, or whatever, have got to go.'

'You want them turned off?'

'No, I want them totally boarded over, solid enough for folks to stand on. And I want those boards sealed tight so nothing gets underneath, and I mean absolutely nothing.'

'Sure, I'll get right on it.'

'Now, do me a favour, pan left and down, let me see those cobblestones.'

In Bristol, Special Agent Craig Bronstein turned his head and examined the ground beneath his feet. The signal from the miniature Motorola video camera hidden in his sunglasses was sent instantly to one of the TV displays in front of Tord Bahr, 3,600 miles away.

'I don't like cobblestones,' Bahr said, as much to himself as Bronstein. 'Too easy to dig up and use as missiles. Can we get asphalt or something poured over them?'

'I doubt it. This whole area's kind of a regeneration project. They're very proud of it. And I don't think the stones are gonna be an issue. They're pretty well secured. You'd need a jackhammer, pickaxe at the very least, to dig them up.'

'Let me think about that,' said Bahr, sounding a long way from convinced.

He switched his attention to another screen: 'Hey, Renee, those four-lane highways, either side of the quay: they're closed to traffic the night before the visit and they stay closed until the President has left the country. If anyone complains about it, tell them it's non-negotiable ... Right, now I want to think about tunnels ... What's under the ground down there? Where are the access points? C'mon, people, talk to me. I need to know ...'

Albanian gangs had been the dominant criminal force in the British sex industry for the best part of a decade and the Visar clan was the most powerful of them all. Of course, not all Albanian immigrants to the UK were drawn to organized crime. For the most part they, like so many immigrant communities in so many nations, survived by taking menial, minimum-wage jobs which the host country's natives refused to consider.

There were, for example, Albanians among the cleaning staff at the Bristol hotel where a Home Office official called Charles Portland-Smyth was staying while liaising with the Secret Service's Presidential Advance Team. On the day, several British police out-fits, including the Royalty and Diplomatic Protection Department, the Met's Counter Terrorism Command, otherwise known as SO15, and the Special Escort Group would all be publicly involved in assisting with presidential protection. Officers from MI5 would also be more discreetly deployed. All came under the overall control of the Home Office.

Charles Portland-Smyth was not a complete idiot. He did not – as so many other government officials have done – leave his laptop on a train, in a pub, or sitting on the front seat of his car, handily placed for any passing thief. He did, however, leave it in his room, unprotected by any password, when he went down for an early-morning workout and shower in the hotel gym, followed by a healthy breakfast of muesli and fresh fruit.

When he got back, the laptop was still there, exactly where he had left it. He had no idea that a memory-stick containing the entire contents of his hard drive was sitting in the apron pocket of an apparently humble housemaid. So it was that all the details of the President's schedule, movements and protection protocols were in the hands of the Visar clan by the time Portland-Smyth was walking through the hotel lobby, smiling ingratiatingly at the small group of Secret Service agents who were waiting for him, and saying, 'Jack, Craig, Renee . . . hope you all slept well. Let's just wrap up the fine points of the plan and then we can all go home!'

24

'He's just chasing rabbits.'

Carver did not know where the words had come from. Maybe he'd dreamed them. But the moment he opened his eyes, he knew there was a reason his subconscious had pushed them to the forefront of his mind.

It wasn't rabbits Buster had been chasing two days earlier. There'd been someone up on that hill.

Carver looked at the bedside clock. It was 05:32. Through a crack in the curtains he could see the first light of dawn. Maddy was asleep next to him. He got out of bed, pulled on his trousers, a sweatshirt and a pair of trainers and walked round the bed to the door.

He had the handle in his grasp when he paused, and walked back to her side of the bed. She kept a handgun in the drawer of her bedside cabinet: she'd told him about it once when he asked about her security. He slid open the drawer and pulled out a Springfield XD sub-compact 9-mm pistol. The barrel was barely three inches long, and the whole gun weighed just a couple of pounds unloaded, making it the perfect handbag weapon: a smart choice by a woman who knew what she was doing. It would suit him just fine, too.

He slipped out of the room, down the stairs and into the hall, where Buster spent the night curled up in his basket. Carver gave a low whistle and the German Shepherd looked up sleepily, no longer hostile but still not certain whether he was happy to be disturbed by this new addition to the household.

'Walkies,' said Carver.

That made up Buster's mind. He scrambled out of his basket, panting with excitement and wagging his tail. Carver led him out through the back door and across the dewy grass towards the treeline a couple of hundred yards away.

The woods rose on a west-facing slope. The dawn sun was behind them and the section of the field nearest the house was bathed in its low, amber rays. Beyond that, the rest of the field and the trees were cast in shadow. Anyone watching from the trees would have a perfect spotlit view of Carver. He, on the other hand, had the sun in his eyes and was looking into relative darkness.

He clapped his hands and said, 'Buster!' in a half-whispered voice. Then he broke into a run and dashed across the field, chased by the dog who was delighted to play along with the game.

There were no shots, no response of any kind from the hill.

As he came closer and stepped into its shadow, Carver was no longer dazzled. The light here was low but even, plenty good enough for his purposes. He headed uphill, trying to re-create the route he and Maddy had taken on horseback. Buster followed, nose down, reacquainting himself with the smells of this part of the forest. Carver paid attention, too, inspecting every inch of the forest floor as he walked very slowly between the trees, stopping to look around at the state of the low-lying branches and undergrowth through which he passed.

There was nothing to see: no footprints, no trampled plants, no sign whatever that anyone had been there. More minutes dragged by, and still nothing out of the ordinary. Maybe he'd got himself worked up about nothing.

And then he spotted it: a scattering of oak leaves on the ground. Nothing unusual about that ... except that some of the leaves were much darker than the others, more rotten, and therefore older. They should have been lying beneath the top layer of newer, paler leaves. Something had disturbed them.

A few yards further on, Carver found a stone lying slightly to one side of a small depression in the earth from which it had been dislodged. There were no hoof-marks nearby: no horse had done this. Elsewhere, a twig from a sapling had been snapped at shoulder height.

They were only tiny deviations from the norm. Under normal circumstances, no one would notice them. Even to a trained eye, like Carver's, the first impression had been subconscious. Only now did he realize that he must, at some level, have picked up the spoor of a man when he was riding through the woods, but refused to register the information.

The sound of barking echoed through the trees. Carver followed the noise until he came upon Buster, working away at the ground. This was the same place he'd run to when they'd last been up there. Beside him was a hole, filled with three or four empty plastic packets of military rations. Buster wasn't paying any attention to them, though. He had found something far more interesting, and Carver realized what it must be. He took five quick strides towards the dog and yanked on his collar, pulling him away from the hole.

Buster snarled at him, furious to have been denied his prize. At the bottom of the hole the top of another plastic bag was poking through the crumbled earth. Carver did not have to take it out to know that it was filled with human faeces. He'd dug enough holes like this in his time.

Someone had been here all right, someone with military training, used to covering their tracks and lying low in enemy territory. He took a look at the ration bags. There were still fresh scraps of food inside. Whoever had eaten them had arrived within the past few days . . . just like Carver. That suggested he might have been the one under surveillance, not Maddy. The trash told him something else: the watcher wanted Carver to know that he had been there. Otherwise, he could simply have taken it all away with him.

But who would want to set up an observation post just to watch him fool around with a new girlfriend? And how could anyone have known he'd be there? He hadn't planned to fly to Boise, the whole thing was a last-minute decision.

He racked his brain, trying to remember the airports he'd been through on the way from North Carolina, hoping he could dredge up more anomalous images: people who'd looked out of place, or followed him, or seemed too self-consciously relaxed when he looked in their direction. Nothing came to him.

Carver was walking back downhill now, Buster following reluctantly and disconsolately behind. There was a gnawing, energy-sapping tension in his gut as the realization struck him that if he really were the surveillance subject there was only one possibility left: the watcher in the woods had been directed there by Maddy herself.

Carver thought back to their first meeting, that chance encounter in the Hôtel du Cap bar. That could easily have been a set-up. Same with the text message a few weeks ago – had it really been as randomly out of the blue as it seemed? And when Buster had caught the scent of the surveillance, out on that ride, hadn't she been just a little too quick to say that it was a rabbit, too eager to change the subject?

The man who'd walked up to her Bronco at the hot-dog stand, standing so close to the car, talking so confidingly: he'd skedaddled right out of there the moment he'd seen Carver turning back towards the car. Sure, he could have been a creep. But he could also have been her control. Her being pissed off by what he'd said certainly didn't contradict that. Carver had argued with the men who'd given him orders often enough.

And take that whole scene at the diner. Maddy goes to the bathroom. A few minutes later two bozos turn up out of nowhere and start an entirely unprovoked fight. Meanwhile, the same grey car is waiting out in the parking lot. What's all that about?

Now that Carver thought about it, he knew nothing about this woman, beyond what she had told him. He had never met the mysterious Mr Cross. In the time they'd been on the ranch, she'd never introduced him to her family, who supposedly lived so close by. And the ease with which she'd fallen for him . . . Carver was not given to insecurity or false modesty, but he didn't think he was any kind of Casanova, either. Beautiful women did not line up to throw themselves at him. Yet this one had.

Or maybe he was just being paranoid.

He walked back to the house, telling himself not to let his suspicions wreck everything. He was having a good time. Just enjoy it.

Maddy was in the kitchen, fixing herself some breakfast. 'I was wondering where you guys had got to,' she said as Buster bounded towards her.

'We just went for an early-morning walk in the woods,' Carver said. 'Looked around a bit. Did some male bonding.'

He was watching her eyes. Looking for any tell-tale flicker of alarm when he mentioned looking in the woods. There was none, just the smile of a woman who's pleased to see her man.

'That's great,' Maddy said. 'You want eggs?'

25

Arjan Visar looked at the men sitting around him at the table. Every one of them could be counted as his competitor. Each would happily have killed any of the others if there was a profit to be had from that death. Now, though, they had been forced together by a greater, common enemy.

Visar was used to making deals with his supposed enemies. He was an Albanian Muslim. Yet he dealt with gangs run by Catholic Croatians, Orthodox Christian Serbs, and his fellow-Muslims in Bosnia and Kosovo. All of those groups hated one another, but all recognized that the continued passage of drugs, women and even weapons was more important than any political or religious dispute. So when he heard about the threat posed by President Roberts's anti-trafficking initiative, Visar understood immediately that any disagreements the men in his business might have were far out-weighed by the long-term threats to all their livelihoods if Roberts should happen to succeed.

The venue he chose for his summit meeting was, ironically, the presidential suite of a seven-star hotel in Dubai, just a few miles from the squalid basement bar where Lara Dashian had been bought and sold and Tiger Dey had swallowed one cocktail cherry too many. The city was geographically convenient for the men Visar had in mind and was, in any case, an informal neutral zone for international crime. Asian, former-Communist and European entrepreneurs whose fortunes came from less-than-savoury activities poured huge amounts of cash into the city and largely desisted from the routine violence which was so central to their business models elsewhere.

Visar's guests around the $25,000-a-night suite's gold-leaf dining table comprised two Russians, a Chinese and an Indian. One of the Russians owned a Premiership football club, another a Formula 1 motor-racing team. The Indian had a cricket eleven in his nation's multi-billion-dollar Premier League. The Chinese possessed a string of racehorses that dominated tracks from Royal Ascot to Hong Kong. All had yachts, jets, old masters and young mistresses of the greatest possible beauty and expense, replaced at regular intervals.

For now, the mistresses could wait. There was business to be done.

The meeting was being conducted in English, since that was the only common language for all five men.

'We all understand the proper way to do business,' Visar began. 'We talk to one another and because we are men of honour, we give our word and we make a deal. But sometimes, there is no deal. There is no talk. Sometimes you must strike fast, like a snake that bites a man before the man can tread on its head. That is why we are here. We must strike, like the snake.'

'And this snake, whom does it bite?' The voice, a deep, guttural rumble, belonged to Naum Titov, leader of Russia's Podolskaya crime gang.

'The American President, Lincoln Roberts,' replied Visar, the calm matter-of-factness of his voice impressing the other men more forcefully than any melodramatic flourish would have done.

'What are you, fucking crazy, man?' Titov exclaimed. President? Forget it. Impossible.'

'Might one ask why you think this is necessary?' inquired Kumar Karn, head of the most powerful Mumbai syndicate, in the old-fashioned, oratorical manner of an expensively educated Indian.

'Because Roberts is the man who will tread on our heads,' said Visar. 'If we do not kill him, he will kill us, or at least kill our business. Roberts is about to make a major policy announcement. Trust me, I know this. He will commit the Army of the United States – also the Navy, Air Force, intelligence agencies, everything – to fight, in these words exactly, "the unspeakable evil of the global slave trade". He is, we can say, declaring war on people-trafficking. I need not tell you what effect this might have on our commercial activities. That is why the President must die. There is no alternative.'

'American presidents declare many wars,' remarked Wu Xiao-Long, the 489 or supreme leader of the global Wo Shing Wo triad organization. 'The wars on drugs and terror failed. Why will this be different?'

'Perhaps because it will not be opposed, night and day, from within America itself,' Karn suggested.

He got up from his chair and walked over to the floor-to-ceiling window from which all the lights of Dubai could be seen, glittering in a dazzling profusion that defied all talk of economic collapse. Karn did not stop to admire the view. Instead he turned back to look at the men at the table.

'Any American president knows that many of his own country's intellectuals, its celebrities and its young people harbour a profound suspicion of any overseas conflict. They feel obliged to oppose it as a matter of principle. The media, also, exaggerate defeats, but ignore victories. They accuse their own soldiers of atrocities while turning a blind eye to those committed against them. Therefore, wherever and whenever America wages war, its campaigns will constantly be undermined by negativity and hostility from within.

'But I think that Mr Roberts has been very cunning in his choice of enemy. For who, in America of all nations, can possibly stand up for slavery? This war will appeal to their bottomless feelings of guilt. The same principle will surely apply to Western Europe as well. The very people who are usually most vociferous in their opposition to Uncle Sam will be those applauding his new venture. It is, I think, a most astute and clever war to declare.'

'Not clever for us,' growled Titov, thinking of the string of brothels he owned in more than twenty major American cities.

'My point exactly,' said Visar, who was Titov's partner in that operation, and the supplier of more than half the women involved.

'Then this is serious for sure,' agreed Wu, refilling his glass. 'My snakeheads will not be happy. Already they get shit from the US Coast Guards, losing many people, hurting their profits. Now it can only be worse. So, Mr Visar, I agree that we must act. But how? At what time, what place?'

'Less than two weeks from now,' said Visar, 'the President is planning to give a speech at a conference on slavery in Bristol, England. This speech has not yet been announced to the public. But the US Secret Service is already in Bristol, preparing for the visit.'

'Then they are surely more prepared than are we,' remarked Karn. 'That must be to our disadvantage.'

'Perhaps so,' Visar conceded. 'But the President is not making it easy for his staff. He will not make his announcement indoors at the conference itself, before an audience of a few hundred delegates. Instead, he will speak to a crowd of thousands in the open air. Lincoln Roberts wants to make his war on slavery a movement of the masses, so that his opponents must battle against a great weight of public opinion.'

'Surely, then, public outrage will be all the greater if any harm should befall him,' said Karn. 'Roberts is popular, indeed he is loved. To be associated with his demise could be counterproductive in the extreme.'

'We will not be associated,' said Visar. 'Any US president has enemies aplenty. Let the Americans argue about which of them did this. Maybe someone will choose to claim responsibility. There is a man who hides in the hills of Waziristan. He would be happy to make the world think he could kill an American president. Or maybe we will find some other man, and place the blame on him.'

Naum Titov grunted in approval. 'Then let us have our killing.'

26

Damon Tyzack was met at Heathrow by a uniformed chauffeur and told that Arjan Visar wanted to meet him. Immediately.

He was driven straight to Farnborough airport, less than twenty miles away, where a private jet was waiting to take him to Málaga on the Spanish Costa del Sol. From there a helicopter ferried him on a fifteen-minute journey to the private landing pad tucked away behind Visar's villa.

Tyzack was not a man given to being impressed, but even he was astounded by the opulence in which Visar lived. The main house was built around a colonnaded courtyard with an ornate stone fountain at its centre. Marble mosaics, crafted in a gaudy profusion of patterns and colours, covered the floor of every room. Massive sofas were strewn with shiny satin cushions decorated with swirls and curlicues of golden thread. The vulgarity of it all was overpowering. This was a retreat fit for a Roman emperor, and a Nero or a Caligula at that.

Arjan Visar, when he appeared, was oddly out of keeping with his home. Small and scrawny with the pallid skin of a sickly child, he was dressed in plain black shirt and trousers. Strands of hair were plastered unconvincingly over his balding scalp. Tyzack could have broken him like a twig. But then, any of the thugs who took Visar's orders could have done the same. And yet they did not. They accepted Visar's control over an operation that he had grown from its beginnings amongst the petty brigands of rural Albania to its current position of dominance over a trade that stretched from the furthest backwaters of China, Africa and the former Communist states to the greatest cities in Europe and North America.

Visar caught Tyzack gazing at his surroundings and smiled apologetically. 'This was my brother's property. It is not to my taste. But my wife likes it very much, so . . .' He shrugged as helplessly as any other henpecked husband.

Tyzack knew that Visar would have his wife killed without a second thought, if he ever thought it necessary or deserved. Rumour had it that he had been behind the death of his own brother, which had led to his taking total control of the clan. That, too, was worthy of an emperor.

A servant appeared at Visar's side. 'You have had a long journey,' said Visar. 'Would you like a drink, some food maybe? Whatever you want, the kitchens can supply.'

'Just a glass of water, please,' said Tyzack, determined to keep a clear head. He had carried out jobs for the Visars many times. But his orders had come from Visar's henchmen, communicating by phone and email. This was his first personal contact with Visar himself. That meant he was either in for very good news, or very, very bad. Tyzack told himself that Visar would hardly have carted him all this way just for a bollocking, or even a bullet in the back of the head. There had to be more to it than that.

'I congratulate you on your recent work, Mr Tyzack,' said Visar. 'Now I have more for you.'

Visar clicked his fingers and another servant stepped silently out of the shadows. He carried a laptop, which he placed on a table in front of Visar and then opened.

'Thank you,' the Albanian said as his servant disappeared again.

He looked up from the screen and caught Tyzack's eye. 'Let me explain . . .'

Tyzack had switched from water to an ice-cold San Miguel beer. He had wolfed down a freshly made club sandwich. And all the time he had been going over the information Visar had given him. Tyzack had never been regarded as academically gifted but, contrary to some of his teachers' scathing reports, he lacked neither intelligence nor application. He simply needed to be interested before he made an effort. The mechanics of killing interested him very much indeed. It was his special subject.

'Yes,' he said, 'I think I can do it. Won't be easy, of course. He's the President of the United States. He has a lot of very clever, well-trained people working very hard to stop him getting hurt. So let's cut out the things we can't do. No point trying to attack Air Force One. There's no aircraft on the planet with better, newer counter-measures against any missile known to man.

'The landing's a no-no, too. He's coming into RAF Fairford. That's actually a US Air Force base and they keep B2 stealth bombers there, so it's already sealed up tighter than a gnat's arse – if you'll excuse the expression. No way anyone's breaking in unless they're on a suicide mission. And I'm not.'

'You did not strike me as that type,' said Visar.

'From Fairford, he'll take Marine One to Bristol, call it twenty minutes' flight time, give or take,' Tyzack continued. 'The exact route won't be determined till the day, which makes it virtually impossible to guarantee a hand-held missile strike. He's landing at College Green, opposite Bristol Cathedral, and you can bet they'll have Cadillac One pulled up right under the chopper's disc. He'll be out one door and in the next in three seconds, and if there's an angle for a shot from anywhere at any point, then some Secret Service agent's made a cock-up. Forget that.

'The President's car itself is totally impregnable. They may call it Cadillac One but the only thing about it that's a Caddy is the badge. That thing is a tank. Even the windows are transparent armour. You can't shoot it, gas it, blow the tyres, nothing. And there'll be twenty-odd motors back and front of it, stuffed with armed men. It's only a few hundred yards from the landing site to the stage at Broad Quay so the motorcade'll be almost as long as the journey.'

'I get the point, Mr Tyzack. You do not think the President can be attacked on the road.'

'Exactly. The only point he's going to be vulnerable is when he's actually onstage. So . . . may I?'

He gestured at the laptop. Visar nodded and swivelled it round so that the screen was facing Tyzack, who spent a few seconds typing instructions before turning the computer again so that both men had a view of the screen.

'Google Earth,' he said, 'best innovation in the history of crime. Gives any man his own private spy satellite. For example, let's find the precise grid references of the point on which Roberts's stage will be constructed. Here we go: fifty-one degrees, twenty-seven minutes and eight-point-five-seven seconds North, and two degrees, thirty-five minutes, fifty-one-point-four-seven seconds West.'

'I can read a reference, Mr Tyzack, is that really necessary?'

Tyzack grinned broadly. 'Oh yes, Mr Visar, it is absolutely necessary. That reference is what will kill the President. And I know just how I'll do it.'

27

'Ten million dollars,' said Visar when Tyzack had finished his explanation. 'That is a very generous figure and it is not open to negotiation. I will pay you half in cash. The other half I will give you in kind: women, territories, rights to certain operations. Over time, these properties will prove far more valuable than a straight payment. Before we conclude our agreement, however, I need to be sure that the technical side of the plan is feasible. Can you be certain of that?'

'Don't see why not,' Tyzack replied. 'I've got a chap who can work out the basic design. But he may not be able to do the actual construction, so I'll need help with that. And someone will have to get hold of the basic components, either buy them or steal them. I have some business of my own to conduct over the next few days. But so long as your men keep to the schedule and do what I ask, we'll be fine.'

Visar nodded. 'Good. But understand this, Mr Tyzack. You cannot afford to be distracted by this business you have to do. You must be in Bristol, and you must do your job. I cannot tolerate failure.'

'But you'll give me the help I need?'
'Of course, anything.'
'Then we're on.'

At Málaga airport, walking between the chopper and the private jet, Tyzack made a phone call. He gave a set of specific instructions, then listened impatiently, his face clouding over with anger, to what the other speaker had to say.

'Are you quite finished?' he said at last. 'Right, then, let me make myself clear. I don't give a damn if you're busy, or you have other things to think about. This is what you're thinking about now. I need that design, so remember those pictures I sent you? Think about them. Think about the people you love. Now go away and do what you're told.'

Tyzack was still fuming as he ran up the steps, barged past the pretty, smiling flight attendant standing at the aeroplane door and slumped down sullenly in the nearest seat.

The attendant turned to look at the co-pilot, who had been watching through the open cockpit door. She raised her eyebrows, widened her eyes in mock-horror, gave an exaggerated sigh and mouthed the words, 'What's got into him?'

At his villa, Visar put in a call to the Albanian embassy in Washington. 'Get a message to Kula,' he said. 'I need him to create an application for an iPhone, a guidance system. The precise specifications will be sent to him soon. Tell him this is a job that will gain him great favour.'

'Consider it done,' said the diplomat on the other end of the line.

28

On their first afternoon in Paris, they got Carver a suit for the wedding. The next morning Maddy went clothes shopping by herself. She said she wanted to give him the morning off. He tried to believe her. A voice in Carver's head told him Maddy wanted to get rid of him so she could meet a contact or speak to her handler, but he was determined not to let his paranoia wreck their trip. If he made himself live in the moment and not think about anything else, several hours at a time could go by without him wondering whether the woman next to him was lying with everything she said and did.

Carver hadn't brought a laptop with him, but there was a computer downstairs in the hotel lounge. He decided to log on to a few news sites and drink a cup of coffee while he worked out how to spend the morning.

The front page of *The Times* carried the usual mix of economic misery and political bluster. The only news that caught Carver's eye was the announcement that Lincoln Roberts was planning a flying visit to Bristol to speak at an anti-slavery conference. At the bottom of the story there was a link to a related feature.

Its headline read: 'Pablo the sex-slave Pimpernel, and...'

Carver grinned: Pablo. It had been a while since he'd heard that name.

He clicked on the link and a page opened up with the full headline. The final words were, 'and a mysterious death in Dubai'.

Well, he could see why people were making that the number-one story. Sex, crime, death, an exotic location and a bloke with a funny name – what more could anyone want?

Carver started reading Jake Tolland's story. It described Lara's enslavement, her rape and her trafficking to Dubai. Then it followed her to a dingy nightclub, where she met an Englishman who was looking to buy a girl of his own. Through Lara's eyes, Tolland described the man. He was slim, not conventionally handsome, but attractive. He had dark hair and green eyes – strange green eyes, said Lara, though she could not describe what precisely was wrong or unusual about them.

By now, Carver was no longer reading for entertainment. As his eyes raced over the following paragraphs, the ache in the guts that he had felt when he first suspected Maddy – and that had hung around him, on and off, ever since – now gripped him more tightly than ever. His throat felt constricted. He felt a stab of pain in his jaw and only then noticed that he had been grinding his teeth so hard that his mouth was virtually clamped shut.

Tolland told how Pablo had freed Lara Dashian, given her money, told her to go to the women's shelter, and then disappeared entirely off the face of the earth. But Lara's pimp had been found shot to death in the hotel parking lot, and Tiger Dey – one of the masterminds of the people-trafficking trade in the whole Gulf region – had been taken to hospital hours later with a fatal attack of what appeared to be ricin poisoning.

'Do you know how it was administered?' Tolland had asked a senior Dubaian police officer.

'Not for certain, no,' the detective had admitted. 'But we believe that the killer may have hidden a small pellet of poison in a cocktail cherry. Mr Dey was very fond of them and ate several while he was in the club that night. We also have witnesses, including Miss Dashian, who testify that the man called Pablo gave Mr Dey a cherry. That may have been the way it was done.'

'But you cannot be certain?'

'No.'

'So you cannot build a definitive case against Pablo?'

'Not at this point,' said the policeman. And then Tolland described the cop as he stubbed out a cigarette, looked up at the reporter and said, 'But I will tell you one thing, Mr Tolland. I believe that this man is a cold-blooded killer, almost certainly a professional assassin. It is my opinion, and that of my superiors, that he represents a significant danger to the security of Dubai and its citizens. And it is my job to protect the people of Dubai. By whatever means necessary.'

29

Carver closed the laptop and leaned back in his chair, staring blankly at the ceiling. He thought about the name Pablo, and the people who knew its significance for him. He took another look at all the phrases used to describe a man whose identifying features were so similar to his own. He checked the date the story gave for that night at the Karama Pearl Hotel. It was a few days before he did the job at Lusterleaf, the job that he could not mention to anyone, and would be denied by anyone and everyone close to the President. Not that it would make any difference what Bahr or even Lincoln Roberts himself might say. When the mysterious Pablo had been in Dubai, Carver had been deep undercover, living off the grid, leaving no trace of his presence anywhere . . . and thus creating no alibi.

Maybe it was all pure chance. But Carver didn't think so, and nor would other people who knew him and would immediately link him to Pablo. He was being framed for another man's hit. It struck Carver that the corny old bumper stickers had got it right. Just because he was paranoid didn't mean someone, somewhere, wasn't out to get him.

He needed someone to talk to. He called Thor Larsson in Oslo and told him what was going on. 'Am I going crazy here? That whole Pablo thing, I don't know, maybe it's just coincidence.'

Larsson was his normal, unflappable, Scandinavian self. 'It's got to be. Look at the odds. How many people call you by that nickname any more, or even know about it? And how many Pablos are there in the world? Picasso, Escobar . . . and lots more no one's ever heard of. It could be any of them.'

'But what if someone really is copying me? That's not good.'

'What's that saying you have in England?' Larsson asked. 'Imitation is the sincerest form of flattery? Take it as a compliment. You're so good at your job that people want to make cheap copies, like a Rolex watch or a Louis Vuitton handbag.'

'Thanks, that's a big reassurance,' said Carver with a humourless chuckle. 'I'm being set up. There are policemen in Dubai pretty much saying they want to kill me.'

Larsson seemed untroubled by the threat to his friend's life: 'But you're not going to Dubai. You're coming to Oslo. We'll chill out and let this all blow over. Look on the bright side. At least you'll be free of this crap soon. I'm getting married for ever.'

'Ha! Let me tell you, if I had to choose between a lifetime with Karin or a single meeting with that Middle Eastern copper, I'm taking the gorgeous Norwegian blonde every time. Believe me, Thor, it's only my deep respect for you as a mate that's stopped me nicking her off you already.'

'You wouldn't stand a chance,' said Larsson confidently. 'You can't whisper dirty Norwegian words in her ear the way I can. Anyway, why do you need to steal anyone's girl? I thought you had a new one of your own.'

'That's true, I do. In fact, I was going to ask you, is it all right if I bring her with me to the wedding?'

Larsson's enthusiasm seemed to vanish in an instant: 'Er . . . yeah, sure, I don't see why not.'

'You don't sound very keen on the idea,' said Carver.

'No, no, I am . . . I was just surprised, I think. I didn't know you were so serious about her. But hey, that's good, you need someone new. Now come on, you haven't even told me her name.'

'Maddy. Maddy Cross.'

'And I suppose she looks like some kind of model or movie-star or something.'

Now Carver's laugh was entirely genuine. 'I think she's pretty stunning, yeah.'

'Then bring her to Oslo and I'll tell you if you're right.'

30

Bill Selsey was beginning to understand that he had entered into an arrangement that was much like smoking a first pipe of crack. You might think you could handle it. But it would soon be handling you.

He was scared – physically scared, with prickling armpits and quivering bowels – whenever his anonymous new master called. He'd been on again that morning.

'So, you got Carver on the run yet?' the man had asked.

'How do you mean?' Selsey replied, stalling for time.

'I mean, has the Firm taken him off its Christmas-card list? Is he persona non bloody grata? Has he been put on a hit-list yet?'

'Not exactly . . .'

'What do you mean, not exactly?'

'It's just that Carver still has powerful friends. One friend, at any rate. He's not convinced yet . . .'

'Have you given him all the information from California yet? The Krebs job?'

'Not yet: I was going to do that this morning.'

'About time. And you make sure you do it well. Go upstairs with it, if you have to, over this friend of Carver's head. Just get the job done.'

'Your boy Tolland seems to be making a name for himself,' said Jack Grantham from behind a copy of *The Times*. The words 'Exclusive: Slavery, Sex and Murder in Dubai: p.23' were printed in bold white text against a blue banner right across the top of the front page. 'I hope he gives you a piece of the action when the film studios come calling.'

He closed the paper, folded it in two and put it down on his desk. Then he looked up at Bill Selsey, standing by his desk. 'So, Bill, what can I do for you?' he asked.

Selsey gave a nervous grimace, a look Grantham recognized at once as a man bearing bad news to his boss.

'It's Carver. You're not going to believe this, Jack, but it looks like he's done another job. America this time.'

'I thought I told you, quite clearly, to find out what he was doing, and tell him to stop it.'

'So would you like to know what I've found out?'

Was Grantham imagining it, or was there an edge to that question?

'Of course,' he said. 'Go ahead.'

'Well, a financier called Norton Krebs had a car accident in northern California last week. He had a massive blow-out, swerved off the road and got himself decapitated by some cattle wire – a real Jayne Mansfield job, by the sound of it.'

'Ouch,' winced Grantham. 'And we care about Krebs because . . . ?'

'In the first place, because he laundered money for a number of extremely unsavoury individuals, several of whom are suspected of having ties to gangs in this country. And in the second place because the local police in Amador County were puzzled to discover that the valves in the car's surviving tyres looked a little unusual. So they sent them off for forensic analysis . . .'

'Don't tell me. The valves had explosive filaments inserted in them. And we all know who uses valves like that, because we had to clean up the mess he made on the M25, last time he did it.'

'Quite,' agreed Selsey.

'But Carver's not the only operator out there who knows that technique.'

'Absolutely, which is why I wouldn't even bring it to your attention, except that Carver arrived in Boise, Idaho—'

'Which is not in California, evidently.'

'No,' said Selsey with only the merest sigh of impatience, 'it isn't. But it is a great deal closer to northern California than, say, Carver's flat in Geneva. And Carver certainly arrived there, two Saturdays ago. Our American cousins have supplied security footage from their airport. I've got a couple of stills for you here. As you can see, he was met by a woman.'

'They don't get any uglier, do they?'

'Apparently not,' Selsey agreed. 'Anyway, this one drove Carver away in a vehicle registered in the name of Madeleine Cross. I checked her record. It appears entirely clean.'

'Or conveniently so,' said Grantham. 'What else have you got?'

'A couple of days after Carver's arrival in Idaho, a second-hand car dealer in Boise sold a Tacoma, whatever that is, to a man who gave his name as Carver and answered to his description. The same vehicle and its driver were seen in Amador County near the crash over the days leading up to the crash. Witnesses say the driver spoke with an English accent. Several remember him mentioning Norton Krebs.'

'And Carver?'

'He seems to have scuttled back to his new woman. Then they both left the country, together. They're in Paris at the moment, with tickets booked through to Oslo.'

'That makes sense. That hippy pal of Carver's with the ridiculous hair – Larsson – he's Norwegian. But I still think this is all too pat. I can just about believe Carver would go back to what he does best. But that's the point – he's very good at it. He doesn't leave clues lying around like losing tickets on a bookie's floor.'

'Not in the old days,' Selsey agreed. 'But maybe times have changed. He's out of practice, getting a bit ragged. The point is, the evidence overwhelmingly says it's him. Why should the evidence be lying?'

Grantham shrugged, conceding the strength of Selsey's point. 'I think it's time we got together with Samuel Carver and had a little chat. See if you can set something up, but very discreetly. Keep this under the radar till we know exactly what's what.'

'I'm afraid I can't do that, sir.'

'I'm sorry?' said Grantham. He and Selsey had worked together for years, always on first-name terms, with barely a serious dispute. Now his deputy was simultaneously calling him 'sir' while disobeying a direct order.

Selsey continued: 'I don't think that it's appropriate to treat Carver's activities—'

'Alleged, unproven activities,' Grantham interrupted.

'I don't think that it's appropriate to treat Carver's alleged activities,' Selsey repeated pointedly, 'as a private matter. If a British citizen is going round killing people in friendly countries, it could have very serious repercussions, particularly if he has links to the Firm.'

'I see,' said Grantham. 'And how would you like to proceed?'

'Formally,' said Selsey. 'I expect to have a full report on Carver's recent movements, finances, associates and suspected activities ready by tomorrow afternoon. It goes without saying that you will be the first to see it. But I want to state now, for the record, my strong recommendation that it should then be passed upstairs, so that a decision can be made at the highest level as to how we should proceed.'

'Your recommendation is noted,' said Jack Grantham in a voice devoid of emotion. 'I look forward to your report with great interest. Now, if that is all, I am sure you will want to be getting on with it.'

As Selsey left the room, Grantham asked himself what had led to this declaration of war. Both men knew that Grantham could not afford to have his relationship with Samuel Carver exposed to close scrutiny. Selsey was now threatening precisely such an exposure. Under normal circumstances, that would simply be part of the normal office warfare by which an ambitious, unscrupulous deputy might seek to undermine his boss. But Selsey had never wanted Grantham's job, and even if he did, he would never get it – he was too old, too long mired in middle-management.

There had to be another reason for this sudden hostility. And the more Jack Grantham thought about it, the more he wanted to know just what that reason might be.

Selsey went for a walk along the Thames, as much to gather his nerves as to find some privacy, before he made the call.

'I think we're getting somewhere,' he said. 'I spoke to ... to Carver's friend. I told him I felt obliged to take the evidence of the two hits to a higher authority. I'm pretty confident that either he'll have to cut Carver loose, or he'll be facing a formal review of our links with Carver. He won't want that.'

'A review?' his contact said, his voice rising. 'That's the best you can do? I don't think you've grasped the urgency of this situation. I'm about to make my move on Carver. And when I do, I want him to know that he's all alone, that no one's coming to rescue him. Forget friends in high places. I don't want him to have a single friend anywhere. Not one.'

31

Larsson met them at Oslo airport. He took one look at Maddy and flashed Carver a quick thumbs-up just to signal his approval.

Like any man, Carver felt no obligation to reply to this compliment with any courtesy of his own. 'Bloody hell, mate, what happened to your hair?' he exclaimed, looking at the short, neatly styled cut that had replaced his friend's wild dreadlocks.

Larsson looked down at them like an amiable giraffe, a rueful smile on his face. 'It was Kari. She said they made me look like an ageing hippy. Apparently, I'm much more handsome now.'

He did not sound entirely convinced.

'Well, I think you look just cute,' said Maddy with a hint of a smile, teasing him a little. 'And you did what you were told, too, which has to be a good thing.'

'Thor, meet Maddy,' said Carver. 'She's a big believer in the chain of command.'

'Damn straight,' she agreed.

'It's all my fault, of course,' said Carver. 'If I hadn't got this man's frozen, half-dead body off an Arctic mountainside and into Narvik hospital, he'd never have met the beautiful nurse who stole his heart . . . and his balls, apparently.'

Larsson laughed, but there was something forced about his good humour, as though he wasn't in the mood for banter. It occurred to Carver that it probably wasn't a brilliant idea, winding a man up about his wife-to-be two days before their wedding, even if he was your mate.

'So how is Kari, anyway?' he said, switching to polite conversation. 'She joining us for dinner?'

Larsson shook his head. 'No, she's got her family down from Narvik. They need looking after and there are all the last-minute things to do for the reception. But you'll see her tomorrow, at the rehearsal.'

'Can't wait,' said Maddy.

Carver looked up at the signs pointing the way to taxis, car-hire, trains and car parks. 'Where are you parked?' he asked Larsson.

'I'm not. We're taking the train. This is a country where the public transport actually works. I'll get you both day-cards for the buses, trams and metro. Costs almost nothing and you can use them as much as you like.'

It took less than five minutes to walk through the arrivals hall, get tickets and settle into their seats. A minute after that they were moving. The whole process had been so swift and painless that Carver almost failed to notice the man standing by the airport information desk in the baseball cap and dark glasses. There was something about that face, the hollow cheeks and slightly petulant, sulky mouth that nagged at Carver's memory, though the answer stayed just out of reach. But there was no doubt the man's head turned and followed them as they walked by.

Well, of course it did, Carver told himself. Maddy had that effect on most men. Get a grip.

On the train he tried not to think about it, concentrating on the instant guide to Oslo Larsson was giving them. He had a tourist's map of the city, taken from a rack at the station. 'OK, here's the station,' he said, pointing to a mass of converging railway lines on the right-hand side of the map. And here' – Larsson's finger pointed to the middle of the map – 'is the royal palace. You see the street that runs almost directly between them? That's Karl Johans Gate. It's the main street in the city, all the fanciest stores are there. That's where we have all the big parades and everything. We're going to have dinner at the King Haakon Hotel, which is about halfway along. It's a little old-fashioned, but you should definitely see it.'

'And they'll let you in now you don't look like a hippy,' grinned Carver.

This time Larsson smiled back. 'Well, that's the real reason I had it done, of course . . .'

He went back to his map, running his finger straight down from the royal palace to the shore of the fjord on which Oslo lay. 'Anyway, round here it's all been redeveloped in the past few years and it looks good, very modern, futuristic almost. The area on the waterfront is called Aker Brygge. It's like a boardwalk. There are trendy bars and restaurants, fancy modern apartments, lots of yachts moored alongside – it's where all the cool people go.'

'Which is why you're not taking us, right?' said Carver.

'No!' Larsson laughed, his normal good humour now totally restored. 'I thought we'd go down there for some drinks after dinner.'

'Sounds nice,' said Maddy.

'It is,' Larsson agreed. 'And the other place you should definitely see while you're in town is the opera house, which is here, by the station. It's very new and it's definitely the craziest-looking place in Oslo. You can even stand on the roof.'

'And that's as crazy as this place gets?' Carver asked. 'An opera house?'

Larsson grinned. 'What can I say? Oslo is a great city. It's clean, it's peaceful and there's fantastic countryside just a few minutes away on the train. But I have to admit, it's not exactly exciting.'

'Don't worry,' said Carver. 'I've had all the excitement I can stand.'

32

Jana Kreutzmann was the last passenger to board the flight from Berlin, dashing through the terminal towards the departure gate, calling out to the ground staff, imploring them not to close the flight, gasping her thanks and apologies as she stood by their desk and presented her boarding pass. She was always late, always rushing, always trying to fit twenty-five hours of passionate commitment into every twenty-four-hour day.

Ten years ago, a boyfriend had taken her to see the E55 highway that ran from Dresden in the old East Germany through to Prague in the Czech Republic. One stretch of the highway close to the town of Teblice, just over the Czech side of the border, had become infamous for the hundreds of East European prostitutes who touted for trade. They clustered in the neon-lit doorways and outdoor drinking areas of countless sleazy roadside bars. They fought for customers, grabbing and embracing the men who got out of passing cars and trucks. The men would grab them back, pawing and prodding the prostitutes like shoppers sampling fruit in a marketplace.

Prices started at thirty euros for half an hour of sex, and rose to 250 for an entire night's pleasure, either at a girl's tawdry room, with thick grime on the window-frames and no sheets on the bed, or at one of the neighbourhood hotels that catered for prostitutes and their johns. All the while, the girls' pimps would lurk in the background, forcing their stables to work harder, making sure that none of the men tried to get away without paying. The entire operation was controlled by criminal gangs. Local police, all bought and paid for, had become an irrelevance.

Jana had been working for Amnesty International then, as had her boyfriend, Dieter. He had hoped that his righteous indignation at the appalling exploitation of innocent young women by evil men would earn him a fuck out of political solidarity, if nothing else. But he had miscalculated Jana's response.

Her outrage, unlike his, was not remotely synthetic. When they got back to their hotel, 20 kilometres away, she pulled out her laptop and went online. It took her just a couple of minutes to find sex-guides advising men how to get to the highway's busiest stretches and what they could expect when they got there.

'Listen to this!' Jana had exclaimed as Dieter lay in bed, wondering when the hell she was going to climb in next to him.

Jana started reading from the screen: ' "Unfortunately, most girls do not show much enthusiasm in bed. At least the prettier ones usually lie passively in bed, but if you show them how you want them to handle you they seem quite obedient. They are also often grateful for tips, because they see little or nothing of your payment, after the bar and her pimp take their share. This may also explain their lack of enthusiasm." Can you believe that? These guys know that the prostitutes are basically slaves, who don't even get paid for letting men abuse their bodies, but they still complain because they aren't enthusiastic. Pigs! Fucking pigs!'

'Don't worry about them,' said Dieter. 'Come to bed, huh?'

'What? And have sex? With you? So you can tell your friends that I am not enthusiastic but, oh yes, I am very obedient when I am told what to do? Are you crazy?'

Jana had never again let Dieter anywhere near her. Instead she had devoted herself to the cause of all the women and children around the world who were trafficked and forced into sex-slavery. Subsisting on occasional donations and fees from speeches and journalism, Jana Kreutzmann had spoken to abused women, confronted the criminals who so cruelly mistreated them and lobbied politicians. She had displayed manic determination and unflinching courage and slowly, as the years went by, she had helped to make a difference. The media that had once regarded her as an obsessive, feminist nutcase now saw her as a twenty-first-century heroine. The criminals who had once dismissed her as an insignificant irritant now saw her as an increasingly dangerous threat to their business.

Official recognition was shown to her too. The European lawmakers in Brussels regularly called her, and paid for her consultancy. Now the Nobel Institute, the organization behind the Nobel Prizes based in Oslo, had invited her to a symposium bringing together academics, campaigners and media experts who specialized in the issue of people-trafficking. Together, they would compile a paper to be presented to the Anti-Slavery Conference. Over the past few days Jana had heard rumours that President Lincoln Roberts himself would be addressing the conference. His support, even if it were little more than a gesture, would be a huge boost to the anti-slavery movement.

As she collapsed into her seat and began her flight to Oslo, Jana Kreutzmann felt for the very first time as though she might just be on the winning side.

33

Presidential speechwriter Bobby DiLivio chewed on the end of a newly sharpened pencil. 'OK,' he said, taking it out of his mouth and tapping it on a legal pad in front of him, 'how about this? "Human trafficking is a scourge in the world, a stain upon the conscience of civilized society." What do you guys reckon – too much alliteration, maybe?'

'How about too many friggin' clichés?' sniped his colleague Josh Grunveld, laughing as he dodged the ball of paper DiLivio flung in his direction.

Over at the far end of the White House writers' room, Thornton Black, the third member of the team working on the President's Bristol speech, paced up and down the carpet, squeezing a black and yellow Nerf ball in his hands.

'Don't worry about the clichés, man. That's Roberts's genius. He turns that trash into pure gold.'

'You calling my work trash?' DiLivio asked, beginning to bridle.

'Man, this is politics, it's all trash,' Black replied. 'So, did you guys see that story in the *Huffington Post*, the one about that sex-slave kid that got rescued in, I don't know, Dubai? Abu Dhabi? Some place like that – Middle East, anyway. Story came out of the London *Times* . . .'

'Nuh-huh,' muttered DiLivio, chewing the pencil again.

Grunveld frowned. 'Was that the one where the dude killed the Indian guy? Yeah, think I remember that . . .'

'So, would it be a totally crazy idea to get that chick over to England for the speech?' Black went on. 'The way the guy wrote it, she sounded pretty cute. I'm thinking a black president with a white slave, that's an image, right? God, that shot's going to be on every front page in the whole damn world . . .'

'Why stop there?' Grunveld asked. 'We could get a little slum-dog and some old Chinese dude, make it a real rainbow nation.'

'Aw, come on, man, I'm trying to be serious here,' Black protested.

'You know, it could even make some money,' said DiLivio. 'If we got enough kids, from enough different countries, we could auction 'em off to Hollywood celebrities after the speech. Get Madonna and Angelina bidding against each other, who knows how high it could go? Pay for the whole trip.'

'Good to know you take the scourge of the century so seriously, DiLivio. Always helps a speech when it's written from the heart.'

'C'mon, Thorn, you know I was kidding.'

'Yeah, well, I wasn't. I honestly think this kid could make the whole thing real. Put a face on the problem, y'know? Give people something they can understand, not just a bunch of fine words and big numbers. The chick was eighteen when she got sold by her own aunt, for Christ's sake. She was flown thousands of miles and forced into prostitution . . . People are going to look at her, think, "Gee, she could be our daughter." That's what I mean – she makes it real.'

'You know, Thorn, that's not a totally dumb-ass idea . . . considering it's one of yours,' Grunveld conceded. 'You should think about it, Bob.'

'OK, I'll take it to Hal, see what he says,' said DiLivio, as

Thornton Black shouted, 'Yes!' and danced a touchdown celebration. 'Now, the speech . . . How about I make it, "Human trafficking is a curse upon the world"?'

'How about we start again from the top?' suggested Grunveld.

'Yeah,' Black agreed. ' 'Cause, Bob, what you've got so far is total shit.'

34

The fifth-floor corridor of the King Haakon Hotel was reserved for the exclusive use of female guests. Men could hardly be forbidden from walking past the rooms, but they certainly were not encouraged to do so.

Damon Tyzack had no qualms at all about intruding. As he made his way along the carpet to the last door on the right he was dressed entirely in black, from his combat boots and his military fatigue pants to his shirt, fleece and ballistic vest – even the cap that hid most of his flame-red hair. He wore gold-framed glasses, a bushy moustache and there was a large and very vivid purple birthmark on his cheek: the kind of thing that people try very hard not to stare at, even though they are unable to see anything else.

Next to him trotted a yellow Labrador, a breed whose remarkable sense of smell and limitless appetite made it perfectly suited to work as a bomb dog. Yellow labs are also disarming. They are so appealing, so smile-inducing that they envelop their owner or handler in their golden glow. When Tyzack had appeared at the front desk claiming to be conducting a check for explosives in Ms

Kreutzmann's room, flashing a fake ID from a non-existent security firm, giving the clerk a confirmatory phone number that was routed through to one of his men, sitting in a van parked not fifty metres away, he was immediately believed.

Tyzack wasn't entirely lying. He really did have every intention of checking the explosives he was going to place around the bedroom, sitting area and bathroom that Jana Kreutzmann would soon be occupying. He wanted to make absolutely certain that she could not possibly survive their detonation. Fräulein Kreutzmann had been causing Tyzack a great deal of trouble with her endless investigations into other people's business. Some of the articles she'd written lately had been getting uncomfortably close to trafficking routes and networks in which he had a direct personal interest. There was every chance that if she were allowed to keep going she might expose him to the kind of public attention that would prove extremely embarrassing. That could not be allowed to happen.

He had been given a pass-key. It let him into a very feminine environment that reminded him a little of the Cross woman's ranch-house in Idaho. It wasn't the specific style of furniture or decoration, just the feeling that someone had worked hard to make things pretty. There were raspberry-pink cushions arranged on the creamy sofa and bright green apples in a china bowl made to look like a wicker basket on the glass table in front of it; softer pink curtains over the window behind; a gold and scarlet patterned bedspread. It made Tyzack uneasy to be in the room – it was all too perfect, as though the women who stayed there were somehow better, even happier than him – but the fact that he was about to smash it all to pieces came as a calming, comforting thought.

He was using shaped charges of cyclotol – a 70/30 mix of two explosives: TNT and RDX – designed to provide an intense, highly focused blast. The largest charge was placed in the toilet cistern, with two smaller back-up devices behind an air-conditioning vent and under the sofa. The key to the whole system was the room's own bedside telephone. Tyzack opened it up and inserted a tiny transmitting device. When the phone rang, the transmitter would send a detonation signal to all three devices. A separate circuit, however, acted as a safety-catch: nothing would happen until it had been remotely activated.

Tyzack wanted to be sure that the target was in place before he let the bomb do its work. He unscrewed the switch outside the bathroom that controlled the lights inside and put another transmitter in it. When the light was switched on, he would know. It would, of course, have been a simple job to link the switch directly to the bombs. Tyzack, however, had other ideas.

Jana Kreutzmann arrived in Oslo shortly after eight in the evening. The Nobel organization had sent a car to meet her and deliver her to her hotel. By nine she had checked in and was heading up to her room. When she got there, she kicked off her shoes and called room service to order a light supper. It would be with her in twenty minutes, she was told. Perfect, she thought, that would just give her time to take a shower. She was longing to wash away the accumulated cares and stresses of another fourteen-hour day, so she walked over to her bathroom, turned on the light, and then let the water run, building up heat, while she slipped out of her clothes.

The transmitter on the light switch worked perfectly, alerting Tyzack as soon as it was turned on. He looked through a pair of compact binoculars to check that the other elements were in place; then he murmured a single word to himself: 'Showtime!'

35

Thor Larsson had reserved a table by the window, equally well placed to watch the passers-by outside on Karl Johans Gate, or inside the café. Carver took off the jacket he'd worn over his plain black T-shirt, jeans and leather Converse sneakers and slung it over the back of his chair. He understood the choice of restaurant when he saw Maddy look around the room, taking in the rich wooden panelling; the swagged curtains; the half-naked statues mounted on the walls between the windows; the splendid arrangements of white flowers dotted around the room, their petals glowing in the light cast by crystal chandeliers; and the murals of Victorian gentlemen and their ladies, eating, drinking and being merry. If there was anywhere in Oslo calculated to please a visiting American, this was it.

They'd eaten their starters and finished the first bottle of wine when Carver's phone trilled, letting him know that he had received a text. He grimaced apologetically and checked it out. The message read: 'Go to hotel lobby. Internal phone. Dial Room 570. Urgent. Grantham'.

The name and number of the sender were withheld. Carver looked up at Thor and Maddy. 'Excuse me one second,' he said.

He tapped out a two-word reply: 'Prove it'.

Less than a minute later a new message arrived: 'M25 McCabe breakfast Mrs Z. Now do it. Fast'.

'Are you OK?'

Carver looked up to see Maddy's concerned expression. He gave an irritable sigh: 'Just a voice from the past,' adding, 'No, not her,' to prevent Maddy jumping to the wrong conclusion. 'Just business.'

The combination of keywords could only have come from Grantham. They referred to a series of events: a road accident engineered by Carver; a fundamentalist maniac Carver had prevented from exploding a nuclear bomb over Jerusalem's most sacred religious sites; and a breakfast meeting with Grantham and Deputy Director Olga Zhukovskaya of the Russian FSB, successors to the KGB, just before he'd taken out McCabe. The tone of the message certainly sounded like Grantham. The snide irreverence of calling Zhukovskaya 'Mrs Z' and the blunt arrogance of his commands were typical of the man. So, for that matter, was his habit of turning up unannounced and unwelcome in Carver's life.

'I've got to take this,' he said. 'Won't be long.'

Carver got up and walked away from the table, leaving his jacket draped on the chair behind him. He passed the bar on his left as he left the café and walked down a winding corridor that opened out into the lobby. It was an automatic reflex for Carver to scan the area, noting the elderly couple pottering in from the street; the businessman making a complaint of some kind to the front desk and the blonde receptionist patiently indulging him; the family looking through the rack of tourist brochures by the concierge's desk.

The concierge directed him to an internal phone placed on a reproduction antique table up against the far wall. As Carver crossed the lobby towards it, he had another flicker of intuition:

that same sense of something or someone just beyond his field of vision, perceived but not identified. He drove it from his mind as he reached the phone and called the room.

He heard one ring of the bell.

And then the very air around him seemed to be ripped to shreds as the thunderous reverberation of a massive explosion shook the old hotel, followed a second later by the tinnitus trilling of fire alarms, the shouts of men and screams of women. The lobby, which had been so peaceful just a second earlier now became consumed by chaos as guests rushed out of nearby hotel rooms and restaurants, a smattering at first and then a flood. More people appeared on the stairs, some stumbling as they hurried down. An elderly lady lost her footing in the mêlée and fell the final half-dozen steps to the ground. She struggled to get up, but no one stopped to help her.

Amidst the panic and desperation, Carver stood still, looking around, his concentration intensified and his focus sharpened. The blast had shattered a large mirror and filled the air with plaster dust, but he saw that there was no structural damage to the area in which he was standing. For most of the hotel's occupants, the greatest danger now lay in being trampled in the rush to escape. Carver, however, had a more pressing issue on his mind.

He'd been set up. The call had been a trigger, he was sure of it. He had no proof, but he'd bet everything he possessed that Room 570 had just been obliterated along, presumably, with its occupant. And he was the patsy who had dialled the fatal number.

He scanned the lobby, searching for security cameras through the dusty air. None were visible. But he was working on the assumption that there would be pictures of him somewhere, complete with date and time-code, standing with the guest-phone in his hand. He had to get out, that second.

But what about Maddy? Carver did not fear for her immediate safety. The blast had come from the far end of the hotel, well away from the café, which had its own separate exit, far from the stampede in the lobby. She should have escaped unharmed, but she'd also be worried sick about him. He wanted to go to her and let her know he was fine, but there was no time. In any case it would be better for Maddy and Thor not to know what had happened to him. That way they would have less to give away, if and when the police caught up with them, and less chance of incriminating themselves along with him. He would find a way of getting word to them later. For now, all that mattered was escape.

He looked around, trying to pick the best way out through the crowd, and then he saw, by the now-abandoned concierge desk, flickering in front of him as people ran across his field of vision, the mocking smile, the pale blue eyes and the flame-red hair of a man who was holding up a phone, clearly enough for him to see; turning it round so that he could clearly see the lens of the camera; taunting him as it flashed.

Only then did Carver become conscious of the weight in his hand. He glanced down and realized that he still had the handset in his hands. Barely ten seconds had passed since the detonation. He hadn't even thought to put it back down.

He flung the phone away, furious with himself. By the time he looked up, the face had gone.

Carver turned towards the door, letting himself be carried along with the torrent of people, out through the hotel's glass doors on to the street.

The pandemonium was even worse out there. The blast had bombarded the area in front of the hotel with a deadly eruption of brickwork, glass, wood and metal. Dead bodies were strewn across the road, bloodied and half buried by falling rubble. Between them, the fatal shards of razor-edged glass glittered in the late evening sun, the prettiness of the flickering light incongruous, even obscene, amidst the slaughter.

Up above a gaping black emptiness had been punched into the hotel. It was fringed at top and bottom by sagging floors and ceilings, their loose planks and beams flopping like unbrushed strands of hair. Yet as shocking as the sight of the atrocity was, the blandly imperturbable look of the untouched façade to either side of the wound was almost as bad. It was as if the rest of the building were simply ignoring the damage that had been done.

Carver heard sirens in the distance as the first police units and emergency services made their way to the scene. He saw a milling group of bemused, leaderless people as the guests fleeing the hotel met both the survivors of the carnage outside and the first rubber-neckers making their way from the neighbouring streets and the great open space on the far side of the road. And then all that was forgotten as he felt the prick of a knife-point in the small of his back, the choking grip of an arm around his neck, and the hot breath against his left ear, as intimate as a lover.

He heard a man's voice, halfway between a whisper and a hiss, 'Hello, old chap . . . remember me?'

And then it all came back to Carver: the voice, the face, the memories.

'Tyzack,' he croaked. 'It's been a while.'

'Hasn't it just. Feel this?' Tyzack pressed the knife a little harder, just enough to draw blood. 'You do know I could kill you, right now, if I wanted, if you tried anything stupid?'

Carver did not respond. Tyzack jabbed the knife again, making him wince.

'I asked you a question. Answer it.'

'I know you could kill me, yes,' Carver muttered.

'Good,' said Tyzack. 'But I'm not going to . . . not yet. I want to have some sport first, a bit of fun, just like you did with me. I assume you recall the occasion. You thought you were so much better than me. Well then, prove it. I've dumped you in the shit, see if you can get out of it. You see, the police know you did this. I just sent them the picture. So they'll be after you. And I'll be after you. And when I've finished with you I'm going to do a job that is so far beyond anything you've even attempted, you're not even in the same league.'

Tyzack paused. It was plain to Carver that he was longing to be asked what the job was. So Carver kept silent. He didn't want to give Tyzack the satisfaction. And anyway, he wasn't interested.

He'd never possessed any regard for Tyzack and didn't give a damn about his desperate attempts to compete.

'Aren't you curious to know what I'm doing?' said Tyzack, betraying a trace of frustration that his achievements still went unrecognized. 'Oh well, mustn't dally. As you once said to me: "What are you waiting for?" Well, come on . . . *get on with it!*'

The blade flashed across Carver's lower back, cutting through his T-shirt and slicing open his skin in a horizontal line, right above the kidneys. He winced, took an involuntary step forward, away from the blade, but there was no second thrust. He turned round to face Tyzack, but he had disappeared again, swallowed in the crowds. When Carver's eye caught a flash of red hair, it belonged to Thor Larsson, maybe thirty yards away.

Larsson's head turned and his eye met Carver for a second. He shouted out, 'Carver!' But Carver had already broken eye contact, as furtive as a petty thief, and was dashing away from Larsson, pushing past anyone who got in his way, oblivious to the broken glass and blood beneath his feet. He knew that Damon Tyzack was right. He had to get out of it. Now.

36

Damon Tyzack's eyes had never left Carver. He wanted to wallow in every second of his misery and confusion. Carver had been kippered and he knew it. He'd been framed good and proper, caught red-handed, still holding on to the phone like an absolute idiot. Back at the hotel, Tyzack had made sure that Carver had seen his smile, just to rub it in, let him know who'd set the trap he'd so kindly walked right into. And then he'd stuck the knife in Carver's back and said his piece, though the words, like the blade, just scratched the surface of what Tyzack had in mind.

Watching him spot Larsson, though, that had been good. Tyzack had read Carver like a book, as even his mediocre mind grasped that he couldn't go back to his American tart and his hippy chum. Tyzack smiled to himself. There was plenty about those two that he knew and Carver didn't; lots more nasty surprises still to come; surprises that would knock that smug, superior expression off his face for good and all.

Tyzack pressed a speed-dial number on his phone. 'He's on the move,' he said. 'Track him. Let me know where he's going. Don't let him out of your sight.'

Next he punched in 22-66-90-50, the number of the Oslo Police District. When his call was answered he said, 'I have important information about the bombing at the King Haakon Hotel. Please alert the detective in charge of the case that the identity of the bomber is now in your possession. A picture of him standing by the telephone used to detonate the bomb was posted to your standard email contact address, along with details of the perpetrator's known associates. You will not hear from me again.'

He hung up without bothering to ask whether the call-centre operative to whom he had spoken had understood what he was saying. He simply assumed that she spoke English. Everyone in Norway spoke English.

When he had finished, he took the SIM and memory cards out of his phone, wiped the handset, made sure that no one was watching him and skidded it along the ground, into a pile of rubble from the explosion.

As he left the scene of the crime, Tyzack had already pulled another phone from his jacket and was talking into it: 'Right, where is he? What's he doing? Come on, I haven't got all night . . .'

He was walking up a side street called Akersgata. A black Mercedes E-Class saloon was parked there, a driver sitting patiently behind the wheel. Tyzack got in. As he sat down, his phone rang. He listened for a few seconds, grunted an acknowledgement of what had been said, then turned to the driver and said, 'Right, let's get going. This should be amusing.'

37

Carver's shirt was sticking to his skin, glued by the blood that seeped from the incision in his back. A wound in the back was the mark of a coward and a quitter, he thought bitterly, and he could hardly argue with that description. He was running away. He was running from the King Haakon Hotel and the savagery that had been unleashed there. He was fleeing from Tyzack's vengeance; from Thor Larsson, who was still trying to chase him down the street; and from Maddy Cross, somewhere behind him in the chaos. He was getting away from his attacker and putting as much distance as he could between himself and the ones he loved. He hoped they would understand that he was doing it for them, saving them from being infected by his guilt.

He needed to go faster.

Beyond the hotel Karl Johans Gate rose uphill and became a pedestrian zone. There were no cars or motorbikes anywhere. But Oslo is a city of bicycles and many of the people who'd been drawn to the explosion by ghoulish curiosity or a more noble desire to help had simply flung their bikes to the ground when they got close. Carver grabbed one of them and started pedalling.

Carver stood up in the saddle and pumped his legs to get him over the top of the hill. Above him a sign flashed the word 'Freia' in swirling script, while a multi-coloured fan of neon lights provided a constantly changing backdrop of red, blue and white that echoed the flashing lights of the police cars, ambulances and fire engines now pulling up outside the hotel.

The people that Carver slalomed around as he rode against the human tide had been hoping for a fun night out. Now they seemed listless, numbed by what had happened and uncertain how they should react. Some were still moving towards the hotel. Others just stood in the street, bereft of the power of decision. Yet others had shrugged their shoulders, accepted that there was nothing they could do and were heading back to their drinks.

He was over the crown of the hill now, and the land fell away in front of him, the broad promenade lined on either side by bars, souvenir shops and clothing stores selling T-shirts and cut-price denims. Carver was pretty sure that the main station was somewhere at the bottom of the slope. He was hoping he could get a night train out of the country, across the Swedish border. Carver was a big fan of the European railway system. The tickets could be bought in cash. There were no customs or passport controls across a vast swathe of the continent, from the northernmost tip of Norway to the furthest-flung Greek island. Trains were a fugitive's best friend.

In the street outside the King Haakon, Thor Larsson put a comforting arm around Maddy's shoulder. 'I'm sure Sam's fine,' he said. 'He'll be back, don't you worry.'

'But he left, and then that happened . . .' She stared up at the ruined hotel, round which police were rapidly creating a formal crime zone while firemen and paramedics ventured into the rubble in search of victims and survivors. Maddy had been calling out to any of their number who came near her, begging for information about Carver, but never getting a reply.

She looked at Larsson, her eyes no longer cool and knowing but wide with uncertainty and apprehension. 'I don't understand. He hasn't come back. I think he's in there somewhere. We've got to find him.'

Larsson strengthened his grip as she tried to run towards the wreckage. 'It's all right,' he said, doing his best to sound calm, repressing any hint of the anger seething inside him. He wasn't going to tell Maddy that he had seen Carver and that he'd been dashing away from the hotel, leaving them both to their own devices. He wasn't going to call his friend a coward. Not after all that they'd been through. Not to his girfriend. Not yet.

'Really,' he went on, 'Sam's been in far worse situations than this. He always pulls through.'

'Then why isn't he here?' she asked, with simple but undeniable logic. 'Why hasn't he come back for me?'

It wouldn't be long now, Larsson realized, before her confusion and fear gave way to resentment. For now, she was concerned about Carver. Soon, she would start wondering whether he had deserted her when she needed him most.

'Come on,' he said. 'There's nothing we can do here. We need to be somewhere that Sam will know to look for us. We'll go back to the hotel. That's the best place now.'

In the front passenger seat of his car, Damon Tyzack burst out laughing as he was given the latest report on his mobile phone. 'He's on a bicycle? Are you sure? Oh, that's priceless. Who does he think he is, ET? Well, just make sure he doesn't fly away, then.'

Tyzack snapped the phone shut and looked out of the window, shaking his head. 'The great Samuel Carver reduced to riding a pushbike,' he said, talking to himself as much as his driver. 'My, my . . . aren't we coming down in the world?'

38

There was no one following him down the pedestrian precinct of Karl Johans Gate itself, Carver was sure of it. But his route was crossed at intervals by roads that were open to traffic. Up ahead of him, he saw two black Mercedes saloons drive slowly across the next junction and then stop, pulling up by the side of the road nearest to him, directly blocking his path. The cars' doors opened and half a dozen men got out. They lined up in front of the cars, each a couple of paces apart, forming a picket line across Karl Johans Gate, waiting for him to reach them. And all of them were armed.

The slope had flattened out briefly, but then plunged down again, much steeper than before. Carver was picking up speed, rocketing downhill. He'd be on them in seconds. He looked back over his shoulder. A third Merc had stopped by the junction he had just crossed, preventing him from retreating back the way he had come. On either side of him, the shops and bars lined the street in an unbroken wall of neon and glass. He was as trapped as a rat in a blocked drainpipe.

The distance between him and the waiting men had halved.

They stood there, waiting for him, a line of broad shoulders, thick necks and impassive, patient faces. He had two or three seconds at most before he'd be on them. And then, like a crafty, resourceful rat, Carver spotted his way out.

The building on the left-hand corner of the junction was being renovated. There was scaffolding all the way up the walls and a skip outside on the pavement. The workmen had used a plank to run their barrows of rubble and waste up to the skip. And to make the job of pushing the barrow easier, they'd put the plank on the uphill side of the skip.

Carver swooped left, straightened up again, picked up the cadence of his pedalling to take his speed even higher, lined up his front wheel with the plank and prayed.

He hit the plank like a tightrope walker sprinting over Niagara Falls, kept pedalling like a maniac to maintain his momentum, and then gave a quick pull on the handlebars as he hurtled into the air.

He cleared the skip. He saw the nearest man in the line throw himself out of the way. For an instant he thought he was going to smack into the side of one of the Mercs, but instead he landed on the bonnet, wobbled for a moment with the impact, and then ricocheted off it on to the tarmac. Carver swerved between two oncoming cars, jerked the handlebars again to get him over the kerb on the far side of the road, and then kept moving downhill on the next stretch of Karl Johans Gate.

Behind him he heard shouts, slamming car doors, revving engines, a squeal of tyres and furious blaring of car horns. One look back confirmed what his ears had already told him. The Mercs had pulled across the road and on to the pedestrian paving. And now they were coming downhill, right after him, scattering the men and women in their path, in machines whose straight-line speed would run him down in a matter of moments.

They hadn't shot at him, though, and it told Carver that they wanted him alive. They wouldn't use their weapons unless they had exhausted all other means of stopping him. But they still had a lot more means up their sleeves.

The leading Mercedes was roaring up behind him, its front bumper almost touching his rear wheel. Carver swung right, picking his way between the people fleeing from the onrushing cars, trying to get some minuscule, temporary advantage from his bike's manoeuvrability.

He was running down the side of Karl Johans Gate now, sticking close to the buildings. Several of the bars and stores had put signs out on the paving. There were metal litter-bins placed at regular intervals. Their frames were firmly embedded in concrete plinths, as were official signs that marked this as a pedestrian zone. They were as immovable as bollards, so Carver ran between them and the buildings, gaining some small degree of protection as the two Mercedes roared along beside him like tigers in a zoo, eyeing up a tasty child kept from them only by the bars of their cage.

Then just up ahead of him he saw a couple sheltering in a shadowy recess he took at first glance for a doorway. A second look told him it was a narrow alleyway between two shops, almost close enough to touch on either side.

'Move!' he yelled.

The guy glanced back over his shoulder, saw Carver and leaped out of his way, pulling his girlfriend with him.

Carver turned into the alley, not even trying to get round the full ninety degrees, but half turning the front wheel and letting it bounce off the far wall and ricochet him into the opening. The alley was far darker than the street, lit only by a single bulb above the back entrance to a clothing store. There were cardboard boxes piled outside it, next to an overflowing wheelie bin. Carver stopped for a second as he went past, leaning over to yank the bin out into the middle of the alley. He kicked out at the boxes, sending them flying, creating as much of a barrier as he could around the bin, then picked up the pace again.

The alley ran slightly downhill and then suddenly fell away down a flight of a dozen steps. Carver stood up on the pedals, letting his bent legs act as shock absorbers as he clattered down, hit the bottom and hurtled out of a narrow opening into an enclosed courtyard, surrounded on all sides by an apparently unbroken square of looming buildings. But there were three cars parked in the yard, so there had to be a way out. He saw it: an arch, in the far corner, diagonally across the yard.

Now there were shouts and running footsteps coming from the alleyway behind Carver. He pumped on the pedals and disappeared under the arch. It opened on to the cross street. The traffic flowed one way from Carver's right to his left, going uphill, back towards the junction with Karl Johans Gate and the two Mercedes. The obvious move for a man on a bike was to turn right, against the traffic, making it much harder for any car to follow him.

So Carver turned left.

There was a tram clattering down the middle of the road, moving as fast as the cars around it. It was modern, smooth and squared-off, painted in two-tone blue, and split into three coaches with concertina links. Carver raced round the back of the tram, then turned uphill, following its path, squeezing his bike into the narrow gap between the tram and the pavement. His plan was simple. He wanted to get up alongside the tram, grab hold of the folding fabric between two of the coaches and then hang on for the ride.

He just hadn't counted on the tram going faster than he was. It was pulling away, leaving him exposed. With every second he was getting closer to the two Mercedes. He had to keep the tram between them and him. He forced his burning thighs to push harder and faster down on to the pedals. His chest was heaving with exertion, his skin burning hot and liquid with sweat.

He was back alongside the last coach now. Just next to him he could see a couple of Oriental girls giggling as they watched his desperate attempts to keep up. They smiled and waved. One raised a camera and took a shot through the window, briefly dazzling him with her flash.

Then he was past them and the joint between the coaches was almost within his grasp. Carver took his hands off the handles, leaned towards the tram, felt the bike start to swerve beneath him, losing its grip on the road surface, then grabbed at the thick, rubbery material and clung on for dear life.

He stayed there as the tram continued across the junction with Karl Johans Gate, past the two Mercedes – Carver snatched a quick glimpse through the window and saw them parked on the paving of Karl Johans Gate, a man standing by one of them, talking into a mobile phone – and on across the top of a square, in the middle of which stood a church surrounded by trees. Now the tram started to slow down. Up ahead, Carver could see a line of people standing by a shelter, just before the next junction. They got up from their seats, picked up their bags and came closer to the edge of the pavement as the tram slowed down for the stop. Carver slowed too, letting go of the tram and pulling over to the side of the road. Then he got off the bike, propped it up behind the shelter as inconspicuously as possible and joined the other passengers as they clambered aboard.

The tram moved off, turning right at the junction before heading downhill again, parallel to Karl Johans Gate, going the same direction Carver had been taking before he'd ducked into the alley. Ahead of him he could see an open, modern plaza and on the far side of that a neon sign over a glass-fronted entrance that said 'Oslo Sentralstasjon'. The word looked strange, but when he said it in his mind it made perfect sense: Central Station.

When the tram stopped again, Carver got off and raced across the paved square, under the awning and into the station. Ahead of him rose an escalator. Above it hung a dark blue sign, printed with Norwegian words in white and English in yellow. Carver read 'Station hall' as he dashed on to the escalator. He stood still on the moving steps, happy to let them do the work as he checked to see if his pursuers had caught up with him.

He couldn't spot any sign of them. He'd made it.

For now, at any rate.

39

Carver stood in the main concourse of Oslo station while his escape plans fell to pieces around him. There were no night trains to Stockholm, or anywhere else outside the country: nothing till seven the next morning. In any case, that was irrelevant. Carver had no money. It had only struck him when he stood in front of the ticket-machine that his wallet was still in his jacket, draped on his chair in the café of the King Haakon Hotel. He'd patted his trouser pockets, in that futile way men have, as if the act of striking their groins with their hands can somehow magic a lost possession into being. Needless to say, the magic had not worked.

He grimaced, hissed a single, heartfelt expletive and then cursed himself for letting his guard down. In the old days, when he worked on the principle that he might be forced on the run at any moment, he never went anywhere without a money-belt round his waist, containing cash, credit cards in at least two identities, matching passports and a clean pre-paid SIM card. Now he'd gone straight, he was as helpless as any other forgetful civilian.

So what did he have?

His most important asset was his phone. There wasn't much battery power left, so he'd have to ration its use, but its text log contained the messages he'd supposedly received from Jack Grantham. They were the only evidence in his defence, the only suggestion that he had called the fatal room-number at someone else's behest.

Besides the phone, his pockets produced his day-card for the Oslo public-transport network, a couple of two-euro coins left over from Paris, and sixty-eight Norwegian kroner in change. So was there anywhere he could go with that? He looked at a route map. The nearest station to the Swedish border was Halden, due south of Oslo. There was a train leaving in eight minutes' time, but the cheapest ticket was almost two hundred kroner. He'd just have to jump it and hope to avoid the ticket-collector once he got on board.

Carver looked around, as he had done repeatedly since he arrived at the station, sweeping the concourse for his enemies. This time he saw one, a man, apparently buying a bottle of water from a newsagent's stand. His back was turned to Carver, but his shaven head and the line of the black nylon bomber jacket stretched over his massive shoulders were familiar. He'd been third from the left in the picket line of men arrayed in front of the Mercedes.

Very calmly, without any sign of haste, Carver walked away from the ticket-machine.

The man put the mineral water back in the cooler and followed Carver, slightly behind him and a few paces to his right.

Carver spotted another familiar face, apparently losing interest in the departures board.

He was still walking quite slowly, as were the men tailing him. They were like competitors in a track-cycling sprint, idling around the track, waiting to see whose nerve would crack first, who'd be the first to try a burst of speed.

Carver walked beneath a sign directing passengers towards the airport express, the left-luggage office and the south exit. Ahead he could see another set of escalators. People were slowing down as they reached them, manoeuvring cases on and off. A mother was taking hold of her small child.

Now Carver ran.

He sprinted up to the start of the escalator, barging one man out of the way. Then he grabbed the long handle of a large roller suit-case and yanked it out of its owner's hand, dragging it behind him as he kept moving. As he stepped on to the downward escalator, Carver swung the case round so that it toppled over, blocking the entrance to the escalator. He got moving again, taking the moving steps three at a time while a barging, complaining, pleading knot of humanity formed around the case.

He reached the bottom and dashed towards the exit. Carver dared not slow down for an instant. He did not need to look behind him to know that his pursuers, whoever they were, had not been long delayed.

40

Tyzack had a vision in his head of how he wanted this to go. He'd make Carver sweat. He'd even give him the illusion that he might get away. But that illusion wouldn't last long. Tyzack had always been the fitter, faster and stronger man: that was one of the many things that had been so unjust about the way Carver had betrayed him. So he'd win, that was inevitable. He'd hunt Carver down, corner him and take him away – he had the place prepared, a farmhouse miles from anywhere. And then, when Carver was tired and hungry, when the arrogance had been knocked out of him and he knew for sure that no one was coming for him, Tyzack would sit down with him and have a little chat. They'd talk about the old days, put a few things straight before Tyzack pulled the plug.

So far, it was all going nicely. Carver had got away from his men in Karl Johans Gate, but that was all part of the game. It would have been a disappointment to catch him too easily. And the momentary illusion of success had only made Carver's failure at the station all the sweeter: it had been a joy to watch him search for the wallet. Only a few minutes gone, and already he was broke. His only shirt was covered with blood, and once he stopped running, he'd feel the evening chill something rotten.

But Carver wasn't going to stop running for a while yet. He'd keep moving till he felt the way they used to on training runs – past the point when you wanted to stop, and the point where you wanted to puke, to the point where you wanted to die. Tyzack would make sure of that.

He'd had enough of leaving it to his men to do the job. As Carver fled from the station, Tyzack stepped out of the fast-food joint from which he'd been observing the main concourse and broke into a steady jog. As he set off in pursuit, Tyzack felt in great shape, well on top of his game. This was a race he was going to win.

41

A motorway ran past the railway station before plunging into a tunnel that hid its traffic out of sight of the city. Carver didn't stop moving, trusting in his agility and the good sense of Norwegian drivers to keep him alive. He crossed the last two lanes and, breathing heavily now, ran beneath a ramp that carried traffic up to a raised intersection. He needed to slow down, get his bearings and gather his strength. As he looked around it struck him that he'd been driven right down to the sea. The men on his trail were like a pack of hounds running down a stag, backing him into a corner till he had nowhere left to run.

Ahead of him, to his left, lay a long thin strip of water that must once have been a dock. Away to his right, past a line of buildings, he could see a car park, beyond which was a much larger expanse of open water. Carver did not believe in stealing cars. He did not approve of petty criminals who preyed on innocent civilians, nor did he enjoy attracting undue attention from the police. But it was a bit late for scruples now. If he was going to get away, he'd need wheels. He turned right, picked up his pace again, and made for the car park.

He was running parallel to a development, which lay between the narrow dock and the car park, the size of a full city block. At first glance, it looked ordinary enough: modern, flat-roofed, maybe half a dozen storeys tall. The lower storeys were glass-fronted, revealing workshops of some kind. As he went further, however, Carver realized that this was actually just a rear extension to a much larger structure. And the more he saw of it, the stranger it became.

The whole thing was an exercise in asymmetry and skewed geometry, with almost no true horizontal or vertical lines: everything was tilted or off-centre. Its angular aggression reminded Carver of a gigantic, architectural stealth bomber, as though all the brain-scrambling planes of stone and glass had been chosen to deflect radar beams. Then he realized that there were people walking along great ramps that ran up the side of the building along and out on to the roof. Some were standing at the very top of the façade, waving down to friends on the ground far below, like figures in a Maurice Escher drawing of staircases that lead round and round in an infinite, impossible spiral.

This must be the famous Oslo Opera House that Thor Larsson had mentioned.

He was approaching the car park now. A narrow strip of water ran like a moat between the car park and the opera house, bridged by a single stone walkway. He looked around, trying to find a car to take, one left in a place where he would not be spotted.

It wasn't going to be easy. A cluster of figures was standing at the near side of the opera house roof, directly opposite him. For now, their attention was directed across the city towards the pillar of smoke and dust still rising from the wreckage of the King Haakon Hotel, but if they ever dropped their eyes, they would have a clear view over the parked cars. There were more people dotted around him, going to and from their vehicles.

A group of sightseers was standing by the sea wall, taking in the view of the opera house and the water. One of them was pointing across to the far side of the harbour, where a giant ferry, belching black smoke from its funnel, was just getting under way, slowly nosing its way out of its berth and into open water. The moment the tourists lost interest in it and turned back in Carver's direction, they'd see him. Meanwhile, the men pursuing him were getting closer. He ducked down between two lines of cars and considered his situation.

He had no money to buy a way out. He had no weapon with which to fight. He had no tools with which to force open a car. His only hope was to hijack a car as it arrived or left the car park. He'd get out of town, dump the car and think of his next move.

Carver was hiding behind a chunky Audi Q7. It was fast, tough and equipped with four-wheel drive: the perfect getaway vehicle but as inaccessible to his bare hands as Fort Knox. He heard the sound of a car coming into the car park, its tyres crunching on the gravelly surface. Raising his head and peering through the Audi's windows, he spotted an old VW Golf manoeuvring into a space. That would have to do.

The moment the engine died, Carver made his move. He got to his feet and sprinted towards the car.

The car door was opening. The driver emerged, a grey-haired, elderly woman. Carver hesitated. Christ, had he really been reduced to beating up old ladies for their car keys?

As he stopped, he heard a shout. He couldn't make out the exact words, but he didn't have to. He turned his head and saw three men walking towards him, sixty or seventy metres away. They were spread out, each walking between a different line of cars and they moved with a calm, purposeful stride as they cut off Carver's line of escape, knowing that they had him.

The middle man of the three was Damon Tyzack. Carver could see that he was smiling, just as he had been at the King Haakon Hotel. But his mocking smirk had given way to the rapacious, scavenging grin of the hyena, made in anticipation of the taste of blood, the tearing of flesh and the cracking of bones against teeth.

The woman looked up, reacting to the shout, and saw Carver standing barely ten metres away. They looked at one another and he saw her eyes flicker with alarm as she locked her car door and hurriedly stuffed the key in her bag. Then she held it to her chest, silently daring him to take it from her. She'd seen the other men and sensed that they were after him. Now she knew the odds were on her side.

Carver could still have escaped. All he needed was three strides; one punch; barely five seconds to grab the bag, rip out the keys, get in the car and go.

He couldn't do it.

He spun towards the sea wall and sprinted in the direction of the walkway that led to the opera house, followed by the sound of hurried footsteps as Tyzack and his men came after him.

The sightseers were watching him now, their eyes fixed on the chase, but their bodies backing away as they struggled between curiosity and fear.

Carver reached the walkway, which was made of the same white stone that had been used on the opera house and the paved area in front of it. Ahead of him, a tourist couple – almost certainly British or American – were waddling back towards him. It wasn't hard to place them. No Norwegian would ever be that grossly over-weight. Carver pushed his way between them, popped out the far side like a cork from a champagne bottle, then turned and aimed a short, chopping kick at the man's leg. He fell to the ground like a tower block being demolished from the bottom, collapsing in on itself. His wife started screaming. Between them, they blocked the entire walkway. Perfect.

Carver heard the squeals of the woman and the pained cries of her husband mix with Tyzack's shouts telling them to get out of the way. For a moment he was almost amused, but then he saw some-thing that dashed any brief flicker of optimism.

Ahead of him, coming round the far side of the opera house, were another three men, line abreast, eating up the ground in a relaxed loping stride. When they caught sight of Carver, they didn't speed towards him, but slowed down. One of them raised a hand to his mouth. Carver couldn't see if he had a phone held in it or was using a wrist-mike, but the upshot was the same. The net was closing in. From their point of view it was just a matter of where they took him and when. He wasn't going to get away now.

42

He was standing at the foot of the marble ramp that ran up the side of the opera house to the roof. On this side of the building, the ramp widened as it rose, flaring away from the glass core. Up its outer edge, marked by foot-level lights, ran a stairway made from stone whose shallow steps were rough and stippled for extra grip. The main ramp was covered with smooth marble, but was still walkable, as the occasional figures dotted about it proved. This would provide the most direct route to the top. Carver started up it, settling into a slow, grim, arm-pumping run.

He'd gone about a quarter of the way up when he looked back over his shoulder. Tyzack was standing at the foot of the slope, speaking into a mobile phone. His two goons had already begun their ascent up the ramp towards him. Carver kept moving. The next time he looked back, Tyzack, too, was heading his way. From where he was, Carver couldn't see the far side of the building. But he was willing to bet that the other three pursuers had taken the ramp that went that way. He was counting on it, in fact.

Close up, Carver could see that the ramp – apparently a single upward sweep – was in fact a series of fractionally crimped and angled surfaces. Its colour was not pure white, as it had seemed from a distance, but a very pale hint of grey. Above his head, the late-evening sky had clouded over so that it was now a virtual match for the marble on which he stood. He felt disconcerted, almost disoriented; running over a surface that was constantly shifting beneath his feet towards a barely perceptible horizon at which stone and sky became one; a monochrome world as cold and alien as an Arctic icefield.

A few paces back, he'd passed three teenage girls coming downhill, arm in arm and giggling, making a game out of trying to keep their feet. Now he heard the tone of the voices change, a shriek of alarm and a jumble of words in which he only understood one: 'Pistol!'

He stopped and looked back down the slope. Tyzack and his men had drawn their weapons, which they held at their sides, pointing down, as they walked. They knew that he was not armed. There was no need to make a show of it. But the girls' words had had an effect. People were turning to look, then backing away from the men when they saw that they were armed. There were more shouts of alarm, a scurry of movement as people tried to get off the ramp and the roof above, looking for a safe way down.

The three men paid no attention to any of it. They were indifferent to everything and everyone except Carver.

He was almost at the top now. Ahead of him were two towers, the lower one about twice his height and faced with pale grey metal tiles covered with raised dots, like Braille. The taller tower, marble-covered like the rest of the building, rose to his right, above the core of the opera house. The other three men would be somewhere beyond and below it, coming up the other side of the building.

The two towers were arranged diagonally to one another – kitty-corner, as Americans say. As long as Carver stood behind one or other of the towers, he would be invisible to anyone on either ramp. He'd reached the shelter of the low tower now. No one could see him. But there was a gap of about three long strides between the tower's two nearest corners. The moment he tried to cross that, the men behind him would spot him at once.

And he needed to cross the gap. His survival depended upon it.

Finally he had a stroke of good luck. Behind the low tower, at the very far end of the roof, the surface fell away about eighteen inches to a path that ran along the edge of the building, below a parapet.

Carver sprinted the last few strides and flung himself on to the path, wincing as his knees and elbows cracked on the marble. He ignored the pain, wriggling forward on his stomach until he reckoned he must have gone far enough to be in the lee of the bigger tower. Then he jumped to his feet and dashed towards it.

As he ran he glanced back across the roof. He could see Tyzack creeping around the low tower, his gun in both hands now, held up to his right shoulder, ready to bring to bear. He was approaching one corner of the tower. The other two men would be round the far side, expecting to catch Carver cowering in its shadow. None of them would be looking in the direction he had actually taken. Not until they discovered he was gone.

He reached the side of the bigger tower and pressed up against it. Now he looked towards the far side of the building, looking for the other trio. They hadn't come into sight yet. They must still be on the ramp. That would place them below him, on the far side of the edge of the central core. How far away, Carver didn't know. But they must be close to the top now. He forgot his pounding heart, oxygen-starved lungs and bruised ankles and ran flat out towards the side of the roof.

At the very edge his path was blocked by a waist-high parapet. He skidded to a halt, placed his hands on the top of the parapet and then vaulted up on to it.

Now he could see the three men below him on the ramp. They were just to his left, their backs towards him, almost at the top. Two of them held pistols; the third had a sub-machine gun, a Belgian P90 by the stubby, futuristic look of it.

They hadn't yet seen him. But Tyzack and his men, away across the roof by the lower tower, had spotted him silhouetted against the pearl-grey sky. There were more shouts and then a couple of sharp cracks of gunshot. Carver's immediate reaction was relief. At that range, if you lived long enough to hear the shots, the bullets had missed.

Then he realized that he wasn't the target. The shots had been an alarm call to the men on the far ramp.

They looked around, trying to work out what was going on. One of them pressed a finger to his ear, trying to hear a message amidst the confusion. Another turned, looked up and saw Carver. He brought his gun up to fire.

But Carver was no longer on the parapet. He was in mid-air.

The two men collided before a shot was fired. Carver's target had long hair combed over a bald spot and gathered in a ponytail. As they fell to the stone, Carver reached for the ponytail with his right hand, twisted it round his fist and then used it as a handle with which he smashed the man's head into the stone: two sharp blows that left him barely conscious.

Carver's left hand was gripping the man's right wrist, his thumb pressing hard into its flesh, trying to loosen his grip on the gun. With his feet, he lashed out in the direction of the other two men, aiming for their shins, connecting with one of them.

Still holding on to the man he'd attacked, Carver flung himself back down the ramp, away from the other two, the two bodies tumbling down the grey-white stone. But Carver's opponent was not yet finished. As they came to a halt, the man's free hand whipped round and punched Carver in the temple, sending a sickening shock of pain through him.

Carver blinked away the fizzing, detuned television blur from his eyes, tightened his grip on the ponytail and put all his strength into one last downwards slam.

The crack of splintering bone and the sudden smear of red blood on the snowy marble told him he would not need another. He prised the gun from inert, slack fingers and rolled away from the corpse, his arms stretched out beyond his head, firing as he moved, hearing other shots crack into the ramp around him.

He came to a halt by the green glass wall of the opera house which ran along one side of the ramp. The other two men were hardly any distance above him. They would have taken evasive action, too. Now it was just a matter of reaction time.

Carver looked up. As he'd expected, the two men had thrown themselves to opposite sides of the ramp, which was much narrower on this side of the building. A stone parapet ran up the outside edge, just as it did on the roof. One of the men was crouched against it, already bringing his pistol to bear. The other was directly above Carver, pressed against the glass. The way he'd thrown himself, he'd got his gun hand stuck slightly behind him, between his body and the side of the building. It would barely take a second to free his weapon, but that was enough.

Carver didn't hesitate. He dealt with the immediate danger: the man by the parapet. Carver put two rounds into his chest, then swung the gun round and shot the other man in the head. He'd just managed to free his gun hand and was bringing it up as Carver fired. They were so close that Carver could see the look of surprise in his eyes.

A little over five seconds had passed since Carver had jumped down on to the ramp. In that time he had halved the odds against him. But the survivors still outnumbered him three to one. He might not get lucky again.

43

Carver got to his feet, shoved the pistol into his waistband, and charged down the ramp until he was close to the bottom. Then he ran to the parapet and vaulted over the side. He dropped fifteen feet and landed on a narrow path that ran beside the opera house and the sea. He turned left, making his way back towards the rear of the building and the motorway beyond that. He stuck as close as possible to the wall of the opera house, so that anyone looking over the parapet, up above, would have to lean right out to see him.

He could hear shouts and running footsteps above him, but they hadn't spotted him yet. In the distance there was another sound, something new: a helicopter, and getting closer, too.

A side door opened and a man walked out, a kid, really, early twenties at most. He was dressed in a red and beige seventies-style Fila tracksuit top, carrying a motorbike helmet. He stopped by a moped propped up against the wall. It wasn't what Carver would have chosen. For urban getaway work, he'd always specified fast, nimble trailbikes, with 400-cc engines as an absolute minimum. This kid's machine had about as much power as an old washing machine. But Carver had long since ceased to be in any position to be fussy.

The kid was bent over, taking the chain off his bike. The helmet was resting on the moped's seat. Carver slowed to a walk, came up behind him as quietly as possible and jammed the tip of the gun barrel into the back of his neck, just below the skull.

'Don't move. Don't say anything. Just listen. OK?'

The kid's head nodded frantically.

'Undo the chain, then place it on the ground beside you.'

The order was obeyed. Carver slid his foot across and shifted the chain out of the kid's reach.

'Now stand up slowly, nice and easy, no sudden movements.'

He waited while the order was obeyed.

'Turn around and face me . . . Now, your keys, please. And again, easy does it.'

Holding his gun in his right hand, Carver took the keys in his left and shoved them into a trouser pocket. The kid began to tremble, his panicked eyes focused upwards at the gun pointing directly at the middle of his forehead. He was trying to grow a beard, Carver saw: little more than a dusting of mouse-brown hair across cheeks still not completely clear of teenage acne.

'Please, don't kill me,' he begged, his voice little more than a whimper.

'I don't plan to,' said Carver, darting a quick glance back down the path. It was clear. They hadn't yet tracked him down. 'Not if you do exactly as you're told.'

'Sure, sure,' said the kid. 'Anything.'

'OK, then, take off the jacket and put it next to the helmet. I'm putting my gun away now.'

The kid was half turned away from Carver, leaving the jacket on his moped. Carver saw the tension ease from his shoulders as he realized the gun was no longer aimed at him. And it was then, at that brief moment of relaxation, that Carver grabbed the scrawny young man and spun him round, kept him moving across the narrow path and flung him into the water. It was hardly any drop, but the slick marble stonework would make it impossible for the kid to climb back ashore. He'd have to swim round to the front of the building, and that would give Carver all the time he needed.

He looked at the kid, who was treading water and looking at him with an expression that had changed from fear to indignation.

'I'm taking your bike,' said Carver. 'But I'm not going far. Go to Aker Brygge. Your bike will be there. I won't.'

Carver went back to the moped, put on the jacket and the helmet, turned on the engine, and moved away. He was thinking about the ferry that had just set sail. That was his way out of Oslo. And he'd worked out how to get on it.

44

'What now?' Police Superintendent Ole Ravnsborg, senior duty officer at the Oslo police headquarters in Hammersborggata, just a short way away from the site of the explosion, looked up at the young officer standing nervously in front of him holding two sheets of paper.

'We just had a tip-off, sir. About the bomb at the King Haakon.'

Ravnsborg was as big and shaggy as a dog with a cask of brandy round its neck. He emitted a rumbling, disgruntled growl and his massive shoulders seemed to slump even lower in his chair.

'Put it on the pile,' he muttered, 'with all the other crazies.'

The youngster stood his ground. 'I think this one might be different, sir,' he insisted. 'They gave us specific names of the bomber, and two associates. There's even a photograph, taken at the hotel, exactly when the bomb went off.'

Ravnsborg gave a little wave of the fingers, as if summoning a waiter. 'Give it here,' he said, taking the paper. A hush seemed to fall on the crowded incident room as the hurriedly assembled investigation team – an ad hoc mix of officers on duty at the time of the blast and other detectives hauled back to HQ as and when they could be tracked down – waited to see what their leader would make of this new information.

Ravnsborg read the email and looked at the photograph, scratching his head through a mat of tousled, dirty-blond hair as he did so. Though his body – a little soft around the edges now, but still possessing vast reserves of strength, like a weightlifter retired from competition – was virtually motionless, his mind was darting from one subject to another with a gymnast's agility.

The bomb had come as a total, devastating surprise. There had been no threat from a terrorist group, nor any warning from the nation's intelligence service, or its anti-terrorism unit. The city's police, fire and medical services were stretched to their utmost just coping with the immediate aftermath of the blast in the vicinity of the King Haakon Hotel. He had no officers to spare for a wild-goose chase, looking for a man who was either an innocent irrelevance or a calculating killer with an escape route planned as meticulously as the attack itself. There had not yet been time or enough available manpower to interview hotel staff. Nor was there, as yet, any forensic evidence linking the explosion to the hotel's internal phone system.

To cap it all, Ravnsborg was profoundly suspicious of the tip-off itself. It had been given anonymously, but who would do such a thing, and to what end? It was, he supposed, possible that the bomber had been sold out by his own people. But, if so, he would surely in turn give up the men who had betrayed him. Perhaps it was a rival group, wanting to undermine its competitors, or a foreign spy, determined to preserve his anonymity. Ravnsborg did not like any of these explanations. Yet he could not afford to ignore a lead as good as this, either.

He looked up to see every eye in the room trained upon him.

'Berg, Dalen,' he snapped. 'Go to the Gabelshus Hotel. It's in Skillebekk. Pick up a guest, an American, name of Madeleine Cross. Also a friend of hers, one of ours, Thor Larsson. Bring them here. Tell them they are wanted for questioning in connection with tonight's bomb attack. They are witnesses, not suspects, at this point, but that may change. Don't let her get away with any crap about calling the American embassy. Just bring them here as fast as you can. Go.'

As the two detectives left the room, Ravnsborg was firing off more orders. All police and security staff were told to be on the lookout for a male, aged thirty-five to forty, six feet tall, dark hair, British, going by the name of Carver.

'Do we have an eye colour?' one of his men asked.

Ravnsborg looked mournfully down at the photograph, which lit Carver in a blaze of flash. 'Red,' he said, then, 'That was a joke.'

There was a nervous ripple of forced laughter. Another order was given to make the picture available to TV stations, along with the information that Mr Carver was wanted for questioning by police so that he could be eliminated from their enquiries.

All the time, phones around the office were ringing constantly with updates from the bomb-site, questions from reporters, interruptions from politicians wanting to get in on the act. Ravnsborg had just finished a short, infuriating conversation with the National Police Commissioner, who had simultaneously wished him luck, promised him promotion if the investigation should turn out well, and assured him of a swift relocation to the furthest, coldest reaches of the nation if it did not, when the young policeman approached his desk again.

'You again,' Ravnsborg sighed. 'What do you want?'

'You're not going to believe it, sir. But all hell has broken loose down at the opera house.'

45

Carver rode the moped at walking pace along the broad esplanade that ran between the fancy food and drink joints and the sea. There was something for everyone down here: steakhouses, pizza parlours, gourmet French and specialist seafood. All the restaurants supplied huge fleece blankets so that customers could sit outside and still keep snug. But there were no cosy couples sharing blankets and stealing kisses. Wherever he looked, Carver saw people huddled round radios and phone-screens, taking in the latest news from the bombing. Some of the restaurants had set up TVs in their dining-rooms, as if admitting that no one would be interested in anything else tonight.

No one paid him the slightest bit of attention as he went by. He felt like a shark swimming unseen amidst seaside holidaymakers: a hated killer who would surely be hunted down and slaughtered if he were ever revealed. He felt stained by guilt. He felt like killing Damon Tyzack. But before he could do that, he needed to get away, regroup, and find a better battlefield.

*

At the police headquarters, the duty press officer completed the release that would be mailed out to all media, along with the photo of the bombing suspect, or 'key witness' as Ravnsborg had decided to call him. She was just about to press 'Send' when her finger paused above the keyboard.

Better get the boss to take one final look at it first. That way her back was covered.

She hit 'Print' instead and waited for the hard copy to emerge from the machine.

Carver could have done with one of those fleeces. The kid's jacket was pretty flimsy and the sweat that covered his body had chilled in the cool evening air. It would be a lot colder out on the water, but there was nothing else to be done for it. He was determined to get as far away from Oslo as he could. Above all, he wanted to be as far as possible from Maddy.

He still didn't know if she'd played any part in the set-up, but it made no difference. Either she was working with Tyzack, in which case he wanted nothing whatever to do with her. Or she was innocent, in which case he had to draw attention away from her, towards himself. If the police saw them together, she would automatically be classed as an accomplice. It was bad enough being dumped in the crap himself, without dragging her any deeper into it.

He wished he could call her up to explain his disappearance. But he had to assume that either Tyzack, or the police, or both, were intercepting her phones. All he could hope for was that Larsson would work out what he was doing and explain it to Maddy. If she understood his desertion, perhaps then she would forgive it.

There was nothing to be done about that, so Carver focused his attention on the matter in hand. He needed a boat, something fast, but all he could see moored alongside the pontoons were sailing boats. Up ahead a bridge curved over a waterway: one of the abandoned docks that cut deep gouges out of Oslo's shoreline. When he reached it, Carver looked down the quayside and his face broke into a smile of grim satisfaction behind his helmet visor. A line of small, fast boats was moored down the full length of the dock, and any one of them would do just fine.

The press officer's face was blandly impassive, but inside she was heaving a sigh of relief. Thank God she had brought the text of the release back to Ravsnborg to be checked. He had received new information. Apparently the bomber had gone crazy up on the opera house roof and started shooting people.

'Make it clear that members of the public are not, under any circumstances, to attempt to apprehend him,' Ravnsborg told her. 'This man is armed and extremely dangerous. If anyone spots him, they must call the police immediately. But they must not do anything themselves. I do not want any dead heroes. OK? Now go. I want this out and on the air . . . Go!'

46

It took no more than a few seconds for Carver to spot what he was looking for: a 25-foot Scorpion RIB with a 90-horsepower Honda engine sitting on its tail. Rigid inflatable boats were the workhorses of the Royal Marines and SBS alike and Carver had spent more hours than he cared to think about sitting in them, going to and from missions and training exercises. When he got off the moped, took off his helmet and got down into the boat, it felt like a kind of homecoming.

Carver had no ignition keys, but he didn't need them. He could get an RIB started with nothing more than his belt buckle.

He began by finding the battery, stored beneath the driver's seat. A red plastic isolator key was inserted in the top. Carver turned it to the 'On' position. Now the boat had power.

Next to the battery was a toolkit. In it Carver found a knife. He used it to cut about four inches off the laces of his All Stars. He relaced his shoes before pulling out the boat's kill-switch, the safety device that shut down the engine if the driver went overboard. Unless the switch was out, the engine would not work. It was held in place by a plastic clip, linked by a lanyard to the driver's life-jacket. If the line was jerked too far, the toggle was pulled, the switch popped back in and the engine died. Carver tied the cut length of lace around the shaft of the kill-switch, ensuring that it stayed out. Perfect.

Moving to the back of the boat, he lowered the engine so that the propeller was in the water. Then he took off the hood and found the starter motor. It was controlled by a solenoid, whose job was to relay power from the battery to the motor. Carver placed his metal belt buckle over the solenoid's terminals. That linked the terminal connected to the battery with the terminal connected to the starter motor. A circuit was formed. The engine spluttered into life.

He'd just hot-wired an RIB.

He made his way round the boat, casting off its lines from the quay. Then he stood at the controls, put the boat into reverse and eased his way back into the dock, swinging the boat round so that its bow was pointed at the bridge.

Beyond the bridge lay Oslo fjord, and beyond that the open sea. Somewhere out there was a Baltic ferry. Carver put the boat into forward gear and increased the speed. Once he had passed under the bridge and gone beyond the lines of pontoons against which all the yachts were moored, he flattened the throttle, felt the boat accelerate up to thirty knots and roared off towards the setting sun.

At the Gabelshus Hotel, Ravnsborg's two men were leading Maddy Cross and Thor Larsson down the steps from the hotel entrance, towards their waiting squad car.

At Oslo police headquarters, the press officer gave the release one last read-through. Yes, she concluded, it was all exactly as her boss had demanded. She sent it off. Within minutes the bomber Carver's name and face would be on every TV station, every news website, every media outlet in Norway. He would have no hiding place.

47

Damon Tyzack was sorely tempted to shoot the two men who'd come with him as he'd run up the opera house after Carver. The chopper he'd whistled up, originally to take him and Carver away, couldn't land on the roof – typical nonsensical modern architecture, not a flat surface anywhere – and they'd had to be winched up one at a time on a rope. It took for bloody ever and did his state of mind no good at all.

He was already feeling stressed that Carver had taken out the other three and vanished. By the time Tyzack had got to the far ramp, Carver had gone. When he heard the sound of the engine, looked over the side and saw a man – it had to be Carver – riding off on a tinpot moped, it was too late for the three of them to make a run for the cars. They'd be better off up in the air. Still, he didn't feel too clever being hauled up to the chopper like some drowning sailor and then having to wait in the cabin while the other two came aboard. Not with the Oslo police sure to pitch up any moment. He seriously considered leaning out of the door and giving his men the old double-tap, there and then. But Carver was still out there somewhere and there was work to do. He didn't want to lose any more people just yet. And one of the men was Foster Lafferty: a total oaf, but he had his uses.

So now what?

Tyzack pulled on a headset and told his pilot to head south, over the water, away from the city. He needed to get away from the heat, find a minute to think. If he made a wrong move now, the whole thing could go tits-up. And he couldn't afford that. Not with a president to kill.

48

Ole Ravnsborg didn't like to tell people that his broken nose was the result of a childhood bicycle spill. He didn't want to disappoint. It pleased everyone to believe that a man built the way he was and with a face so battered must be a tough guy. And that helped when dealing with criminals, most of whom had an essentially bestial, Darwinian view of life. It instilled a degree of respect and it blinded his opponents to the fact that he might just be smarter than them, too.

With women, of course, the dynamic was different. Ravnsborg felt able to display the more thoughtful and to him more authentic aspects of his personality. Those qualities, too, provided their own smokescreen.

He interviewed Maddy Cross in the presence of a female detective. He took his time sitting down and getting himself set. He wanted to take a look at her, not for any prurient reasons – though he was not blind to her attractions – but simply to get a sense of her as an interview subject and possible adversary.

She was confused and uncertain, that much was to be expected, either as a natural reaction to being dragged off to a police station in a foreign country, or as a pose adopted by a professional criminal, playing the role of the vulnerable female. There was something in her eyes, though: not the truculence of a habitual offender, perhaps, but a certain coolness. She had strength in her, this woman; she was self-possessed. Whether that made her anything other than an innocent bystander, only time would tell.

He began by sliding a picture of Carver's face, cropped from the emailed photograph, across the table between them. 'Do you know this man, Mrs Cross?'

She looked at it, frowning: 'Yes, but . . . I don't understand. Why am I here? I've done nothing wrong. Do I need a lawyer?'

Her voice was rising in pitch as she spoke, anxiety creeping in with every sentence. Ravnsborg was deliberately casual in reply.

'I don't know. Do you? I can say that at the moment you are here as a witness. You have not been charged with any offence. What do you have to worry about? Just tell me the truth and everything will be fine. So . . . what is his name?'

'Samuel Carver . . . but, what is this? Is he in trouble?'

'Possibly. Do you know where he is now, please?'

She shook her head. 'No . . . no, I don't. He just . . . disappeared . . .'

Ravnsborg nodded, tapping the table with his fingers as he pondered Carver's vanishing act. He was not taking notes of the interview, though the female detective occasionally jotted down words in a notebook.

'Where were you when this disappearance happened?' he asked.

'In the café, at that hotel . . .'

'The King Haakon?'

'Whatever, the one where . . . you know, the explosion . . . Is that what this is about? Because I don't know anything about that.'

'We'll see . . . So, Mrs Cross, how would you describe your relationship with Mr Carver? Are you, how should I say . . . together?'

Maddy ran her hands through her hair, pulling it back from

her face. 'I guess. I mean, I thought we had something . . .'

'And you came to Oslo, why?'

'For a wedding – his friend Thor's wedding.'

'That would be Mr Larsson?'

'Yes.'

'So they were old friends.'

'Sure. Sam was going to give a speech at the wedding.'

'This wedding was the sole purpose of your trip?'

'Well, we stayed in Paris for a couple days. We did some shopping. Then we came here. It was just a vacation, you know. That's what he told me.'

'Quite so,' said Ravnsborg, noting the distancing of herself from him, the first indication of doubt. 'And you arrived in Oslo at what time?'

'About four in the afternoon, maybe a little after. It was the SAS flight, you can check.'

'I will. And then?'

'We took the train into the city and got a cab to our hotel. Thor came with us, then he went off to do wedding stuff. We were both a little tired, still jetlagged, you know? So we stayed in our room, resting, till it was time to get ready for dinner.'

'When did you leave the hotel?'

'I don't know, around eight, maybe.'

'And you were in your room until then . . . resting?'

'That's right.'

'So there were no witnesses who saw you there.'

'I would hope not.'

If she was telling the truth, thought Ravnsborg, that left no time for Carver to place a bomb at the King Haakon Hotel. Of course, he might have had accomplices who did it for him. Or she might be lying. He made a mental note to have her alibi checked as soon as possible. But if true it made the evidence against Carver less secure, for now at least.

Ravnsborg returned to the interview: 'Who suggested the café for dinner?'

'That was Thor. He said it was kind of touristy, but we'd like it anyway.'

'So it was not Mr Carver's idea?'

'No. I don't think he'd ever heard of the place before.'

'And you were having a nice time there?'

'I thought so.'

'Nothing unusual, out of the ordinary?'

'No, we talked, had a bottle of wine, it was … it was nice. Everything seemed fine.'

'Was Mr Carver nervous, or edgy at all – anything unusual about his behaviour at that dinner, or over recent days?'

There was a momentary hesitation before Maddy spoke, but her words, when they came, were hurried and over-emphatic. 'No, not at all, he was fine.'

'You're quite sure about that, Mrs Cross?'

'Well, maybe he was a little distant, you know, tense. But it was our first trip together. I just assumed he was the kind of guy who takes time getting used to being in a relationship. If he was hiding anything, I got the impression it had to do with me, with us.'

'I see. So, to return to your meal. He left the table. Why was that?'

'Sam got a message on his phone.'

'How did he react to this message?'

'To tell you the truth, he seemed pissed about it. He sent another text straight back and waited till he'd got a reply. He said it was a voice from the past and that he had to take the call. So he got up and left the room. And that . . . that was the last time I saw him. He's all right, isn't he? Tell me he wasn't hurt.'

That concern sounded genuine to Ravnsborg's ears. She still cares for him, he thought. He said, 'I can't tell you anything for sure. Mr Carver has not been formally identified, alive or dead. I can, however, say that a man who might have been him was seen at the Operaen, that is our opera house, a little over ten minutes after the explosion.'

The bafflement in Maddy Cross's voice sounded authentic, too.

'What are you talking about? You're saying he is alive? But what . . . I don't get it . . . what was he doing at the opera house?'

'If it was him, Mrs Cross, he killed three men.'

The words hit her like a slap in the face. 'No! Please . . .'

Ravnsborg began to apply his pressure now, not by any obvious displays of aggression, but simply by giving her a crisp, impersonal recitation of facts.

'My men have been interviewing witnesses. A man answering to Mr Carver's description was observed being chased into the area of the opera house. There were three men following him at first. They were joined by another three men. All six were armed. None of our witnesses report seeing Mr Carver with a weapon. Yet three of the men were killed and he escaped.'

'So he was defending himself?'

'It would seem so.'

Ravnsborg looked at his interviewee. She seemed relieved. Yet she had not questioned the account he had given.

'You know, Mrs Cross, you do not seem entirely surprised by this information. Why is that? What do you know about Mr Carver?'

'Not much . . . I know he used to be in the military. He told me he worked as a security consultant now.'

'But that could mean almost anything, no?'

'I guess.'

'Would you describe him as a violent man?'

There was a fractional pause, the hesitation of an interviewee editing a response before she said, 'Not with me, never. He was very caring, very thoughtful.'

Ravnsborg leaned forward. 'And yet, according to your evidence, he left you in that café. He just got up and walked away. Has he made any effort at all to contact you since then?'

'No.' That sounded like an admission.

'Has he tried to communicate through Mr Larsson, do you know?'

'I don't think so.'

'Really?' Ravnsborg's tone was one of surprise, but its irony was obvious. 'That does not seem very caring to me; not very thought-ful. If I took you to dinner, I would not leave you without warning. But if by some chance I had to leave – if I were called away to a case, maybe – I would try to call you to explain. That is the least you should expect, no?'

She nodded in agreement.

'So now let me tell you something else about your Mr Carver. Shortly after he left you in that café, he placed a telephone call. Here is a photograph of him doing that . . .' Ravnsborg slid a copy of the full image towards her. 'You will notice the time-code in the bottom corner. At that exact moment, the hotel bomb was detonated, killing seven people and injuring another thirty. Three of the injured are not expected to last the night.'

'But that . . . that could be coincidence.'

'It could, yes. Lots of people must have made calls at that moment. But only one of them is currently wanted for the killing of three more men. So let me ask you, Mrs Cross, how well do you really know Mr Carver? How much can you trust him? Because it looks to me as though he has used you. He has turned up in your life, worked his way into your affections, persuaded you to come to Oslo . . .'

'For the wedding!'

'Yes, the wedding – how convenient it is, the timing, the location . . . That bothers me, I will admit to you, Mrs Cross. I worry that it is too much of a coincidence. But I do know something for sure . . .'

'Yes?'

'I know that if I were you, I should be very suspicious, very angry. I would wonder if I had been used by a mass-murderer. I would ask, "Why am I here, being interviewed by police, while he is running away?" Tell me, have these questions crossed your mind?'

Her silence provided its own response.

'No, you are right, there is no need to answer,' Ravnsborg said. 'Although, of course, there is one other possibility . . . We are assuming that Mr Carver has used you and Mr Larsson. What if he is an innocent man who has himself been used?'

'Used by whom?'

'Used by you, Mrs Cross, or by Mr Larsson, or both of you. Is that the truth of what happened?'

'No! I swear . . .'

Ravnsborg leaned back into his chair and looked at her, just as he had when he first entered the room. The ease with which Carver's identity and apparent guilt had fallen into his lap struck him as too good to be true. In his experience, that usually meant that it was.

'Well, we shall see, I am sure,' he said, as much to himself as to Maddy Cross. 'For now you will give a statement, please, to my colleague here. Then you will sign it. After that you will be free to return to your hotel. And I hope you enjoy the wedding.'

49

Carver had sent a single text message while he was chasing after the ferry. It went to a number he hadn't used in years. Chances were it wasn't even in use any more, but if it was, its owner might just clear his name.

He'd been doing some thinking, too, going over the events of the past few weeks, doing the old Sherlock Holmes trick: eliminating the impossible until what he was left with, however improbable, had to be the truth. The conclusion he'd come to was improbable all right. It damn near broke his heart. But he knew he was right, and he knew, too, that he'd been terribly wrong before. He just hoped he'd get a chance to put things right and repair the damage his stupidity had caused. First, though, he had to get away.

The lights of the ferry were clearly visible no more than half a mile away when another thought entered into his mind – one repressed during his desperate flight from the city: the memory of Tyzack talking about a killing that would put him in a different league, something bigger than Carver had even attempted. Carver had ignored him out of pride and ego, and now he realized that his arrogance had blinded him. It had been an act of unforgivable folly. If he'd satisfied Tyzack's longing to boast he would have known for sure what he was planning to do. Now he'd have to work it out for himself.

There were two ways Tyzack might, in theory, outdo him: by the sheer number of people he killed, or by the significance of a single victim. But Tyzack was not a terrorist, motivated by religion or ideology. He killed because he was paid to take out individual targets: any other victims were simply collateral damage. Many had died at the King Haakon Hotel, but Carver would have bet everything he had that there was only one real target. Even he had just been a distraction.

That left significance: Tyzack hitting someone so powerful, or so famous that – in his mind at least – it trumped anyone Carver had taken out. In theory, that might apply to any number of politicians, religious leaders, celebrities or monarchs. In practice, however, there was only ever one target whose elimination could guarantee an assassin the sort of perverse immortality Tyzack craved: the President of the United States.

The terrible realization struck Carver that having once subjected Lincoln Roberts to a fake attack, he might now have exposed him to a real one. A man he admired, whom he had worked to make safe, could now be in mortal danger. But what could he do about it? Carver was a man on the run, with nothing but his guts to go on. No warning he gave was ever going to be taken seriously. Yet somehow he had to make himself heard.

He'd come up behind the stern of the ferry now. Her name, *Queen of Jutland*, was painted across the full width of the vessel over the raised vehicle-loading ramps, and was lit by the glow from eight large portholes that ran above the lettering.

Carver slowed his engine to the pace of the ferry. He looked up at the massive hull, which loomed over his RIB like an elephant over a mouse as it rose straight up as high as a ten-storey building into the evening sky. The ferry filled Carver's entire field of vision. The noise of its engines, the buzz of his outboard motor and the rushing of water and wind all but deafened him. He just had to ignore the clamour and concentrate, searching for a way in.

Flanking the entrance through which cars and trucks rolled on and off, two massive metal buttresses protruded backwards, on either side of the stern. The buttresses curved up to the main bulk of the hull like gentle slopes at the foot of a sheer cliff. Above the top of the buttresses, where they joined the stern of the main hull, were two recessed winches, from which mooring ropes were run when the ship was in port.

Directly above them a rectangular opening had been cut into the hull, about three times wider than it was high. It was unglassed. Three similar openings ran down the flank of the ferry, creating a small promenade deck where passengers could take the air or smoke a cigarette. Carver hoped to God that at this time on a damp, chilly June evening they'd all be in the bars and restaurants, getting hammered like any normal human being.

On the way from Oslo, Carver had cut a short length of rope from the RIB's lines and placed it by the boat's controls. Next, he'd taken the anchor chain out of its storage chest, undone the shackle that fixed it to the boat, and carried it amidships so that it now lay piled behind him on the deck between the two seats.

Carver steered the RIB over the ship's wake until it was alongside the buttresses, as close as he could get to the stern opening. He tied one end of the rope to the steering wheel and turned the wheel so that the boat was virtually on the same course as the ferry, but turning slightly in towards the hull. Then he tied the other end of the rope to the chromed steel windscreen-frame, locking the steering wheel in place.

The RIB was nuzzling up against the ferry, but it would only stay in position for a matter of seconds, so Carver had to move fast. He grabbed the anchor chain and then clambered up on to the seats till he was standing astride the boat, one foot on each seat, leaning backwards so that his calves were resting against the seat-backs, taking the strain as the RIB bucked and lurched against the seething waters at the stern of the ferry.

He gripped the chain so his right hand was just below the anchor and a short length of chain hung between that and his left hand. Then, slowly at first, but with increasing momentum, he began to rotate his right arm, gradually paying out the chain, raising it above his head until it was swinging through the air like a lasso above the boat. Carver felt the cut in his back open up again under the strain of the movement, but ignored it. He gave a final, mighty heave and hurled the anchor at the opening.

50

Oslo is sheltered by a belt of islands, stretching the full width of Oslo fjord, just south of the city. Tyzack's pilot headed straight for the shelter of the nearest island, flying low and getting into its lee, so that the helicopter could not be seen from the mainland. He flew slowly, creeping between the outcrops of land until he reached the fjord's main shipping channel. That was when he saw the massive hull of the *Queen of Jutland*, to the right of his aircraft, steaming towards him from the north.

The light was fading now and it had started to rain, making the visibility still worse. So it took the pilot a couple of seconds to spot the RIB coming up behind the ferry's stern, and a few more to realize that whoever was driving the boat wasn't going to miss the *Queen of Jutland*. In fact, he was ... well, for a moment it looked like he might be trying to board it.

'Take a look down there, boss,' he said to Tyzack, pointing towards the ocean. 'There's some bloke on an RIB playing silly buggers. Total bloody lunatic.'

Tyzack rolled his eyes and then, like a parent indulging an attention-seeking child, did as the pilot asked.

He looked down towards the ferry.

And that was when he burst out laughing.

51

The anchor clanged against the ferry's hull just below the opening, fell down, slid along the buttress and splashed into the water.

As he pulled it out, Carver realized that he'd miscalculated his speed. It was set fractionally slower than the ferry. The RIB was steadily losing ground, sliding back along the buttress. Very soon he would have lost contact with the ferry completely. He could reset his speed and course, but that would mean untying and retying the rope around the steering wheel, and the longer he hung around the back of the ferry the more certain it was that he would be spotted.

No, he'd keep the boat set exactly as it was. Have another go and pray he could get aboard in time.

Once again he arced the anchor chain through the air, giving it even more speed this time and an even greater effort on the final throw. It flew into the air, hit the top of the opening and disappeared into the ferry like a football going in off the crossbar.

The RIB was still sliding backwards. First the outboard motor was into open water. Then the boat began to come free of the ferry, inch by inch. Very soon it would unbalance, swing round and be swirled helplessly in the ferry's wake.

Carver tugged at the chain and felt a reassuring resistance as the anchor caught against the inside of the hull. He felt the seats beneath him buck up and down and swerve from side to side as the RIB became progressively less stable.

There was no time left.

He gave one last heave on the chain and leaped out across the RIB towards the ferry. He smashed against the hull with an impact that knocked the breath from his body. For a moment he loosened his grip on the chain and slipped down until he was almost to his waist in the sea, the saltwater stinging as it splashed up against his open wound, every swell of the wake drawing him away from the hull and then crashing him into it again.

Christ, the water was cold! No wonder that kid had looked so furious when he was thrown into the sea by the opera house. Carver was chilled to the bone within seconds.

Behind him Carver saw the RIB swirl off into the darkness like a twig in a racing stream. He had nowhere else to go now. He had to get to the top of the chain or he would be washed away to his death.

He lifted one hand above the other, then tensed himself for the next crash against the hull.

As the water moved him away from the hull again, he moved his other hand a little further up the chain. And so it went on: the agonizingly slow movements up the slippery chain; the repeated slips as his wet, cold-numbed fingers lost their grip; the terrible shivering as the chill of the water seeped ever deeper into his body; and all the time the constant battering of flesh and bone against plate steel. Finally, though, Carver hauled himself almost clear of the water and now he could lean back on the chain and place his feet against the side of the buttress and haul himself up, pace by pace, hand over hand, until he was standing at the foot of the final sheer stretch up the hull to the opening.

He gritted his teeth to stop their incessant chattering, wiped the seawater and rain from his eyes and reminded himself that when he was in the SBS he'd think nothing of training exercises that required him to climb up the legs of a giant North Sea oil rig, or the hull of the *Queen Elizabeth II*. All he had to do now was get up a lousy bit of steel.

And then he heard a new sound, the clattering of a helicopter rotor. Still holding the chain, he twisted round so that he was looking away from the ferry, out to sea, and instantly saw the chopper, outlined against the last fragments of light on the western horizon. It was hovering, inquisitively, some way off, watching and waiting with all the cruel patience of a cat at a mousehole. Carver leaned back, placed his feet against the hull and started pulling himself up towards the opening, taking the strain on his shoulders, arms and thighs.

Now the predator swooped. The helicopter moved much closer to the boat. A searchlight cut through the darkness and rain, picking him out against the dazzling white backdrop of the hull and forcing him to screw his eyes shut to keep out its scorching glare. Directly above him, barely an arm's length away, he heard a sharp, percussive rattle, like stones catapulted against a sheet of corrugated iron. Someone was shooting at him. Carver flinched, dreading the impact of a ricochet. The gunman in the helicopter fired again, even closer this time. There was no noise or muzzle-flash from the weapon, just the same rattling stones. It didn't take a genius to work out the choice that Carver was being given. By the time the third salvo was fired, he had let go of the chain and was falling towards the water. This time the bullets hit the hull exactly where his body had been.

The ferry steamed away; the helicopter hovered directly over Carver and a rope was lowered down to him. He trod water, held a hand over his eyes to deflect the buffeting down-draught and saw Tyzack standing in the doorway smirking down at him. Carver was being mocked and, as the rope dangled in the water in front of him, he suddenly understood why. He'd got the whole thing wrong and everything he had done – not just tonight but for days, even weeks

– had been based on lousy, idiotic, unforgivable stupidity. He was so angry with himself, so frustrated, that he almost didn't reach out for the rope. It was an admission of defeat. Problem was, he didn't have a better idea. Besides, the closer he got to Tyzack, the easier it would be to wipe that stupid grin off his face.

But when he was finally pulled inside the helicopter, Carver didn't get to wipe anything at all. Instead, he was grabbed by two pairs of hands and shoved down into a chair. Someone stuck a gun up against the side of his head. And the last thing he knew was Damon Tyzack leaning over him with a syringe in his hands sighing, 'Sadly, this really won't hurt at all . . .'

52

Ole Ravnsborg looked down at the damp, huddled figure wrapped in a rough woollen blanket, sitting on a metal chair in his office and shivering unhappily. The young man's hands were wrapped around a mug of hot coffee. It did not appear to have done much to raise his spirits. So Ravnsborg began by giving him the good news.

'We found your moped, Mr Olsen,' he said. 'It was abandoned in Aker Brygge, at the end of Stranden, just as he promised. He even left your helmet.'

Per Olsen looked up, feeling better than he had done for some time. He almost managed a grin. 'That's great,' he said. 'Can I take it away now?'

'Afraid not,' Ravnsborg told him. 'We need to do forensic tests and then we may have to hold it as evidence, in the event of a trial.'

Olsen looked downcast again. 'But that could be months!'

'It could, yes, I am sorry about that. But you will get it back eventually . . .' He thought for a moment. '. . . Assuming there are no appeals.'

'Thanks a lot.' Olsen was now plunged into the pits of that

melodramatic, self-pitying despair that is reserved for those in their teens and early twenties.

Ravnsborg pulled up a chair and sat down opposite him. 'Now, tell me exactly, in detail, what happened to you.'

'Why should I?' Olsen sulked.

'Grow up,' said Ravnsborg. 'I am not your father, having some stupid argument. I am a police officer attempting to understand two violent, criminal incidents in which at least ten people died, and I am not interested in playing childish games. Either you talk to me, or I throw you in a cell overnight for obstructing my investigation. And, no, you will not be given dry clothes.'

'All right, all right . . . I get it.'

It took Ravnsborg a while, and there were points where even he, who prided himself on his non-violent nature, was tempted to grab Olsen by the neck and shake some sense into him, but in the end he had a clear picture of events.

'There is just one point I want to be completely certain of,' he concluded. 'The man who stole your moped was armed. He placed his gun against the back of your neck . . .'

'The barrel was hot,' Olsen said, 'I just remembered.'

'So he had already used the gun. In fact, you may be interested to hear, he had just shot two men dead and killed a third with his bare hands.'

'My God . . .' Olsen wrapped the blanket even tighter around his body, as if it could protect him.

'And yet he did not shoot you. In fact, he did nothing to you, except throw you in the water.'

'That wasn't nothing!'

'Oh yes, I think it was. And he even told you where you would be able to find your moped afterwards.'

'I shouldn't have told your men that. I should have waited and just gone to get it myself.'

'But then you would have been committing a crime, so it is as well that you did not. As it is, you have been a great help to me, Mr Olsen. Thank you. And I will have one of my men drive you home, so you won't even miss your moped.'

When Olsen had been led away, Ravnsborg sat for a while in silence, letting the many apparently contradictory elements of the evening's events sort themselves out in his mind. Olsen's survival was just one of these. If Carver were really a heartless killer, why had he not killed the young man when stealing his ridiculous little moped? It would have removed a witness. Ravnsborg wished there were some way of seeing precisely what had happened around the hotel and up on the roof of the opera house. Oslo was not littered with CCTV cameras every few metres: the Norwegian government, unlike so many of its counterparts, still trusted its people to go about their business unobserved.

Ravnsborg was musing on this fact when a thought suddenly struck him. The government might take that view, but the people, particularly the young, were just like their counterparts everywhere else. They photographed or videoed every single moment of their lives. And then they put it online.

The massive policeman lumbered off to the incident room. He looked around, mentally sorting through his officers until he found two detectives who looked particularly juvenile and, to his eyes, badly dressed. He thought they would understand the task best.

'You, you . . . come here!' he snapped. 'Go on the internet – Google, YouTube, Facebook, Twitter, all those places. Find everything you can relating to the bomb at the Haakon, and the shoot-out at the Operaen. Oh, and anything that anyone took between those two points. In fact, find every damn frame of material taken in Oslo tonight. Stick it all together. Then come and get me.'

It was amazing, Ravnsborg mused, this total change in the way the world perceived itself, and it had happened almost overnight. There had been no massive advertising campaigns, no government policies: just a spontaneous global decision to make everyone visible everywhere, all the time.

Already there were six different YouTube entries that showed the actual moment of the explosion, and more than twice as many dealing with the aftermath. The first group all began with something extraneous in the foreground: a girl posing awkwardly for her boyfriend, trying not to look embarrassed; two teenage lads pulling silly faces at the rich folk gathered inside the hotel café; an elderly couple arm in arm, smiling at the grandchild recording them on his phone. But the next scene was always the same: a blast of light and flame; a tremor as the force hit the person holding the camera or phone; the boom of the blast, followed by screams and shouts of alarm. The YouTube films all kept rolling. In the post 9/11 world, everyone understood the value of live disaster footage. But there was another film, retrieved by detectives at the site itself. Immediately after the blast, this one switched to a single, unchanging shot: the night sky seen through the blood-smeared filter of the glass that had killed the young woman behind the lens.

It was now possible for Ravnsborg to assemble a sort of montage that showed the run-up to the explosion, the blast itself and the aftermath from a series of different angles. He knew now that Madeleine Cross had not been lying when she described the events at her café table. He could see her behind the face-pulling boys. Larsson, too, was there. And, yes, there was a third figure, just rising from the table as the film began. That must be Carver.

It was only when he had spent more than two hours watching the same few minutes of footage again and again that Ravnsborg spotted a fourth individual, a red-haired man, standing outside the café, tapping out a message on a phone. That same figure was on another film, walking into the hotel, barely a second before the blast. He could be seen emerging fifteen seconds later. So, too, was a man who appeared to be wearing a T-shirt similar to the one worn by the man in the café that Ravnsborg had identified as Carver. He stood for a moment outside the hotel, a single point of stillness among the confusion all around him. Then the red-haired man came up behind him.

That took him by surprise, thought Ravnsborg, zooming in as close as he could on Carver's face.

The other man was very close to him, whispering in his ear. Were these instructions, perhaps? Or was he making threats? For Carver's face twice winced as though he had been hurt. Ravnsborg wished he had a shot that could give him a view from beside or behind the redhead, just so he could see what he was sticking in Carver's back. The obvious assumption was a knife, for Carver then jerked forward, arching his back and pulling his hands round to protect his kidneys.

Ravnsborg could then see what Carver had not, the red-haired man sidling back into the crowd and disappearing down the street. Carver, meanwhile, looked around. He saw someone – Ravnsborg knew from his witness statement that this must have been Larsson – then ran.

But why? Was this the natural reaction of a fugitive, fleeing the scene of a crime? Or was Carver fleeing something else?

The answers to his question, Ravnsborg felt sure, lay up on the roof of the opera house. He went and poured himself yet another black coffee, then settled down again. He was using a workstation equipped with a widescreen the size of a large domestic TV. It enabled him to get several different shots in front of him at the same time.

His young officers had collected all the material they had found into folders covering specific times, places and incidents. Sipping on his coffee as he worked, he clicked on the one marked 'Operaen'. There were nine different video files, and 114 photos.

Ravnsborg rubbed his aching eyes. He slapped his hand against his cheek to sting himself back awake. And then he got down to work.

53

Karin Madsen lay in bed at three in the morning watching the man she was about to marry emerge from the bathroom and walk towards her. There was barely any light in the room, but even so she could tell just by the set of Thor Larsson's shoulders and the heavy, sighing sound of his breathing that something was wrong: something above and beyond the obvious stress of the past six hours.

She propped herself up on one elbow and asked, 'What is it?'

'What's what?' he mumbled, almost as if he were making a point of sounding exhausted.

'Do you think I won't notice something's wrong? Come on, Thor.'

'I'm just wrecked, OK? It's been a long day, and a night from hell.'

'I know, darling, it must have been terrible. I understand. But that's not what I mean. I know you too well, Thor Larsson. I've changed your bedpan and wiped your backside. You can't fool me. Something's wrong.'

He sat down on the bed. 'Yes, Kari, something is wrong,' he said irritably, stating the blindingly obvious. 'My oldest friend has disappeared. The police say he is responsible for a terrorist attack. His girlfriend doesn't know if he is alive or dead, innocent or guilty. I have been interviewed by the police, and they told me they may speak to me again. And I'm probably going to have a whole bunch of cops as uninvited guests at my wedding. So yes, something's wrong.'

Well, it was a reasonable explanation, but it wasn't the whole story, Kari was sure of it. Something else was eating at Thor. But whatever it was, he wasn't going to tell her now. If she pressed him any harder it would only lead to an argument and she didn't want that, not two nights before her wedding.

'I'm sorry,' she said, reaching out to rub his back. 'Come to bed now. I'll hold you till you fall asleep.'

But it was Karin who slept first, and Thor Larsson who lay in the darkness, guts churning, eyes staring blankly up at the ceiling for hours until exhaustion finally claimed him.

54

Arjan Visar had received the technical specifications for the weapon that would be used to kill Lincoln Roberts within seventy-two hours of Tyzack's departure from his villa. He was impressed. Tyzack might be an animal, but it had taken cunning and imagination for him to devise his means of attack, and initiative to commission the design he had in mind.

The finished device, however, depended on an existing piece of technology that could not be purchased without attracting undue attention. So it was that a modest commercial premises tucked away in a mostly residential area of detached family homes in the English Midlands was burned to the ground as a result of an electrical fault. Amidst the damage caused by the blaze itself and the efforts of fire crews to put it out before it could spread to nearby houses, no one noticed the absence of two small units from the company's inventory. Within a couple of hours of the theft, they had been taken to a small engineering company, whose workshop was located under a railway arch in Manchester, and work had already begun on their conversion from the peaceful uses for which they were designed to the deadly intent conceived by Damon Tyzack.

As the engineers were getting down to work on their conversion job, Jack Grantham was at Heathrow trying to find a seat on an early-morning flight to Oslo. It wasn't easy. The news that the Norwegian police were looking for an English male – they hadn't specified that he was a suspect, but that was the only inference that could be drawn – had suddenly given what would otherwise be a shocking but relatively minor tragedy a much more powerful domestic angle. When, in the early hours, Oslo University Hospital announced that two of the seriously wounded victims of the King Haakon Hotel bombing had both passed away, and that they were a British pensioner couple, that just added to the feeding frenzy. It had taken a discreet conversation with a senior British Airways executive to squeeze Grantham on to the 7.20 plane, leaving a big-name newspaper columnist fuming as he was bumped on to a lunchtime departure.

On the plane, Grantham returned to the subject that had been nagging at him for hours. He'd spent the previous evening at the movies: even intelligence officers, after all, have wives and social lives that need to be attended to occasionally. When he left the cinema he forgot to switch his phone back on. It wasn't till he was home that he remembered and picked up the text Carver had sent him, which consisted of three short messages topped by two questions and a statement: 'Was this you? If not, who? Framed.'

The answer to the first question was easy: no, it damn well hadn't been him that sent the messages to Carver. So who was it? Well, 'Mrs Z' herself, Olga Zhukovskaya, was still a Deputy Director of the FSB, and strong, reliable rumours suggested she would soon be its Director. Yet there seemed no reason that Grantham could think of why she would want to stage a bombing in the middle of Oslo (and he had spent half the night going through the bombing's casualty list trying to find one), still less plant it on Carver. He had got her out of a very nasty hole in the

Waylon McCabe affair. She had no reason to feel anything but gratitude towards him. That wouldn't stop her screwing him if she could gain sufficient advantage from it, of course. But try as he might, Grantham could not think what that advantage might be.

On the other side of the Atlantic, there were senior officers at the CIA who knew about Carver's role in disposing of McCabe. They might well have uncovered Zhukovskaya's involvement by now – Grantham had hardly publicized it at the time – but again, he could not see how the Cousins stood to benefit by what had happened in Oslo. After all, one of the victims – the presumed target, according to some reports – had been a prominent anti-slavery campaigner, and President Roberts was about to go balls-out against slavery.

Grantham was a professional conspiracy theorist. Experience had told him there was no explanation so bizarre that it could not, in fact, be true. So he was willing to consider the possibility, however grotesque, that some headcase at Langley had decided that the death of a photogenic campaigner against human trafficking would give the President's crusade some handy advance publicity. It was not inconceivable, either, that this was a cover-up of some kind. One of the grubbiest aspects of this sordid trade had long been the involvement of senior UN officials, military personnel and corporate leaders in facilitating the passage of trafficked women through territories like Montenegro, Kosovo and Bosnia. Plenty of respectable men, with no desire to be embarrassed, had procured women for themselves. It was not inconceivable that their allies in the CIA might wish to snuff out any embarrassment. But using a man with known links to SIS, the Agency's closest ally, well, that was just bad manners.

And then there was a third possibility. One man knew every detail of Carver's activities, because he knew virtually every detail of Grantham's own working life: Bill Selsey. Grantham hoped, very much, that this had nothing to do with Selsey. They may have had their differences of late, and his deputy's sudden interest in playing office politics had come as an unpleasant surprise, but there was a big difference between professional rivalry and active involvement in cold-blooded murder. Surely Selsey would never have crossed that line?

Still, someone had crossed the line, and Grantham wanted to know who it was. He was flying to Oslo in the guise of a Foreign Office official, concerned about the involvement of Her Majesty's subjects in this unpleasant event. At the airport, a first secretary from the British embassy, who just happened to be the Secret Service's representative there, led him to a waiting Jaguar.

'Are we all set up?' Grantham asked as the car purred away from the terminal.

'Oh yes,' said his officer, who was showing a distracting amount of bare thigh beneath the hem of her skirt. 'Everything's arranged. The detective in charge is called Ravnsborg. He's quite an interesting man, actually, quite subtle – you know, for a policeman. Anyway, he seems very happy to help. In fact, I get the impression he's really keen to meet you.'

'Oh great,' said Grantham, 'an enthusiastic copper. Can't wait.'

55

Carver came to with his brain as numb as a novocained tooth, his mouth as dry and malodorous as a chicken-house floor and his bladder as uncomfortably swollen as a porn star's boob-job. He'd been seated on a plain wooden kitchen chair. There were no restraints on his hands or feet. Tyzack was standing no more than ten feet away, bending over a small metal-framed table, arranging something on it. Carver couldn't believe his luck. He leaped from the chair, took two quick strides towards Tyzack . . .

. . . and was jerked back by a sudden, choking tug at his throat so violent that at first he lost his footing and thrashed around like a condemned man on the end of a noose before he could get to his feet and retreat, coughing and gagging, back to the chair.

Tyzack was convulsed with laughter as he turned to face Carver. 'I'm sorry, but that was priceless!' he gasped, trying to catch his breath. 'Excellent kit! It's bungee-jumping cord, in case you were wondering, and much too strong for you to have any hope of breaking it. The item round your neck is what's known among the sado-masochist fraternity as a slave collar. They tell me it's very comfy, nicely padded. I dare say that's why you didn't notice it straight away. It's padlocked at the back, incidentally, and I filled the lock with superglue, so you won't be picking it. Oh, and the shackle at the end of the cord, where it joins the collar, has been welded shut, so that won't come undone either.'

Carver looked around. He was sitting in the middle of a small wooden barn, maybe twenty feet by forty, illuminated by sunlight streaming through an open window high up on one wall.

The table at which Tyzack had been standing was directly opposite Carver. It was flanked by two large plasma-screen TV sets, angled towards him. More sets were arranged in a circle, surrounding him.

On the table stood a fifteen-litre bottle of mineral water, the kind that sits upturned in an office water-cooler. Next to it Tyzack had placed a single plastic cup and beside that a small cardboard box on which the word 'Japp' was printed in red and gold script. The final item, to the right of the table, was made of white plastic and stood about a foot tall.

'It's your bog,' Tyzack said, spotting where Carver's eyes were directed. 'Do you fancy a slash? I bet you do. You were out the best part of twelve hours. Must be bursting. Go ahead, don't mind me.'

Carver remained exactly where he was. Tyzack wasn't the only man with an agenda in the room. Carver was determined to get him to name Lincoln Roberts as his target. That meant messing with Tyzack's head, keeping him talking, getting under his skin, no matter what it cost him, or what pain he had to endure. Carver was used to pain. It didn't hurt half as much as the knowledge that he'd screwed up.

Tyzack shrugged. 'Suit yourself. Only here's the thing. You're going to be here quite a while, and very soon you'll be totally alone. I won't even be in this boring little country and there are no other houses for miles around. When I leave here I will activate a booby-trap system. A friend of yours installed it, top-quality work. Once I flick the switch, anyone who tries to get in or out is going to meet a very sticky end. So if you want to live, you've got to be able to get to that water and pray that I decide to come back.'

Tyzack gestured towards the cardboard box. 'I'm a generous man, so I've also left you some nice choccy bars, just in case you get peckish. They're called Japp, but they're really just Mars bars for Norwegians and I never met a soldier who didn't like a nice Mars. Helps him work, rest and play. But now I come to look at it, I have a feeling I made a mistake. I put this table too far away from you. Well, I must have done, otherwise you'd have got to me by now. Now, I'm prepared to move it all a bit closer, so you can eat and drink. But how much closer, that's the question. One has to be precise about these things and I'm going to need your help. What you're going to do is get up and see how far you can go before you get pulled back by the bungee cord, or strangled by the collar. Come on, up you get!'

Carver stayed exactly where he was. Tyzack glared at him. Then he walked round behind Carver, took three quick steps towards him and kicked the wooden chair out from under him. Carver fell to the floor, felt the cord yanking at his neck and was forced to scramble to his feet. There wasn't enough slack to let him sit on the ground, still less lie down.

'You don't get it, do you?' Tyzack shouted, returning to a point beyond Carver's reach. His mask of sophisticated, gentlemanly civility had slipped and all the years of suppressed rage and resentment were seeping out like the pus from a septic wound. 'I'm in charge now. Not you. Me. So you do what I say, right now . . . or I leave you here for the duration, without anything, until you're too thirsty, too hungry, too bloody knackered to stand it any more and you'd rather be dead. Now do you get it?'

'Kill me,' said Carver, matter-of-factly. 'Kill me now.'

Tyzack smiled. 'Giving up so soon? Really? What is it, want the easy way out?'

'No. I'm just thinking of your welfare. You'd better kill me now, because if you don't, I'm going to hunt you down and tear you limb from limb . . . you worthless, gutless, psychopathic piece of shit.'

Tyzack let the words sink in, and then he laughed again. 'Well done, defiant to the end! But how are you going to hunt me down if you're dead on the end of a rubber rope? How does that work? Do yourself a favour . . .' Tyzack had walked round behind the metal table while he was talking and shifted it fractionally towards Carver. '. . . See if you can reach it now.'

Carver had no choice. His only hope of staying alive long enough to find a way to beat Tyzack was to do as he said. So he got up and stepped gingerly towards the table until he felt the pulling on his neck. Then he stood with one foot in front of the other, the front leg slightly bent at the knee to brace him, took a deep breath, and leaned forward, hands outstretched.

He pushed his head and shoulders forward till the pressure on his throat was so strong he felt as though his windpipe and larynx would be crushed. He stretched his arms till they were almost pulled from their sockets. He held his breath until his chest felt close to bursting and sparks danced before his eyes. But still his fingertips were nowhere near the top of the water bottle.

He stepped back and crouched, bent over, hands on his knees, desperately dragging air down into his lungs.

'I don't think you're really trying,' said Tyzack with an exaggerated air of disappointment. 'I believe you need some encouragement. An incentive, so to speak.'

He walked away to the wall of the barn. Carver raised his eyes and noticed something else, lying on the floor: a thin, flexible bamboo cane, five or six feet long. Tyzack picked it up. He strode back towards Carver and stood calmly as Carver turned to face him. Then Tyzack lunged his left foot forwards so far that he was almost down on one knee and brought his right arm round in a fast, low, whipping motion.

The cane lashed into Carver's legs, just below the knee. He screamed in pain, lost his footing and then the screams were transformed to retching gasps as he fought against the cord and the collar pulling yet again at his unprotected neck.

Tyzack stood up straight and almost danced round Carver, as agile as a boxer. The next lash of the cane ripped into his lower back, the excruciating agony of a blow to the kidneys made even worse by the knife-tear that it reopened.

Carver screamed again . . . and again as a third strike of the cane cut into his shoulders.

'Try again,' said Tyzack, quite calmly, almost encouragingly. 'See if you can reach the bottle.'

Carver tried.

He pulled and choked and strained every muscle, while Tyzack flayed his back with the cane: once, twice, half a dozen more times.

Still he could not reach the bottle.

Finally Tyzack lowered the cane.

Both men were breathing heavily now, a sheen of sweat glistening on their faces and soaking their shirts.

'I think we've established that it's still not close enough. I'll make it a little easier for you,' Tyzack panted.

He shifted the table forward another few inches. Then he gave a sudden exhalation of breath, as if something had just occurred to him. 'Who's a silly boy?' he said. 'I almost let you get away with it. Can't have a cap on the bottle, can we? That way, you'd only have to pull it off the table once, pull it towards you and keep it at your feet. Can't have the choccies in a box, same reason.'

He unscrewed the top of the water bottle and threw it away. He also detached the white plastic carrying handle. Finally he emptied the box of Japp bars on to the table.

'Knock the bottle off now, and you'll be in serious trouble,' Tyzack observed. He picked up the cane. 'Now, let's try again.'

It took barely ten minutes. But it felt like a lifetime of pain beyond anything Carver had ever known, an eternity of craving as he begged for breath, living on the very edge of unconsciousness, the blood and sweat mingling and stinging as his back became a pulpy intersection of cuts and welts etched and slashed across his skin. He pissed himself at some point, he didn't know when. But finally the table had been moved to a point where he could – just, if he went beyond the point where his body was telling him it was about to black out, into a new realm of agony – reach the water, and the chocolate bars, and even lift the lid of the chemical toilet.

'You'll be able to pee,' said Tyzack, who seemed strangely calmed by his physical exertion, his tensions temporarily released. 'You won't be sitting down on it, though, sadly, so it could get a touch Bobby Sands in here, if you catch my drift. Still, I'm glad we got that sorted. Now, why don't you sit down?'

Tyzack winced as he saw Carver's reaction to the contact between his flayed skin and the chair back. 'Oh, that's got to hurt,' he sympathized. 'Can't be helped though, eh? So . . . let's have a little talk.'

The sting of Damon Tyzack's hand slapping against his cheek cut through the fog of pain that was clouding Carver's mind.

'Wake up,' Tyzack insisted. 'We're going to chat, talk about old times. Ironic, though, isn't it?'

'Isn't what?' Carver mumbled.

'Me dragging you from the water. I mean, the helicopter, the ship – there's a certain symmetry to it all. The only difference is, I'm in charge now.'

Carver forced himself to straighten his whipped and bleeding back and look Tyzack in the eye. 'I never wanted to take you. Didn't think you were up to it. Trench disagreed. He denied it, but the truth is he'd got a soft spot for you because of your father . . .'

'I really don't think we need to talk about him.'

'Maybe, but he was ten times the soldier you'll ever be.'

This time, when Tyzack hit Carver, it wasn't just a slap.

Carver spat the blood from his mouth. 'Suit yourself,' he said. 'But the fact remains, I didn't want you. Trench did. Afterwards, of course, he admitted I was right.'

'Oh really, is that so? Well, I tell you what, since you're so keen to tell your side of the story, why don't you do that? And then we'll examine the evidence, compare it with my account, and see who's telling the truth . . .'

56

Back then he was not yet known as Carver. He was still Paul Jackson, the name given to him by his adoptive parents. His friends and brother officers in the Special Boat Squadron, the waterborne arm of British Special Forces, used his nickname, Pablo. So did Quentin Trench, Carver's commanding officer.

'Pablo, I want you to take Damon Tyzack along with you as your second-in-command on the *Maid of Dumfries* job,' he'd said one evening at SBS headquarters in Poole while they were in the officers' mess, drinking their after-dinner coffees.

'Are you sure that's wise?' Carver replied. 'He's never had a job like this before.'

'Well, he's got to start somewhere. This should be a pretty straightforward operation. Tyzack's fully trained for it. And you're just the man to make sure he doesn't let himself or anyone else down.'

Carver stuck to his guns. 'You know how I feel about him. It's a character issue. I don't trust him to react the right way under pressure. Don't think the other men do, either. He's not well liked.'

'Well then, it's a good thing this is a military unit, not a bloody popularity contest,' Trench snapped. 'Your reservations about Second Lieutenant Tyzack's character were noted during the selection course. But so were the rest of his results, and they were superb. His powers of endurance are remarkable. He's a first-rate swimmer-canoeist, his marksmanship is outstanding and he breezed through all the technical, tactical and theoretical aspects of the course. Scored rather better than you did when you first got here, as a matter of fact.'

That was a cheap shot and Trench knew it. 'Look,' he continued, trying to smooth things over, 'I know there are other issues. I served under Tyzack's father, best commanding officer I've ever known. But I'm sure you don't think I would favour a man just because I knew his dad . . .'

'No, sir.'

'Good. Take Tyzack. Give him some responsibility. Let's see how he handles it.'

Three days later, Carver and Tyzack were both among the six men seated in the cabin of a Westland Sea King helicopter, flying low over the black waters of the Bay of Biscay. The wind was blowing about fourteen or fifteen knots: a good breeze, but no more than that, with the waves no worse than choppy. Rain was falling steadily, just enough for the clouds to obscure a waning crescent moon. Somewhere up ahead was the *Maid of Dumfries*, a 72-foot trawler, rigged for tuna-fishing. According to the intelligence, passed on to the SBS from the brains at MI6 who had come up with the idea for the operation, there were no fish in her hold. Instead, the *Maid of Dumfries* carried a far more valuable cargo: an estimated three tons of cocaine, with a street value in the region of forty million pounds.

'ETA, two minutes,' the pilot announced, and the aircrewman standing by the sliding door in the flank of the chopper yanked it open, letting in a blast of cold, wet air. He signalled Carver to move into position. A heavy hemp rope about two inches thick hung from the roof of the cabin and fell to the floor where it sat in thirty feet of coils. Carver grabbed hold of the rope and held it as he leaned out of the opening and peered forward into the darkness.

Then he saw it, the stern light of the *Maid of Dumfries*.

The trawler was cruising normally, heading north-east at around ten knots. A boat this size could be handled by a crew of three and it didn't look as if any of them were aware of the Sea King sneaking up behind them, the clattering din of its approach masked by the sound of the ship's own engine, or blown away on the wind. Well, that was about to change.

The *Maid of Dumfries* had its superstructure and bridge in the middle of the boat, with gantries fore and aft for hauling nets aboard, and only a few bare, flat patches on the decks on which Carver and his men could land. But the gantries were relatively low, less than twenty feet high, and the wind was still benign. The helicopter hovered over the stern at forty feet, keeping pace with the trawler, but out of harm's way. The green light went on above the door. Carver threw the rope out of the opening, watched it hit the deck below, then stepped out into the void.

He descended the standard SBS way, as fast as possible, using only a pair of heavy leather gloves as brakes. As soon as his feet hit the deck, he moved forward, away from the rope, knowing that Tyzack was only seconds behind him.

Even while he was still on the rope, Carver had seen the doors opening on the ship down below: one at the rear of the bridge, above a set of metal steps that led down to the deck; a second at deck level, on the far side of the yellow-painted superstructure. Carver was targeting the bridge.

As he moved forward towards it, a man emerged at the top of the steps, carrying a gun. He looked towards Carver and the men descending like black-clad wraiths from the helicopter that now loomed over half the length of the boat.

Carver tried to shout over the noise of the engines, the rotors and the wind, 'Put down your weapon, now!' But before the words were out of his mouth, the man – acting out of courage, desperation or sheer blind panic – had started firing, his shots spraying randomly as he tried to keep his balance while his ship moved beneath him.

Carver did not hesitate. The moment his hands had let go the rope, he had torn off his gloves and reached for the Heckler and Koch MP5 strapped across his chest. A flashlight was attached to the barrel of the gun. Now Carver swung it to his shoulder, let the light pick out his target and fired a three-round burst that hit the drug-runner full in the chest, sending him back a couple of staggered paces before the boat pitched up into an oncoming wave, and sent him falling down the stairs.

His body came to a halt just above the deck, held by a boot that had caught in one of the steps. The dead man's forehead was bumping into the bottom step with every movement of the *Maid of Dumfries*. For some reason that steady, repetitive impact seemed more disturbing to Carver than the three gaping exit wounds his bullets had ripped from the corpse's back.

Carver forced his concentration back to the matter in hand.

To his left, on the far side of the deck, he saw Tyzack raise his own MP5 and fire. Tyzack flashed him a quick OK with his thumb and forefinger. A second man was down.

Carver nodded in acknowledgement and gestured to Tyzack to keep moving. Then he turned to the men behind him and started signalling more orders, his hands moving like a tic-tac man at a racecourse betting stall.

The six men now split into three pairs. Carver took one man and moved to secure the bridge and take control of the vessel. Tyzack and his back-up were tasked to enter the superstructure to clear the cabins and engine-room. The final pair would secure the holds and start the search for the drugs that were the justification for the entire operation.

When Carver and the man behind him reached the bridge, it was deserted, the boat moving forward on automatic pilot. So where was the third crewman?

The question had no sooner crossed Carver's mind than it was answered by a burst of gunfire from the cabin below. The last echoes died away. Then there was another short, sudden blast of firing. Then silence.

'Stay here,' Carver said to his partner. 'Keep an eye out. Make sure we don't bump into anything.'

Then he went back out of the bridge, stepped over the dead body now lying on the deck at the foot of the steps, and made his way towards the sound of the guns.

57

'Very interesting,' said Tyzack. He was standing a couple of paces from Carver, looking down on him. He'd adopted the attitude of a QC cross-examining a witness. Carver wondered how long he'd been dreaming of this moment, working on his delivery, polishing up his questions.

'So you admit that Trench knew that I had superior military skill to you?' Tyzack went on.

'That was his opinion, yes. You were good under training conditions. I always felt combat would be a different matter.'

'And yet, when we landed on that boat, we advanced together and both of us took out our designated targets.'

'Yes.'

'And those were certainly combat conditions.'

Carver nodded. 'Yes, you were doing a good job at that point.'

'It was my first kill, you know. Do you remember your first kill?'

'Yes.'

'Did you enjoy it?'

'Not particularly.'

'Really?' said Tyzack. 'I thought it was an amazing moment. I'd heard all about that sort of thing, of course. Growing up in my family, I could hardly avoid it. But it's a bit like sex, isn't it? Until you've actually done it, you really have no idea . . .'

'If you say so.'

Tyzack ignored him. 'I can still see the way the rounds hit their target. There was much more blood than I expected. I'd allowed for the wounds going in, you see, but not for the mess coming out the far side. The poor chap I hit, his body sort of rippled with the impact; it was the most extraordinary sight, filled me with absolute, pure pleasure. But you say it wasn't the same for you?'

'No.' Carver leaned back a fraction and the open wounds on his back touched the frame of the chair. He gasped with pain.

'I'm so sorry,' said Tyzack with exaggerated concern. 'Painful, is it? Well, concentrate on what you're saying, why don't you? Take your mind off it. Tell you what, I'll give you a little drink just to wet your throat. I really can't say fairer than that.'

Tyzack walked across to the table and poured a dribble of water into the bottom of the paper cup. He gave it to Carver, who gulped it down in one swallow.

'There,' said Tyzack, 'we've got a little system going, water for talk. So let's talk some more. Answer me this: if you hate killing so much, why do you keep doing it?'

Carver smiled wearily. Tyzack was not best pleased.

'Did I say something funny? I wasn't aware that I'd been trying to amuse.'

'No,' said Carver, shaking his head. 'I've just heard that one before.'

He thought back to a clinic by the shore of Lake Geneva and the sessions he'd had there. Carver's mind had been torn apart by unendurable trauma. A psychiatrist called Karlheinze Geisel had helped to put it back together. He'd harped on about Carver's deadly profession, too. So Carver gave Tyzack the same answer he'd given the shrink.

'I do it because it's the thing I can do. I look on it as a curse, for what it's worth. I wish I had another saleable talent. And if you want to know how I justify it, I'll tell you. The people I take out have got it coming. The world is a better place for them not being there.'

'Not always, it isn't,' said Tyzack, a teasing smile playing around the corners of his mouth. 'Dear old Percy Wake told me how you once killed a certain well-known woman in Paris. That was hardly a service to mankind. And all those poor people at the hotel last night. Did they have it coming?'

'No, they didn't. But both those times, I was set up, and you know it.'

'Oh, I see. They were unintentional killings?'

'Yes.'

'What about all the people who've died just because they happened to get in the way? How do you justify it when you trot off to Canada and take out a plane with someone on it you think deserves to die and – oh dear! – the pilot dies too, and the chap next to him, and the poor little trolley-dolly, and a couple of passengers too? This is an actual case I'm quoting . . .'

'I know.'

'You were trying to get a man named Waylon McCabe.'

'That's right.'

'But he was the only person who walked away. Dearie me, that was a bit of a mistake.'

'Yes . . . yes, it was.'

Tyzack stepped forward till his mouth was just inches from Carver's right ear. 'So why, when I make a mistake, just one mistake . . . a mistake which harmed far fewer people . . . why did you have to ruin my entire . . . fucking . . . life?'

58

Carver took a second gulp of water and went back to the story of the *Maid of Dumfries*.

'Even when I was topsides I knew that the weapon I'd heard was an MP5 set to automatic fire – one of ours. So I went below decks, came through the door of that cabin and your oppo, McWhirter, was standing there saying something like, "Oh Jesus . . . what the fuck have you done?" This tough Glasgow bastard, seen it all, done it all, and whatever he'd just seen, it had shocked him to the point he was almost in tears. Then you caught sight of me and said – no, that's wrong, you whined: "He had a weapon."'

Tyzack stepped back, away from Carver's chair, and started pacing up and down the floor of the barn. He looked agitated, twitchy, on the brink of another loss of control.

'Would you like me to stop?' Carver asked, the victim briefly inflicting more damage than his torturer.

'No,' snarled Tyzack. 'Keep going. Tell me the lies you told Trench and the rest.'

'Whatever you say. So, I was looking for a man with a weapon.

And I was puzzled, because I couldn't see him anywhere. And then I noticed something. There was a padded bench, ran most of the way round the cabin wall. And something had been flung on it. At first I thought it was a pile of dirty rags. And then I realized that the dirt was blood and the pile of rags was this little kid. God knows how many rounds you'd put into him because you'd practically cut him in two, poor little beggar.'

Now the anger was rising in Carver too and it was emotion that constricted his voice, not the collar round his neck as he said, 'And next to the kid was the weapon, except it wasn't a weapon, was it, Tyzack? It was a plastic toy gun. And in front of the kid, on the floor, was a woman, the mother. She'd tried to protect her baby, and you'd given her a burst too. Once I'd seen that, what else did I need to know?'

'You could have asked me what happened?' said Tyzack, still pacing up and down. 'You could have let me explain.'

'All right then, explain. Tell me why you couldn't tell the difference between a grown man with a gun and a small child with a toy.'

'Because it was dark down there. We were all using goggles, remember? No lights on at all, just the flame from that gas hob in the corner. There was a cooking pot on top, so I reckoned there had to be someone there. Plus, we'd been told to expect a minimum crew of three, and there were only two down, both of them armed. And I didn't see a kid. I just saw something moving across the room, I saw a gun barrel, and I heard the sound of firing—'

'Do me a favour,' Carver interrupted. 'You heard the sound of the kid's toy. He probably thought it was all a big game. And if you think a toy gun sounds anything like the real thing, you need your ears examining, as well as your head. How about muzzle-flash, see any of that? Notice any bullet holes anywhere, any ricochets? You were in a cabin no more than eight foot square. If he had been firing a real gun, you'd have known all about it.'

'I didn't have time to work that out, did I?' Tyzack protested. 'I don't know, maybe I thought he had a suppressor. And there was at least one adult in the cabin. They could have been armed, too. I couldn't afford to take chances.'

'Bollocks,' said Carver, quite calmly. 'I'll tell you what happened. You were on your first mission. You'd just had your first kill and you were practically coming in your pants with excitement. You couldn't wait to do it again. So when you saw two people in that cabin you let rip. And all the training you'd ever done went right out the window. How many hours had you spent in the Killing House, training for exactly this kind of moment? That's why we did it, so we didn't kill the wrong people. And if you really want to know, what pissed me off was not just that you were such a blatant bloody psycho, it was that you were a total amateur. You're just a fucking awful soldier.'

Whatever scenes Tyzack had played out in his mind, that hadn't been in the script. He came to a halt, turned to face Carver and there was outrage in his voice as he protested, 'That's not true! You said it yourself, my assessment scores were better than yours. I was just inexperienced. If I'd been given a chance, I wouldn't have made mistakes like that again. But you never gave me the chance. You humiliated me in front of the other men, and then you had me kicked out.'

Carver shook his head in disbelief. 'That's what all this is about, is it? I'm sitting here because I'm the man who got poor, mis-understood Damon Tyzack his dishonourable discharge? You moron. You'd still be in prison if it wasn't for me. I didn't ruin your life. I saved your bloody neck. '

59

Carver had said nothing when he saw the bodies. He stepped across to the light switch, turned it on, and took off his night-vision goggles as the cabin suddenly filled with the harsh glare of an unshaded bulb. Then he put a hand up to his face and massaged his forehead, the movements of his fingers alternately smoothing and deepening the single deep furrow on his brow, the outline of his goggles still visible on his skin. When he removed his hand and opened his eyes, they looked as chilly and green as the ice in a glacial crevasse.

'You're very lucky,' he said, looking straight at Tyzack. 'This is a secret operation, and we don't want it compromised by a murder inquiry, or getting in the media. So we're going to have to destroy the evidence. I want you to place charges on the fuel and water tanks. If you've got any spare, put them against the inside of the hull, below the water-line, ten-minute fuses on the detonators. When they're set, open the seacocks, so the boat starts flooding. That'll do most of the work. The charges will just blow the buoyancy out of the tanks and give us a bang for the fly-boys to see.'

There was a clattering of boots behind Carver and another SBS man, Sergeant Hirst, appeared in the doorway.

'We found half of Colombia down there, boss,' he shouted. 'Tons of the stuff. You'll never . . .'

Hirst fell silent as he took in the scene in the cabin.

'This ship's got to have a life-raft,' said Carver. 'Find it. Launch it. And get the lads together. We're scuttling the ship.'

'But, boss, the cocaine . . . it's worth millions . . .'

'Makes no difference. Customs are only going to burn it anyway.'

Hirst gave a shrug of his shoulders and left the cabin, shouting orders as he walked up on to the deck. Now Carver was on the radio, talking to the helicopter pilot.

'We found the cocaine. Two crew, both dead. Bad news is, they stuffed the ship with enough C4 to sink the *Titanic*. I don't know if they managed to set the fuses before we hit them and I'm not waiting to find out. Nor should you. Get well out of range. We're going to abandon ship and take the life-raft. We'll give it the standard thirty minutes. If she blows, you can come and pick us up. If she doesn't, we'll get back on board. Got that? Over.'

'Absolutely. Have a jolly cruise. Out.'

No one would question the story. Drug-smugglers routinely scuttled their boats if they thought they were going to get caught. That way they destroyed the evidence, and when they were found floating on a raft maritime law defined them as rescued sailors, not suspected criminals, so no charges could be pressed.

'What are you waiting for?' Carver snapped at Tyzack. 'I thought I told you to sink this boat?'

'Yes, sir.'

'Well, get on with it. The sooner you do it, the less distance you'll have to swim to reach the life-raft.'

'You're not waiting?'

'You heard what I told the man. The ship could explode at any moment. I can't risk the safety of my men, can I? And you, Lieutenant, can't risk this ship not sinking. Can you?'

Carver did not wait for an answer before he left the cabin. It took

Tyzack several minutes to set the charges and open the seacocks. By the time he dived over the side, into the cold, choppy waters of the Bay of Biscay, Carver and the other men in the life-raft were barely visible in the distance. He was still swimming when the *Maid of Dumfries* exploded and sank to the bottom of the sea.

60

'Oh I see, you were doing me a favour, were you?' Tyzack sneered. 'And I'm the amateur, am I? But even I know that a true fighting man doesn't let his brother warriors down. That's why I was willing to let the matter rest. All right, so you humiliated me in front of the men and risked my life making me set up the charges and swim to the boat. But never mind, I'd have let bygones be bygones. But no, you felt obliged to deliver a full report to Trench. And that meant he was obliged to have a court martial. He didn't want to, but you left him no alternative. Trench told me that in a letter. I've still got it. He even said he'd put in a good word for me with my old man . . .'

'Did he really?' Carver gave a weary, humourless laugh. 'Sounds like Trench. Hope you didn't believe him.'

'Didn't make any difference either way. My dear old daddy just did what he'd always done. He got out his horsewhip and thrashed me . . . rather like I've thrashed you, actually. I always thought to myself I'd pass on the favour one day, so that's one resolution kept. My mother, of course, just stood there, doing nothing, just fiddling with her pearl necklace while he beat the hell out of me. I should have killed him then, of course. I don't know why I didn't, because I was more than strong enough, but I . . . I . . .' Tyzack sighed. 'For some reason I couldn't fight back. Why was that, do you suppose? I just stood there and took my beating like a man. That was my father's great phrase: Take it like a man. Oh well, I made him take it a few years later. I thought about my darling parents and made an executive decision. I had to let them go.'

'You killed them?' asked Carver.

'No, I sent them on holiday to Barbados. Oh, for goodness' sake, do I have to spell it out?'

'I just wanted to make sure. And by the way, in case you've ever wondered what happened to Trench, he tried to have me eliminated, but I got to him first.'

'Really?' asked Tyzack, genuinely interested. 'What did you do to him?'

'I fired a flare gun into his face at point-blank range and turned him into a human torch.'

A smile crossed Tyzack's face. 'And you loved it, didn't you? I can tell.'

'Yes, I admit, that one did give me a certain satisfaction. So there have been times when I've gone too far. Innocent people have died. But if you think that makes me anything at all like you, you're wrong. I may cross the line, but you don't even know the line is there.'

Tyzack laughed. 'Do you have any idea how absurd you sound, giving me your little lectures?'

Carver cracked a battered smile. There was something he needed to know from Tyzack. This might be the chance to get it.

'You think I'm absurd? You spend years obsessing about the harm I'm supposed to have done to you. And all the while, you know what? You never even crossed my mind. Not once. I just didn't give a toss. Why would I care about a loser like you?'

Tyzack's jaw tightened. His breathing became heavier. The mask was cracking again as he fought to contain the rising tide of rage.

At last, after everything he'd been through, Carver had pushed Tyzack to the brink. Come on, he thought. Spit it out. Tell me just how great you are.

'You really shouldn't say things like that,' rasped Tyzack. 'You should know by now what I can do. Just look at yourself. You're a murder suspect in three different countries. Your friends don't want anything more to do with you. You're hanging by the neck from a bloody great rubber band, like a Thunderbird puppet gone spastic . . . I put you there, and I'm going to leave you there. And while you're busy dying, I am going to . . .'

Yes, yes! the voice in Carver's head was shouting. What are you going to do?

Tyzack stopped dead. A smile crossed his face, his air of superiority suddenly restored.

'Oh, very good,' he said, as though he had been able to hear the screaming in Carver's brain. 'You nearly had me there. Almost got me to spill the beans about . . . the big one. Well, I've changed my mind. I think it's more amusing to leave you in suspense.'

Tyzack glanced at the cord from which Carver was hanging. 'No pun intended,' he added. 'Don't worry, though, you will be kept fully in touch with my success, and your failure, as it all unfolds. Watch!'

He removed a remote control from his trouser pocket and aimed it at the nearest television, which sprang into life, as did all the other sets ringing Carver. They were all tuned to the BBC News channel.

'Well, I thought that was only right, don't you think? Mother country and all that. Still, I think it could be a bit louder. I wouldn't want you to miss anything.'

He pressed the volume control and suddenly Carver was assaulted on all sides by a voice promoting a forthcoming *Hardtalk* interview with an Israeli politician. Wherever Carver turned, he couldn't escape the screens, all carefully positioned just beyond his reach.

'Excellent,' said Tyzack, raising his voice above the television babble. 'But I do think that you need to be taught one last lesson before I go. I've done my best, but I fear you've failed to grasp some of what I've been trying to teach you. I suspect you're not very bright, to be honest. Our relative positions still don't seem clear to you. So let me explain. I've beaten you once . . .' Tyzack picked up the cane and walked up to Carver's chair.

Carver couldn't help it. He flinched. That was all the encouragement Tyzack needed.

'. . . I . . .' He swung the cane, hitting the arms that Carver raised in a desperate bid to protect himself.

'. . . can . . .' Carver had bent forward, leaving the raw, hamburger meat of his back exposed. So that's where Tyzack aimed the second blow.

'. . . do it . . .' As Carver howled in pain, Tyzack kicked the chair away again, swinging the cane at him and grinning in delight as his desperate attempts to escape only forced him to the limit of the cord's tolerance, gagging him and forcing him back within Tyzack's range as he shouted, '. . . again!'

The last blow hit Carver just below the diaphragm, doubling him up, and then jerking him back up again as the cord rebounded, a wounded marionette at the mercy of a sadistic puppet-master.

Tyzack stepped back and examined his handiwork. Carver's refusal to accept his version of events had angered and frustrated him, but he had exacted a more than satisfactory price. He was going to have to leave soon. Visar wanted him working on the Bristol job and he couldn't afford to disappoint the Albanian.

He took another look at Carver, who was scrabbling around, trying to reach his chair, which was lying on its back, several feet away from him. Tyzack walked round the barn until he was standing right by the chair, paying very close attention as Carver – now apparently oblivious of his presence – fought the choking power of the cord.

Yes, Tyzack thought. It would be hard and it would hurt a very great deal, but Carver would get the chair. And if he had the chair he could live – or exist at any rate – for a few more days, being driven mad by the pain of his back, the choking frustration of his collar and lead and the unstinting blare of the TV sets. That was perfect. And so, feeling happier than he had done in years, Damon Tyzack walked out of the barn, leaving Carver to his pathetic struggles and padlocking the door behind him.

61

Hans and Gudrun List were ardent ramblers, still blessed with wiry physiques and tanned limbs despite being well into their sixties. Natives of Salzburg, Austria, they had grown up striding across the spectacular alpine landscape that surrounds their home town. Now they were walking across southern Scandinavia, from Stockholm to Oslo, enjoying the perfect weather of early summer and the rural scenery as they made good progress along the northern shore of Tvillingtjenn lake, just a couple of hours' walk from the Swedish border. Above all the Lists took pleasure in the peace and solitude; the cool, muffled calm soothed them as they walked between the trees along the water's edge.

And then the silence was shattered by a terrible howl of pain, a scream so primal that it might have come from an animal. 'What was that?' Hans asked. But the question was superfluous. The Lists both knew at once that this was the sound of a man in agony.

'It came from over there,' said Gudrun, pointing away from the lakeshore into the trees.

They took a few more tentative paces into the woods, torn

between the desire to help a fellow-human and the fear of whoever, or whatever, had ripped that terrible sound from his body. Then another scream rang out, more raggedly this time, as though the man's vocal cords no longer had the power to communicate his suffering.

'Look,' said Hans, pointing ahead of them. 'Over there.'

Gudrun saw it now: a small wooden building, a barn perhaps, or a garage. It looked drab and nondescript, apart from an incongruously bright pair of green doors, whose colour was echoed on the gable-ends of the roof. The fact that they could see the barn made the Lists themselves feel exposed. They retreated back down the path as a third scream, weaker again, seemed to call them, wordlessly pleading for their help.

'We must do something,' Gudrun insisted, waving her husband forward as she crept back towards the building, leaving the path and moving from the cover of one tree to another. They came to a halt behind the trunk of an ancient spruce and peered ahead of them. When what sounded like a very loud TV set was switched on they looked at one another in confusion. Then, a minute or two later, both flinched as the green doors opened and a man appeared, his head topped with a shock of fiery red hair. He turned back to lock the doors, then walked away from the barn. As they watched him go, the Lists realized that there was another, bigger building behind the barn, more like a chalet or farmhouse. More men emerged from it and followed the red-headed man as he kept walking. Silence fell for a while and then the thunderous racket of a powerful engine started up. There was a rise in pitch as it got up to speed, followed by a clatter of rotor-blades and then a helicopter rose from the forest and roared away over the trees towards the east.

As the sound of the chopper disappeared in the distance, the Lists turned to one another.

'He's still in there; we must do something,' Gudrun insisted.

'But if he is there, then surely there will still be someone in the main house. They would not just leave him.'

235

'Unless he is dead. We should go and look, to make sure.'

'Why, what good could we do? My dearest, this is a matter for the police.'

'But that poor man . . .'

'Exactly. Think about what they did to him. They could do it to us, too. Come, we must hurry away . . . Come on!'

Neither of the Lists' phones could get a signal where they were. It took another half an hour of brisk walking, every so often breaking into an undignified jog, before they were able to get through to the Norwegian emergency number, 112, and report what they had heard and seen.

The case was assigned to the nearest police station at Bjørkelangen, seven miles away. The inspector on duty there was about to send a car to investigate when he recalled one of the alerts that had been sent from Oslo in the hours after that terrible hotel bombing: something about a helicopter that had been seen over the opera house. Maybe this was the same chopper? It was a long shot, but it never hurt to be over-careful. And if he did happen to have found it, well, that might help him get a big-city posting.

He got on the line to Oslo right away.

62

Damon Tyzack's helicopter was over the Swedish border within three minutes of take-off. It swung south, flying low over the hilly, lake-strewn landscape of Värmland. The scenery there is some of the finest in Sweden, but Tyzack had no interest in enjoying the view. He was too busy checking his watch and urging his pilot to squeeze every last knot out of his machine.

Thinking about the task that lay ahead of him, he didn't see himself coming back to Norway any time soon. So he wouldn't get the chance of one last heart-to-heart with Carver. That was a pity. On the other hand, there was the consolation that Carver would die horribly, all alone, after long pain-filled days in which he'd have nothing else to think about but how much he'd fucked up. By now, he'd probably worked out who'd really shopped him. He'd be tormented by the loss of his best mate and his woman and he'd be all alone with the cuts on his back going septic, the pain in his neck getting worse and worse and not even a drop of water to drink without putting himself through hell.

Tyzack laughed aloud at the thought of such a satisfying

revenge. He felt it was a good sign. Things were moving his way. Now he just had to hit the ultimate target for any assassin: Mr President himself. If he pulled that job off, he would not only have destroyed Carver but utterly overshadowed him.

He'd got a text from one of Visar's people. The goods had been procured and conversion was taking place, it said. Excellent.

Foster Lafferty was with him in the helicopter. 'I've got a job for you,' Tyzack said. 'It means going back to Bradford, having another pow-pow with the Pakis.'

'You want me to smack 'em around again?' Lafferty asked.

'On the contrary, I want you all to become the very best of friends. Tell the Pakis they can have their tarts back. But I need something from them in return . . .'

The helicopter landed half an hour later in a field north of Gothenburg. A car was waiting for him there. It would take him the four hundred miles down the Swedish west coast to Malmö, across to Denmark on the Öresund bridge and tunnel, and then west to a private airfield close to the North Sea coast. From there he and his men would be flown to a similar field in northern England, their route carefully planned to avoid airspace controlled by the National Air Traffic Service.

He didn't have any worries about getting into the country un-detected. England's immigration and border controls were a joke. He got illegals in every day of the week. He could get himself in easily enough.

63

Jack Grantham had wondered how he was going to play this policeman, Ravnsborg, and how much he would reveal to him about
Carver. Would he, for example, show Ravnsborg the texts? They
were clearly important, even crucial evidence that suggested very
clearly that Carver had been duped. On the other hand, they were
bound to make any detective ask the obvious question: 'Why did
he send them to you?'

'Let's just say we know one another,' Grantham replied, when
Ravnsborg did, indeed, ask precisely that.

'He works for you, does he, at the . . . Foreign Office?'

There was a half-smile on Ravnsborg's weary face as he spoke.
Grantham got the impression that the big, sleepy Norwegian was
enjoying the break in the grinding, relentless pressure of coping
with a major disaster. It struck Grantham that this was a man he
could have a drink with, or fight alongside and know that his back
was covered: a man he could trust. And trust was not one of Jack
Grantham's natural emotions.

'No, Carver's not an employee of Her Majesty's Government,'

he replied. 'But he has carried out a couple of assignments, unpaid . . . favours, if you like. Big favours.'

'And in your estimation, Mr Grantham, is he a man who would blow up the King Haakon Hotel?'

'He's not a man who'd get caught blowing it up.'

Ravnsborg chuckled. 'Quite . . . And we have yet to determine that Carver was the man who we believe planted the bomb at the hotel yesterday afternoon. Of course, even if he were not, that might only tell us that more than one man was involved in the plot. I know only two things for sure. First, that Carver's call triggered the bomb. That has now been confirmed. And second, that he is capable of killing, because he attacked and killed three men last night.'

'Sounds like him,' Grantham agreed.

'On the other hand,' Ravnsborg continued, 'these text messages tally exactly with what other witnesses have described . . . You can assure me, I take it, that you did not send them to him yourself?'

'Would I be here if I had?'

'You might, I suppose, but I am too exhausted at the moment to work out why. Tell me, do you know this man?'

Grantham got up and walked round to Ravnsborg's side of the desk. A series of shots of Damon Tyzack appeared on the policeman's computer.

'Doesn't ring any bells,' said Grantham. 'Bluetooth them to my phone and I'll send them back to London. We'll see if anyone can put a name to the face.'

'At the Foreign Office?'

'I was thinking the Home Office, actually.'

Grantham would normally have sent the picture-files straight to Bill Selsey, but that hardly seemed wise under the present circumstances; and if he could not be trusted, the whole department was compromised. Grantham sent them to a different agency altogether.

Then he murmured, 'Hang on,' to Ravnsborg and hit a number on his speed-dial.

'Agatha,' he said when he got through. 'Jack Grantham here. Look, I wonder if you could do me a favour . . .'

Dame Agatha Bewley, the newly appointed head of the British Security Service, or MI5, was several rungs up the Whitehall ladder from Grantham, but the two of them had worked together in the past. They had history, and shared secrets, particularly where Samuel Carver was concerned. So it was as much out of self-protection as any collegial feeling towards a brother officer that she listened to what Grantham had to say and replied, 'Of course, I quite understand. Don't worry. I'll set the wheels in motion right away.'

In Oslo, Ravnsborg waited patiently until Grantham had finished his call.

'So . . . you think Carver has been framed, correct?' he finally asked.

Grantham nodded.

'Me, too. This is a problem, because he is a convenient, obviously guilty man, and I have everyone up to the Prime Minister telling me to arrest him so that he can be convicted as soon as possible and the public can feel safe again. But it seems to me that they would be safer if the right man were in prison. Excuse me . . .'

His phone had started ringing. Ravnsborg took the call. At first he said nothing beyond a few grunts of acknowledgement and understanding before firing a series of short, incisive questions in Norwegian. He wrote something down on a pad in front of him. Then, with his pen still hovering over the paper, he asked another couple of questions, evidently checking that he had written down the details of what he had been told correctly. When he put the phone back down, he looked up at Grantham.

'I was about to tell you, before that call, that we had lost track of Mr Carver. Last night, his movements were traced right up to the point where he attempted to board a ferry bound for Denmark. A passenger on that ferry, who had stepped outside for a smoke, saw him being lifted from the water by a helicopter. Well, I think we know now where that helicopter took him. And if the reports are correct, he is still there. A man with red hair was also spotted at the same location. That is the good news.'

'And the bad news?'

Ravnsborg ran his hands through his hair, leaving it even more dishevelled. He sighed like a man who was way past the end of his tether. 'The bad news,' he said, 'is that your Mr Carver may very well be dead.'

64

As soon as Bill Selsey got to work and realized that Grantham had scurried off to Oslo, he knew that it was time to make his move. The head of SIS, Sir Mostyn Green, had been chosen more for his willingness to tell the Prime Minister precisely what he wanted to hear than any great gift for intelligence. Selsey had been among those appalled by the way Green had been parachuted into Vauxhall Cross over the heads of men and women far better qualified for his position. Now, though, he was delighted that his boss was a political crawler, who dreaded public embarrassment above all else.

Selsey put himself through to Green's gatekeeper, a junior toadie built in his master's image.

'Morning, Jason, can you squeeze me in with Sir Mostyn for a few minutes, soon as poss? Something's come up.'

'I'm afraid he's tied up all morning. He's got the Foreign Secretary at eleven, and then they're both attending a JIC meeting. Is it urgent?'

'Well, it's an internal matter. Pretty delicate, actually,' Selsey replied in the confidential tone of a man about to pass on a particularly juicy piece of gossip. He had always known, as a matter of principle, that knowledge was power. Now he understood that power first hand.

'It's Grantham,' Selsey went on. 'He flew to Oslo this morning. He's gone to meet a chap called Samuel Carver.'

It took a second for the penny to drop.

'What, the one who's wanted for that hotel bombing?'

'Precisely.'

'But why would Grantham . . . ? Oh Lord, are you suggesting that the Service might be exposed to some kind of embarrassment?'

'Exactly, that's what's causing me concern. I can't go into details now, but Jack and Carver go back a while. They've got form. That's why I need to see Sir Mostyn.'

'In that case, I'll see what I can do.'

'Thanks, Jason. Knew you'd understand.'

65

Madeleine Cross put a hand on the basin and leaned towards the bathroom mirror. God, she looked wrecked.

She hadn't slept a wink. The whole night had crawled by with the same thoughts going round and round her brain without her coming to any conclusions: always the same questions, but never with any answers. She wished she knew where Carver was and whether he was alive or dead. She wished, too, that she knew who Carver was: the man she'd thought she could love, or the vicious killer she'd heard described on CNN. She kept going back to that moment at the ranch, when she'd felt his hands grip her body tight and watched him struggle to overcome his desire: he'd never been more attractive to her than at the precise instant he let her go. But against that proof of self-restraint and consideration she thought of the brutal efficiency with which he'd dispatched the two rednecks in that roadhouse south of Cascade. The man who had done that might just be capable of bombing a hotel without even losing sleep. And yet she still heard Ole Ravnsborg's voice in her head, asking, 'What if he is an innocent man who has himself been used?'

When the morning came, she hauled herself off to the bathroom and stood under a blistering hot shower until the fatigue and stiffness had melted from her neck and shoulders. Then she yanked the control to the far side of the dial and made herself stay there under the blast of freezing water. Now, as she stood by the basin and dabbed a concealer wand at the sacks under her eyes, her mind at last reached a point of clarity and the answers she was seeking seemed to fall into place like the tumblers of a lock.

It was just a matter of getting enough evidence to convince Ravnsborg that her answers were right. And to do that, the first thing she needed was a chat with the future Mrs Larsson. Time they had a good girl-talk.

The hotel was surrounded by TV crews and reporters. Maddy had to persuade the management to smuggle her out of the rear service exit like a scandal-ridden celebrity. She dashed to a waiting taxi and was driven up through hills dotted with smart suburban homes to the Holmenkollen Chapel, a starkly beautiful construction of black-stained wood topped with heavy wooden crosses.

'What do you think?' asked Thor Larsson, who met her outside the entrance.

'About this place?' she replied, looking up at the looming silhouette of the chapel set against the pale blue sky. 'I think it looks like a cross between a church and a haunted house. Or do you mean: what do I think about being here, at this damn rehearsal? Because, honestly, I don't know how you can go ahead with a wedding, after last night.'

'You think we should cancel it?' he asked.

'Yeah, don't you? Ten people died last night. We were there. Oh, and your best man is accused of the crime.'

'Ten people will die on the roads in this country over the next two or three days. Ten people die on a good day in Iraq. Should we cancel everything for them too?'

'But we were there.'

'Yes, we were having dinner in the café. But we didn't make the bombs go off. And what about Karin? Am I supposed to tell her: Sorry, darling, you'll have to send all your family and friends a thousand kilometres back to Narvik because some guy let off a bomb? It doesn't make sense.'

There was a tension in Larsson's voice, a desperation almost, which was out of keeping with everything Sam had told her about his laid-back personality; everything she had seen herself at the airport and over dinner. She wondered if the person he was really trying to persuade was himself.

'What about Carver?' she asked as they walked into the chapel.

'Do you think he was responsible for what happened?' Larsson replied.

'No . . . no, I don't. I can't.'

'OK. But if we cancelled, that would be like an admission that we were linked to the guilty man. We can't do that to him.'

'What if he's dead?'

'I don't think he is. I've known him a long time and he always pulls through. So we're going to do this rehearsal, OK?'

Ahead of them, Karin was looking up at the altar, lost in thought.

'Wait a minute,' Maddy said to Larsson. 'I just need to say hello to Karin, all right?'

'I'll introduce you.'

'No, it's OK, I can do it.'

Maddy walked towards Karin, wondering what to say to her. At any other rehearsal she'd tell the bride how pretty she looked and giggle sympathetically about the stress of it all. But now? Maddy decided that she might as well be honest.

'Weird, isn't it?' she said. 'I mean, doing all this . . . now . . . after last night.'

'Oh God, I'm so glad you said that,' said Karin, bursting into tears. She sounded distraught, but also relieved, as though a great burden of lies and pretence had been lifted from her shoulders.

Maddy hugged her. 'It's OK . . . Come on, sit down here.'

She led Karin to the altar steps. She told her everything was going to be fine, though she knew neither of them believed it. There was only one thing Maddy truly wanted to talk about.

'Can I ask you a question?'

Karin nodded as she wiped away her tears.

'How long have you guys been engaged?' Maddy asked. 'You must have been planning this for the longest time.'

'Actually, no,' Karin replied. A weary smile played around her face. 'You know, marriage is not so important here as maybe it is in America. In fact, it's a little old-fashioned. But Thor just proposed to me, only a month ago, right out of the blue.'

'I didn't know he was so romantic!'

Karin laughed. 'Oh God, I'm sorry!' she said, acutely conscious of her red eyes and runny nose.

'It's fine,' said Maddy, touching Karin's arm sympathetically. 'It's my fault for suggesting your husband-to-be is romantic.'

Karin smiled again, this time without apology. 'Well, I don't think Thor is romantic, exactly,' she said. 'But he was trying to be, I guess. He'd gone to so much trouble. He'd even checked up the dates when the chapel was available.'

'He'd even picked a date? Oh my!' said Maddy, doing her best to sound cheerful. 'Well, I guess you had to say yes to that!'

'I didn't know what to say at first, it was so sudden. But he was very persuasive.'

Maddy nodded sympathetically. 'I'm sure,' she said. 'And I'm so glad we could talk.'

She leaned across and pecked Karin on the cheek, then got up, walked right over to Larsson and asked him, 'Do you want to tell her, or shall I?'

'Tell her what?'

'That the wedding is a scam. That it was only set up to get Carver here on the right date, the same way you got us to go to that restaurant last night, so he'd be there when the bomb went off. So he'd get the blame – your best friend. How could you do that to him? Why?'

Maddy was ready for Larsson to react violently. But he did not even argue. Instead he seemed to crumple before her: his face, his shoulders, even his legs seemed to buckle a little.

'Come with me,' he said, 'please. I don't want Karin to hear anything.'

Maddy walked with him back down the aisle and out into the open air.

'I swear I didn't know what was going to happen,' Larsson said when they got outside. His voice was pleading but there was also relief there that he could finally get things off his chest. 'I was just told to find a way to get Carver to the hotel that evening, that was all. And some other stuff, you know, designs . . . like I did for Carver . . .'

'But why did you agree?'

'I was sent photographs of Karin . . . at home, at work, walking through town, everywhere. If they had threatened me . . . I mean, I'm not like Carver, but I can look after myself. But I could not look after Karin, not every minute of the day . . . And there was something else . . .' He leaned closer to Maddy and barely whispered, 'Karin's pregnant. Our baby . . . that was too much to lose. I had to do what he asked.'

'Who was he, this guy?'

'I don't know. He never gave me a name. But, Madeleine, you have to believe me. The bomb, blaming Carver . . . I didn't know anything about that.'

'Oh come on, you must have guessed!'

'Maybe I did not want to admit it. But even when I found out for sure, last night, I told myself Carver would escape. He would win. Like all the other times.'

'Do you know where he is now?'

'No . . .' Larsson closed his eyes and screwed up his face. Maddy could see there was a battle going on inside him, as if part of him was resisting one final admission.

'Come on, Thor, you know something. I can tell . . .'

'OK, assuming Carver is alive, if he's free, he'll go back to Geneva. But I've been calling pretty much constantly. No answer.

If he's not free . . . If this man has got him, well, I think I know where he is. But I hope I'm wrong.'

'We've got to call the police, tell them everything.'

'But what about Karin? The wedding?'

'You think she'll care about that, once she knows what you did? You've only got one chance, Thor. With her, with me, with Carver . . . You've got to tell Ravnsborg everything. Now.' She held out her phone towards him.

Larsson shook his head. 'It's OK, I've got the number too.'

He took out his phone and dialled the incident room at Olso police headquarters. Maddy watched as he spoke, not understanding the words but picking up the change of mood, from introduction, to explanation, to exasperation and finally anger.

'There's a problem,' he said, when he ended the call. 'Ravnsborg isn't there. He left the station about five minutes ago, with some English guy, they wouldn't say who. He's on a mobile, but they won't give me the number. They just say that if I leave a message, they'll pass it on in due course.'

'So what did you tell them?'

'I told them to tell Ravnsborg his life is in extreme danger, and so is Carver's. They didn't seem to believe me.'

'So now what are we going to do?'

'We are going to drive like crazy to a lake called Tvillingtjenn. We have to get there before Ravnsborg. People's lives depend upon it.'

'Well, if we need to get there quickly, you'd better let me drive,' Maddy said.

'For heaven's sake!' snapped Larsson. 'Are you crazy? You don't know the way. You don't know the country. It's my car. You won't be quicker than me.'

'Believe me, I will. Just give me the keys.'

66

If Carver stood up, directly under the beam, the pull of the bungee cord against his slave collar didn't hurt his throat or restrict his breathing. If he sat on the chair, absolutely upright, trying to ignore the rasping agony of his open wounds rubbing against the rough wooden chair-back, it felt no worse than a tight dress-uniform collar. The moment he tried to do anything else the trouble began.

If he slumped his shoulders, or lowered his head, for example, the pressure increased against his Adam's apple, making him want to gag. Sleep, or even the slightest relaxation, would be impossible.

There was a part of him that almost admired Tyzack for the thoroughness with which he'd thought the nightmare through, right down to the ceaseless jabber of the TV sets that surrounded him like medieval peasants jeering at a man in the stocks. He'd already seen a report from the site in Bristol where the President would give his speech in a little over forty-eight hours. Regular updates had been promised, an inescapable countdown to the moment when Tyzack struck.

Carver wondered what state he would be in by then. The pain

and exhaustion would increase hour by hour, steadily draining him of the will to live. Yet it would be equally hard to kill himself. The elasticity of the cord and the padding of the collar allowed no possibility of a quick hanging. It might be possible to asphyxiate himself, but it would take a long time – several minutes at least – and an implacable, unrelenting death-wish. That, too, would surely be beyond him. He had no choice but to endure a half-life, a purgatory that would continue until Tyzack returned. Assuming that he ever did. He could just leave Carver to rot. Or he might be arrested or killed on his mission, whatever it was.

Carver's heart was pounding now, his breath coming in shallow gasps. He'd let his thoughts run away with him and now he was close to panic.

'Come on, get a grip, you wanker!'

His voice was little more than a husky rasp through his battered vocal cords. Shakily, he got to his feet, straightened his back, ignoring the protesting shots of pain, pulled back his shoulders and let out a single, voice-cracking roar of pain and frustration, holding it until his lungs were empty. When he breathed again, the panic was gone and his pulse was steady.

His throat, though, felt as if it had been scrubbed from the inside with wire wool. He needed a drink. The prospect of enduring another fight against the cord as he dragged himself towards the table, where the plastic container sat taunting him with its fifteen litres of cool, fresh water, sent another shot of fear through his system. Yet far from putting him off, the fear only drove him on. If he was to survive, he had to turn the desperate scrabble for water into a routine. He had to find a way of normalizing the experience. Better yet, he could try moving the water closer to him, a lot closer, so that he could get to it easily – or as easily as he could do anything in Tyzack's chamber of horrors.

Carver told himself to start with the basics: get a drink.

He took three deep breaths, flooding his lungs with oxygen. The fourth breath he held and stepped forward towards the table, his total concentration focused on the water bottle. He felt the grip on his neck tighten and willed himself to ignore the sensations of nausea and asphyxiation. All the while the cord was pulling at him, trying to force him back.

He was still barely halfway across the open floor between his chair and the table.

Carver leaned forward into his next step. His blood was pounding in his ears and the edges of his vision were becoming blurred. For a moment he craved the vicious sting of the cane on his back, forcing him to go onwards whether he wanted to or not. It was even harder making himself do it.

One more step: he pushed his left foot ahead of him as far as it would go, till the toe of his shoe was almost touching the table. Then he leaned forward one last time.

He could almost feel his larynx collapsing under the pressure from the collar. His craving for oxygen was as desperate as a drowning man's.

He reached out his arms, joints and tendons straining, fingers outstretched, and somehow his left hand managed to curl around the neck of the bottle, while his right fumbled for the little plastic cup beside it.

Carver was close to blacking out as he lifted the cup to the lip of the bottle.

He tilted the bottle towards him. Water gurgled up the spout, but did not reach the lip. He would have to tilt it further before any came out.

The bottle tipped over another few degrees. Now Carver felt as though he was fighting a war on two fronts. The weight of the bottle was dragging him downwards, just as the cord was pulling him up and away.

He was desperate for air now. But if he let go of the bottle, he might never manage to get it again.

He had to get the water into the plastic cup, but still it wouldn't come out.

He tilted the bottle a few more degrees, the strain becoming worse as its centre of gravity shifted over.

And then something gave.

What went first he didn't know. But suddenly his back foot was slipping and scrabbling for purchase on the wooden floor. The bottle was sliding on the table.

There was even more tension pulling against his throat. The full weight of the bottle was bearing down on his fingers wrapped around its neck. As the bungee cord pulled him inexorably away, his fingers lost a fraction of their purchase. But that was enough.

The bottle slipped from his grasp, teetered for a fraction of a second and then toppled over, thudding against the top of the table and then rolling sideways, water now pouring from its spout, and all Carver could do was watch as it fell from the side of the table, crashed down on to the floor and poured its precious cargo over the pine boards.

A pool of water spread across the floor, too far away and too low for him even to touch, let alone scoop into his hands.

The water gurgled. It splashed. It puddled. And every drop of it was wasted.

He could only stand and watch despairingly as little by little it slipped between the cracks in the floorboards and seeped, agonizingly slowly, into the soft, pale wood.

Carver lunged despairingly, trying to reach the overturned bottle and the last litre or two that remained within it. He strained until he felt that his shoulder sockets would be torn apart and his head torn from his body. He fought against suffocation and unconsciousness. But it was no good. The bottle remained out of reach, untouchable, its open top staring blankly at him.

He knew then that it was over. Tyzack had won. He would hit the President. And Carver was going to die within the next few days. From now on it was simply a matter of exactly how and when.

67

The road map of Oslo's northern suburbs looks like a maze in a children's puzzle book. The roads twist and switchback as they snake across the hills. Some side roads link back into the system, while others run blindly away to dead ends. Had she not had Thor navigating for her in the passenger seat, Maddy would have become hopelessly lost. Instead he gave her instructions in a voice as irritatingly calm and emotionless as a sat-nav, while she channelled her anger and desperation into the business of getting to Carver as fast as humanly possible.

Larsson owned a Volvo XC90 4×4 whose engine growled like an angry bear as Maddy flung it round corners, slicing across the oncoming traffic, seeking out the racing line. She braked like a racing driver, too: one decisive deceleration, then straight back on the power and a slingshot round the bend, trusting the Volvo's four-wheel drive to keep it on the blacktop. She broke every rule in the book, overtaking on blind corners, aiming for tiny gaps between vehicles, playing chicken with trucks and buses. Her face was a tight mask of concentration, the only outward signs of her tension coming from the occasional flicker of her cheek, just below the left eye, and the clenching of her jaw as she worked the wheel and the brakes.

The ground was flattening out and the individual detached chalets that lined the streets on the edge of the city, each with their patch of garden, were giving way to more tightly packed housing when Larsson spotted a run of shops a hundred metres or so ahead.

'Pull in there,' he said.

'Are you outta your freakin' mind?' Maddy shouted, her temper pumped up by the adrenalin flooding her system.

'Just do it,' Larsson insisted. 'If you want Carver to live.'

Fuming, she pulled into a small line of parking spots.

'I won't be long,' Larsson said, jumping out of the car and running over to one of the shops. Maddy couldn't work out what the sign on the front meant, but, from the gear displayed in the window, it looked like a tool-hire store.

Larsson emerged from it barely a minute later carrying what looked like a gigantic, super-vicious pair of orange kitchen scissors, with a chainsaw where the top blade would be.

'Alligator loppers,' he said, by way of explanation.

'Yeah, I know what they are,' she said dismissively. She'd already started the engine as he was walking towards the car and was now pulling back out into the traffic.

Within a few minutes they were on the ring road that ran around the north of the city, still going fast, but travelling more smoothly. Larsson didn't have to give directions any more. He tried making conversation.

'Where did you learn to drive like that?'

'Back home, when I was a girl. I come from the boonies, didn't Carver tell you? Oh, no, I guess he didn't have time. Look, just don't talk to me, all right? Don't tell me how it's all a terrible mistake. Don't try to justify yourself. Just shut up unless you're giving me directions.'

Larsson lowered his head for a moment, cradling it in his right hand. Then he took a deep breath, pulled himself back together and sat back in his seat.

'Yeah, I get it,' he said. 'So, where are we?' He glanced out of the window. 'OK, turn left at the next exit. Take the E6. Follow the signs to Lørenskog and Lillestrøm. Got that?'

'Uh-huh.'

'Fine then, I'll shut up.'

68

The police Saab 9-5 was powered by environmentally conscious biofuel, but that didn't seem to slow it down as Ravnsborg raced down a country road on the way to Tvillingtjenn. He leaned forward and looked up through the windscreen as a helicopter clattered overhead, painted in drab, military green.

'The anti-terrorist boys!' he shouted over the noise. 'Let us hope they manage to control themselves until we get there. Not long now.'

Another car, filled with Ravnsborg's own people, was hurtling after them. The local force from Bjørkelangen had already established a perimeter around the farmhouse and barn where the Lists had reported hearing sounds of violence and seeing a helicopter take off. Grantham was on the phone, listening more than talking.

'Thanks,' he said at last. 'Appreciate it. Sorry if I caused you any grief. Speak to you later. Bye.'

He put his phone away and turned his head towards the driver's seat.

'The man's name is Damon Tyzack,' he said. 'He's an all-purpose nasty piece of work. Suspected links with various unpleasant gangland activities, including trafficking of people and drugs. He's also rumoured to work on the side as a hitman, though no one's ever got enough evidence on him to bring charges. One interesting thing, though: he's an ex-marine, spent some time in the Special Boat Service, but got cashiered, kicked out. Seems like a mission went wrong, though the SBS didn't release any specific details. They like to keep things close to their chests, those boys, but friend Tyzack must have been a very naughty boy indeed, judging by the speed with which they shoved him out the door. There's one other interesting wrinkle. It was the commanding officer on the mission who insisted Tyzack had to go. Guess who that was . . .'

'I thought you said Mr Carver did not work for Her Majesty.'

'That's right, he doesn't.'

'But he did once? In the SBS?'

'Bingo.'

'And Tyzack has never forgiven him for destroying his military career?'

'Well,' said Grantham, 'that's certainly a possibility.'

'We may soon find out, one way or the other,' Ravnsborg said, hitting the brakes and bringing the Saab screeching to a halt at a police roadblock. Up ahead, to the left of the road, a long, narrow stretch of water was lined with rows of trees rising up into jagged, rocky hills. Three fire-engines and a couple of ambulances were lined up along the side of the road, their crews standing around, chatting, smoking, or lying on the verge, soaking up the sun.

Ravnsborg opened his window and showed his badge. One of the officers manning the block leaned down and gave directions, pointing across the water towards the trees. Ravnsborg turned off the road on to a dirt track and drove the car, much more gingerly now, around the narrow end of the lake and along the far bank.

The track had taken them round the back of the property, up to the patch of open ground now occupied by the anti-terrorist unit's helicopter. It led past the farmhouse and round to the barn, which was just visible through the trees in the distance. Black-uniformed and helmeted assault troops and local police were lined up behind a line of squad cars opposite the farmhouse. A couple of the men were pointing guns at the building, but most were standing round with the unmistakable air of men awaiting orders and wondering when something would happen.

As Ravnsborg parked and got out of the Saab one of the black-clad figures walked towards him with a tough, purposeful stride in keeping with his menacing appearance. A pot-bellied policeman followed after him, almost having to jog to keep up. Ravnsborg was a superb detective, but it didn't require a man of his talents to deduce that this was the local inspector.

'Morten,' snapped the anti-terrorist officer, shooting out a hand towards Ravnsborg, who shook it and introduced himself.

'Inspector Petersen,' said the policeman, presenting a sweaty paw. He spoke a couple of further sentences in Norwegian. Grantham did not understand a word, but he didn't have to. A nervous, eager-to-please subordinate sounded the same in any language.

'This is Mr Grantham . . . from London,' Ravnsborg said, in English, with a wave of his hand. 'He may be able to help us with the man in the barn.' He gave one of his weary smiles. 'If he is who we think he is . . . If he is there at all.'

Morten gave a grunt that seemed to convey disapproval of Ravnsborg's apparently vague manner, and scepticism of Grantham's value to proceedings, all without a word being spoken.

'Hope I can be of assistance,' said Grantham, offering his own hand and noting Morten's reluctance to take it.

'Now that you are here, we can proceed,' Morten said, also switching to English. 'We have reconnoitred the main building thoroughly. No heat-signatures of any occupants have been detected, nor any sounds. With your permission, we will secure this building, then move on to the barn.'

Ravnsborg shrugged. 'That sounds perfectly reasonable to me. Mr Grantham?'

'Fine by me,' said Grantham with a smile whose graciousness was calculated to irritate Morten still further.

He told himself he really shouldn't be winding the poor bastard up like this. They all had serious work to do. But it was fun. And Grantham was a great believer in trying to enjoy his work.

Morten turned on his heel and walked back down towards his men, shouting orders. He was efficient enough, Grantham had to grant him that. There were already men posted on all sides of the farmhouse, covering every possible exit. Now the personnel behind the cars were transformed in seconds from bored layabouts to fast-moving fighting men. Three of them scurried across the open ground towards the front door while the rest stood behind the cars, guns pointed towards the house, ready to fire at the slightest sign of trouble.

The first blast, however, came from a shotgun blasting the lock on the door. It was followed by the crash of a hand-held battering ram.

'Close your eyes and cover your ears,' Ravnsborg said to Grantham just seconds before the deafening blast of a flashbang erupted from within the front hall of the farmhouse.

The three men by the door were already moving into the house before the last echoes had stopped ringing round the surrounding hills. Three more men raced across from the cars, following them into the building. Barely a minute later, Morten was taking a message on his headset.

Ravnsborg was standing next to him.

'The building's clear,' Morten reported. 'No occupants.'

'Good,' said Ravnsborg. 'Now for the barn. And fast. Someone may still be alive in there. There's no time to waste.'

69

The road from Bjørkelangen to the lake at Tvillingtjenn described two sides of a crudely drawn right-angled triangle. The third side was formed by rough, heavily wooded country. That was the way that Maddy and Larsson took, hoping to make up time by cutting the corner. Their route was comprised, at best, of rutted, potholed dirt tracks. When they ran out Maddy had to drive between the trees, jinking between the biggest trunks and simply smashing the big Volvo through the lighter undergrowth.

If her technique on tarmac had been as impressive as it was terrifying, her off-road skill was something else again. Maddy drove at motorway speeds down tracks barely wider than the car, using the rally-driver's knack of drifting round corners in a controlled sideways skid, oblivious to the frantic scrabbling of the tyres as they swung out over precipitous hillside drops. She took hairpin bends using handbrake turns, locking the rear wheels and letting them swing round to push the car through an angle far tighter than its steering lock would allow.

'Are you sure you're not really Scandinavian?' Larsson shouted over the roar of the engine and the constant clattering of stones, solid rock and knotted tree-roots against the underside of the car. 'I thought we were the only people who were crazy enough to drive like this.'

Maddy didn't say anything. She was racing through the woods, heading directly towards the trunk of a massive old tree. Larsson suddenly realized that he had never been so frightened in all his life. He was certain that he was about to die. There could be no doubt of it. She was taking her revenge for his betrayal of Carver by killing them both.

The tree got closer and closer until it seemed to fill the entire windscreen. In the last fraction of a second before impact, Maddy flicked the steering wheel sharply to the left and then equally fast to the right. The sudden shifts in direction were enough to destabilize even the Volvo's four-wheel drive. For an instant, all traction lost, the Volvo turned broadside on to the tree. Maddy seemed to be hurling herself sideways into its trunk. Then she slammed her foot down on the accelerator, the wheels spun frantically, grabbed a fraction of purchase against the forest floor and the car slid past the tree, still moving sideways till she turned hard left again and swung the nose of the car round and they could carry on again, careering through the trees until they hit another track.

'OK, almost there,' said Larsson, his voice shaking. He looked across at Maddy and saw the whites of her knuckles against the steering wheel. Her face was more taut and mask-like than ever. She was only just keeping her emotions in check. It occurred to Larsson that the nerve-shredding tension of driving so fast in such difficult conditions was, for her, a distraction from the far greater fear of what might have happened to Carver.

How had it come to this? Larsson thought about the steady escalation of threats and demands to which he had been subjected. At first it was just a matter of getting Carver to arrive in Oslo on a particular day. Then came the order for the bombs and their triggers: not just the hotel device but other ones, too, incendiaries.

There had never been any explicit connection between the various commissions. Larsson had feared, of course, that Carver might be the target for the bomb, but not knowing it for sure had enabled him to pretend that it might not be so.

Finally he had been taken up to the barn and had been forced to install the booby-trap system the man demanded. Larsson had seen that the barn was intended as a torture chamber, but there was still no certainty that it would be Carver hanging from that cord and sitting on that simple wooden chair. The only certainty was that Karin and their unborn child would be made to suffer if he, Larsson, did not do as he was told. That had overridden everything else. But then there was the other thing, the design job he'd been given just recently. That didn't fit with any of the others. It was intended for something else, he was sure: something just as bad as the atrocity at the King Haakon Hotel. If only he knew what, that might give him a chance to atone for what he had done.

Then the track came out of the trees and joined another path that was running through an open field with a helicopter parked at its centre. He knew where he was now, recognized the house that stood beyond the line of parked police cars.

'Down there!' he shouted, pointing ahead and to the right. 'He's in the barn!'

Maddy gave a fractional nod of the head and flung the car down past the house, oblivious to the unarmed police officers, shouting and waving at them, and the black uniformed figures lifting their automatic weapons to their shoulders.

When one of them fired a pair of three-round warning bursts that just missed the car, Maddy finally hit the brakes.

Larsson hardly noticed the men or their weapons. He was too busy grabbing the alligator loppers, kicking the door open and running towards the barn. He was watching the black-clad figures crouching by the double doors at the front of the building. His eyes were wide in horror at what he was seeing. His mouth was forming the word 'No' and he was screaming it.

But the sound of Larsson's voice was drowned by the blast of the shotgun and then, as the door was rammed open, the sound of an explosion and a sudden whoosh and a crackle of timber as the whole barn was engulfed in a blazing yellow and orange sheet of flame.

70

Samuel Carver did not believe in regret, any more than he believed in guilt. There was no point in feeling sorry about something that could not be changed, and even less in mourning an action that could still be put right. Stop whining and do something about it: that would be his reaction. And if you've got regrets, but too few to mention, then just stop singing and shut the fuck up.

Like guilt, regret was also a self-excusing emotion. People felt better about themselves for being sorry about bad things they'd done, their character failings, their wealth, or their full bellies when others were starving. They were often so proud of themselves for displaying all this guilt that it seemed to be enough in itself: they saw no need to actually change anything.

Yet as he confronted his death and tried to make peace with himself amidst the pain, the thirst and the noise that assailed him, there were three things Carver wished he'd done before it was too late. Getting the warning through about Tyzack's hit on Lincoln Roberts was one of them and in the greater scheme of things perhaps that was the most important. But to Carver, the people he loved mattered more.

He wished he'd been able to sit down with Thor Larsson, pour him a beer and ask him a simple question: why? There had to be a good reason Larsson had shafted him. He wouldn't have done it for money, surely. Unless he'd suddenly developed a cocaine habit or a dangerous taste for casinos, Larsson wasn't short of cash and anyway he stood to earn more from Carver alive than dead.

Maybe it was something personal. He and Larsson had had the odd fight in their time, but nothing that had left any lasting resentment, not that Carver was aware of anyway. And though Larsson was slow to anger, when there was something eating at him, he wasn't shy about letting Carver know, even if it meant grabbing him by the throat and shaking some sense into him. Carver smiled to himself as he thought about a night in Geneva when Larsson had done just that. Carver had barely been out of the clinic an hour and he hadn't been thinking straight, to put it mildly. That was when you knew you had a true friend: when he had the balls and the honesty to let you know you were making a total tit of yourself.

It must have been a threat, then. He'd been frightened into the betrayal. And since he knew that Larsson was no coward, Carver knew it had to be something to do with someone he loved, and that meant Karin. Christ, why hadn't he just got in touch? Together they could have dealt with anyone. Except they couldn't have, could they? Larsson had told Carver about his upcoming wedding just a few days before Carver had started work on that Lusterleaf job. He'd been totally wrapped up in that. When his best friend had needed him, he hadn't been there.

Same with Maddy. If he'd been any kind of normal man, he'd have moved heaven and earth to get back to her after the bomb went off. Instead he'd found every way he could to rationalize running away, and every single one of those reasons had been nothing but crap. The truth was, he just couldn't deal with the possibility that a woman might actually love him.

But all he wanted now was to put his arms round Maddy one last time. He wanted to feel her, smell her, hear her whispering something filthy in his ear, both of them laughing as they rolled into one another's arms. He wanted to say sorry for being such a dick and putting her through so much when all she'd wanted was to be together and have a good time. He closed his eyes and concentrated on recalling her with all his senses, hoping that would help him forget the pain, the exhaustion and the fear that racked his mind and body, and buy him a few moments of peace.

That was why it took him a few seconds to register the sound of the helicopter coming into land, loud enough to be heard over the TVs, and a while after that to conclude that it was a different, bigger aircraft than the one that had taken off just after Tyzack had left him. And if it wasn't him on that chopper . . . A surge of hope flooded through Carver. Someone was coming for him!

He shouted out, 'Help! Over here! I'm here!' but it was only when he'd shouted the same few words over and over again that he realized no one could possibly have heard him. His voice had been reduced to a husky, almost silent croak. Someone standing where Tyzack had been, just a few feet away, would have had a hard time making him out. There was no chance at all of his cries carrying to anyone outside.

Still, it wouldn't be long till they found him, surely . . .

. . . would it?

Time went by, the seconds stretching out like faces in a hall of mirrors, and nothing happened. Carver thought he heard cars arriving. After that . . . nothing.

He strained to pick up scraps of information from the brief moments of silence between words and music on the BBC news report. Several minutes later two more cars arrived. The next thing Carver heard was the familiar sequence of a forced entry. OK, he thought, so there was another building nearby. That made sense. If this was a barn, there had to be a farmhouse to go with it. They were clearing the buildings one by one. Whoever was out there, they'd get to him soon enough. It was just a matter of keeping cool until they arrived.

It struck him that he would probably be arrested. They were looking for a bomber, not the half-strangled, beaten victim of a psychopath's obsession. He didn't mind. If he could just write to Maddy, call her, maybe have one prison visit, that would give him the chance to explain.

The sound of running boots on the path outside and orders being barked told him it would not be long now. Then he heard another engine, the sound of a car being driven right on the limit and he knew – absolutely knew with the certainty that comes from a lover's deepest instinct – that Maddy was in that car. His heart soared . . . and then crashed back down again as he heard two short bursts of gunfire. The engine died away.

'Oh God, please, oh no-o-o-o . . .' Carver pleaded. He thought for a second he could hear a voice outside, one he recognized, echoing his own. But then there were more footsteps, the blast of a shotgun against a lock.

And the next thing Carver knew, he had swapped Damon Tyzack's personal vision of hell for the fires of an all-too-real inferno.

71

Thor Larsson did not stop running. While the men in their black uniforms fled from the blazing barn, he kept moving straight towards it. When he got to the doors, he kicked out at them, sending his foot through the flames that were racing up the green-painted wood and forcing them open so that he could charge right through and into the building itself.

Larsson looked like a man who was already halfway to damnation. His face bore a look of such manic intensity that his old self was all but unrecognizable. Fire was licking at his trouser legs and he held some kind of weapon in his hands. Carver flinched like a whipped dog confronted by a man's passing boot, but then he saw that the weapon was not intended for him as Larsson reached over him, gripped the bungee cord in the alligator's teeth and turned on the chainsaw. He was shouting something, the same words again and again, but the rasping buzz of the saw biting at the toughened rubber was so loud in Carver's ear that he could not make out what it was. It was only by lipreading that he worked out Larsson was repeating, 'I'm sorry,' in an anguished mantra of apology.

The air was rippling with the scorching heat that had turned the barn into a cross between a sauna and a pizza oven, and smoke was curling up walls that had been transformed into satin curtains of gold and scarlet by the roiling flames and snaking over the inside of the roof. Carver's eyes were watering and he was choking as his battered lungs tried to extract oxygen from the scorching, toxic atmosphere. The flesh on his back, exposed by Tyzack's cane, felt as though it was cooking, basting in the sweat that poured from the pores of his remaining skin, the burns adding a whole new layer of pain to his torment.

At the end of the barn, by the doors through which Larsson had entered, a roof-beam gave way, eaten through by fire, and crashed to the ground, bringing a sheet of corrugated iron roofing down with it. Carver glanced up and saw that the beam from which he was hanging had caught fire. It would give way soon, and he would be directly underneath it.

'Hurry up!' he croaked.

Larsson grimaced. There were burning embers floating down on his head but he ignored them as the loppers tore all too slowly through a cord designed to resist the massive stress imposed by a human body falling hundreds of feet through the air.

The flames were creeping across the floor towards them, forming a predatory circle around the two men. The roaring fire and crashing timbers were now as loud as the chainsaw, but Carver just made out the words, 'Almost there!'

Larsson's demonic transformation was complete. He had become a creature of flame, all but consumed by the inferno his own incendiaries had created. The last strands of the cord gave way. Larsson threw the loppers away and shouted, 'Go! Go!'

Carver looked around, searching for a way out, but there was none. The flames were everywhere. Their only hope was to race towards the doors and pray that they could get through to the outside world before the fire consumed them. Carver took a first tentative step towards the blaze, girding himself for the final effort.

And it was then that one end of the beam gave way. It swung

downwards, as if on a hinge, hitting Larsson with a sickening impact, caving in the left side of his skull and dropping him to the ground before it crashed to a halt. Larsson lay motionless on the floor. The beam was angled over him, one end on the floor, the other jammed against the far wall. Calling up the last reserves of strength that adrenalin always provides, the berserker energy that is any fighting man's last resort, Carver dragged Larsson's long, spindly body out from beneath the beam. He got down on one knee and hauled Larsson over his shoulder, then forced his legs to straighten, pushing him upright.

As he faced the wall of fire, an image suddenly came into Carver's mind. He saw Tyzack grinning at him and heard his mocking laugh. 'Screw you,' Carver said, and ran full speed into the flames.

It was only twenty feet to the door. Call it five racing strides, eight maybe with a man on his back. An Olympic sprinter could do it in a little over half a second. Carver took five. He had his head down and his eyes closed: a blind, broken man with an even more ruined creature on his back. The noise, the smoke and the heat seemed to engulf him as he charged on.

And then he was through, stumbling out into the cool, clear air and falling to the bare earth. He had just enough self-possession to land on his front, protecting both Larsson and his own griddled back. As the two of them lay there, side by side, Carver saw Larsson's blistered right eyelid open a fraction, just for a moment, and his lips move as he whispered, 'The sky. Look to the sky . . .'

Then the black-uniformed figures were on them. Someone was covering Carver's body in a thick blanket. Dimly he realized that they must be putting out flames, but then there was a pinprick in his upper arm and oblivion wrapped itself around him in a blissful, soft cloak of darkness. And he was out.

72

Jack Grantham could hear the sound of sirens in the distance, the fire-engines and ambulances racing to the blazing barn and the casualties it had contained.

He looked around frantically, saw Ravnsborg talking to Morten, the anti-terrorist officer, and sprinted towards him shouting, 'Stop them! The emergency services – make them stop!'

Ravnsborg's face was a mixture of puzzlement and irritation. 'Why?'

'They mustn't see what's happened here. Not yet. If you want to catch the man who did all this, for God's sake stop them!'

Ravnsborg picked his phone out of his pocket, pressed a speed-dial button and snapped out an order. Seconds later the sirens fell quiet.

He looked at Grantham. 'You have one minute. Then they come. There are seriously injured men here. They cannot wait.'

'They're dead,' said Grantham.

Morten shook his head. 'Larsson, maybe. His injuries are terrible. He won't make it. But the other one, Carver. He'll live.'

'No,' said Grantham. 'That's the whole point. He's got to die. As far as the rest of the world is concerned, the man who bombed the Haakon Hotel died here. He killed himself when surrounded by the police. Case closed. Pats on the back all round.'

'But then the other man, Tyzack, will get away,' said Ravnsborg.

'There's no "will" about it,' Grantham pointed out. 'He already has got away. And he's not coming back. But if he thinks Carver's been blamed for the bombing, then he'll be feeling pleased with himself, a little bit cocky. So he won't take the precautions he'd take if he knew he was wanted for mass murder.'

Ravnsborg nodded. 'OK, so you will help us track him down, yes? If he returns to Britain, he will be arrested and deported back to Oslo for trial.'

Jack Grantham was almost certain that Damon Tyzack had recruited Bill Selsey and compromised the Secret Intelligence Service. He had no intention of letting him anywhere near a criminal court, particularly not one in a foreign country with no concern for British security. But there was no point getting into that now.

'Exactly,' he said in a spirit of international co-operation. 'That's just what I had in mind.'

'But what about Carver?' asked Ravnsborg. 'How can we say he is dead, when obviously he is not?'

'No, he isn't,' said Grantham, making Ravsnborg frown at the apparent tone of regret in his voice. Grantham's face brightened: 'But that's not a problem. The man who died in that barn isn't Samuel Carver at all. Samuel Carver doesn't exist. He's Paul Jackson, late of the Royal Marines and the Special Boat Service – just another twisted, embittered special forces veteran who came to a sticky end. There's a lot of it about these days. And Jackson certainly does exist. We'll give you all the paperwork you need: service records, photographs. Just say the word and it's yours. By the way,' he added, looking at his watch, 'it's been more like three minutes than one.'

'I know,' said Ravnsborg, with the faintest trace of a smile. 'And if we wait another three the fire will have destroyed the building completely. And, sadly, much of the forensic evidence will be destroyed, too.'

'What about Larsson?' Morten asked.

'Put him on your helicopter, fly him out,' said Ravnsborg. 'It will be faster, anyway.'

'And Carver?' Grantham asked. 'He's going to need treatment, but he can't go anywhere near a hospital. We need someone discreet who can be trusted absolutely . . .'

Ravnsborg made another call. When it was over, he said, 'It's done. There will be a doctor waiting for us, a man who has worked for the police for years. He is retired now, but only recently, and he was the best. He will meet us at his house. But we need a way of getting Carver there without attracting attention.'

'How about that?' said Grantham, nodding towards Larsson's giant Volvo. 'Lie him down in the back, there's plenty of room. The woman who came with Larsson, is she Carver's?'

'She has a relationship with him, yes,' said Ravnsborg. 'Her name is Madeleine Cross. She is American.'

'He gets around, that boy, I'll say that for him,' remarked Grantham. 'Come on then, let's go and have a word with Ms Cross.'

'No need,' said Morten. 'She is coming to us.'

Jack Grantham knew no more about the workings of the female mind than any other male. But he didn't need to be an expert to see that Madeleine Cross was one shocked, distraught and furious woman. She aimed for Ravnsborg, the only man of the three she recognized, and launched right in.

'What's the matter with you people? Where're the ambulances? I heard the sirens but they stopped and there are wounded men down there. They're going to die and you're just standing around doing nothing. What's going on here?'

Ravnsborg let her anger crash him like the waves against a cliff. Then he gently placed two huge hands on her shoulders and said, 'I understand your distress, Mrs Cross. But please, do not be concerned. Look, do you see the men near Mr Larsson?'

She turned to look back the way she had just come. Members of the anti-terrorist unit were placing Larsson on a stretcher. From beyond the main house came the sound of a helicopter engine.

'He is being airlifted to Oslo,' Ravnsborg continued. 'It is his best chance. We are getting Mr Carver treatment, too. And you, Mrs Cross, are going to help us. Come, let me explain . . .'

Ravnsborg led her away towards the Volvo. Grantham was just about to follow them when Morten grabbed his arm. 'Just a moment,' Morten said. He waited until the other two were out of earshot before he spoke again. 'Your plan is very clever, Mr Grantham, but you have forgotten one thing.'

'Really?' said Grantham with studied casualness. 'What might that be?'

'Larsson. Whether he lives or dies, he has to be explained. Armed personnel surround a building where a terrorist is hiding and not one of them is even scratched. But a civilian is killed while they all stand around doing nothing. How does that happen?'

Grantham chuckled condescendingly. 'Yes, I can see how that might be a problem . . . particularly for the man who commands those armed men. But don't worry, I think you'll find that Mr Larsson died a hero. He's some kind of weapons expert, as I recall. I dare say he was called in to defuse the booby-traps, something like that. Brilliant man, terrible loss, deeply missed, that's the big picture. I'll think of the details. Don't worry, Morten, that's what I do. Now, if you don't mind, I've got a Volvo to catch . . .'

Jack Grantham strode away towards the car. By the time he got there, Carver's unconscious body was already being lifted aboard.

73

'Is he dead?'

Maddy nodded. 'They switched off the life-support. I'm so sorry
. . . I just spoke to Karin. At least she saw him. That's something, I
guess.' Her eyes were red from crying, her cheeks still lined by the
tracks of mascara-stained tears. She swallowed, chewed her lip and
then said, 'She's pregnant with his baby. Ten weeks.'

'Oh God . . .'

Carver closed his eyes and his face slumped back down on to the
padded examination table on which he was lying.

'I'm sorry,' he said, his voice muffled. 'Dragging you into all this
. . . I had no idea . . .'

He was finding it hard to talk. He'd been drugged unconscious
twice in twelve hours and he couldn't clear the narcotic fog from his
brain. There were things he wanted to say to Maddy – explanations
at least, if not excuses – but the right words wouldn't come. There
was something else, too, something he had to do, but he couldn't
remember what.

His body was naked, and numb from the neck down with local

anaesthetics. A grey-haired doctor, glasses perched on the end of his nose, was working his way down Carver's back, buttocks and legs, repairing the damage wreaked by Tyzack's cane. He had been introduced to Carver as Dr Rolf Lyngstad. His wife Greta, a former nurse, was assisting him. The hundreds of stitches combined with the lines of the wounds to create a brutal cross-hatching over Carver's shredded skin.

Maddy glanced up at Lyngstad, who caught her eye and then very deliberately turned away, devoting his full attention to Carver's back. Whatever she was about to say, he was not going to hear it.

She crouched down by the end of the table until her head was level with Carver's. Quietly, but with fierce insistence, she said, 'Look at me. Look me in the eye.'

His head tilted up again.

Now her voice was somewhere between a whisper and a hiss. 'I know you kill people. The cops told me. Three guys last night. That's true, isn't it?'

He didn't deny it.

'But the sick bastard who did all this to you, who killed Thor, he's still out there.'

A fractional nod.

'And he's been planning . . . all this, right? He's been working on it a while. That British guy who knows you, Grantham . . .'

Carver's eyes widened: 'He's here?'

'Yeah. He told me about Damon Tyzack. He said it looked like he'd been setting you up, not just here, but other places. He said Dubai was one. And California. The sick bastard was in the States. And it made me think. That day at the hot-dog stand, the guy who creeped me out, that was him, wasn't it?'

'I don't know for sure.'

'But it might have been . . .'

Carver nodded again.

'He knows where I live. Doesn't he? He knows where I fucking live!'

'Yeah . . . I think so.'

'Was he there? When we were together?'

Carver didn't have to reply. The look on his face told her all she needed to know.

'Shit! That's just . . . I mean, what am I supposed to do now? Where am I supposed to go?'

'I'm sorry,' Carver repeated.

'Sorry? Oh, screw that. Sorry doesn't begin to cut it. No, I don't want you being sorry . . .' She knelt down in front of him again. 'I want you to kill him, Carver. Do you understand me? I want you to blow his sorry ass away. I want Damon Tyzack dead. I want him in pieces. I want to know that he's never coming back, that he can never find me, or hurt me. And if you can promise me that he's gone then maybe, just maybe, I might let you back in my life. Because right now, I wish I'd never met you.'

Carver looked at her, trying to see some sign of forgiveness or hope for him in her eyes. Maddy had rested one of her hands against the table to balance herself. He reached up to hold it, but she snatched it away.

'Just kill him,' Maddy said. Then she got up and walked out of the room without a backward glance.

Jack Grantham peered round Dr Lyngstad's back, screwing up his mouth in squeamish disgust. 'Your back,' he said, 'looks like a badly darned sock.'

'Piss off.'

'Oh dear, feeling sorry for ourselves, are we?' he said, getting closer to Carver while Lyngstad, not best pleased by the criticism of his handiwork, shot a venomous look over the top of his glasses. 'Woman trouble, I bet. I passed that American piece of yours in the hall and she didn't look too happy. I don't know . . . every time I ever meet you, there's some girlfriend or other giving you grief.'

'Has it ever occurred to you that you might be the reason why?' Carver asked. 'Telling her Tyzack had been in the States . . . Now she's convinced he'll be after her next, and she blames me.'

'You say that as though she's wrong. So, is she gone for good, you reckon?'

'As long as Tyzack is still around, she is.'

Grantham could not keep the smirk from spreading across his face.

'Jesus wept . . . That was what you wanted,' Carver snarled. Grantham had managed to irritate him as much as usual but there was one compensation: the anger was cutting through his brain like Drano down a blocked pipe.

'That's not quite fair,' said Grantham. 'I honestly thought she had a right to know that there was a possible threat to her safety. But yes, it did occur to me that there might be consequences. And I wasn't entirely unhappy about that because experience has taught me that if I want you to do something, well, let's just say you tend to need an incentive.'

'To get Tyzack?'

'Who else?'

'You don't think that the fact my best friend is dead because of Tyzack is enough of an incentive? Or that I might feel like killing him just for what he's done to me?'

'Yes, but I wanted to be absolutely sure.'

'I see. So where is he?'

'Ah, well . . .' A look that came as close as Grantham would ever get to embarrassment crossed his face. 'I was hoping he might have told you something about where he was heading next.'

Carver closed his eyes, forcing his mind back to the barn. And then it came to him, the warning he had to relay: 'No, I don't know where he is now. But I think I can tell you where he's going to be in two days' time. He'll be in Bristol. And he'll be trying to assassinate Lincoln Roberts.'

A look of incredulity crossed Grantham's face. 'He told you this, did he?'

'Not in so many words, no,' Carver admitted.

'So how, then?'

'He said he was going to do a job that would put him in a

different league. He also said it would be "the big one". He wouldn't be more specific than that, though I knew he was longing to tell me everything. He's trying to prove that he's better than me. In his mind that means taking out the world's number-one target. And that's always going to be the US President.'

Grantham shrugged. 'Not necessarily. Could be any number of people ... the Queen, the PM, bin Laden, the Pope. Could be a celebrity.'

'Yes, it could be,' said Carver, 'but Damon Tyzack has no reason to kill any of them. Let me ask you something: have they worked out who the target was last night?'

'Yeah, some German woman, name of Kreutzmann. She was a journalist, one of those campaigning types. The bomb was in her room.'

'And what does she campaign about?'

'People-trafficking,' said Grantham. 'Evidently she's against it.'

'Right, and that job Tyzack did in Dubai, the targets were a people-trafficker and a pimp. Maddy said you told her Tyzack had worked in the States. Who was the target?'

'Chap called Norton Krebs. He was some sort of financial consultant.'

'Oh yeah? Who did he consult for?'

'Well, some of his clients were pretty unsavoury.'

'Slave-traders?' asked Carver.

'I honestly don't know. But it's possible.'

'OK, let's forget about him. That still leaves Tyzack and the people who are paying for him up to their necks in the slave trade. Meanwhile President Roberts is flying into Britain to give a speech at a conference about slavery and people-trafficking. I don't know, maybe it's a coincidence. But if I'm wrong, I just look paranoid. If you're wrong, Tyzack takes a potshot at the President.'

'Point taken,' said Grantham. 'But suppose it is the President, all he's doing is giving a speech. Why would anyone need to kill him?'

'Depends what he's going to say.'

'Well, no one knows the answer to that,' said Grantham. 'The speech has been totally embargoed. The Yanks won't even tell Number Ten. It's really put the PM's knickers in a twist. He even wanted us to see if we could find out what was in the bloody thing. We had to tell his office that we'd love to oblige, but sadly we don't have any bugs in the White House and it's a bit short notice to try and turn one of his staff.'

'For you, perhaps,' said Carver. 'But maybe I can help.'

74

It had been mid-afternoon in Washington, DC when the bomb detonated at the King Haakon Hotel. It took diplomats from the local US embassy a couple of hours to establish that there had been nine US citizens listed among the hotel guests. None of them had suffered anything worse than mild shock, along with a few cuts and bruises, most of which had been acquired in the scrum as the hotel's occupants tried to leave the stricken building. The news was passed to relieved officials at both the State Department and White House, who could now relax knowing that there would be no domestic political repercussions from the incident and that media coverage would be limited. Sure, it was an outrage, but there were no signs of involvement by any known terrorist group. All the evidence suggested that this was a criminal attack, to be handled by local police. It wasn't headline news in Peoria.

So the aide who handed Harrison James a briefing document on the bombing did not think she was giving him anything of any great significance or sensitivity.

'We drafted a statement, right there on the top sheet,' she said.

'Fine,' said James, not bothering to look at it. He was up to his neck in final preparations for the President's trip to England.

The aide turned to leave. She had almost reached the door when James, as an afterthought, casually asked, 'They got any idea who did it yet?'

'No name,' she said. 'But the police released a photograph of a guy they said was wanted for questioning. They said he was armed and dangerous. Seems he killed some other folks, too, making his getaway.'

'Hope they catch him then,' said James.

A few minutes later, sighing with irritation, he told himself he'd better look at the damn briefing package before he took it into the President. The statement was fine, though he knew Roberts would add a flourish or two of his own. The information was pretty straightforward. James raised an eyebrow when he read the account of the gunfight on the opera house roof and the apparent disappearance of the hotel bomber. Then he turned a page and saw the shot the police had released. The copy in front of him had been taken from an internet download. The quality was poor. But Harrison James did not need high resolution to recognize that face.

Now the bombing had his attention.

He called Tord Bahr, from one private mobile phone to another, keeping the conversation off the White House and Secret Service logs.

'We have a situation,' he said. 'And I want you to make it go away.'

Plenty of men Harrison James had worked for swore by the principle of deniability. The less their subordinates told them, the safer they felt. Lincoln Roberts took a very different view. The first time they'd discussed working together, he'd told James, 'I don't see any excuse for ignorance. When there's something I need to know, tell me. And if I don't need to know it, well, tell me anyway.'

So James told his boss about the picture of Samuel Carver

holding the phone from which he'd triggered the Oslo bombing. Roberts didn't rant and rage. He didn't demand immediate action. He didn't blame anyone for risking his life with a mass-murderer. He sat at his desk, steepled his fingers and took a moment to reflect, like a university professor considering a philosophical proposition. The first word he said was: 'Interesting . . .' He thought some more and added, 'I guess there are two possibilities here. Either my ability to judge another man has totally broken down, or they got the wrong guy.'

'I'd say your judgement is pretty good.'

The President smiled. 'Yeah, that's what I'd say, too. But I could be wrong. And if anyone finds Carver, I'd sure feel better if it was us.'

Tord Bahr spent the night getting nowhere. Carver had disappeared. No one knew where he was. There were no satellite images, no communications intercepts, no leaks or leads from anyone, anywhere. He finally crashed out at three in the morning. At five he was woken by a call from his office and told that the Norwegians had just announced that the suspect in the Oslo bombing had died when cornered by police. Bahr sank back on to his pillow with his face wreathed in something perilously close to an actual smile. He wasn't bothered that the man's name had been given as Paul Jackson. A guy like Carver would have multiple aliases. All that mattered was that the face of the man the Norwegians were talking about was unmistakably his. If Carver was dead, he couldn't possibly cause any trouble to anyone. The big brown clouds that had threatened an almighty shitstorm had passed and the sun was shining on Tord Bahr's little world.

Bahr thought about trying to grab a couple of hours' more sleep, but it wasn't in his nature to take it easy. Instead he got up and went for a three-mile run. He showered, dressed and ate his customary bowl of granola and fruit. He got to work shortly before seven and spent an hour working on the final details of the President's trip, talking to his people in London and Bristol, and to the Brits with whom they were working, most of whom struck Bahr as pompous, arrogant, lazy and incompetent. Plus, the way they spoke, every last one of them sounded gay.

He had just put the phone down on some asshole police commander when he got a call on his cellphone.

'Tord Bahr?' said a British voice, one that sounded oddly familiar.

'This is he.'

'Hi, this is Samuel Carver.'

75

'I thought you were dead,' said Bahr. He sounded disappointed.

'That's the theory,' Carver replied. 'But here I am.'

'Pity, for a moment there my life just got a whole lot simpler. So, you want to tell me what the hell is going on?'

'Certainly. I'm trying to work out whether there's a highly trained psychopath trying to kill your boss. Wondered if you could help me with that.'·

Bahr had a short fuse at the best of times. These were not the best of times. 'Is this some kind of joke?' he snapped. 'Your famous British sense of humour? Listen, I got a lot of work to do. I don't have time for this shit.'

Carver took a deep breath and fought the urge to get angry right back at him. With studied calm he said, 'It's not shit. It's a legitimate threat, a man called Damon Tyzack. He served with me, briefly, in the SBS. He got sacked and blamed it on me. It was him who set up the Oslo bombing, tried to frame me for it. So yesterday me and Tyzack had a little chat, and shortly before he said goodbye he told me he had a job to do. I believe that job is the assassination of Lincoln Roberts.'

'Whoa! Hold up there. You say you had this guy and you let him leave? Are you frickin' nuts?'

'Well, I didn't have much choice in the matter. I was his captive, not the other way round.'

Tord Bahr yawned. With his free hand he tried to rub the sleep from his eyes.

'Wait a second,' he said. 'Run this by me from the top. This Tyzack is some kind of professional killer?'

'Correct,' said Carver.

'He had the same training as you?'

'Yes.'

'And you served together in the military?'

'That's right.'

'But he captured you, which tells me that he's better than you . . .'

'Yeah, that's what it tells him, too,' said Carver. 'Personally, I doubt it.'

'Kind of similar, aren't you? Like brothers or something.'

'I sincerely hope not. Listen, Bahr, Tyzack is a man you should take very seriously. Technically, he's very accomplished. Morally, he's sociopathic. That's a dangerous combination.'

'And you think that's unusual?' asked Bahr. 'My whole life is dealing with people like that.'

'So Tyzack's not unique. But you're about to go with the President to a conference on people-trafficking, and trafficking is what Damon Tyzack likes to do when he isn't killing people. So the question is: will the President do anything, or say anything in Bristol that would make him the next target?'

'Honestly, I don't know,' said Bahr. 'I'm not in the loop on the President's speaking plans. He's restricting the contents of his speech to an absolute need-to-know basis. And I don't need to know what he's going to say. I just need to keep him alive while he's saying it. So, tell me, what actual, concrete evidence do you have that Tyzack is planning a hit? And, if so, what is the target, date and location of the attack?'

'Concrete evidence? None,' said Carver. 'He just told me that he
was about to do a job and implied it was a big one.'

'And from that you figure it's Lincoln Roberts?'

Carver knew how feeble his warning sounded. He tried to make
it anyway: 'Look, I know it sounds crazy, but—'

'But nothing,' Bahr interrupted. 'You know how many threats we
are currently investigating against the President? I mean real, confirmed threats, with credible evidence of hostile intent? More than
six hundred a month, that's how many. We've got everyone from
the Aryan Nation to al-Qaeda under observation. Lincoln Roberts
is like a magnet for nut-jobs and we follow them all up, every last
one. Maybe your guy is dangerous. But I don't know, because you
have nothing to tell me beyond, "He said he was going to do something big." What am I supposed to do with that? You give me some
real facts, I'll take a look at them. But this kind of bullshit, forget
it. No use to me. So, Carver, enjoy your life. This conversation is
over.'

'Charming, isn't he?' said Jack Grantham, who'd been listening to
the conversation on the speakerphone.

Carver was still lying on his front on the examination table,
though the doctor had finished his handicraft. He reached out and
handed Grantham back his phone. 'Oh yeah, Bahr's a fun guy all
right,' he said.

'How did you get to be such great chums?'

'I helped him out with some security work. It didn't end well for
him. I was hoping he'd got over it. Apparently he hasn't. So now
what?'

'What's next,' said Grantham, 'is we go back to London and I
spend some time playing bureaucratic games in Whitehall, trying
to persuade people that even if the Yanks won't take the threat of
Damon Tyzack seriously, we should. I'll see if I can get this in front
of the Joint Intelligence Committee, point out it wouldn't do much
good to trans-Atlantic relations to have the US President killed on
British soil by a British assassin. There's an outside chance that

might scare the powers-that-be into action. Trouble is, unless I have something better to give them, they're liable to react the same way Bahr did. I mean, he wasn't exactly tactful, but one could see his point.'

'Well, there is one other possibility,' Carver said. 'If Tyzack persuaded Thor to work for him against me, maybe he involved him in the job he's about to do. I mean, that's what Thor does . . .' His voice trailed away.

'Did,' said Grantham, not unkindly.

Carver pulled himself together. 'Has anyone checked his laptop? He had everything on that. If he was working on something, that's where it'll be.'

'Ravnsborg already thought of that. He's brighter than he looks, that man. Anyway, his people went to Larsson's apartment. They found his computer, but it was protected by iris-recognition.'

Carver had a hard time getting the next question out. 'Couldn't they . . .' He sighed; tried again. 'Couldn't they remove his eyeballs and use them?'

Grantham shook his head. 'Apparently not. The system only works with living tissue. Besides which, Larsson's eyes were pretty badly damaged. Might not have worked anyway. They've got their boffins trying to hack into the computer. They're working on the phones, too.'

'Forget it,' Carver said. 'Whoever they've got, I guarantee they won't be as good as Thor. The guy was a bloody genius – a big, geeky, hippy . . .'

Grantham nervously placed a hand on an undamaged area of Carver's left shoulder. 'I'm sorry,' he said. 'I know he was your friend.'

'It's just . . . we never had the chance to talk, to put it right. He died thinking I hated him . . .'

Carver's voice drifted away. Grantham reached out his arm again, but Carver brushed it away impatiently.

'I'm not looking for sympathy,' he said. 'I'm trying to think. Larsson did say something, just before they put me under . . .

something about the sky . . . That's it, got it: "Look to the sky."'

'Is that all?' asked Grantham. '"Look to the sky"? You're sure there was nothing else?'

'No, that was it.'

'But that could mean anything. He could have meant something spiritual or religious. You know, look to the sky, to heaven, God, angels, all that kind of thing.'

'Thor Larsson didn't believe in God and angels.'

'It's amazing how dying can suddenly make someone start believing.'

'No,' said Carver, 'that wasn't the point of what Thor was saying. He was giving me a warning. He knew that something was going to happen. It's got to be Tyzack. Whatever it is he's doing, it's coming from the sky.'

76

Lara Dashian was living under siege. It had begun slowly in the first hours after Jake Tolland's piece appeared in the London *Times*. Local TV stations had asked for interviews with her and been turned down by Sadira Khan. So had the Dubai stringers for the major news agencies and international press. But then Jake Tolland arrived and said that he had been offered one hundred thousand English pounds to write a book about her story. He said he would share it fifty-fifty with her. Lara was not really interested in a book. She did not understand why anyone in England would want to know about her. But she had trusted Jake, and when he came to her offering to share his money that trust deepened. Her experience of men was that they wanted to abuse and exploit her. The notion that a man might treat her as an equal was far more exciting than any book.

Tolland promised he would keep the book project quiet. But someone took a photograph of Lara saying goodbye to him at the gate of the House of Freedom. When that hit the internet, along with a report of an upcoming book – now said to be worth half a million pounds – the reporters all came back. Once the first murmurings of Hollywood interest in her story began to surface, reporters started flying into Dubai from Britain, Europe and the States. Several prominent young actresses were said to be vying to play her. They knew that the part of a raped and abused prostitute rescued from hell and triumphing over her suffering had Best Actress Oscar written all over it. By the time that Jake Tolland's agent was unwise enough to get drunk at a launch party and boast that he was about to do a series of deals that would make both his client and Lara multi-millionaires, the House of Freedom had effectively become a prison, its inhabitants entirely blockaded on all sides by hordes of media, police and onlookers.

And then the delegation from the US embassy arrived.

The two women in their knee-length skirt suits were hustled into the refuge compound by a team of large men with black suits and buzz-cut heads. They kept their heads down and faces obscured. When they got into the courtyard they had to keep running, just to get out of range of the photographers up trees, on ladders or shooting from the roofs of nearby buildings. And then they had to get past Sadira Khan.

She stood opposite her two compatriots, hands on hips, watching them disdainfully as they brushed themselves down, straightened their clothes and checked their hair. 'You wanna say why you're here?' she asked.

One of the women came forward and held out a hand. 'Hi,' she said, 'My name's Renee Sorenson. I'm with the embassy in Abu Dhabi. This is Chantelle Clemens. She works with Harrison James. He's the White House Chief of Staff.'

'It's OK, hon, I know who he is. I'm still a registered voter. So let me guess, this is to do with Lara, right? Or did you come all this way to congratulate me on my selfless work for abused women?'

'Er, no, ma'am,' said Chantelle Clemens as she shook hands. 'We're here at the President's particular request. We'd like to speak to Miss Dashian.'

'The President, you say?'

'Yes, ma'am.'

'He gonna rescue us all from this madhouse?'

Clemens smiled. 'Anything's possible. But first, please, we really do have to talk to Miss Dashian.'

'You know I've turned down every single request since that story came out?'

'We heard, yes.'

'I'm trying to protect the kid, you understand? She's been through hell. She's still very fragile.'

'I understand, and so does the President,' said Clemens. 'You can rest assured that we are very aware of the suffering she has been through, and we respect that totally.'

While the women had been talking, the House of Freedom's inhabitants had been gathering in the background, whispering to one another, fascinated by these new arrivals in their home.

Sadira Khan turned and looked at the girls, who retreated a few paces. Some slipped back through doors into other rooms.

'It's all right,' she said, and the girls came a little bit closer again. 'Lara,' she went on. 'Come here, sweetheart.'

Two of the girls stood to one side to let Lara through. She stood still for a moment, sticking by her friends, examining the American women through her big, brown, bush-baby eyes. Then she looked at Sadira Khan seeking reassurance, found it and stepped forward.

Chantelle Clemens watched the slight, nervous figure step across the hall towards them. Was this really the sex-slave who'd been bought, sold and raped, the way the story claimed? In her cheap T-shirt and tracksuit bottoms she looked about fourteen.

The woman from the White House smiled as she said, 'Hi, Lara, my name's Chantelle.' She almost had to bite her lip to stop herself adding, 'So you're what all this fuss is about?'

77

Greta Lyngstad placed a large bowl of spaghetti covered in tomato sauce and Parmesan cheese in front of Carver and said, 'Eat. You need it.'

'Thanks,' said Carver and piled in. Greta wasn't the best cook in the world, but he didn't care. Almost eighteen hours had passed since he'd been rudely interrupted, halfway through his dinner, and not a morsel of food had crossed his lips since. He was famished.

They'd moved from the doctor's study into his dining-room. Carver was bandaged like an Egyptian mummy from his shoulders to his waist. There were padded dressings on his buttocks – Greta had tactfully left a soft cushion on the dining-chair just to make him more comfortable – and more bandages round his thighs. Grantham and Lyngstad were standing at the far end of the room, by a window that looked out over a small, well-tended garden.

'So, is he fit to go?' asked Grantham, nodding in Carver's direction. He did not seem bothered by the fact that Carver was sitting at the other end of the tables well able to hear every word that was said.

'I am afraid that I can only discuss my patient's condition with him,' Lyngstad replied. He had clearly not forgotten Grantham's description of his stitching and was not going to forgive him any time soon.

Grantham sighed irritably. 'Oh, for God's sake. You ask him, Carver.'

'Ask who what?' said Carver innocently.

'You know.'

'Dr Lyngstad,' said Carver, 'first may I thank you for taking such trouble to patch me up. It must have been very difficult work. I appreciate it.'

'You're welcome, Mr Carver,' said Lyngstad with a little nod.

'I was just wondering . . .'

'Yes?'

'How long do you think it will be before I can go back to work?'

'Hmm . . .' Lyngstad gave a contemplative sigh, relishing the impatience that was radiating from Grantham as obviously as the light from a bulb. 'That would depend on your job. For example, if you were a civil servant, in a government department, I would say that you should take at least one month, possibly more, to recuperate – on full pay, of course. On the other hand, if we were at war, and the enemy were at the gate, so to speak, then I would look at your wounds, vicious as they are, and say, "They're a long way from your heart."'

'You mean they won't kill me?'

'Quite so, Mr Carver. You will experience considerable pain and discomfort for some time. It could be many weeks before the wounds are properly healed and months, or even years, before the scars begin to fade, if they fade at all. But so long as you keep the wounds clean and bandaged and take painkillers when necessary, you are in no danger. You still have almost full mobility. Your senses are not impaired. No vital organs have been damaged. So if this were a war, and the situation was very serious, then I would send you back to the front line. And since I note both that you are in excellent physical condition and that your body bears clear signs of previous injuries, I should say that you are closer to a soldier than a civil servant.'

'So he is ready to go then,' said Grantham.

Lyngstad ignored him. 'Does that answer your question, Mr Carver?'

'Yes, thank you, doctor.'

'Right,' said Grantham. 'We're off. I've already had your bags collected from the hotel. No need to hang around.'

'No,' said Carver.

'What do you mean, no?'

'Exactly what I said. Mrs Lyngstad has made me this excellent bowl of pasta. I can't just leave it here uneaten, that would be rude. Besides, I'm starving. So first I finish the pasta. Then I go.'

'Well said, Mr Carver,' said Lyngstad.

Just then, Greta appeared in the doorway that led to the kitchen, holding a saucepan. 'I've got a little bit more if you'd like it,' she said.

78

On his flight to England, Damon Tyzack considered the whole issue of loose ends. So far they had been looking after themselves quite satisfactorily. He'd been tracking news-feeds during the drive into Denmark and had been delighted to learn that so far as the authorities were concerned, the Oslo bombing case was closed. Both Carver and Larsson were dead. The manner of their passing, however, disturbed Tyzack. The official account stated that Carver, who was referred to by his original name Paul Jackson, had died when surrounded by police at his hideout close to the Swedish border. The use of Carver's old name had niggled at Tyzack. He couldn't help wondering also how the police had found that hideout. An Oslo police spokeswoman had stated that they were alerted by members of the public walking in the area, but to a man of Tyzack's conspiratorial temperament, that account seemed too straightforward. There had to be more to it than that.

Even if there weren't, the very fact that he was worried told Tyzack something. He was operating much closer to the surface than ever before, straying uncomfortably into the public eye. It had begun with Jana Kreutzmann and her damned investigations into people-trafficking. Then there had been the whole business about Pablo the Pimpernel. He'd ordered Selsey to discredit Carver among his allies in MI6, and to send a message that Carver himself would see. But the whole thing had spiralled infuriatingly out of control. Lara Dashian was rapidly becoming the most famous whore in the world. People were talking about books and films about the grotty little tart. Unbelievably, the latest reports were even suggesting she might appear on the podium with Lincoln Roberts at his Bristol speech. That, Tyzack thought, would actually be doing him a favour. He could get them both at the same time.

That left Selsey. Tyzack was under no illusions at all about the MI6 officer's long-term reliability. If a man could betray one master, he could just as easily betray another. Of course Selsey did not know that Tyzack was his paymaster, but he knew enough to make it much easier for others to uncover connections that might make life very difficult indeed. In the meantime, buying Selsey's silence could well prove an expensive proposition and Tyzack never liked spending money when there was another, simpler option.

It might be necessary to deal with Selsey personally. And if he was going to do it, the sooner the better. Once the President had been hit, things might get a little hectic and he'd be wanting to lie low. He knew where Selsey lived. Tonight he'd pay a house call.

Bill Selsey wished for nothing more than the chance to go home. He wished he'd never gone down to meet that manipulative old bastard Percy Wake. He wished he'd never been seduced and deluded by the prospect of easy money and a cheap thrill. He wished he'd never harboured such childish resentments against Jack Grantham, and, even more, that he'd not been so stupid as to believe that he could outwit Grantham in a contest of wills and cunning. And he wished he'd never walked into Sir Mostyn Green's office and seen him sitting there with a face like thunder while Dame Agatha Bewley introduced herself and said,

'We've never met, but I feel as though I know so much about you.'

And now here he was, tied to a chair in a windowless basement while the man opposite him, with the soft face and the steely eyes, loosened his tie, took a drink of water and said, 'Right, Bill, let's go over this one more time. We found the money, all of it. You hadn't even moved it out of the account it had been paid into. I mean, I'm sorry, Bill, I know you were never out there in the field, but even so, that's bloody stupid, isn't it?'

Selsey gave a sad, beaten shrug. 'Maybe.'

'No, Bill, not maybe: certainly. There's no doubt at all you were bloody stupid. But what I want to know is, who put that money there? Eh? Who paid you all that lovely dosh?'

'I don't know,' Selsey pleaded. 'I swear I was never given a name.'

'Oh right, so the money just arrived, did it? Maybe the Easter Bunny put it there, is that what you think? Or the Tooth Fairy? Or Father fucking Christmas?'

The man got up and walked right up to Selsey's chair till he was looming over him.

'I don't like your attitude,' he said. 'You know what I think? I think you're taking the piss. I think you know, but you just don't want to tell me. So, one more time: the money, who gave you the money?'

'I really don't know,' whimpered Selsey. 'I don't . . . I don't . . .'

And then he started to cry.

79

Assistant Commissioner Peter Manners, commanding officer of the Metropolitan Police's Counter Terrorism Command, SO15, cleared his throat, the way a man does when he's about to state a position and wants the world to know it. 'No disrespect, Dame Agatha, but I have to say I take the same view as Tord Bahr. I've got a lot of time for the man, he's bloody good at what he does, and I can assure you that we have been working with his people to ensure that there are no loopholes, no weak spots, no opportunities for anyone to make an attempt on the President's life. It's a responsibility we all take very, very seriously.'

'I know you do,' said Dame Agatha Bewley in a conciliatory tone that was almost maternal, as if she were settling a fight between argumentative children. 'But I must say I'm surprised Bahr refused to pay any attention to what Mr Carver told him. After all, it doesn't hurt to take precautions, no matter how implausible a threat might be.'

'It's a personal thing,' said Carver. 'We had a run-in recently. I made him look stupid in front of his boss. He'll never admit I could be right again.'

'His boss . . . really?' asked Dame Agatha, her eyebrows arching as she leaned forward on her desk and looked at Carver over the top of her reading glasses. 'Might one ask . . . ?'

'Afraid not,' said Carver. 'Confidential. But you can take it that I'm personally familiar with the President's security arrangements. And I want to keep him alive. That's also personal.'

'I try not to get personal myself,' said Manners. 'I look at this professionally, and I'd ask a simple question: suppose Bahr believed you, Carver, how would that change anything? He's already done everything he can. Unless he has specific information to go on, what else is there?'

'He could keep an eye out for Damon Tyzack.'

'Don't worry, we'll be doing that. Crowd control and observation is a police responsibility and I've already entered every available picture of Tyzack into the facial-recognition software we'll be using for the event. If he's there, we'll spot him. You seem amused, Carver, why's that?'

'I'm not a big believer in facial-recognition programs. They're too unreliable, too many ways to throw them off, particularly when you're working in real time. In the lab, after the event, yes, then you might get something you can use. But live, well, I'd back myself to get past any system that I know of, and Tyzack will too.'

'Maybe we have systems you don't know about.'

'Try me.'

'That's enough!' Dame Agatha's voice cut through the verbal wrist-wrestling match. Mother was losing her patience. 'I find this pointless male need to compete deeply, deeply tedious. It is my judgement, which is shared by the Home Secretary, that we need to consider Mr Carver's information seriously. And I would add that both I and Mr Grantham have reason to respect Mr Carver's professional abilities, if not always his tact. Let us assume, for now, that we are facing a threat from a former member of the special forces whose personality is amoral, cunning and utterly ruthless. Let us also suppose that he may be making some form of airborne attack. So, Assistant Commissioner, perhaps you would be good enough to talk us through the existing precautions, before we move on to anything else?'

'Certainly,' said Manners, getting to his feet. A 50-inch screen was fixed to the wall at one end of the room, linked to a laptop. Manners bent over the keyboard and aerial images of south-west England, followed by central Bristol, appeared on the screen. Just as Tyzack had done when talking to Arjan Visar, he described the journey that would bring Lincoln Roberts on Air Force One to RAF Fairford and then on by helicopter to College Green. Then he turned his attention to the presidential motorcade.

'Basically it's a combination of British and US vehicles and personnel,' he began. 'In the lead we have armed motorcycle out-riders from the Royalty and Diplomatic Protection Department. They're followed by three cars containing our officers from SO15, running in front of and to either side of Cadillac Two, which is one of the presidential limousines. The Chief of Staff will ride in that, along with the Emergency Satchel. Inside the satchel is everything the President needs to order the launch of a nuclear war, so we try to keep it safe.'

'So I should hope,' muttered Jack Grantham, who had remained silent during Manners's argument with Carver, preferring to enjoy it as a form of spectator sport.

Manners chose to take the remark as a joke and gave a forced chuckle. 'Absolutely! Wouldn't want to lose that. So . . . There then follow several more escort vehicles, split between SO15 and the US Secret Service. Their occupants are very heavily armed, and trained in close-quarters combat. With the greatest of respect to Mr Carver and Mr Tyzack, they are capable of taking down any conceivable ground-attack short of a full-scale military assault. Anyway, these escorts drive fore and aft of Cadillac One, in which Mr Roberts will be riding. There will also be a number of minibuses filled with White House staff and members of the press, all vetted in advance, of course.

'I have to say that the only form of attack that I can envisage having any sort of success against this motorcade would be some kind of guided missile, though it would have to be very powerful indeed. Cadillac One is as well armoured as a Challenger battle tank. Serious question, Carver: does Tyzack have access to that kind of ordnance?'

'I doubt it,' said Carver. 'And I don't see him going for a missile, even if he could get one. Whatever he does, he'll want to be there. This is about him as much as the President.' Carver gave a wry chuckle. 'With Damon Tyzack it's always personal.'

This time Manners's smile was genuine. 'Well, in that case, he'll be looking for an opportunity at the speech itself.'

He put another image up on the screen. 'This is Broad Quay. They're putting the stage at the waterside, here, facing inland, with the President's back to the water. As you can see, there are a number of newly completed or renovated towers along the right-hand, eastern side of the quay. These contain offices, hotels or residential properties. All will be repeatedly searched in the run-up to the speech. All rooms with windows giving a clear line of sight to the stage will be emptied and secured. All roofs will be occupied by our people and/or US Secret Service. Aside from that, the site comprises an open expanse where the crowd will gather, with wide roads on either side, running back several hundred metres, wider by the stage, but narrowing the further it gets inland. On the west side of the quay, that's the left as you look at it, there's nothing but low buildings all the way back, very few of which have flat roofs. So there are virtually no potential shooting positions, even if any would-be assassin could get in those buildings in the first place. And we will be making sure that he can't.'

'How about underground access to the site?' asked Carver.

'All checked, rechecked, guarded and sealed,' said Manners. 'Every sewer, every drain. The rats must be wondering what hit them. So, to continue . . . Once the President arrives, all the close guarding work will be handled by his Secret Service personnel. Our efforts will be concentrated on the crowd. We're planning body, bag and shoe searches, very much like airport security, with walk-through scanners, explosives dogs and extensive video monitoring of the crowd. And don't worry, Mr Carver. We'll be relying on good old-fashioned human observation as well as fancy technology, and we'll be watching out for troublemakers, known terrorists, anyone who even scratches their arse in a suspicious manner. And just in case anyone does get a gun past security, and makes it somewhere near the stage, the President's autocue will be a reinforced, bullet-proof shield. As I say, we're taking this very seriously indeed.'

80

Damon Tyzack was a man for whom the phrase, 'I know where you live,' was more than a figure of speech. He had long known exactly where Bill Selsey went at the end of a working day. Now he was also certain that Selsey had been blown. All the more reason, then, to dispose of him as soon as possible.

One of Tyzack's men, Ron Geary, had trailed Selsey from the moment he stepped on to the street outside the MI6 headquarters at Vauxhall Cross, obeyed the signals that took him across several lanes of rush-hour traffic and stepped up to the platform at Vauxhall railway station, where he took a train to the terminus at Waterloo. There he made the five-minute walk across to the suburban services at Waterloo East, spent ten minutes browsing magazines at a WHSmith bookstall and buying a cup of Earl Grey tea before getting on his regular evening train to Lee in the south-east suburbs of London.

Like most of Tyzack's more reliable employees, Geary was a Special Forces veteran. He was therefore well able to spot the tail that MI6 had put on Selsey and make sure that he was not spotted himself. Along the way, he sent pictures of both MI6 officers from his phone to Tyzack, who was being driven south in the back of a white Ford Transit van, as anonymous a form of transport as the roads of Britain provide.

Geary stayed on the train, handing over the surveillance to another one of Tyzack's people, who picked up Selsey as he came out of Lee station and turned right on to Burnt Ash Road. Neither Selsey nor his MI6 tail noticed the harassed-looking woman smoking a cigarette and pushing a baby-carriage who followed them along the busy commuter route, still laden with the last dregs of evening traffic trying to get on to the South Circular.

Her name was Raifa Ademovic. She had arrived in Britain five years earlier as an illegal immigrant, imported by Tyzack just as he was establishing his own trafficking network. With her greasy hair, prominent nose and almost permanent scowl, Raifa was never going to be of much value in the brothel to which she was first shipped. But the remarkable number of credit cards, banknotes, driving licences and wallets that she managed to lift from her paltry clients suggested that she might have other, exploitable talents. When she reacted to a john who tried to give her a playful smack by punching, clawing and biting him into the nearest A&E department that impression was confirmed. Tyzack had been making good use of her bad attitude ever since.

Raifa turned into the side road on which Selsey lived and watched as he approached and entered his semi-detached home. With a sullen defiance typical of her character, she stopped directly opposite the house, in full view of anyone inside it, or standing guard outside. She walked round to the front of the baby-carriage and briefly made encouraging noises at the small child – borrowed from a friend – who sat there, doped to the gills with motion-sickness tablets. Then she lit another cigarette, turned her back on the captive toddler and dialled a number on her mobile phone. In the genteel, middle-class area where Selsey lived, plenty of respectable citizens might disapprove of such blatantly bad mothering, but none would suspect her true purpose.

'He is in house now,' she told Tyzack. 'I see three other men. One following Selsey, he go inside house with him. Another man, he meet them at door, stay in house also. Final man in car outside. He watch Selsey go by, raise hand to say hello to man following, then make call. I guess he tell boss, OK, they get here.'

'Are they armed?' Tyzack asked.

'Man following Selsey, he carrying gun for sure. Other two, I could not see. But if they trying to protect him, why not carry gun?'

'Why not, indeed. Thank you, my dear. I really don't know what I would do without you, even though you really are quite remarkably unattractive.'

Raifa spat on the ground, loud enough for Tyzack to hear the hawk. 'Hey, fuck you too!' she said, and then hung up.

In his Transit van, now circling London on the M25, Tyzack laughed. There were very few people in the world he would ever allow to be so rude to him. But there was something so relentlessly unpleasant about Raifa Ademovic that he found himself admiring her more than any other woman he knew. There was none of that cringing desire to please that oozed from so many females, not the remotest attempt at seduction, just an unbending hostility. That, thought Damon Tyzack, is my kind of woman.

81

'Thank you, Assistant Commissioner,' said Dame Agatha, who was both the host and chairperson of the meeting called to discuss the appropriate response to Tyzack and the potential threat he posed to the President's life. 'I think we can all agree that every possible precaution is being taken. Rear-Admiral Johnstone?'

Manners stepped back from the screen and his place was taken by a short, stocky man in naval uniform, his rank denoted by the thick golden band around the wrist of his dark blue uniform jacket, topped by a thinner, looped band. He stood with his feet apart, as if Dame Agatha's office on the top floor of Thames House, an office building on the north bank of the river Thames, might at any moment be hit by a rogue wave or sudden squall.

'I'll be dealing with the joint Navy–RAF response to this new threat of air attack,' he said in a calm, reassuring Scots accent. 'Essentially, we will be stepping up the level of protection that was already in place. Eurofighter Typhoon jets from 3 (Fighter) Squadron, based at Coningsby in Lincolnshire, are ready at all times to scramble within three minutes as part of their Quick

Reaction Alert capability. The original plan was thus to keep them on the ground, awaiting the order to scramble. Three Typhoons will now be patrolling the airspace above and around Bristol before, during and immediately after the President's speech.'

A soft smile crossed his ruddy, square-jawed face. 'We have assured the Americans that the Typhoons will be close enough to protect Mr Roberts, but not so close as to drown out his voice.'

As a gentle murmur of amusement rippled around the room, Johnstone continued, 'We will be telling the media about the RAF presence over Bristol. We think it will make for a good wee story. It will also distract them from the Navy's contribution. I don't know how many of you are familiar with the Type 45 destroyer. This is the first of them, HMS *Daring*. She's a very rare lassie. We originally ordered twelve Type 45s. That order was cut to six, for financial reasons. And now, in the current climate, we'll be lucky to see three. But she's a very splendid lassie, too, for all that.'

A picture appeared of a long, low hull topped by a series of huge triangular towers.

'Looks like a bloody great grey Toblerone,' mused Grantham.

'Aye, she's not the prettiest of craft,' Johnstone admitted. 'But she's clever enough. Her radar can track more than a thousand targets at once and her missile systems are so accurate and so fast that they can detect and destroy a projectile the size of a cricket ball travelling at three times the speed of sound.'

Carver gave a low whistle. 'So they could detect a man in freefall, then?' he asked.

'Och aye, no trouble.'

'Ouch!' Carver winced, thinking of that night above Currituck Sound.

'Do you think Tyzack might attempt some kind of parachute jump?' asked Manners.

'Something like that. But it seems he'd be ill advised.'

'Aye,' said Johnstone with gentle relish. 'That he would. And if he tries he'll get a very nasty surprise.'

'Which leaves us with Mr Tyzack himself,' said Dame Agatha.

'Jack, perhaps you would bring us up to date on efforts to find him?'

Carver could see Manners frown. Grantham was an MI6 man. Domestic security was not his business. That was strictly an MI5/police affair.

Grantham saw his reaction. 'I appreciate my involvement here is unusual,' he said. 'But we've been tracking Tyzack's movements for some time, although, while we were doing so, we were not aware of his identity.'

'How do you mean?' asked Manners, sensing that Grantham was trying to avoid going into details, and determined not to let him off the hook.

'Tyzack carried out a series of assassinations, the most recent of them in Oslo, the night before last. On each occasion he did so in such a way as to frame Carver for the killings. He was able to do this because he had subverted one of my officers, whom he used to pass on misleading information, designed to focus our attention, and that of local police forces, on Carver. The officer in question has, however, been apprehended and has spent the day in interrogation. Ironically, he is unaware of Tyzack's identity. He was recruited through an intermediary and although he spoke to Tyzack, never met him.'

'So what have you done with your officer?' asked Dame Agatha, nothing in her voice betraying her involvement in Selsey's capture.

'He's been sent home,' said Grantham.

'What?' Manners gasped incredulously. 'You just let him go?'

'No,' said Grantham. 'We used him as a staked goat to catch a tiger. It's just possible Tyzack may try to contact him. We will be monitoring all communications, and have officers outside and inside the house. If Tyzack calls, we will pin down his location. And if he goes near the property, then we aim to get him in person.'

There was a clock on the wall of the office. It gave the time as a little after nine in the evening. Carver glanced up at it, and then asked Grantham, 'What time did you send your man home?'

'About ninety minutes ago,' Grantham replied.

'And you're sure he's still alive?'

'He certainly was when he arrived home.'

'Well, I hope he still is now,' said Carver. 'But I wouldn't count on it.'

'I told you,' said Grantham, 'I've got people covering the property, inside and out.'

'I'm sorry, didn't you hear what I said about Tyzack?' Carver asked, getting to his feet. He nodded towards the desk: 'Dame Agatha, gentleman, it's been a pleasure, but we've got to get going.'

He paused and looked at Grantham, who was still rooted to his chair. 'Or don't you want your traitor to live?'

82

There were thousands of cars all over south London that looked just like the ten-year-old Vauxhall Corsa parked across from Selsey's house, a little way down the road. Its body was bulked up by body panels and flared arches intended to give a small, harmless car the appearance of a serious muscle machine, as if it had been given a course of fibre-glass steroids. The windows were blacked out, and the muffler had been removed from the exhaust in an attempt to give the engine an intimidating roar, over which the thumping bass of the oversized sound system could clearly be heard.

There were countless men who looked just like the one who got out of the car and leaned against the bonnet, drinking from a can of Stella. The close-cropped hair, Fred Perry shirt, faded jeans, chunky gold jewellery and extravagant tattoos weren't exactly an original style statement.

From the bedroom window of Bill Selsey's house, the man could clearly be seen as he finished his beer, threw it into the gutter and reached into the car for another can.

'What's he doing there?' asked one of the men observing him.

'Dunno. Think it's worth going down and having a word?'

'Not yet. No need to draw attention to ourselves unless it's absolutely necessary.'

'Oh, hang on, I think we just got our answer.'

'Bloody hell, that's a terrifying sight.'

Raifa Ademovic was walking down the road. The baby-carriage was gone and she'd changed since her last appearance. Her hair had been pulled into a tight pony-tail, a proper Croydon face-lift. Her face was adorned with heavy scarlet lipstick, false eyelashes and dangling gipsy earrings and her body was clad in a stretchy black nylon boob tube, a microscopic leopardskin mini-skirt and teetering white plastic heels.

'No wonder the poor bastard needs a couple of beers first,' the MI6 officer went on as Raifa reached Ron Geary, who did not bother to get up off the bonnet to greet her. She threw her fag-end on the pavement and ground it under her shoe. He chucked his can away. She leaned over him and they kissed. He groped her backside. Then they disappeared into the car.

'And people say romance is dead.'

'You know, that was the bird who walked by earlier with the pram,' said the other officer.

'So she's left one brat and gone out to make another. That's nice.'

'Not necessarily. She could be an au pair.'

'Illegal, I bet.'

'Either way she'll be living off benefits. Him too, most likely.'

The car started rocking.

'Our taxes are paying for that.'

'I know, makes you sick.'

Inside the car Raifa Ademovic was sitting in the passenger seat, her legs pressed against the floor, pushing back and forth to make the car move. Between pushes, she leaned forward and spat the taste of Geary's lager out of her mouth. If it had been any other woman gobbing in his motor, Geary might have given her a slap, but he knew better than to get into a fight with that mad Bosnian bitch. He also had a job to do. He got on the phone to Tyzack.

'No movement, boss. They're all still in there. What d'you want us to do?'

'Give the lovely Raifa a good seeing-to, why don't you?' Tyzack replied mockingly. 'But be quick about it. I'm on my way.'

Bill Selsey was having dinner with his wife, sitting at the kitchen table. His desperate attempts to make conversation had come to nothing. Now they were left in silence, just the scraping of the cutlery against a china plate as Carolyn Selsey pushed her food around, trying to work up the appetite to put some of it in her mouth. She managed a couple of desultory mouthfuls before she gave up the struggle. Then she looked at the stranger sitting in the chair where the husband she'd thought she knew once used to sit and asked, 'What have you done?' And then again, her voice half stifled by unshed tears: 'What have you done?'

'For Chrissakes, don't you have a siren or something?'

Carver was humming with frustrated energy, grateful of the seat-belt that kept him pinned down and stopped him bouncing off the walls of Jack Grantham's Jag. They were trying to cut south-east across London, but every short burst of progress was brought to a grinding halt by a jam at a set of lights, a bus taking an age to set down and pick up its passengers, or any one of the countless delays and obstructions a crowded city can provide.

'No, I don't,' Grantham replied. 'See, we're meant to be the Secret Service. That means we don't want people to know we're around. Sirens, flashing lights – that would pretty much wreck it, don't you think?'

'Ha-bloody-ha . . . He's coming. I know he is . . .' Carver screwed up his face. 'Bloody hell, my back hurts.' He shuffled in his seat trying to find a comfortable position.

'Take a couple of painkillers, maybe they'll calm you down.'

'You got any guns in this car?'

'One. Mine.'

'Can I have it?'

'Piss off.'

Carver leaned forward, peering through the traffic as though he could will a path through the wall of vehicles. 'Come on,' he said. 'Come on . . .'

Damon Tyzack had made quick progress round London on the M25 and was now on the A2, coming back into the city, heading for Lee station and the Selseys' house. He put in a call to Ron Geary. 'Any developments?'

'No, boss. No one's gone in or out.'

Tyzack laughed. 'Oh dear, did Raifa say no?'

'No, boss, I meant the house.'

'Oh for God's sake, Geary, where's your sense of humour?' Tyzack sighed and ended the call.

His driver leaned back, half turned his head and spoke over his shoulder. 'So Ron didn't get any joy, then?' He cackled with laughter.

'I'm not sure I'd describe an act of sexual congress with Raifa Ademovic as joyous, exactly,' Tyzack dryly observed.

'Yeah, know what you mean. She's a fucking loony, that woman.'

'Precisely . . . That's what I like about her.' Tyzack put on a baseball cap and pushed the peak down over his face to hide it from any traffic cameras. 'Pull up, the next chance you get,' he said. 'We'll be there soon. I want to move up front.'

He got back on the line to Geary. 'Check your weapons, and be ready to move on my signal. Won't be long now.'

Then he took out his own gun and racked the slide. He had a round in the chamber. He was ready to go.

From the house the watchers saw the front window of the Corsa descend a fraction. A red-nailed hand appeared and threw out a cigarette, and then the window closed again.

'That's the bloody limit, the post-coital ciggy . . . I could bloody use a cigarette myself.'

'You can't, it's illegal.'

'What?'

'We're working, right? So this house is now a place of work. That means no one can smoke here. Not even Selsey.'

'Sod him, it's me I'm thinking about.'

'Well, the law says you can't smoke.'

'And this is the country I risk my life to defend . . . unbelievable.'

Just past New Cross, with darkness finally falling at the end of the long summer evening, the traffic began to thin. A new spirit of urgency seemed to get into Grantham and he started driving more aggressively, flashing his lights at the oncoming traffic as he raced down the wrong lane, overtaking anyone who looked likely to impede him. He ran a red light. He cut up a truck on a roundabout, earning a blast of the trucker's horn and a V-sign out of the cab.

'That's more like it,' said Carver.

Grantham was doing close to sixty as he raced down Lee High Road, slowed briefly to turn right, across the oncoming traffic, into Burnt Ash Road, then hit the gas again.

Three blocks down, Grantham swung right again, ignoring the white Transit van waiting to turn into the same side road and getting an angry flash of the Transit's beams in his face, briefly dazzling him. The Jag screeched to a halt by Selsey's house. Grantham and Carver got out.

Grantham walked up to another parked car, a Ford Mondeo, and leaned down by the window to talk to the MI6 officer inside. Carver stayed where he was and looked up and down the road. As he did, the white van came towards him, slowed briefly opposite the house, then sped up again and moved away down the street. Carver watched it go. Something nagged at him, an instinct that told him Tyzack had been in the van.

'Grantham!' he shouted. 'Give me your keys!'

Grantham looked up from the Mondeo. 'Why?'

'That van! Tyzack was in it. I'm sure.'

Grantham stood up, shaking his head. He looked at Carver and started walking back towards him, just as the lights on the Corsa came on, its engine started and it too pulled out into the road and drove away.

'This is getting out of hand,' Grantham said when he'd reached Carver. 'You're jumping at shadows.' There was something close to sympathy in his voice as he went on, 'Look, I understand. You've had a hell of a time and he's given you a proper beating. I'm not surprised you're traumatized, but you've got to calm down. There's been no communication between Tyzack and Selsey and nothing's happened apart from a couple of chavs having a shag in a parked car.'

Grantham put a hand on Carver's shoulder and looked him in the eye. 'Tell me, honestly, are you sure about this whole US President business? Because I've gone a long way out on a limb for you and I don't want it cut out from under me.'

Carver closed his eyes. For a second he felt almost overcome by a wave of exhaustion. Maybe Grantham was right.

No . . . he wasn't going to give in now. He hadn't imagined what Tyzack had said, and he knew, in his bones, what it meant.

'Don't worry,' Carver said. 'I'm fine. And I'm right about Tyzack. I'm sure of it.'

'All right, I believe you. But I still don't think you're doing anyone any good charging round London chasing paranoid delusions. I'm going to check in with the people here, make sure everything's good, then I'm taking you back into town. We'll get you a hotel room. And then I want you to rest. The President lands in approximately thirty-six hours and I need you fighting fit by then.'

It was only a couple of hours later, as he was lying in bed, on the cusp between wakefulness and sleep, that an image flashed into Carver's head. It was the man in the passenger seat of the white van, driving past Selsey's house. He'd been looking into his glove compartment, so Carver hadn't seen his face. But he had seen the cap and he'd recognized the badge: the New York Yankees. He'd seen the same badge, the same cap somewhere else: outside the hot-dog stand in Cascade, Idaho . . . the creep who'd walked across to chat up Maddy.

Carver opened his eyes and looked up at the ceiling as he whispered two words to himself: 'Damon Tyzack.'

83

Chantelle Clemens let Jake Tolland know exactly where he stood and she didn't mince her words. 'I just want you to know, if it were down to me, you wouldn't be getting on this plane,' she said as they stood at the foot of the steps that led up to the US Air Force C-37A Gulfstream jet that would be taking them to England. 'The only reason you're here is because Miss Dashian made a personal request for you to accompany her. Seems the one person in the whole Western world that this young woman trusts is a journalist. Guess that shows how much she's got to learn.'

She glared at Tolland, just daring him to deny it. Young as he was, he had the good sense to stay silent. Clemens went, 'Humph!' and then returned to reading the riot act. 'Here's the deal. You do not, repeat not, have any press privileges on this flight, nor at any time leading up to the President's speech. Everything that happens stays private, and I mean a total embargo. One word gets out before the speech, you're out on your skinny white ass and I don't care what Missy says. You hear me?'

'Absolutely. My lips are sealed. But how about after all this is over, can I write about it then?'

Clemens looked at him as if he'd just broken wind. 'Maybe,' she conceded. 'No promises at all, but maybe. And only after you have received explicit clearance from the Chief of Staff's office. Now get aboard the damn plane before I change my mind.'

Tolland ran up the steps, followed more sedately by Clemens. As she reached the cabin he was already strapping himself into a set facing backwards, directly opposite Lara, who was smiling at him in a way that made her whole face light up. Suddenly she seemed a totally different creature to the shy, suspicious, obviously traumatized girl who had shuffled across the front hall at the House of Freedom.

Oh my Lord, thought Chantelle Clemens. I do believe that crazy child is sweet on the boy. She sighed, shook her head in wonderment at the resilience and optimism of youth, and made her way to her seat. Then she summoned the steward and said, 'You can tell the captain we're ready to go.'

Lara was flown into Fairford airbase well before dawn and shown to a guest suite. Someone told her they'd give her a few hours to rest, but Lara was so filled with a mixture of nervousness, excitement and sheer confusion at the dizzying pace of events that she lay wide awake until someone knocked on the door to take her to breakfast.

She'd been smuggled out of the House of Freedom with a blanket over her head and the only photographs of her that had reached the media were some blurry old family snaps, touted by the same aunt who had sold her into slavery. Yet somehow all the people in their military uniforms, going about their work or lining up for food, seemed to know who she was, and they greeted her as someone special, even precious.

Lara had been used by plenty of Americans in Dubai, and she couldn't understand how those crude, drunken oafs could have been produced by the same nation as the impeccably neat and sober Air Force personnel who were now smiling at her, shaking her hand and calling her 'ma'am'. They told her what a privilege it was to be taking care of her. They insisted that she should let them show her round the base. They even helped her choose what to eat when she was overcome by the sheer profusion of choices on display.

She found herself looking round every so often, just to make sure that Jake was still close by. He would give her hand a little squeeze and that would be enough to make her feel safe until the next time she was overwhelmed by it all. In the meantime, she was happy to let Chantelle Clemens tell her what to do now, what would happen tomorrow and what her role in proceedings would be.

'You'll meet the President when he arrives here and you'll travel with him to Bristol,' Lara was told. Clemens must have seen the look of alarm on her face because she added, 'Don't you worry yourself about Mr Roberts. He's a good, kind man, and he's got kids about your age. He'll make you feel right at ease.'

Lara nodded, saying nothing as Clemens continued, 'When we get to Bristol, I'll be there to look after you and show you where to go, OK? Good. Now, you'll be introduced onstage during the President's speech. We wrote some words for you to say, if you think you can manage that. But if you can't that's fine. Take a look, why don't you? I've got them here.'

Clemens handed Lara a sheet of paper. 'What do you think?'

Lara read aloud, speaking quietly: 'My name is Lara Dashian. I was taken from my country, Armenia, against my will. I was bought and sold. I was made to do terrible things. If I did not do what my owners wanted, I was beaten.'

She stopped for a moment, unable to go any further.

'Take your time,' Clemens said.

Lara nodded, took a deep breath to compose herself and continued. 'But I was lucky, I was rescued. Many other girls, just like me, are not so lucky. They are still slaves. Please, I beg you, do everything in your power to help rescue them.'

She fell silent, the arm holding the sheet of paper loose at her side, her head down, biting her lip.

'Please excuse me,' Lara said. She walked a few paces away and then slumped down against a wall. She ended up on the floor, with her head in her hands.

Clemens gave the girl time, then went over to her, crouched down on her haunches and put a hand on her shoulder. 'Are you all right?' she asked.

Lara nodded.

The two of them stayed silent and motionless for a few seconds, then Lara looked at Chantelle Clemens and said, 'I will say those words. For the other girls, the ones who are not so lucky, I must say those words.'

84

Damon Tyzack heard the explosive crack echo around the rolling Cotswold landscape and watched as a puff of orange smoke billowed up into the air. He cursed under his breath. The dummy explosion had detonated on a patch of grass at least ten yards from its target, a crude structure built from scaffolding, planks and hay bales. It stood at one end of a field far from any public roads at the heart of an estate in Gloucestershire owned – via a complex series of intermediaries – by the Russian mafia leader Naum Titov. The loan of his field was Titov's contribution to the death of Lincoln Roberts. To Damon Tyzack, however, the simultaneous removal of Lara Dashian was at least as important an objective.

He spoke into a walkie-talkie. 'Let's do that again. This time I want more height at the point of release, and a longer delay on the fuses. See if that achieves the desired result.'

Tyzack had been hard at work for several hours, calibrating his equipment and checking that the combination of stolen goods, back-street engineering and software mailed in from the far side of the Atlantic could do the job for which it was intended. Not yet, was the answer. But it would, even if he had to stand in that damn field all night. The only weapon he would be taking into the kill-zone tomorrow would be the iPhone on which Bobby Kula's custom application was installed. He watched the screen one more time, hit a button, waited a few seconds . . . Crack! This time the smoke rose from a point just beneath the foot of the stage. They were getting closer.

'And again,' he said into his handset.

As he waited for the next run, Tyzack thought about the events of the previous night. He had to admit, he'd got a hell of a shock when he'd looked through the Transit's windscreen and seen Samuel bloody Carver getting out of a Jag thirty yards up the road. The man was supposed to be dead. What in God's name was he doing alive and well outside Bill Selsey's house?

Tyzack had ducked his head just in time, thanking his lucky stars that his face was partially hidden by his cap. Carver's arrival had significantly altered the odds and made the attack on Selsey un-acceptably risky. If that was all he had to do, Tyzack might have gone ahead, just to take on Carver and put him down for good. But with so much else at stake, that was one pleasure he would have to deny himself, for now at least. He'd shouted at his driver to keep going, then told Geary to abort the mission.

And it had not been an entirely wasted effort. Tyzack now knew a lot more than he had before. MI6 had obviously not only broken Selsey, they had also used him as bait. Selsey did not know who had hired him, but Carver would have worked it out in an instant. Tyzack went over what he had told Carver about the Roberts hit. No name had been mentioned, but he'd certainly given enough clues. He'd wanted Carver to work it out and be tortured by the thought that there was nothing he could do to stop it.

That had been a mistake, Tyzack had to admit. But again, he had learned something, too. They were expecting him. That was useful to know. Especially since there was absolutely nothing that anyone could do to stop him.

*

About thirty miles to the south-west, a slender blue-grey and black XSR48 speedboat was cruising at a fraction of its potential 100-mph top speed upstream along the river Avon. Its destination was a berth on a pontoon at a boatyard located off The Grove in Bristol. The man at the controls had no idea why he was making the delivery. That was none of his business. His orders were to get the boat to where it was meant to be, make sure it was refuelled and ready to go, then take a cab to Bristol Temple Meads station and get on the first train to London. He carried those orders out to the letter.

In Bradford, Foster Lafferty, sitting in a Bangladeshi curry house on his interracial diplomacy mission, was equally clueless as to what any of it was about. Not long ago Tyzack had wanted him to teach the Pakistani gangs a lesson. Now he was supposed to offer the same men a hundred grand just to do Tyzack a favour. Lafferty had never known the boss let anyone off the hook like that before. But he'd been around a long time, and both his instincts and his experience taught him that the best thing to do was say, 'Yes, sir,' and leave the thinking to the high-ups. When the deal was finally concluded, he heaved a sigh of relief and ordered a couple of onion bhajis, a chicken tikka bhuna (extra hot) and a pint of Kingfisher. That, at least, he understood.

85

Carver spent the day just trying to fill the hours. It was a feeling he knew well from his military days, the point when all the plans and preparations have been made and there's nothing to do but wait until it's finally time to go into action. That's when boredom becomes a soldier's biggest enemy.

Grantham had booked him into a nondescript three-star hotel just off Kensington High Street. Carver slept late, piled into a full English breakfast, choosing fried bread rather than toast, then worked off the cholesterol with a run that took him on a massive figure-of-eight through the parks of central London, via Hyde Park Corner and Buckingham Palace. In the afternoon a doctor came round to his room to take a look at the dressings on his back and make sure that the wounds were clean.

The doctor told Carver to take it easy. 'Don't worry, I will,' he replied. And for the next few hours, at least, he kept his word. He watched some cricket on TV and then went to a movie, sitting in the dark, munching popcorn and watching actors fake the things he did for real. Afterwards, he had a couple of pints, ate Chinese for dinner and went to bed early. Grantham was picking him up at five the next morning to drive him down to Bristol, so by ten in the evening he was getting into bed. Carver wasn't prone to anxiety before a big day. He went out like a light.

Air Force One was wheels-up from Andrews shortly before midnight, local time. The President conferred briefly with his staff before retiring to his personal quarters, intending to spend most of the six-hour flight asleep. Elsewhere in the aircraft, Tord Bahr did not allow himself that luxury. It was already dawn in England and his people were all getting into place. Earlier in the day, he'd spoken to the Brits' anti-terrorist chief, Manners. It seemed they were taking Carver's warning about this Damon Tyzack guy seriously. Manners assured Bahr that they had the situation covered. He also told Bahr the same thing he'd told Carver. It made no difference what Tyzack was or was not planning to do. They'd already prepared for every conceivable attack scenario.

Bahr had double-checked. He'd been on to Homeland Security, the Feds, the CIA and NSA. None of them had any intelligence whatever about any hit being planned by people-traffickers; nothing about Tyzack, either. The only indication anywhere that Tyzack might be planning something was an unsubstantiated, unreliable claim made by a man who had just suffered extreme physical and psychological abuse. But as much as he hated to admit it, to himself or Carver, Bahr didn't think Carver was the kind of guy who invented allegations for no good reason. There might be something to what he said, despite the lack of any supporting evidence. Either way, it was an uncertainty, and it niggled away at Bahr's mind. He got an hour's sleep, was woken just before landing and felt like shit as he got off the plane and set foot on British soil.

86

Carver was supplied with a flak jacket, just in case Damon Tyzack really was in Bristol and felt tempted to take a shot at him. They gave him a pair of binoculars so that he could search for Tyzack in the crowd. He had an earpiece and mike so that he could report any sighting, or receive information from Peter Manners, who was co-ordinating the British end of the operation. What he did not possess was a weapon of any kind. So far as the authorities were concerned, Carver was a civilian like any other. And British civilians are not allowed to bear arms in any city at any time, especially not when there's a US President in the vicinity.

Jack Grantham had been assigned the job of minding Carver. 'You got him involved in this, you can bloody well babysit him,' Manners had said.

The two men managed to get through the entire journey down the M4 from London to Bristol without a single argument thanks to an old soldier's trick: the ability to go to sleep whenever the opportunity arises, no matter what the surroundings. Grantham drove. Carver dozed. One hundred and twenty miles sped by in ninety minutes of silence. Carver woke as the car slowed down, driving into Bristol. The first words he heard were Grantham muttering, 'What the hell is that?'

A line of coaches was crawling down the inside lane. As Grantham overtook them the two men saw that signs had been placed in each of the rear windows with slogans like 'British Muslims Against Slavery', 'Bradford Unites Against Oppression' and 'American Satan, You Are Slave-Master Now'. Carver counted ten vehicles, all of them packed. And every one of the passengers appeared to be a young Asian male. At the front of the line was a police car, its lights flashing, acting as an escort.

'Holy shit,' said Carver, still looking out of the window. 'What are the plod going to do about that?'

'What can they do?' said Grantham. 'They can hardly keep them out. Everyone gets to see the President, except the Muslims? That would go down like a cup of cold sick.'

'But they'll have to strip-search the lot of them!'

'And then they'll start claiming discrimination—'

'Which it is.'

'Up to a point. You noticed any Hindu terrorists on our soil lately?'

'But those people will say they aren't terrorists, they're upright British citizens. What a mess.'

'I know,' said Grantham, his face wreathed in a broad smile. 'And our good friend Assistant Commissioner Manners has been lumbered with it.' He sighed contentedly. 'I knew this was going to be an entertaining day.'

The Bradford convoy was directed to a special area of the coach park where a line of policemen diverted from other duties was waiting for them. Each vehicle was carrying at least fifty passengers. When the luggage holds were opened it was revealed that every one of those passengers had a rucksack and many were also supplied with large placards and banners, some carrying slogans like those on the coaches, others bearing the flags of Iran,

Iraq, Syria, Afghanistan and Pakistan. A police inspector was foolish enough to order the men to leave their belongings on the coaches and proceed to Broad Quay empty-handed. At once, he was surrounded by half a dozen irate community leaders.

'Look!' shouted one, pulling out a woven mat from his bag. 'Prayer mat! You telling me I cannot pray? This is religious hatred! This is harassment!'

'What about all them lot?' said another, his accent pure Yorkshire, pointing at a line of young white people, many of them carrying bags no different from those being taken from the coaches and waving banners emblazoned with peace signs and pictures of Lincoln Roberts. 'Tha's not stopping them. That's racism, that is.'

A group of more than fifty furious young men gathered around their leaders, shouting and waving fists at the now-terrified inspector, whose own men moved in to rescue him from the mob. As a stalemate was reached at the coach park – a seething mob of Asian Yorkshiremen on one side, a nervous line of police on the other – word of the confrontation reached Peter Manners in his command centre, and Tord Bahr, newly arrived at Fairford.

'Get them out of there, right out of the city!' Bahr shouted. 'These are the people who let off bombs in London. They're Islamic terrorists. I don't want them anywhere near this thing.'

'I'm afraid it's not that easy,' said Manners, trying to keep his cool. 'In the first place, the government does not acknowledge the concept of Islamic terrorism, the official term is "anti-Islamic activity"—'

'You have got to be kidding me!'

'And in the second, any attempt to remove around five hundred fit young men would require all the manpower I have available, quite apart from the potential for widespread public disorder if the riot spreads. Just let us handle it. We'll let them in, but not before we've made certain that they can't do any harm.'

Half an hour was spent organizing the Bradford contingent into a line, complete with all their baggage. They were marched down to the security checks under massive police escort. More chaos ensued as all were subjected to bag and body searches whose severity slowed down the entire crowd as they waited to get into the speech site, causing shortened tempers and raised voices and adding to the confusion.

The tallest building on Broad Quay, a new office development, was also the closest to the stage. The building had been closed to the public, its occupants given the day off whether they liked it or not. Up on the roof three men, all wearing variations on the theme of black urban-combat uniforms, were peering back up the quay through binoculars, trying to get a look at the chaos.

Two of the men came from a Secret Service counter-sniper team. They bore small Stars and Stripes patches sewn on their packs and uniforms. Their handguns were carried in holsters strapped to their right thighs, directly below which their gold badges were displayed. One of the pair was standing by a custom-made sniper's rifle of a type known as a JAR, or 'Just Another Rifle', because its manufacturer and specifications are confidential.

'Man, you guys have sure screwed this up,' he said.

'Oh, I wouldn't worry,' said the third man in a languid upper-class English accent. 'I'm sure we'll have it all more or less under control by the time your boy gets up to say his piece.'

One of the Americans rolled his eyes at the other, who nodded back. The arrogant and often unjustified air of casual superiority affected by some British officers had become a publicly acknowledged source of irritation to their US Army counterparts in Iraq and Afghanistan. Now they were going to have to spend a whole day stuck on a roof getting their chains yanked by this mousy-headed, sulky-faced jerk-off.

Damon Tyzack, however, couldn't have been happier, even if he had been obliged to dye his hair. He had counted on the fact that the weak spots in the security for any major event occur along the fault-lines between different nations and agencies, all of whom mistrust, despise and compete with one another to a greater or lesser degree. At the very least they fail to communicate fully. So if the system were put under unexpected additional stress, he'd felt certain it would crack.

The Bradford Pakistanis had done their job perfectly and were well worth their hundred grand. Tyzack had confidently sauntered past an overworked gatekeeper with a single flash of a well-forged military ID card. Once he was inside the security cordon, looking as though he knew what he was doing, no one had asked him any questions. Now he'd found himself a grandstand seat for the big event, up here on the roof. Everything was proceeding exactly as he had planned.

Tyzack's iPhone was encased in a black rubber housing which gave it a military air. He used it to call Ron Geary, who was sitting with two other men in the back of the white Ford Transit, parked near an open expanse of playing fields, all deserted on this weekday morning, to the north-east of the city.

'Confirm your status,' he said.

'Ready to go, boss. Just say the word.'

'Await my command,' he said. 'Out.'

Everything was in place. All he needed now were his targets.

87

'Hello, Lara, my name is Lincoln Roberts. Well, don't we make a pair?'

Jake Tolland had to smile at that. Roberts was the epitome of an African-American patriarch: physically imposing, exuding a commanding dignity, with a full head of hair lightly dusted with silver threads among the black. Next to him, Lara looked tiny, very young and utterly vulnerable. The White House stylists had deliberately gone for the most innocent, girl-next-door look they could find, rejecting anything that even hinted at sexiness. So she'd been dressed in flat shoes, loose-cut jeans, a plain T-shirt and a knitted cotton cardigan to ward off the cool of a grey day in June. Her hair was tucked behind her ears and the make-up artist had given her face just enough definition to show up under the stage lights, without adding any glamour whatever.

Even so, Tolland thought, Lara looked wonderful and he agonized for the umpteenth time about the fact that his heart did a backflip every time he set eyes on her. It was inappropriate in every way. She was too young for him. She had been appallingly abused by men. They were supposed to have a dispassionate, professional relationship. If she wanted anything from him, it was protection. Yet he could not deny what he felt and the detached, observing side to his nature saw that she was the perfect poster-girl for Roberts's campaign. The world would fall a little in love with her, too. And for a black President to be fighting for the rights of a white slave girl, well, Tolland reckoned that was a stroke of public-relations genius.

'And you must be Jake Tolland . . .'

Tolland realized with a start that the President was talking to him. He just managed to splutter an answer: 'Er, yes, Mr President.'

Lincoln Roberts looked him in the eye, and as he looked into that strong, warm, wise face Tolland found himself overawed, almost hypnotized by the sheer charisma of the man.

'You wrote a good story, Mr Tolland. I could tell that you were being true to your subject. I admire that. I can see why Lara trusts you. You be sure to keep deserving that trust.'

'Yes, Mr President, I'll do my best.'

'Good for you. So, you guys gonna ride with me to Bristol?'

Jake Tolland gulped and nodded, unable to speak. He was twenty-six years old, at the very start of his career, and the President of the United States had just offered him a lift.

He was vaguely aware of a woman laughing softly just behind his right shoulder.

'Don't worry,' said Chantelle Clemens as she walked by. 'We've all been there. The man has that effect on everyone.'

Forty-five minutes later, the presidential motorcade pulled up backstage at Broad Quay. Roberts got out and walked to a special media area where he posed for press photographers and TV crews with the British Prime Minister, who was basking in his reflected glory. A huge roar rose from the crowd as Roberts's face appeared on the massive screens that were arrayed at regular intervals along the full length of the quay, followed by a few desultory boos for the PM.

Two hundred feet up on the office-block roof Damon Tyzack saw the images on the screens and spoke a single word into his phone.

'Go!'

88

Carver's frustration had been growing with every minute and hour that passed. He and Grantham were atop another building, about half as tall as the one on which Tyzack was positioned, and sixty yards further north, roughly a third of the way back along the quay from the stage. Ever since he had taken up his position, he'd been scanning the tens of thousands of faces within range of his binoculars, but had seen no sign of Tyzack. Carver wondered whether he had made a total fool of himself. He told himself to take it easy. His damaged pride was of no consequence if Lincoln Roberts delivered his speech safely.

Another eruption of noise burst from the crowd as the stage was suddenly lit in a blaze of spotlights that glowed bright against the drab grey backdrop of the city and the cloudy sky. A voice that sounded as though it belonged at a heavyweight boxing match rather than a political gathering boomed across the speaker stacks arrayed alongside the video screens. 'Ladies and gentlemen, the President of the United States!'

The crowd leaped to their feet. The noise of their applause rose even higher and a blast of 'Hail to the Chief' rang from the loudspeakers as Lincoln Roberts strode to the front of the stage and waved to the vast mass of humanity stretching back from the stage as far as the eye could see. One of the screens was positioned directly below Carver's position. The volume it produced combined with that of the crowd was deafening.

And then, as the music died away and tens of thousands of people settled down to listen to what the President had to say, and he stood there calmly, smiling at the TV cameras, letting the mood subside a little before he began his oration, Carver heard a whirring, buzzing noise above his head and something very much like an oversized insect zipped past him, just a few feet overhead.

'What the hell was that?' he shouted.

'What?' asked Grantham.

'That thing that flew by, like a cross between a mosquito and a miniature helicopter.'

'Oh, that,' said Grantham, nonchalantly. 'Probably one of the spotter drones. The cops use them to observe the crowd. They've got video cameras. Clever little buggers. They use electric motors, very quiet, and they're only a couple of feet across, so you can't see them from the ground.'

Realization dawned on Carver, just as Lincoln Roberts began his speech.

'More than two hundred years ago, my ancestors were taken captive on the shores of Lake Chad in central Africa, in a land then known as Bornu. They were marched overland many hundreds of miles to the barracoons of Lagos, then sold to the white slavers who would transport them across the oceans to the colonies of the Americas and the Caribbean. They made the terrible crossing of the Atlantic, the dreaded Middle Passage, and were sold again in the slave market in Charleston, South Carolina. The people who shipped my ancestors across the Atlantic, and brought the profits back to cities just like this one, were white. The people who owned, worked and whipped my ancestors in the plantations were also white . . .'

Carver could almost feel the shame rising from the audience, the consciousness of a sin that could never be expunged or atoned for. But he was only half listening to Roberts. Instead, his concentration was focused on the sky above the crowd as he swept his binoculars slowly back and forth, looking out for the drones.

'But white people were not the only sinners in the slave trade, nor Africans the only victims,' Roberts continued. 'No white man had ever ventured close to Lake Chad at the time my folks were seized. They were first enslaved by their fellow-Africans, who probably traded them to Arab merchants along the way. And this trade flowed in more than one direction. Over the centuries, hundreds of thousands of white Europeans, many of them from England, were captured by raiders and taken to be sold in the slave markets of North Africa. This is how it has been since the very dawn of mankind. Slavery is the original form of human oppression. And it is still among us, on a greater scale than ever before, right here in the heart of our civilization, right now in the twenty-first century.

'So it is time we made a stand . . .'

As the crowd started getting to their feet, clapping and cheering as they rose, Carver shouted at Grantham, 'How many of these drones are there?'

'Dunno. Two, I think.'

'It is time we said, "Enough is enough!"' Roberts declared.

The crowd noise rose another level as Carver yelled, 'You sure?'

'No,' Grantham replied, having a hard time making himself heard. 'Why does it matter?'

Roberts's voice grew stronger still: 'It is time we put an end to slavery. And that is what I, and you, are going to start doing today.'

Carver's throat, still suffering the after-effects of Tyzack's torture, felt as though he'd just swallowed a cocktail of acid and barbed wire and his voice was starting to go. 'Don't you get it?' he rasped. ' "Look to the sky." That's what Thor meant. Tyzack is using a drone!'

Grantham cupped a hand to his ear and screwed up his face to indicate that he couldn't hear over the din. Then the noise subsided as the President stood silently again so that he and everyone else could all catch their breaths.

'It's the drones,' Carver repeated. 'That's how Tyzack is going to do it.'

'You sure? They're not armed or anything,' said Grantham sceptically. 'But call it in if you think you're on to something.'

On stage Lincoln Roberts was moving to the next section of his speech. 'Pretty soon I'm going to tell you all how I believe we can use the power of our armed forces and the strength and justice of our cause to beat the people-traffickers and slave-traders. But first, I want to show you what slavery looks like today; what form its victims take. I'd like to introduce a very special, very brave young woman whom I had the privilege of meeting earlier today. She comes originally from the land of Armenia. Some of you may have heard or read of her story . . . how she was betrayed by a member of her own family and handed over to men of unspeakable evil and brutality . . . how she was bought and sold just like my ancestors were . . . how she was forced into prostitution against her will; beaten, raped and abused. To understand this young lady's courage, just know that as we were coming here I showed her the words that I have just spoken to you, words that describe her shame and degradation. Yet she still agreed to stand by me today because she felt that it was her duty so to do – her duty to the women who still suffer as she once did. It is my profound honour to introduce to you . . . Miss Lara Dashian!'

While Roberts was making his introduction, Samuel Carver was trying to get a message through to Assistant Commissioner Manners. The officer to whom he spoke did not have his name on the official list of the communications system's approved users. He certainly wasn't willing to disturb his commanding officer at such a vital point in the day's proceedings. And anyway, he could not hear, let alone understand what Carver was saying over the cacophony of background noise. In the end, he cut Carver off without a word of warning, still less apology.

*

On HMS *Daring* one of the seamen operating the Sampson radar displays called over an officer. 'There's something odd going on here, sir. It's the area directly above where the President is giving his speech. I'm seeing three spotter drones.'

'Yes, what's the problem?'

'There are only supposed to be two.'

'So which one isn't meant to be there?'

'I don't know, sir. The drones don't carry any kind of identification beacon, they're too small. They're only the size of model airplanes, sir.'

'What's the altitude?'

'About one hundred and fifty feet, sir.'

The officer thought the problem through. Even if there was an extra drone, and there was something suspicious about it, they didn't know which one it was. Even if they did know, they could hardly blast it out of the sky: that close to the ground, the exploding missile would cause a host of casualties in itself.

In the circumstances, he did the sensible thing. He covered his backside, called the ship's bridge, informed them of the situation and passed the problem up the line.

89

Damon Tyzack felt just fine about what he was going to do. If there was one thing he really hated, it was pompous, sanctimonious moralizing. This President Roberts was the worst kind of preachy, self-righteous politician. It would really be doing the world a favour to get rid of him. And . . . ah, perfect! Here came little Miss Dashian, looking very nicely scrubbed-up and respectable. He thought of the whore he'd carried to his hotel bed in her high heels, micro-skirt and painted tart's face.

You don't fool me, my dear, Tyzack thought. You'd still be anybody's for five hundred dirhams.

He looked down at the iPhone. Its screen displayed a map of the Broad Quay area. A moving, flashing dot showed the position of the drone that Geary and his men had launched from the playing fields. It was moving towards the stage, its precise location tracked by a pair of ever-changing co-ordinates at the bottom left of the screen. After yesterday's practice runs, Tyzack knew precisely where the drone had to be, at what altitude, and at what speed it had to be travelling to ensure the delivery of its payload to the precise spot where the President and the whore were standing.

And now she started to talk. 'My name is Lara Dashian . . .'

'Well, that does it,' murmured Tyzack, his finger hovering over a digital 'Fire' button displayed at the screen's bottom right.

The drone had settled on a course that aimed it directly at the stage. It was moving in.

Just a few seconds to go now.

Carver had been reduced to screaming down the microphone, 'Get him off the stage! Get the President off the fucking stage!' But the people at whom he was shouting either could not or would not hear him.

Lara Dashian had begun to speak. This, Carver realized, was the perfect moment for Tyzack to strike. He must think Christmas had come early, being able to get rid of his prime target, the President, and an inconvenient witness to a past crime.

There was only one way to stop this.

Carver stepped right up close to Grantham and yelled in his ear, 'Give me your gun!'

Grantham shook his head.

'Give me the bloody gun!'

Grantham turned and pushed Carver away.

Carver stepped back, away from Grantham's hand, fractionally adjusted his balance and then sprang forwards. As he moved he swung the heel of his right hand, slamming it into Grantham's face, just to one side of his chin. The blow caused Grantham's head to jerk round, wrenching the tendons of his neck and sending his brain bouncing off the inner walls of his skull like a pea in a whistle. Grantham was lifted off his feet and flung back across the roof until his body slammed to a halt against a raised air-conditioning vent.

Carver walked across and removed Grantham's gun from its shoulder holster. SIS must have taken advice from the Special Forces because the gun was a SIG-Sauer P226, precisely the same model that Carver himself always used. That would make life easier.

Something had to, because what he was about to do was verging on the impossible.

He stepped to the edge of the roof and looked over the parapet to the stage, at least one hundred yards away. The distance was at the very furthest limit of the gun's effective range. He was shooting downwards, into and across a stiff breeze coming in off the river behind the stage.

But he had no alternative.

Carver raised his gun, aimed it at Lincoln Roberts, President of the United States, and fired.

90

'No!' shouted Damon Tyzack as four gunshots rang out and one of the clear perspex screens that acted both as the President's autocue and his shield shook with the impact of the bullets.

On the display in front of him the drone was still five seconds away from the point at which the two anti-personnel grenades mounted in place of the conventional surveillance equipment could be released.

Before the sound of the shots had died away, the first Secret Service man had hurtled across the stage, grabbed the President and was manhandling him away. Roberts appeared to be trying to stop him. He was reaching out towards the girl, but the agent, now joined by two of his colleagues, had virtually lifted their charge off his feet and was carrying him to safety.

Two seconds left and Tyzack – his system surging with a toxic cocktail of rage, impotence and overwhelming frustration – thought about firing on the President himself. But his own gun was still holstered. It would take too long to draw, aim and fire. In any case, unless he shot the three Secret Service men up there with him before aiming at their President he would be signing his own death warrant. There was certainly not time to hit all four targets. From now on in it was strictly a damage-limitation exercise.

He could hear the Americans talking to their headquarters.

'I saw muzzle-flash,' one was saying.

'I have a location,' the other added, virtually simultaneously.

At the front of the crowd, the dignitaries nearest to the stage were desperately trying to get away and their panic had already begun to infect those around them.

Meanwhile the whore had barely moved at all, paralysed by indecision and fear. All was not yet lost. At least he could get her.

Tyzack pressed the red button on his display and the grenades were released. For a fraction of a second, as he launched the attack, his gaze had dropped to the iPhone. When he looked up there was another figure on the stage. A tall, spindly young man in glasses was racing towards the whore. He wrapped his arms around her, held her tight and then leaped off the front of the stage.

An instant later the grenades struck the stage at exactly the point where Lincoln Roberts had been standing. They detonated in a pair of orange and yellow fireballs that blasted superheated fragments of steel shrapnel through the air, shredding the screen that had withstood the gunshots, destroying the backdrop, ripping into the lighting rigs above and to the sides of the speaking area and killing several members of the stage crew, as well as a Secret Service agent who had not yet got offstage.

The main force of the blast, having exploded some ten feet above the ground, went over the heads of the crowd in the immediate vicinity, though several people further back were killed and many more wounded by shrapnel particles that travelled up to two hundred yards from the impact point. Tyzack's attention, however, was concentrated on the foot of the stage where the whore's body lay motionless on the ground, next to that of the young man who had tried to rescue her.

For a moment Tyzack felt a brief flutter of hope, a tiny scintilla of optimism amidst the bleak disappointment of the failed mission.

But even that shred of good news was taken from him as the whore slowly pulled herself out from under the man's body, staggered to her feet and then, when she saw that the figure was utterly inert, started screaming with a desperate despair that seemed to Tyzack to echo his own feelings.

Perhaps he should put the silly bitch out of her misery.

There was nothing to stop him shooting her. It was a fiendishly tricky shot but there was no risk from the Secret Service. They knew that their President was safe. Tyzack could always claim to have aimed at a fleeing suspect.

He unholstered his weapon and then stopped as he heard one of the Americans say, 'I have a visual on the roof from which the shots were fired. There is a man down, repeat a man down. Another man appears to be vacating the area. He is approximately six feet tall, slim to medium build, dark brown hair, wearing civilian clothes: black pants, possibly jeans, and some kind of grey top.'

Carver, thought Tyzack with rancid bitterness.

Forget the whore. It was time to go. Tyzack wasn't afraid of being caught by any British or American security forces and he certainly wasn't scared of Carver. But the absolute certainty of Arjan Visar's displeasure, and its potentially fatal consequences, meant that he needed to disappear. Starting right now.

He walked towards the door that led to the stairway down to the top floor of the building. When he got there he turned and said, 'Bye, chaps.'

The two Secret Service men turned towards him, an automatic reflex, acknowledging his farewell. Tyzack killed them both with two single headshots. It was time, he decided, that he made sure witnesses were definitely, undeniably dead. Furthermore, it was always a delight, the sort of thing that only a true connoisseur could appreciate, to see the fractional look of surprise on the face of the second of two victims as they realized what had just happened to their companion an instant before it happened to them, too. And finally, he was seriously pissed off, and the sheer pleasure of inflicting death took the edge, at least, off his anger.

91

Just as he was about to get off the roof, Carver heard two shots from high up the tower closest to the stage. He looked up and saw a male figure on the roof; only the top half of him visible above the parapet. From that distance Carver was unable to make out his face. Nor could he see the distinctive flash of red hair. And yet he knew, without a shadow of a doubt, that it was Tyzack. His outline, his movements, everything about him had become so familiar and their relationship had, in its own warped way, become as inter-twined as a pair of lovers, so that awareness of his presence was automatic, instinctive. The location made sense, too. It was the highest, closest point to the stage, the perfect vantage point from which to direct a low-level aerial attack.

In his earpiece Carver was receiving a babble of frenzied chatter as different units reported in on the current position of the President and other VIPs, the state of the crowd and the arrival of emergency services at the stage.

Then he heard: 'All units be aware, we have reports that the initial shots were fired by a white male, height six feet, medium build, answering to the description of Samuel Carver, a civilian consultant on the security for this event. He is believed to be armed and extremely dangerous. Approach with extreme caution.'

Carver was racing downstairs now. He switched to transmit and said, 'This is Carver.' He was painfully aware how strange his voice must sound, his throat wrecked and his breathing ragged as he hurtled down the stairwell. 'Yes, I deliberately fired at the President's protective screens. But in case you morons hadn't noticed, I saved his life. I'd been trying to warn you he was about to be attacked and you refused to listen. What else was I supposed to do?'

'Carver, this is Assistant Commissioner Manners. Give yourself up, immediately. That's an order. If your story is true, you have nothing to fear.'

'Forget it. I'm going after Tyzack.'

'Tyzack? Give it a rest, Carver. He isn't here. To be honest, I wonder if he even exists.'

'Really? Then who planted two grenades on the stage you were tasked to protect? Who has shot at least one, possibly two people on the roof of that tower right by the stage? I heard the shots. I saw Tyzack. Go on, do a flypast with one of your drones. Tell me I'm wrong. But I'm not coming in.'

Carver had reached the ground floor of the building. He was halfway across the main foyer, heading for the front entrance, when a West Country voice came over his earpiece: 'We have a visual, two men down, as reported.'

'Is the drone still in the area?' Carver asked, pushing open the door. 'If so, do you see a man wearing black special forces combat uniform anywhere near the foot of the building? He's trying to get away, so he'll be moving fast.'

As he said the words, Carver was aware how absurd they sounded. All around him were tens of thousands of people trying to get away from Broad Quay, all moving as fast as they could go. This was like the scene inside the King Haakon Hotel, magnified a thousandfold. If Tyzack had half a brain he'd have done what

Carver had not and left by a rear entrance, on to one of the back streets, away from the quay.

'Look to the east and south of the building!' he shouted. 'Got anything?'

Carver didn't wait for an answer. He was already fighting his way through the mass of people, moving past the tower where Tyzack had been positioned. Then he heard a crackle in his ear followed by, 'Yes! We have a possible sighting, moving south along King William Avenue in the direction of Queen Square.'

Carver thought back to the presentation Manners had given in Dame Agatha Bewley's office. Queen Square was somewhere to the south of where he was now. He looked up at the sky. It was midday. Wherever the sun was, that was south.

There was no sun. The sky was grey with low-lying cloud. But one patch of cloud looked marginally less dismal than the rest, as though some light was trying to force its way through. Carver ran in the direction of the light. He forced his way past another group of people and suddenly he was on a virtually deserted street. Ahead of him was a small pedestrian area, laid out in paving stones between patches of grass, that lay at the foot of a couple of office buildings. As he ran on, he saw that there was a gap between the buildings and at the end of it was the corner of a much larger open space, surrounded by trees. That must be Queen Square. He kept moving through the gap, across a road, up to the trees and then flung himself to the ground as he heard a crack of pistol-fire, followed by a stinging sensation on the right-hand side of his face as it was hit by splinters from the impact of a bullet on the tree-trunk right beside him.

'We have you on our screen,' said the voice in his ear. 'Tyzack is ahead.'

'Thanks,' muttered Carver. 'I gathered.'

'He's moving again, approximately sixty to seventy metres ahead of you, along the same line of trees.'

Carver got to his feet and started running down the road side of the line of trees. He could not see Tyzack, so he cut though the trees on to Queen Square itself to get a better view. Now he spotted Tyzack, almost at the end of the square.

Tyzack stopped, aimed and fired three shots. He set off again, ducking back into the trees, out of Carver's line of sight.

The pattern of bobbing, weaving, firing and taking cover continued as Tyzack turned left along the southern border of the square. But Carver seemed to be dropping behind with every step. The punishment he had taken in the barn might not have done him any fatal harm, but it had seriously weakened him. This was a race he was going to lose. As he reached the south end of the square, Carver looked around. Tyzack had disappeared. He'd lost him.

'Where is he?' Carver panted, barely managing a jog.

'Hang on, can't see him . . . wait . . . yes! Got him! He's heading for the pontoon at the end of Grove Avenue, about a hundred metres from where you are now. He's on the pontoon now. We've got units heading in that direction. He can't get away unless . . . He's got a boat. He's casting off the lines.'

Carver wasn't going to make it to the dock in time. But there was another way to get him.

'There's a bridge somewhere round here. How do I get to it?'

'Prince Street Bridge, yes. From where you are, turn right. The junction with Prince Street is about forty metres ahead.'

'I can see it.'

'Turn left on that and follow your nose. You can't miss it.'

Carver was out on his feet. Then he thought of Thor Larsson's burned and mutilated body lying next to him outside that barn. He thought of Karin and their unborn child. He heard Maddy snarling, 'Just kill him.' And he ran again.

He sprinted round the corner and on to Prince Street, ignoring the warning signals of screaming pain from his lungs, his legs, his wounded back and his overworked heart. He kept pumping his arms and legs, desperately trying to squeeze out more speed as somewhere to the left he heard the deep, throaty rumble of powerful engines starting up. As he dashed on to the bridge he caught his first glimpse of a sleek dart of a boat, with a long, arrow-like bow and a low cabin roof sweeping back over the driver's cockpit with the sensual curve of an Italian sports car. It was reversing out of a berth.

Now it was turning to face downstream, towards the bridge.

As Carver reached the middle of the bridge, the boat began moving towards him. It was no more than the length of a football field away and the gap was narrowing with every second, shrinking still faster as it picked up speed.

Carver fired off four more shots in quick succession, aiming at the figure he could just make out in the cockpit behind the raked-back windscreen, and then the gun clicked as the magazine emptied. Grantham hadn't kept it fully loaded.

There was no time to worry about that now. Though its windscreen had shattered, the boat had not slowed down or deviated from its course. It was aiming straight for the single narrow span of clear water at the centre of the bridge, directly below where Carver was standing.

Carver couldn't believe that Tyzack would make it. The bridge sat just a few feet above the water. It had to be lifted to let boats through. But Tyzack wasn't slowing down. As the bow came almost within touching distance of where he stood, Carver turned and ran across the bridge.

He leaped up on to the sturdy cast-iron parapet and then jumped as the speedboat sped by in a blazing shower of sparks, ignited as it scraped along the underside of the bridge.

The cockpit had a short roof, immediately above the driver and co-driver's seats, but was then open all the way back to the stern where there was a shallow transom above the frothing white water churned up by twin stainless steel propellers. Carver landed hard on the transom, half in and half out of the boat, driving all the air from his lungs. His head was hanging over the steps that led down on to the aft deck and the lower half of him dangled terrifyingly close to the propellers. If his legs touched those flashing blades they would be pulped into a flesh smoothie, like a banana in a food processor.

Damon Tyzack's head peered round from the high, carbon-fibre driver's seat. He coughed, put his hand up to his mouth, flashed his most disarming smile and shouted over the roar of the engines, 'Welcome aboard.'

92

The Type 45 destroyer is an air-defence specialist. It does not carry any anti-ship missile systems. But it has a little friend that does, the Lynx HMA8 helicopter that it carries in a hangar amidships, which is armed with four Sea Skua guided missiles. The radar on HMS *Daring* had spotted the two hand grenades on their brief journey between Tyzack's drone and the presidential stage. The information had been relayed to Manners and from him to Tord Bahr, confirming Carver's story and making Damon Tyzack the prime suspect. The moment Tyzack got into his boat, HMS *Daring*'s Lynx was ordered to intercept him. The only question now concerned the rules of engagement. Would the Lynx be allowed to use deadly force? That was a decision that would have to go right to the very top.

93

Tyzack ordered Carver forward over a deck littered with broken glass. His right hand was grasping the steering wheel. His left was covering Carver with a gun that still had ammunition in its magazine.

'Take the co-driver's seat,' Tyzack said, his gun gesturing towards the empty seat to his left. 'Do up the safety harness. Now place your hands between your legs and the seat. Don't move, or I'll be obliged to shoot.'

As they passed the Bristol docks and the Floating Harbour, Tyzack leaned forward and used the palm-heel of his gun hand to push the twin throttles, opening up the engines and making the boat leap forward with a new surge of speed, a blast of cool air racing in through the broken windscreen. For a second, more of Tyzack's upper body was visible, exposing the ragged scarlet hole in his upper chest, just beneath his right collar-bone.

Tyzack caught Carver's eye. 'You got lucky,' he said and coughed again, spattering the pristine white leather around the steering wheel with a fine spray of blood.

'For God's sake,' said Carver, 'give up. You can't get away. There's a bloody great destroyer sitting out in the Bristol Channel and a squadron of Typhoon jets up top. One way or another, they're going to blow you out of the water.'

'Won't be the Typhoons,' Tyzack said. 'Technical problem. They can only hit ground targets if they're given warning and prepped before take-off. They were up there to protect Air Force One. They won't be able to get me.'

'The destroyer then . . .'

'Yes, that could. Probably will, in fact.'

'So stop. Get that lung fixed. You'll live.'

Tyzack's smile was almost melancholy now, in its recognition of his inevitable fate. 'No, I won't. Doesn't matter where they put me. Visar will get me. I'm a dead man in jail.'

Carver could not hide his surprise. 'Visar? Christ . . .'

It took Tyzack a couple of seconds to make the connection. 'The hit on his brother – that was you?' He broke into a hacking, blood-spraying laugh. 'Oh, that's priceless, that really is!'

'For God's sake, man,' Carver implored him. 'Hasn't this gone far enough?'

'No,' said Tyzack, with definitive certainty. 'It hasn't. You're right, I'm going to die very soon. And the one thing that makes that prospect even remotely bearable is the sure and certain fact that you're going to die with me.'

The Prime Minister had been complicit in decisions that sent his country to war. He had happily signed off on defence cuts whose effects on equipment procurement condemned scores of in-adequately protected servicemen and -women to needless, avoidable deaths. But when it came to giving the order for a specific use of military force, he suddenly lost his appetite for decision-making.

On the one hand, he did not want a man who had tried to kill Lincoln Roberts to escape the grasp of justice. On the other, he led a party that was viscerally opposed to capital punishment and had little natural sympathy for US presidents, no matter how charismatic. Besides which, he was the leader of a European Union state, and the EU forbids capital punishment. Indeed, many of its nations virtually forbid their armed forces to fight.

It took a pollster to put the PM out of his misery. The British people, he suggested, would not take kindly to a leader who let a would-be assassin get away with it. On the other hand, the vast majority of the population would have no trouble at all with the idea that such a villain had been blown to shreds by the Royal Navy. This was still, after all, a country whose biggest-selling daily newspaper, at the very height of its circulation, had greeted the sinking of an Argentine battleship with the single word: 'GOTCHA!'

'Gotcha it is, then,' said the Prime Minister morosely. 'But wait till the target reaches open water. I don't want a pleasure-boat full of pensioners or a family taking a river cruise getting caught by the blast. That would not be good for our ratings.'

'No, not very,' the pollster agreed.

94

The speedboat flashed under the Clifton Suspension Bridge and headed for Avonmouth, where the river met the sea, roughly six miles away. With the engines at maximum power they would cover the distance in under four minutes. Off to the west, the *Daring*'s Lynx was now airborne, aiming for a position offshore, directly in line with the river.

'How does it feel?' asked Tyzack. 'Confronting your death?'

'I wouldn't know,' Carver replied. 'I'm not planning to die.'

His earpiece burst into life again. The words that followed were barely audible over the engines, the wind and the slamming of the hull against the water, but 'barely' was enough to get the point.

'Carver, this is Manners. Don't know if you can hear me. If you're on that boat, get off it. The PM's given the order. The moment you reach open water, the Navy's going to take you out . . . Good luck. Out.'

'You're right,' said Carver. 'It's the Navy. For God's sake, for once in your life, do something sensible and stop the bloody boat.'

Tyzack turned and his blood-caked lips cracked into a leering smile below eyes that now burned with a feverish intensity. 'Now you're confronting it,' he cackled.

'Look out!' Carver shouted.

Immediately ahead, the river made a dogleg turn to the left. Tyzack did not slow the boat at all, hurling it around the bend with such abandon that Carver thought they would capsize. For a second, the sheer force of the turn unsettled Tyzack and he began coughing again, even more violently than before, the blood now gushing from his mouth. Carver was working out when to make his move when the river swung again, this time to the right, shaking him so violently that he was for the first time glad Tyzack had forced him to strap himself in.

But that was the last of the turns. The bows were now pointing directly down a final, almost dead-straight stretch of river that ran under the brutalist concrete span of the M5 motorway bridge. Carver could see one final, relatively innocuous kink in the river and ahead of that the open sea.

Death awaited on that choppy brown estuary water, but Tyzack wasn't slowing down to avoid it. He was charging gleefully, exultantly, onwards. Hardly turning his head, he pointed his gun in Carver's direction.

'Shall I put you out of your misery now?' he asked.

The crew of the Lynx had been tracking the speedboat's progress on their radar. Now, as it emerged into the mouth of the river, they had visual contact. The pilot's orders were clear. Ensure that the target was well clear of any civilian water traffic, then shoot at will. He was planning to let it go a mile out to sea. At that point it would be two miles from where his helicopter was waiting. Then he would fire. His Sea Skua missiles travelled at close to the speed of sound. Less than ten seconds after their launch the speedboat would be blasted from the face of the earth.

There was a manic glee about Damon Tyzack as he sped towards oblivion. His head was held high, his hair blown back by the wind rushing in through the shattered screen. His arms stuck straight out from his shoulders at right-angles, like the arms of a clock at nine: one hand on the wheel, the other holding the gun. His bright blue eyes were fixed in a fevered stare and his blood-smeared lips were twisted into the wild grin of a man embracing his own damnation.

Carver was waiting, calculating, praying that he still had time, knowing that there were just seconds in it. He could see the helicopter in the distance, hovering just above the horizon. How long would it wait?

And then he saw something else, much closer; the prospect of salvation.

The XSR hurtled out of the river and hit the first waves coming in from the sea. The bow reared up into the air, hurling both men back in their seats, off balance.

Tyzack's gun was jolted upwards by the impact. Carver yanked his arms out from under his legs and lashed the side of his right hand into Tyzack's left wrist. The blow sent the gun spinning from Tyzack's hand. It fell to the deck and skimmed away over the bucking, rearing wood surface.

Carver unclipped the buckle of his safety harness then clambered upright. Tyzack made no attempt to stop him, or to resist in any way. His chest heaved in a convulsive hack, spraying Carver in a deep pink spume of foaming blood. Then he let go of the wheel, spread his arms wide as the boat started veering round in a circle and wheezed, 'Go ahead. What's the worst you can do?'

Carver didn't punch Tyzack. He wasn't worth breaking a knuckle over. He just slapped his head three times, left-right-left with great swinging blows that left Tyzack slumped barely conscious in his seatbelt.

'This is for Thor Larsson,' said Carver, pulling the plaited leather belt from his jeans and tightening it around Tyzack's neck. He pushed the pin of the buckle between two strands of leather and wrenched the buckle round behind Tyzack's head.

Carver undid Tyzack's harness and pulled on the belt, yanking his head forward until he was doubled up. Then he began tying the loose end of the belt to the blood-spattered rim of the boat's steering wheel.

Tyzack was coming to. He turned his head and looked up at Carver through unfocused eyes. He tried to speak, but all he could manage was a feeble, wordless croak.

Carver bent down and asked, 'How's it hanging?'

In the Lynx the pilot watched the sudden apparently random change in the speedboat's course with alarm. He wasn't sure if the pilot had lost control or was trying to escape. And he wasn't going to wait long enough to find out.

'Fire!' he commanded.

The Sea Skua missile scorched away across the sky.

Carver caught a quick flash of light in the corner of his eye as the rocket engine ignited.

He took one last look at Tyzack, suspended from the steering wheel like a discarded puppet. Then he raced back towards the stern, grabbing hold of the passenger seats and physically dragging himself through the cabin as it juddered with the impact of each fresh wave.

A mile away, the Skua acquired its target before plunging into its final death dive.

Carver reached the stern and flung himself into the water, diving away from the thrashing propellers then staying underwater as the missile hit the boat. The shock waves from the blast punched Carver in the back, driving the breath from his lungs and pushing him still deeper, fighting for control until he was finally able to kick upwards again and emerge, gasping for air, on the surface.

He took one quick look to get his bearings and struck out for the shore.

95

They took Thor Larsson home to rest alongside his ancestors in a treeless, windswept graveyard that lay atop a headland overlooking the Norwegian Sea. At its centre stood a church, a simple construction of white-painted wood with a modest spire at one end. The houses of the village where Thor had grown up were wooden too, coloured deep russet red, yellow ochre and green: gaudy bursts of brightness against the featureless landscape of scrub and sand and the constantly shifting whites, greys and blues of the limitless sky and the sea.

Carver wore the suit he'd bought for Larsson's wedding and a black tie he'd bought at Heathrow.

Maddy was waiting for him by the churchyard gate. They didn't say anything at first, didn't even shake hands.

'I didn't think you'd be here,' he said. 'I expected you to go home.'

'Oslo was safer. It was the one place I knew he wouldn't be. And Karin needed help with, you know, everything. So . . .' She shrugged, and then said, 'I would have told you if you'd called.'

'No phone,' he explained. 'Tyzack took mine and I never got round to buying another. Had other things on my mind.'

Carver's words blew away on the breeze coming in from the sea. They faced one another in an awkward, unaccustomed silence.

'Oh Christ,' she said, 'don't just stand there.'

And then they hugged.

'I thought I'd lost you,' he whispered, holding her tighter to feel the soft press of her body and breathe in the scent of her hair.

'You had,' she murmured, her mouth against his shoulder.

'And now?'

She didn't answer, but stepped out of his embrace, running her hands through her hair to push it back into place.

'I saw you on TV with the President,' she said. 'Him shaking your hand as you were sitting up in that hospital bed.' She smiled. 'I was proud of you.'

'You were?' he said, as if he couldn't quite believe his ears.

'Uh-huh.' She grinned. 'Even if the news guy said you were just "a bystander, injured in the bombing".'

Carver laughed. 'Yeah, I heard that too.'

'You're all right, though?'

'Sure. They just insisted on keeping me in overnight for observation. That reporter kid was in the same ward as me. He spent the whole time on the phone to his agent. Every time it rang, he got a little bit richer.'

'Well, he did a very brave thing,' said Maddy, taking his arm as they slowly walked up towards the church. 'So did you.'

'That's what Roberts said, too. Well, almost. His exact words were, "Son, you must have *cojones* of steel if you think the way to save a president is to shoot at him."'

She giggled. 'The President said that? Really?'

'Absolutely. But very quiet, with his head right by mine, so the reporters wouldn't hear.'

Carver felt as if they were getting back to their old selves. They still weren't all the way there yet, nowhere close. But give it time.

Maddy held his arm tight against her. They couldn't talk any more now, because there were introductions to be made and condolences to be expressed. Carver murmured all the proper expressions of sympathy as he was introduced to the family, but he knew they must resent him for being alive when their beloved Thor was dead. Everyone had been told about his heroic self-sacrifice. No one knew about the betrayal that had come before.

It had been Karin who had insisted on Carver speaking at the service. She came up to him now and told him, 'Say all the good things, like you would have done at . . . at our wedding. Tell the jokes, even if they are rude. Make him live for me again, just for a few moments . . . please.'

When the time came for him to speak, Maddy gave his hand an encouraging squeeze. He stepped up to the lectern, past the coffin in which Thor's remains lay, offering a silent prayer that he be allowed to get through his words without breaking down. As he looked out over the congregation, he paused for a moment to collect his thoughts and gather his strength, and it was then that he saw, right at the back of the church, a flash of golden hair beneath a black hat. The woman beneath the hat must have sensed his gaze upon her for at that instant she raised her face and her clear blue eyes looked straight into his. He felt his stomach flip and told himself it was only natural that Alix should be here. She and Thor had become very close. There was nothing more to it than that.

Carver swallowed hard, coughed and thanked God for the fact that his emotion would be read by the congregation as understandable nervousness. He felt their eyes upon him, and the weight of their expectations. Somehow he had to find a way to acknowledge the loss they had all suffered and the joy they had taken in the person who was gone. He thought of what Karin had said: 'Make him live for me again.' So he set aside the notes he had made and stepped back down from the lectern. Then he stood beside the coffin, looked out at the people crammed on to the hard wooden pews and told them about his friend.

Author's Note

This book is explicitly and unambiguously a work of fiction and its characters entirely imaginary. Nevertheless there are elements in it that are based on fact. So far as possible, for example, I have tried to make the descriptions of the slave trade – the abusive techniques of the traffickers; the experiences of the women; the facts and figures; even the price for which a sex-slave can be bought in an airport coffee-shop – as accurate as possible. The facts are so appalling that they need no exaggeration.

Amidst a great welter of research material, three books in particular gave me some small measure of insight into and understanding of trafficking: *McMafia: Crime Without Frontiers*, by Misha Glenny; *The Natashas: The New Global Sex Trade*, by Victor Malarek; and *Selling Olga: Stories of Human Trafficking and Resistance*, by Louisa Waugh. All are strongly recommended to anyone wanting to know more about the trade and the criminals who operate it. The US State Department's annual *Trafficking in Persons Report*, available online, is also an invaluable source of data on global slavery. Finally, my fictional House of Freedom was inspired by a report in the *New York Times* on the work of Sharla Musabih, founder of the City of Hope refuge for battered wives and trafficked women in Dubai. Ms Musabih dedicates her life to the real-life Lara Dashians who suffer appalling exploitation in Dubai, just as they do all over the world – Britain, Europe and the USA included.

Anyone who has ever visited Dubai, Oslo, London, Bristol or even Cascade, Idaho will, I hope, recognize those places from my descriptions. Nevertheless, they will also spot the many liberties I have taken. I would, for example, strongly advise anyone lucky enough to own an XSR superboat, a fabulous piece of kit for which they will likely have paid in excess of a million pounds, not to attempt to drive it under Bristol's Prince Street Bridge.

Likewise, to the very best of my knowledge, there is no Karama Pearl Hotel in Dubai, nor a King Haakon Hotel in Oslo. On the other hand, the Oslo Opera House is even more astonishing than my meagre powers of description can suggest, and the Gabelshus Hotel certainly does exist. I recommend it for its elegant surroundings, charming staff and free breakfasts, afternoon teas and buffet suppers. Those familiar with the boggling restaurant prices in Oslo will understand the significance of the word 'free' in this context.

One other inaccuracy, however, was entirely unintended. The air-defence systems that I attribute to HMS *Daring* certainly are those planned for deployment on the Type 45 destroyers, of which she is the first. Yet it emerged after the book was written that thanks to delays, cost overruns and the matchless, life-threatening incompetence of the Ministry of Defence, HMS *Daring* has actually taken to the seas without her main Viper missile system. I can only hope that the Navy's meagre budget has run to a Lynx helicopter and its Sea Skua missiles. If not, any real-life Damon Tyzacks will stand a very good chance of getting away.

Tom Cain, Sussex, 2009